# There's No Place Like Hell

## Janis Hill

---

## Book 2 of
### *The Other World series*

THERE'S NO PLACE LIKE HELL

Book 2 of *The Other World seriese*

Copyright 2019 Hague Publishing

Hague Publishing
PO Box 451
Bassendean Western Australia 6934
*Email:* contact@haguepublishing.com
*Web:* www.haguepublishing.com

ISBN: 9780648050360

Cover Art: 'There's No Place Like Hell' by Jade Zivanovic
http://www.steampowerstudios.com.au/

Typeset Garamond 12/14

This one's for you Mom.

# Chapter 1

HEROES come in all shapes and sizes. We're not all super, nor do we wear our underwear outside of our pants. Some of us have actually been asked not to wear track suit pants out in public as much as we actually do. But it is what I am all the same: a hero, a protector of the weak, and those in need of help. Though I prefer being called Stephanie than 'Protector', especially when my full title of 'Protector of Souls' is used. I have no problems with having the title or being what I am, said Protector. Must we, however, use this name in front of the whole world? As it *so* doesn't do me much good out in the general public, not even store credit or the ability to queue jump at the local grocery store.

But here I am, living in an old lay-in hospital owned by the Temple of Isis — located just around the corner — and I am indeed a protector of souls. The Goddess Isis herself decreed it. And — despite not name dropping her to said general public — it is an honour to hold such a title.

Without starting to sound too kooky, or appearing the sort who really *should* be wearing their underwear outside of their pants, I walk in the Light and I believe in some of the more far-fetched things in this world. I would rather not believe in things like Isis, vampires and ghosts but when you've met them personally, it does make it hard to keep disbelieving in them. Especially when some of them are out to kill you via your undead sister. But the less I go back to *that* moment in my life six months ago, the better I can sleep at night.

Still, I am a Protector of Souls, and almost daily I find myself up against the Darkness that opposes the Light I walk in. And, sadly, today just seems to be another one of those days.

\*\*\*

"Package for Stephanie Anders, Protector of Souls?" intoned the rather bored looking delivery driver. He was holding a large brown box in both hands on my door step when I answered the ring of my bell. Admittedly his eyes did brighten in question a little when he took in my appearance of tracksuit pants, oversized baggy t-shirt, and elbow length, tight fitting, black leather gloves. I just returned his bored look until the question died in his eyes and then patiently held out my hands to receive the package.

"Actually, I think I should be taking that for you," announced a crisp and neat voice from behind the delivery man. As he turned questioningly toward the voice, I was unable to stifle my groan. Did I mention demons were real too? And that I had happened to be able to control them to some extent? Like the deal I had with the demon dressed as a small, neat little gentleman now politely taking the parcel from the delivery driver and signing for it.

"Ugh, who is it this time Mr Vontant?" I asked in a tired voice. See, the deal I had with this particular demon was that he would protect me from any and all who walk in the Darkness that may wish me harm. . . plus a bit more. If he was here to take a parcel for me, and not let me touch it, there was a good bet something nasty was in it. It's not as if this was the first time he'd signed for parcels for me in the last six months either. And I had learned the hard way that it was better I didn't have him open the parcel to prove what it contained was indeed a gift from those who walked in Darkness. I shuddered at the memories while awaiting his answer.

"Birdfolk of Wroth," Mr Vontant replied, returning the signing device to the delivery man and dismissing him with a look of disdain. Despite him being one right evil, little bastard who I only dealt with because I *had* to, I was impressed by the power of his look, which sent the delivery driver scurrying back to his van and screaming it out of my quiet little street.

"Be seeing you," Mr Vontant said as he stepped down from my front step and vanished. I didn't ask how, I really didn't want to know — as the more I knew of this strange new Other World I'd found myself living in, the more I wished I still didn't know.

Well, that was the morning's *fun* dealt with. I gave my peaceful neighbourhood a quick once over before retreating back inside my little stone cottage, shutting and bolting the door. This act of securing my door during daytime hours was from habit now, after learning the hard way that Mr Vontant didn't always get there in time. And that not all bad things came to me in small brown packages via delivery men. I still had a scorched doormat to remind me of that now.

I slowly peeled off my leather gloves while wandering back down the hall to finish my breakfast. My life hadn't always been so odd, but despite all the pain and sadness that had brought me to where I was now, it hadn't really been much of a life either. More an endless repetition of dull routines, stretched out to give the impression of living.

As I sat to finish my toast and much needed fourth coffee I pondered over what those Birdfolk had against me. Yes I had threatened to turn one of them into a feather duster by cramming their feathered clothing — who wears *just* feathers — down their throat until they came out the other end. But it's not as if this was the only group I had said or done such things to. I'd had a busy past six months establishing myself in the Other World and had released and successfully banished several earthed demons, laid a couple of ghosts to their final rest and all in all pissed off quite a few groups who walked within the Darkness. Meh, what can I say? They started it. Why the Birdfolk suddenly had their feathers ruffled again was a mystery and one I felt I should add to my 'to do' list at some point.

I finished my breakfast while looking at the latest text message from Roxanna, the High Priestess of Isis. Technically I was employed by her, and even received a small salary — as well as free room and board in this cottage — and I always received her texts with trepidation. She was my friend as well as my sort of boss, and second only to Isis herself within the society I now lived. But she only ever sent me a text message when there was some Other Worldly thing she wanted me to sort out. Oh well, time to get kitted up and on with the job.

Despite not liking the hero badge that much, it did mean I'd had to change my wardrobe a little. I mean, how I presented myself to the general public wasn't a problem, but how I was perceived by those of the Other World was. Image being one of their big things, along with always getting the wording right — something I'd had to learn the hard way. Still, they got what they got with me as I felt I had to be comfortable when saving souls. So I donned some neat, tailored pants, a pretty but not-too fancy blouse, and a decent pair of fancy running shoes. Yes, who needed all leather and spiked shoes to totter about on when you often had to run like the blazes and were often soaked in salty water? It was the least of the nasty things I had found myself covered in too I may add. Sure I didn't really look much like a Protector of Souls and more like the accountant I used to be, but a lot more had to be at stake before I started dressing like some of the more colourful Other Worlders I knew. Feathers were one thing, white bed sheets and lace curtains another. This outfit allowed me to blend into both worlds. What truly now marked me as to what I was in the Other World were the items I put on last.

As I walked to the front door I donned my elbow length black leather gloves and grabbed my giant handbag. The bag was essential, as you never knew what you had to carry and, well the gloves were just second nature to me these days. There were very few things in the Other World — I had discovered — that you should really touch with your bare skin. The gloves didn't exactly go with any of my outfits, and I really *had* tried to mix and match, but they were more than essential. Besides protecting my bare skin from some rather unwholesome unholies, they showed the world who I was in some strange way, and gave me comfort in what I had to do.

It was only a few streets to the Temple of Isis. Not only did I shamelessly use the back of their estates to park my car for free, but the priestesses of the temple made purified water as part of their daily ritual, meaning I didn't need to. Yes, I had given up making my own batch in the bath each day, when stopping by to swap some bottles over was so much easier. Plus, they seemed to enjoy doing it for me, and who was I to spoil their fun?

"Good morning Protector," came the ever-happy voice from the back door of the temple as I approached. I hid my grimace behind my best fake smile as I approached.

"Jasmine, so nice to see you as always," I greeted the middle-aged woman politely. I had never really got over Mr Vontant possessing her to come and help me within the temple — demons being unable to enter its sanctified ground — but what worried me the most was she seemed so much more bearable when possessed by a demon than when left alone in her own body. When solo, she was just some silly, lost, middle-aged woman wearing white bedsheets and lacy curtains.

Keeping the conversation to a minimum to avoid showing her how I truly felt, I thanked her for my daily purified water and headed to my car. Gone were the days where I felt silly carrying bottles of salty water around in my bag, even if these glass ones did chink and jingle in a way that let everyone know they were there. Still the other option was to wander about with the old milkman's wire framed basket containing glass bottles of purified water, which is how I received my daily half-a-dozen. I often felt it was meant to be an amusing prank, something the High Priestess was known for, but I just wasn't going to bite.

I put the wire rack of bottles down on the floor of the front passenger seat of my car, another new addition within the past six months after a demon — not Mr Vontant — had destroyed my last one. I was just not going back to those memories either, as what I ended up doing to *that* demon still gave me goosebumps.

Sliding behind the wheel of the car I glanced at my unkempt hair and serious expression in the mirror. It was time to go sort some nasties of Darkness out. Here's hoping I could get it done by lunchtime.

# Chapter 2

———————⑤———————

I SURVEYED the shopping centre sceptically. It wasn't an area known for catering to the Other World. In fact it was in the tourist trap area of the city and full of your typical boutique type shops that sold unnecessary fripperies to those with more money than sense. There was one of those expensive crystal figurine shops, a 'genuine souvenir' two dollar shop, some kind of Asian general store with an overabundance of kitsch ornaments and furniture on display out the front. There was also a store that seemed to purely sell TV and movie merchandise, and the Irish shop I had come to investigate. I mean, I had been annoyed at such shops when they had been popular. But seeing one surviving now after all the Celtic craze had settled just had my teeth on edge. Usually this was a good sign that something Other Worldly was going on in a place. But I *really* did hate such places in general. I was fairly certain most people had a little Celtic in them, as their rampaging was as renowned as that of the Vikings. But to use that as an excuse to wear green in March and to tattoo shamrocks on your backside? Pass!

Actually, the on edge feeling I was starting to get didn't just stem from the little Irish memorabilia shop in front of me. I was starting to get that itch at the back of my neck that tended to mean someone had spotted me, and they were also a card carrying Other Worlder. As Mr Vontant was yet to make an appearance, I was guessing it wasn't someone who walked in the Darkness too deeply, but still I was starting to get into one of my very bad moods.

I glanced back toward the Asian shop behind me, had someone just ducked out of sight? Right, well once I had the Irish shop sorted out, I would go see what was going on in there too. I mean, why just pick on one nationality a day?

"Top o' the mornin' ta you!" chirruped the ruddy complexioned, curly haired gentleman behind the counter as I entered the shop. I wasn't too sure if it was my outfit or my expression that stopped him from continuing with his phoney accent and cringe worthy clichés.

"Uh, is there anything in particular you be after?" he tried, as my expression changed from scowling at his 'Kiss me I'm Irish' t-shirt to the neutral expression I took on when trying to sense the bad stuff I was meant to sort out.

"Just browsing," I replied calmly, taking in the shop and all its little knick-knacks. It was your typical Irish shop containing the range of cheap and nasty kitsch through to your overly expensive handcrafted silver and leather goods. Some of it wasn't half bad, when you got into the leather and jewellery section. Still, that wasn't helping me and I tried to focus more as I wandered the few shelves the place had.

Roxanna, in her usual manner of being deliberately obscure, hadn't actually told me what I was here to do. Simply that there had been reports of 'items of Darkness' being sold from this shop. Bravo Roxanna, we both knew that could mean anything!

"You sure dere's nottin' te take yer fancy?" asked the shop owner again as I finished my circuit of the store and approached the counter once more. I did my best to keep my expression neutral, despite the overly annoying fake accent. I was just thinking through the best *polite* response when I got a tickle at the back of my neck and my eyes were suddenly drawn to a large display of eggcups. They were little white ceramic cups with poorly attached transfers of landmarks in Ireland, which would normally have them in the cheap and nasty section. But they had a warmth and glow to them that made me want to reach out and touch them, to feel them and see why they were just *so* attractive.

"Ah, me pretty little wee cuppies. One of me best sellers if I do say so ma'self," chirruped the fake accent as the man came out eagerly from behind the counter and over to where I stood. "Feel free to touch them my lovely. None of dat silly 'break it buy it' malarkey in *my* shop!"

I pulled my gaze from the eggcups and raised a cynical eyebrow at the man.

"I'd appreciate you dropping the act," I said, keeping my tone quiet as I turned back to the cups and reached out for one.

"Ah, sorry about that. It's just what most of my customers expect. But they are lovely cups aren't they? Have a feel, see what you think. Nice bit of balance to them. Perfect for the whole family."

I picked up one of the little ceramic cups and tried not to notice the sharp intake of breath from the man at my side. I flipped it over to see the price tag on its underside and blinked a few times at the three figure sum.

"Made in Ireland, are they?" I asked casually, turning my attention back to the man, my face all sweet smiles and innocence.

"To be sure, to be sure." He grinned then his face clouded as he studied my expression further. There was always just a *little* bit of strain around the edges when I plastered happy over pissed off.

"And you'll be buying it now surely?" he asked, scampering back to behind the counter to the cash register as I followed and placed the cup down on its glass surface.

I made a show of glancing about his shop and even feeling along the nearby door jamb for engravings.

"I don't see your signage for selling Fae ware," I said pleasantly. "May I see your licence for dealing with Other World goods in a mainstream environment?" My smile widened naturally as his expression paled and he realised he'd been rumbled.

"Licence?" he mumbled, starting to pat at his shirt and pants as if trying to find a piece of card. "But surely you just want to pay that *very* reasonable price for the eggcup?"

Was there an edge of panic now in his voice? Oh yeah, I did so love it when they got that edge of panic!

"What? This piece of tat?" I asked and picked up the cup, tossing it at him. He gave a squeak and dodged to one side so that the eggcup smashed on the tiled floor at his feet. I did my best amused cat like stare — I'd been learning it from Roxanna — and casually wandered back over to the display of cups and grabbed another.

"Clumsy me," I smiled, placing the new eggcup on the counter. "Perhaps you should put this one in bubble wrap while you get that licence," I said sweetly and pushed it toward him. He recoiled with a stricken look. Our eyes met and I let my sweet and innocent expression fall and my look of distaste show. He recoiled further into his little corner behind the counter.

"So let me get this straight, you little Irish wannabe," I started coldly. "You know what they are, or at least what they make people do. But you don't have a warning up that your shop contains them and you're such a greedy little newb you actually *believed* me when I said you needed a licence to be a member of the Other World?"

"I was just. . . My rent. . . I needed to. . ." He wilted under my gaze. "The man who sold them to me said no one would know and that it did no real harm."

I raised a sceptical eyebrow at him. "These are Fae cursed cups." I stated bluntly flexing my leather gloved fingers as if spoiling for a fight. I then picked the object in question up again. "It means anyone who touches it, with their bare skin I may add, will be overcome with the overwhelming need to own it no matter what the cost." I gave him my best nasty look. "And how on *earth* is charging four hundred and fifty dollars per eggcup *not* harming someone? Even in this day and age that is a *lot* of money."

The shopkeeper slumped even further into his corner and looked resigned to whatever fate I was about to give him.

"I'm sorry. I just wanted to keep my shop and it seemed too good a trick not to try!"

He did seem to be someone green to the Other World who was more interested in making money than dabbling in the Darkness. I sighed and picked up the eggcup again and put it back on the shelf.

"You're lucky I'm in a good mood," I said resignedly, and returned to the counter and fished in my voluminous handbag for a business card. "I will give you a week to take all, and I *do* mean *all*, your stock of Fae ware to Friar Thomas here to be destroyed." I handed over the business card for a Catholic monk in the know over on the South side. For being a man of the cloth for a religion that usually scoffed at the existence of the Other World, he was still a nice guy. He also knew a couple of useful ways of safely disposing of cursed items.

"And I assure you I *will* be checking up on you in seven days' time and expect to see his receipt in your hot little hand." I gave the shopkeeper a stern look. "Oh, and don't think of just running or trying to hide from me." I warned him, time to instil a decent bit of fear in the fellow. "I know who you are, I know where you live, and I have a few demons who owe me a favour."

He gulped and looked rather scared, oh *good*.

"Wh. . . Who are you?" he stammered, gently taking the card from me.

"Someone you should learn to respect," I told him curtly. "You are dabbling in the Other World and I strongly suggest you stop while you just have your toes wet. I'm known as the Protector of Souls. And if you don't watch how you tread, I can assure you we will be meeting again. And the next time we do, it may be because your soul needs my protection." Words were important, even when addressing a newb, as they really needed to learn about it all before it was too late. "I may walk in the Light, but I can still decline to help someone who pisses me off too much." And, with my best meaningful look, I turned and walked out. Yes the jingling of glass bottles in my bag may have detracted from the dramatic effect I had been after, but I really did feel I'd got my point across. Especially as he immediately shut the door behind me and took a box and, hand wrapped in a t-shirt, started carefully removing the eggcups from off the shelf. I only knew this as I had stopped outside to collect myself and my thoughts.

People like him got me so frustrated that I always felt the need to just stop and take a few deep breaths after dealing with them. Yes I was fairly new to the Other World, and yes I made some dumb mistakes when at the newbie level too. . . but Isis damn it, *I* had at least tried to realise exactly how deep in the mess I had been to try and stop myself sinking further. Those who felt they could just *dabble* in the Other World for their own gain and profit — and not have to deal with the payback — were not just stupid, but usually dead soon after they did it. And, as with most things, ignorance was *no* excuse. Words and appearance may be important in this Other World I now worked in, but it basically all came down to weights and balances, Darkness and Light. To survive in the Other World and still be able to live in what was laughingly known as the 'real' world, you had to truly know what you were doing and take responsibility for your own actions. Otherwise you ended up facing me in my gloves and bag full of glass bottles of salt water, or became a smear on the bottom of something's foot.

Flashing one last frustrated look back at the man in the shop, now carefully removing the eggcups with an occasional worried look over his shoulder at me, I moved off. As I did so I took out my phone to not only put a reminder in my calendar to indeed come back and check up on the shop in seven days, but to text Roxanna I was done.

'Fae cursed cups. The man was an idiot.' That pretty much summed it up. Just because I walked in the Light didn't mean I always had to be polite.

As I slipped my phone back into the back pocket of my pants I got that usual itchy feeling that meant someone was watching me. I turned back to the Asian general store I'd spotted earlier and gave it a good hard look. It didn't *feel* like it had anything Other Worldy about it and, quite honestly, when you found one shop dabbling in the Other World in an otherwise mainstream area, you didn't tend to find another. Glancing about there wasn't a sight or sound of Mr Vontant so I guessed nothing too dire was threatening to happen and so stepped toward the shop.

Although giving it the generic title of 'Asian' store suited its mishmash of items, it did seem to have a leaning toward Chinese objects. As I approached I ran a casual hand over the wooden tables and chairs out the front and had to stifle the stab of pain I got from the carved wooden boxes on display. Despite the very first ghost I had freed being one of the biggest pains in the arse, he had helped me through a lot. Because of him, I often found myself making a cup of tea and just sitting and watching it steam away when I was feeling at my loneliest and most lost. Though I would obviously never admit doing it if anyone ever asked. Instead I just fobbed it off as a cup I'd made for myself, and then forgotten. Not everyone believed me but hey, Roxanna tended to be even more sceptical than me.

Shaking off the pang of emotion I often felt when missing Trishna, I strolled into the shop with my best 'casual shopper' look. There didn't seem to be anyone there. Inside was much like outside, but the shelves were more cluttered. Half the shop appeared to hold the furniture and knick-knacks that people wanting an Asian look or feel to their home would buy, while the other half contained traditional Asian foods.

Not entirely realising I was doing it, I found myself wandering toward the tea section to browse the various types they had. I did like the smell of Darjeeling in the morning.

Suddenly the prickling sensation began again, from behind me this time and I almost cursed out loud for allowing myself to get distracted and letting whoever it was sneak up behind me. Even as the arms grabbed me from behind by the shoulders and twisted me around, while pinning me to the wall, I wasn't as worried as I should have been. I mean, Mr Vontant would be pulling them off me and ripping them a new one shortly, right? I then realised that only counted for those who walked in the Darkness of the Other World and, sadly, your everyday criminal didn't exactly fit into that category. Damned demon loopholes!

I braced myself for the attack, despite it all happening so quickly, but was still admittedly stunned when my supposed attacker leaned in and planted a rather overly passionate kiss right on my mouth. It's not as if he, and I was fairly sure it was a he, smelled or was greasy or something but still. On. My. Mouth. Uninvited. It got my blood boiling in just the right way that had me start to struggle against him as he moved his body closer to mine. So occupied in what he was doing, my would be passionate assailant was standing in just the wrong way. I proved this when my left knee rose swiftly between his spaced apart legs and impacted soundly with the area I was fairly certain he was currently thinking with. Seriously, just because I'd not been kissed in years didn't mean any weirdo would do.

As my attacker wheeled away, crumpling to the ground as he went, I stood there too stunned to know what to do next. Despite his aggressive and thoroughly inappropriate behaviour, there was something to the fellow that didn't make me want to scream rape at the top of my voice. And so I blinked down at him, shivering as the adrenaline surge slowed and I caught up with the world around me. There was another tingle mixed with this shiver, something vaguely familiar and yet not tangible enough to help me figure out what the hell had just happened. That was, of course, until the man at my feet opened his mouth.

"You little fetid whore monger's daughter. Is that a way to treat an old friend, you hairy arsed end of a hippo?" Oh my God, I mean *Isis*. It wasn't that he was insulting me. . . it was *how* he was doing it.

"Trishna?" I asked weakly, staring down at the prone man with more disbelief than I thought my sceptical brain would allow. I prodded him with my foot. Yep, definitely a man, a solid form. Not a ghost and definitely not the ghost I had laid to his final resting place six months earlier. They weren't meant to come back, were they? No one had mentioned dispatching the dead meant they'd pop up later on as a real person. And, sweet Isis, I hoped this wasn't going to happen to all the ghosts I'd released as not all of them were entirely happy with me when I had done it. I prodded him with my toe again, I couldn't help it.

"Kneeing me in the pants is one thing, but if you're going to put the boot in frizz features, you're doing it all wrong."

I almost swung my foot for good measure at that remark, but remembering I was supposed to be one of those who walked in the Light instead stepped forward to help him to his feet.

"You can't be Trishna," I stated propping the, still obviously in pain, man against a nearby shelf. I mean, he was of a similar looking age and

Chinese but other than that there was no similarity. Except for the potty-mouth of course. And since when did that make him the solid form of a ghost I had sent on to be reborn as part of his Buddhist faith?

"And as you're not Trishna, what the hell did you think you were doing grabbing me like that?!" I gave him a hard thwack on the shoulder. Hey, people who walk in the Light can lose their tempers from time to time too you know. "And, actually, if you *are* Trishna — what the hell are you doing kissing me like that!" Another thwack.

"Just let me catch my breath you frazzle-haired harpy so I can explain!" he wailed and I took a few steps back to give us both some personal space. I was suddenly thankful Mr Vontant wasn't here to witness it all as I was sure he'd have been on the floor with laughter by now. I spent the next few minutes staring suspiciously at the man across the aisle from me and tried to calm down by counting slowly from ten. The man looked *nothing* like Trishna, I could see this the more I watched him. He was taller, skinnier, had hair that was in need of a cut — from the way his fringe hung over his eyes — and a shave from the sprinkle of whiskers under his nose and on his chin.

My anger at his assault started to mix with the anger and bitter disappointment I felt over tricking myself into suspecting this man had anything to do with Trishna. He was gone, and good riddance — he had been a horrible companion. That was, until the end and he had helped me face the pain I tended to keep deep inside me. Had given me his strength to help me face my sister and release her from the vampire who possessed her. And then there was what he had done with our auras moments before he went to his resting place. . . damn it, I was getting tears welling up in my eyes now and this was *so* not the right time to have to face any of those memories again. And so I did what I normally did and shoved them deep down inside myself and stormed off. He was no threat, he was not someone walking in the Darkness. He was just some stupid shopkeeper with busy hands one step away from being a rapist. Let the real world cops deal with his sort.

"Stephanie, wait!" his pleading call reached my ears as I stepped through the door of his shop and back into the main part of the shopping centre. I stopped. Eyes closed, anger keeping a tight lid on all the other emotions. It was my cloak and protector that way. How did he know my name?

"Stephanie?" his voice was a lot closer now, less pleading, more questioning. I wasn't going to turn, I was going to just keep walking and get the hell out of there until I had to come back to check on the jolly olde worldy shoppe keeper in his stupid fake Irish store in a week's time. I glanced over at the shop in question, it was still closed but from here I couldn't tell if he'd finished clearing that shelf. Maybe I should just go and check once more?

I fought to ignore the hand that gently touched my shoulder, trying to turn me back to face my Asian shop assailant. But something inside me made me turn all the same. I refused to believe it was the odd tingle I felt from his hand touching me. Faint, but still familiar.

"How?" I asked, never one to faff about with questioning. This man was Trishna. I don't know how or why, but he bloody well was and I didn't know how I felt about it.

"Words are important, dumb arse," he smiled at me, as if that was meant to explain it all.

"You do realise that, in solid form, there are worse things I can do in response to your language than just burn a tea bag," I told him coldly, not wanting to let my guard down on all this. I mean, it's not as if I would have flung myself into his arms or anything. I didn't think of Trishna in that way *at all*. . . despite his parting gift. I just didn't want to have him back in my life again, have him as an emotional crutch, then whisked away when I felt I needed him the most. I had enough weird crap happening in my life without needing to add him back into the mix.

I realised he was smirking at my comment and despite him being a different man, and having a different face, it was still Trishna's smirk and, with tears in my eyes, I realised exactly how much he had used to piss me off with that look. Still, being in solid form did mean I was able to, possibly childishly, stomp hard on his foot and take off back to my parked car before he could catch up.

Seriously, when a ghost is sent to their rest, I expected them to stay there, not open up a shop in tourist town and kiss me. That was so *not* on the Protector of Soul's job description!

# Chapter 3

---⊖---

"AND you say it was Trishna?" Roxanna said, sometime later as I sat in her office within the Temple of Isis. I always felt like a naughty school girl sent to the principal's office when I was there. Not that I'd ever experienced that when I *was* a school girl. No, I was usually there to pick up my sister who *had* been that sort of school girl.

"It was him," I replied dully. We'd had this same conversation about eight times now and there were only so many times I felt I could say the same things without it getting boring. And that had been at about the fifth time we'd said it all. Still, Roxanna had a way of circular questioning me that often helped us both eventually find the answers to things we didn't think we *would* find answers for. So I went through it all — again.

"You could see his aura and knew it was him?" she asked, offering to top up my coffee, which I declined by holding my hand over my cup. The last thing I needed was caffeine induced heart palpitations to end an already shitty day.

"No, I couldn't see it." Yup, I'd already said this as well. "But I could *feel* it, and it was him. That same tingle of shared energy and strength we used to have."

Roxanna frowned, this was a different expression than the last seven times, so that was good. . . right?

"But the binding between you and Trishna would have been broken when his box was burned and the spell destroyed," Roxanna said, thinking it through as she spoke. What she was saying now was new, so I started to pay attention again.

"Okay, now this time try saying it in a way that makes sense," I asked politely. It's not as if it had been the first time I'd had to ask her to dumb down Other World stuff to my level.

"It means," Roxanna replied patiently, "that he shouldn't have been able to share his energy with you. Only a soul bound to another can do that. The fact that he could do it as a ghost doesn't mean he should have been able to do it as a human."

"Because a ghost's soul is mere energy and is able to be used as a tool to increase the powers of the person who possessed them, unlike a body which is a whole other kettle of fish, right?" Okay so I had started off sounding like I knew what I was talking about but stumbled along the way. Roxanna was used to this.

"Something like that," she smirked. "And, he said 'words were important'? I just wish I could remember what it was you'd said exactly when you released him," she mused. "Because I'd put money on that being the reason he's back."

I gave her my best unamused look. So, yes I had had a little trouble with grasping how important words were to the Other World when I had first started out. I felt, however, I'd got it down pat by the time I'd sent Trishna to his last resting place. And hang on, a Priestess of Isis could bet too? Was there anything forbidden in this place?

"Oh, it was something along the lines of 'I wish for you to find peace as you return to your point of death and find freedom there'," came an amused voice from the doorway.

I jumped; I physically leaped an inch out of my chair with the shock of not knowing he had been standing there. Roxanna just calmly turned her head to the door with an eyebrow raised in question. Hey, you didn't get to be the High Priestess of Isis by being surprised so easily.

"Trishna I presume?" she asked the wiry Chinese man leaning against her door jamb. How long had he been there? I turned to face him, angry he had figured out where I would be.

"High Priestess, long time," he said with a smile at Roxanna, and then calmly walked into the room to take the chair next to me.

"Released 'to your point of death'. . . yes, I can see how that would have done it." Roxanna returned to the conversation as if some rude and complete stranger hadn't just barged in and sat down uninvited.

"Please tell me she's got better at the wording of things since then," Trishna said, grinning at Roxanna and deliberately ignoring me. I gave him my best pissed off look.

"She has." Roxanna actually returned his smile with one of her own. "Her demon, Mr Vontant, has been very educational in his assistance and tends to make a face at her when she's getting it wrong."

"I'm right here you know. And he is *not* 'my demon'." I felt the need to point this out as they seemed so absorbed at discussing my flaws as if I wasn't present. Besides I *did* get the words right these days and it wasn't due to Mr Vontant. Well, not always. It was just the more I'd learned about all the Other World dos and don'ts, I'd tended to find the right rhythm in what I was meant to say. Then there were the times the words just came, as if it wasn't me saying them. So what if Mr Vontant winced over a few things, it barely influenced the outcome. I think.

"It is very hard to miss you when you're sitting right there," grinned the man who would be Trishna, eyeing me over in a way I wished he wouldn't. That kiss was still rather fresh in my memory and it made me squirm. It was like being kissed by a cousin who got the wrong idea about mistletoe at Christmas, and boy was *that* a bad enough memory.

"Nice gloves by the way," he added. "They complete your outfit and make you stand out like a complete crazy lady with crap hair *so* well." If he wasn't Trishna, he was doing a very good impression of him.

"Okay," I sighed, deciding to ignore him as best I could, and focused my attention on Roxanna, "Tell me where I went wrong. You're both obviously reading from a different part of life's little script than I am, so spill."

Amusement sparkled in Roxanna's eyes and her imitation of cat playing with a mouse increased. "When you release a ghost, what is the wording you use?" she asked me calmly.

"She's released more than just me? Buddha help us!" muttered Trishna *sotto voce*.

"I tell them to go to their final rest and be at peace with the world," I replied, racking my brains for where I went wrong with Trishna and hoping like hell they weren't all coming back.

"You don't tell them to go back to their point of death and find freedom there?" I could tell by Roxanna's tone she was pointing out my obvious mistake and waiting for me to see it. I thought over her words a moment and then groaned. Had I really done that? Was it really possible for it to have happened?

"I sent him back one hundred years to when he died and he just continued on his path to enlightenment through reincarnation from there to modern day. . . didn't I?" I sighed glumly at the stupid wording and sat on my hands to prevent myself from flipping the bird at Trishna when he laughed.

"By Jove, I think she's got it!" Trishna said.

Oh screw him with bells on.

"I don't suppose you made this mistake with any of the others?" Roxanna added casually, looking amused as I sank lower in my seat, feeling a complete fool. "I mean, that Cavalier bound to a stone from Leeds castle someone was using as a doorstop was rather cute and seemed to have a thing for you."

Oh, yeah, Gerald. Wasn't he just a hum dinger? Until I'd found the right way to release him he'd sat on my bed every night reciting poems of love. Gag! I'd ended up storing his stone down in the crypt of the Temple just to avoid him. That was, until I'd released him properly.

"No, no. . . Fairly certain I just told him where to go in the nicest possible way," I added, attempting a casual tone myself. "Go being to his final resting place, of course."

"Sure it was," Trishna smirked.

Why did I suddenly have the urge to set fire to something tea like?

"Okay, look I'm sorry! I stuffed up!" I near yelled this at them both as I sat up straight in my chair. "I would like to point out I'd been doing reasonably well at all the Other World stuff at that point, what with only having been doing it a few days and having just killed my sister and all."

"You didn't kill her, she was already dead," Roxanna pointed out sympathetically. "You merely released her soul from the vampire that would have taken it to purgatory."

I sighed. When you worded it like that I didn't always feel so bad.

"And then there was that releasing thing you did on Jamal in the Tormented Whore," Trishna added in tones that just screamed it really was him. I still don't remember giving my leg the order to lash out and kick him in the shins, but gosh it felt good.

"Children, please," admonished Roxanna amused. "We are a Temple of peace and understanding after all." Part of me had wanted to complain that he had started it, but the more mature side of me kept it quiet and I just gave him a stony stare as he rubbed his bruised shin.

"Well, this has been. . . pleasant," I said, rising to my feet to leave. "And now that we've established the cheesy guy in the Irish shop was selling illegal Fae wares to the unsuspecting, and the sleazy guy in the Asian store was just Trishna in a new incarnation, I best be going. I've got a load of washing to hang out and some items to purify in my Inner Sanctum." Yeah, I actually had one too, fun huh?

I waved to Roxanna and deliberately ignoring Trishna walked out, it was that or I *would* flip him the bird. Well, at least I tried to walk out. I got as far as the doorway before Roxanna cleared her throat in a way that stopped me in my tracks. I turned meekly and gave her an innocent look.

"Trishna, if you don't mind me calling you that, even though I'm fairly sure that's not your current name, is there any restitution required from Stephanie to apologise for making you relive that last one hundred years again?"

By Isis that was a mouthful, even for Roxanna. Uh-oh. . . restitution, relived the last century? I really didn't like the sound of that.

"Mark, Mark Luò," Trishna replied, "but around you two, being Trishna feels okay." He glanced over at me as I tried to casually slink back into the room, awaiting my obvious punishment. "And to be honest, it's not been the last one hundred years that I've remembered who I am." Here he shrugged and seemed to be focusing on something within himself for a moment. "I mean, I've always gotten snippets of things my Granny said were part of a past life and which I should use to ensure I didn't stray from the path to enlightenment. Most of the time I felt she was just being a strict Buddhist and Grandmother. It wasn't until I saw Stephanie outside my shop today that I got one almighty headache and all my visions and things coalesced into. . ." He stopped and stared helplessly at the two of us, for the first time looking like the stranger he was and not the ghost I had known.

"So you haven't been living Trishna's life all over again," Roxanna said relieved. "That would explain why you've never come to us before now. I can't say you feel like someone who's walked the Other World's path before."

"I *am* Trishna though," Mark said quietly. "At least now I am. I just wasn't when I got up this morning." Another helpless look. "I am Mark too. But up until an hour ago I didn't really feel like I was who I was meant to be. Now, it seems to have all clicked."

I stood there staring down at him as he stared up at me as if I was offering him a life line.

He shook his head. "You have been an imaginary friend in my life since I was five years old. Then, when I saw you, *really* saw you today. . . all the emotions and relief and joy. . . I thought I was meant to kiss you as you were what I'd been waiting for."

I supressed a shudder as I started to realise exactly how badly I'd stuffed up his life. . . lives?

"He kissed you?" Roxanna sounded startled more than amused. Yeah, I'd kind of skipped over that part and just said he'd attacked me.

"I shouldn't have," Trishna admitted, while I tried to find the right words. "I just didn't know how to handle the emotions and happiness I felt at seeing Stephanie again, finally. The happiness. . . the. . . energy I felt."

"We are linked." I was surprised that small sentence had come out of my big mouth. Man I hated it when part of my brain was able to follow the Other World conversations better than the rest of me could.

"Whatever it was I did, we did, we're linked," I said, sitting back down in the chair next to him, facing mine toward his this time, not toward Roxanna's giant desk. Our knees bumped as he turned his chair toward me too. Suddenly I realised what was going on and just needed to find the words to explain it. It's why I was what I was in the Other World — a Protector of Souls.

"I'm sorry that I sent you all the way back to when you died," I said slowly. "But your lives since then have been sheltered, been at peace. That's what I told you to be. It also meant you didn't remember. But hell, how many people — even the truly devoted — remember their lives from past incarnations?" I glanced at Roxanna, almost expecting her to give me a figure.

"But, when you came back to this time line, the connection grew stronger as I was already here." Yes, I could tell he was obviously younger than me. Not that I was a cougar or anything, okay? I tried not to think about how I suddenly knew all this and just focused on saying it.

"What had happened here, before you were released, has been humming about in that Other World energy pool we all draw on and so you've been getting flashbacks the closer you've come to when we first met. And seeing me again today just broke through the mist of memories and. . . here you are." Wow, had I really just said that? And how did I know it was all correct? 'Other World energy pool'? Huh?

"By Isis that rings such a tone of truth you've just given me goosebumps Stephanie," Roxanna murmured. "I am always amazed when you come out with these things."

Oh, um, that had been a compliment, right?

"So, did you miss me?" Trishna asked quietly.

I allowed myself to meet his gaze as my eyes filled with painful tears. "More than I would think I should have," I told him, choking up. This wasn't the reuniting of lost lovers, but the emotions were still pretty high. He had been there for me, had given me the strength to be what I had to be through my darkest and nastiest thoughts. Had been my link to the Light when I was smothered by the Darkness I'd been holding within me. And then I had had to say goodbye as I'd promised to free him from his ghostly imprisonment. I had been left alone when I'd still needed that support. The last six months seemed to suddenly catch up with me. They had been really hard for so many reasons. But I had never dreamed of giving in and turning my back on my new vocation. Despite the grim duties I often found myself performing, I was working in the Light and I *was* protecting souls. But I had been doing it without the safety net I had started out with — Trishna. I had been living on the edge and had been afraid of teetering into the Darkness the more time I spent with people like Mr Vontant to show me the way.

Trishna touched my hand and I felt that old tingle somehow, that sensation he was giving me his energy.

"I'm back now," he said quietly. "And you're sure as shit going to find it a lot harder to get rid of me this time." And that was all it took to have me burst into tears. So much for this protector of souls being as tough as nails!

***

It had taken me a while to recover from our reunion, so by the time I let myself back into my little cottage, it was late afternoon. I also had a guest with me.

"Quaint, in an overly religious and rather under-furnished sort of way," Trishna grinned, as he dropped a duffle bag just inside the front door and watched me as I locked and bolted it. I hadn't really wanted to lock and bolt it with him on the inside, heck I didn't want him here at all. But the burn mark on the floor was always there as a reminder as to why I *did* lock and bolt it.

"Demon?" Trishna asked, pointing to the burn.

"Misguided hate filled fireball," I replied as casually as one could when discussing a curse that focused someone's negative energy into a small corporeal ball of fire that could be thrown at will. Or at me, as had been the case on that occasion.

"Really? You pissed off a Black Witch coven?" he asked and I was surprised at how nice it felt to turn such weirdness into a normal conversational topic.

"It's not as if I started it," I complained. Actually I rarely ever *did* start it. "They stupidly summoned Mr Vontant for some full moon ritual and, according to that deal I have with him, I rocked up and freed him. The fact they'd summoned a couple of other demons for the ritual too and were using the ghost of a twelve year old Roman slave girl as a familiar just pushed me over the edge. I mean, a *twelve year old* trapped as a ghost for a couple of millennia. Poor thing had been terrified her whole afterlife."

"Fair enough," Trishna said, with an odd look of amusement on his face. "How about you give me the quick tour and then show me what sort of putrid floor sweepings from an incontinent weasel you serve as tea around here."

Ah, and to think I'd thought his potty-mouth had mellowed.

I sighed at this, remembering he had decided to come and stay with me, using the excuse of me owing him restitution to do so. I mean, we could still be the old team we used to be, with him still living at his own place, right? I had thought so, but was apparently wrong as here he was. I got the feeling he'd been living with that strict grandmother of his and any excuse to flee her wrath was good enough. Oh well, despite the emotional day I had caused, it was nice to have him back. . . sort of.

"So," I announced, clearing my throat in a way hopefully designed to clear my thoughts as well. "This is the burned front door." I waved at it. "This is the hall." That was self-explanatory as we were standing in it, "That is the lounge room, formerly known as the parlour. And the next door along is the study." I waved to two doors to my right as we moved down the hall. "That is the box room, though not in the way you may think." I pointed to the first door to the left. My house laughingly called a 'cottage' had, until recent decades, been a lay-in hospital. Meaning where women came to have babies, rest for a few days and then go home to the drudge life of the housewife. It was a large building, and the 'box room' was actually the former pharmacy-cum-laboratory. And let's just say I still used it for a little of those things when I had the time. Trishna let out a low whistle as he opened the door and gave it a quick glance. Yeah, I still didn't know what I was meant to do with half the stuff, but the Temple of Isis' Apothecary had stocked it and I was slowly working through her hand written notes on what it was all about.

"This next room is the Inner Sanctum. I recommend you only go in there when you really have to," I advised as the tour continued.

"Okay, things given that name — especially when capital letters are used — never fill me with joy," Trishna muttered. He eyed the door for a moment before opening it and stepping inside. The sanctum looked more like a store room to the untrained eye. Books, cups, ornaments and weapons were arranged about the room while the central part was just bare floorboards with a diagram known as 'the circle of the moon' painted onto the floor in a mixture of salt, sea chalk and silver. As I watched from the doorway, not entering myself, I noticed Trishna's expression change and then stepped aside as he blanched and fled back to the hall I was standing in.

"What in a demon's left testicle was *that?*" he asked me as I gently closed the door and tried not to smile. I *had* warned him.

"That room was the original birthing room, when this was a lay-in hospital. It was used for almost one hundred years and many thousands of lives began in that room," I explained. "The stone walls absorbed some of that beginning of life's energy, along with the emotions the events caused." Here I had to pause, remembering my own experience, and feeling the pain of others locked into the wall. Not all births had a happy ending. I felt Trishna's comforting hand on my shoulder before I realised what it was and was thankful he was there again.

"So the walls now store that force to such an extent it's a tangible presence," Trishna said softly, understanding not just about the room, but about my silence. "So I'm guessing all your really good shit is kept in there, right?" If he was trying to bring me back to the present by continuing to swear, it worked.

"Quite," I answered weakly, removing his hand — but giving it a brief squeeze of thanks as I did — so I could continue on the tour. Just after the Inner Sanctum there was a crossroad hall.

"Guest bedrooms are to the right," I continued, as calmly as I could. "Feel free to choose between the two of them as they're both unoccupied." I then waved a hand down the left side of the new hall. "My room and the bathroom on this side. Feel free to use the bathroom, but stay out of my room." As if I really needed to say that.

I led the way down the flight of four steps that led into the cottage's newer extension; basically a large, light and airy kitchen and dining room in a modern, open plan style. Most of the light came from the back walls made of glass. It had been built about twenty years ago but still looked and felt fairly modern due to the lack of use until I moved in. And I barely used the dining room area, it contained a heavy oak table that easily sat eight and I honestly didn't know that many people I'd really want over all at once. I mean, if I wanted to hang out with the Priestesses of Isis, I'd head on over to their restaurant style refectory. Heck it saved on the shopping, cooking and washing up if nothing else.

The kitchen itself was clean, white in colour, and had a small table for two sitting just outside its benched in area. That was where I ate when in a 'meals for one' frame of mind. I was yet to stoop to returning to eating in front of my TV. As a protector of souls, I did have an image to uphold.

"Kitchen, dining room, breakfast nook, and back door out onto paved area only ever used to cleanse things by moonlight. . . and an over-grown garden with high fences that the Temple's Apothecary tends and apparently loves that way." I waved my hands about one last time. "And I really recommend you *don't* go out into the garden. Not only is the Apothecary a bit of a grump if you accidentally step on one of her favourite weeds, I've seen what she uses to grow some of them, as well as what some of them are." Here I met Trishna's amused look and found I could leave the rest unsaid. It's not as if she was growing anything exactly illegal out there, but some of her methods — like comfrey grown in a sheep's skull on a bed of compost made from its brains — yeah, I just didn't want to know.

"Okay, nice, neat, not as anally precise as I had expected from you," Trishna mused as he wandered into the kitchen and looked through my cupboards, why *did* people find the need to do that?

"Oh, you want precise, that's definitely the study," I replied. There was no question that some of my old neat freak accounting hang-ups had followed me to my new life as that room, as overcrowded as it was, had been organised by me to within an inch of its life. And Isis help anyone who dared move even a pencil out of place. I spent many hours of my solo evenings in that room reading the old texts, making notes, and trying to get my head around the many things that made up the Other World. No there wasn't exactly an encyclopaedia on everyone or everything that was the Other World, but there were some reference books on rituals and routines that had helped. Plus I'd started my own 'Dummies book of the Other World' as I found making notes on all the craziness helped.

"Stop going through my cupboards and sit down, I'll make the tea," I announced, not because I wanted to, but because I *did* want him out of my cupboards.

"I would have thought I owed you enough cups of tea that I'd be making them for at least the next six months," Trishna grinned as he moved to the small table and sat down.

I shrugged, he was right but hey. I peeled off my gloves, thankful to be in a safe place again and went about the tea duties. Not knowing why I wanted to show off so much, I took down two small, eggshell thin porcelain tea cups of Chinese origin and a matching teapot. Once the kettle had boiled and the pot had been warmed, I added the tea known as Buddha's Tears, which got an approving whistle from Trishna, and then served it. Sitting down next to him I found myself smiling at his look of pleasure as he inhaled the steam.

"I was half expecting you to hate the damned stuff, having been trapped so long with it as your only comfort," I said, idly pulling my biscuit jar toward myself from the middle of the table and wondering if I'd eaten all the peppermint Tim Tams.

"There are some things that stick with you as their comforting presence is so strong." he said, giving me a look that made me feel uncomfortable. "I think that's why I probably started working in that Asian shop. I felt a connection to it and loved the discount I got on the tea."

I felt even more uncomfortable, not knowing what to say as it was my fault he'd been so messed up with those mixed memories. So I focused my attention on rummaging through the small biscuit jar.

"Any jam fancies?" he asked, taking the tin from me once I'd extracted a Tim Tam with a look of triumph. It was an odd feeling knowing he now had the ability to pilfer my biscuits. Still, if it helped with the restitution for what I'd done. . . why not! I could always buy more Tim Tams.

# Chapter 4

———————————S———————————

THE next morning it took me a moment to figure out why I could hear singing and smell bacon coming from my kitchen. I mean, yes, Mr Vontant occasionally just popped into being in my home but he'd never bothered to make me breakfast before.

I was able to stifle the groan as I rolled over onto my back and the memories of the previous day bitch-slapped me in the face. Trishna: new and improved, sort of. It had been. . . interesting.

We'd spent the afternoon with him listening to me drone on about what I'd been up to in the past months. How I'd learned to differentiate between hexes and curses, the demon releasing and all the rest. He had almost fallen off the chair from laughing so hard when he saw the little black book I kept with all the deals I'd made with demons before releasing and banishing them. Roxanna had raised her eyebrows when I'd first mentioned it to her too, but seriously, if you're going to do a favour with the scum of all evil, they should owe you one in return. And it's not as if I was using their favours to walk in the Darkness at all. It was usually simple things like them rugby tackling and taking back to Hell anything that wasn't willing to go when asked — nicely or otherwise — by me.

Trishna had then spoken briefly of his life as Mark Luò, his strict grandmother, and working at his richer cousin's shop. He'd led an apparently quiet and normal life, despite the dreams, and had felt he was almost in some sort of holding pattern until his full memories as Trishna hit him. My gut twisted a little at this as I once more felt the guilt of such a green mistake. Still, I was fairly certain I'd not made any stuff ups of that magnitude since. All the same, perhaps I needed to start carrying a little voice recorder around with me and then write out transcripts of all releasings and banishments. You know, in case I ever needed to follow up on another one?

We'd ended the evening with a meal at the Temple of Isis' refectory, after which I excused myself to work in my study while listening to

Trishna bitch about the lack of channels on the television in my lounge. He only stopped after I threatened to shove the remote somewhere. Yeah, a classy way to end the night with a man I owed restitution to. Just because I owed it though, didn't mean I had to be nice to him all the time, did it? I sighed realising I may just have to look that one up as maybe being nice to a jerk *counted* as restitution.

"Morning lazy bones!" Trishna said, as he burst into my room with far too much energy for the hour. And it was a mere seven in the morning may I add. I started up in bed and clambered into a sitting position with my best scowl as he placed a cup of steaming coffee next to me on my bedside table before throwing himself down on the bed next to me. This whole ghost with a solid body thing was going to take some getting used to. Especially when that body was only wearing pyjama shorts and a loosely tied dressing gown, and I was in just one of my oversized t-shirts.

"Sleep well?" he asked, and I just continued to scowl as wasn't that something I, as the host, should have been asking him?

"Seriously, even when not sleeping in a crumb-bum motel after spending most of the night guarding a vampire possessing your sister, you're a sour face in the morning." He grinned, leaning back into the pillows.

"I'd say bite me, but I'm a bit worried you would," I grumped. I really wasn't a morning person when it meant I had to spend said morning with others before I'd got a chance to reboot my politeness. I'd once had a nightie that had 'Don't poke the bear!' daubed on its front. I'd loved that nightie, as it really said it all when it came to me and interacting with people first thing.

"We've been over this Steph, I'm here for the restitution not sex. Although. . ." Urgh, he waggled his eyebrows at me and was lucky it was a pillow, and not my steaming cup of coffee, that was thrown at him.

"Out!" I demanded, as he rolled off the bed into a standing position. "I admit to owing you the best restitution I can possibly give. But I can assure you I need a bit of a run-up to 'nice lady' mode in the mornings."

"You have a 'nice lady' mode?" Trishna cocked an amused eyebrow at me. I think I preferred him with the shaved head; his eyebrows hadn't been so annoyingly mobile in that form. He caught the look in my eye and was off out the door before I stained the door jamb with said coffee.

\*\*\*

"So, what are the plans for the day?" Trishna asked me some time later, as I finished demolishing my second egg, bacon, cheese, and sweet chilli sauce white bread sandwich. Just because I walked in the Light didn't mean I had to eat healthy. And it wasn't as if I pigged out like that every morning. But if someone cooks me bacon for breakfast, a girl's got to do what a girl's got to do.

"Dunno," I replied, mouth full and licking sauce off my fingers. "Haven't checked my phone for messages yet, but pretty sure there'll be something there from Roxanna."

Rising to my feet I gathered all the dirty dishes from the small table, wondering idly if clearing someone else's plates counted toward restitution points. And were there such things as restitution points, I mean, there were brownie points, right?

After the spot of domesticity I needed in the mornings to keep the house at a decent level of cleanliness I sat down and looked at my phone. I'd actually checked in with Roxanna before coming to breakfast, but had enjoyed the naked anxious suspense building up in Trishna. So possibly there went my current restitution points, but watching him jiggle impatiently and eye my phone hopefully had been enjoyable.

To my surprise there was actually a new message from Roxanna and when I read it I was suddenly glad I'd been sitting down.

It read: 'Do you know Simon Welsh? He is trying to contact you.'

"Obviously someone you *do* know?" Trishna said with a mixture of curiosity and concern as he read the message over my shoulder. I was fairly certain he was responding to seeing all the colour drain from my face when I'd opened the message.

Simon Welsh, as much as I did my best not to stoop to Trishna's sewer level of the vocabulary, that name sure as shit made me want to have a damned good go at it.

"He was my ex-husband's best friend," I eventually replied, having fought down the desire to add a few colourful words to that description.

"Oh," was all Trishna said, surprising me with his tact.

"And chief instigator of our divorce."

"Oh!" Trishna said with more surprise, but still refrained from adding any extra nasty words.

"He convinced my then husband it was 'no big deal' that I'd lost our baby before she could be born. It wasn't true loss if we hadn't had a life to lose. When I couldn't get over it, he encouraged my husband to just up and leave. . . which he did."

"Well here's hoping he's looking to volunteer to be the next pin cushion for the Hellcats of Prin, and your ex can be the one after that. The pair of them are obviously lower than a turd scraped off of the wart riddled foot of a puss filled whore of hell." O-kay, so he didn't manage a whole conversation without adding his own special touch. As much as I winced at the description I actually agreed with him. Theo, my ex, didn't *have* to listen to that *dear* friend of his and ignore the personal hell I'd been going through. But he had, and I'd come to peace with it some time ago and basically regretted ever meeting him or that he still breathed. But hey, even a girl who walks in the Light and is a Protector of Souls can bear a grudge, right?

"I suppose I should call Roxanna and see what it's all about," I said, and sighed deeply. Why couldn't I just be left to deal with one problem from my past at a time? If it had anything to do with Theo trying to get back in touch with me, screw him. He'd had his chance and burned that bridge too long ago for me to want to listen to him now.

Roxanna answered my call almost immediately, and from her tone it appeared she'd been hoping I'd call sooner.

"Simon, huh?" I asked in way of greeting. "Would I lose my 'walking in the Light' privileges if I refused to talk to him?" I was rather proud there was no whine in my voice.

Trishna was looking impatient so I told Roxanna I was switching to speaker phone so he could be part of the conversation. Obviously the super duper hearing Trishna had had as a ghost hadn't carried across to the newer model.

"Unfortunately, in this matter I fear it would," Roxanna said reluctantly. "As it has nothing to do with your past and everything to do with your current path in life."

"We're talking about Simon Welsh here, right? Annoying, smug, pretty boy from a wealthy family who brought him up to have more money than sense, feelings or the consideration for others, Simon Welsh? A man who would only give you his time if you could turn it into a good one?" I realised I was now ranting *and* venting at the same time and bit back the rest of the words I'd wanted to use. There was some dirty laundry I didn't want to air in front of even Trishna and Roxanna.

"Although I can't vouch for all of that *delightful* description, he is indeed the Simon Welsh who was friends with your ex-husband," Roxanna said soothingly.

She could tell I was pissed and wanted to keep me focused. I'd been getting better at reading her tones so took a deep breath and let it out slowly. As I tried to calm myself Trishna placed a cup of tea in front of me. I inhaled the steam, Darjeeling, the bastard. It took me to the calmer memories of watching him in the Buddhist temple and as he placed a comforting hand on my shoulder, like in the 'old days' I felt the calm from these memories wash over me and bring my focus back to the fact this was a job for the Protector of Souls, otherwise Roxanna wouldn't be asking me. I glanced up at Trishna and smiled my thanks, wishing he hadn't been able to do that so easily.

"How can I, as Isis' chosen Protector of Souls, help him?" I said, trying for an attitude of calm professionalism. Perhaps if I didn't actually say his name I'd be fine.

"He learned from your parents of your new vocation and came here looking for you. He's. . . in a bad way."

Uh-oh, I didn't like the sound of that at all, Roxanna actually sounded uncomfortable.

"Define 'bad way.'"

"He has been taken under the wing of the Birdfolk of Wroth," Roxanna replied slowly.

If it hadn't been for Trishna's sharp intake of breath over that statement, I would have gone into a rant as to why those feathered fruit loops had it in for me.

"I'm guessing that's a bad thing, even for the Other World line of bad things?" I replied, inhaling more of the tea's steam in the vain hope of re-capturing my slowly diminishing calm.

"A very bad thing," Trishna replied. The worry in his eyes shredded the last of my calm. "How did he manage to enter the temple?" he asked.

"With great difficulty," she replied, her tone still holding an edge I didn't like. "I have some priestesses still cleaning up the vomit, but he thankfully didn't stay that long."

"Vomit?" I asked. Why, I really don't know.

"Think Exorcists type possession when it comes to holy ground," Trishna replied, "I'd guess he was only in the first stages if he was even able to get as far as seeking your help."

Okay, mental note to wear some old clothes when meeting Simon.

"I sent him to Shortens Park, two blocks east of here and said I would send you over," Roxanna added, hope now in her voice. "Though I must warn you Stephanie, once a person has been chosen by Wroth, there isn't much that can be done for them."

"And yet, as the Protector of Souls, I'll lose my licence if I don't at least give it a damned good try, right? Despite it being for some feckless idiot who probably deserved it." Yes, I was getting angry again, but this anger was now focused on the evil bastards ruining the life of a — and I was using the term rather lightly — innocent.

"I can assure you Stephanie, despite what this man may have done in the past, *no one* deserves a fate like this."

The reproach in Roxanna's voice had me try and focus my anger on what was important.

"Fine," was all I said, possibly a little more curtly than Roxanna deserved. "So tell me, any special equipment needed for this meeting? Or do I just turn up with my best professional smile and some wet wipes?"

"As always, go how you feel you should," Roxanna replied, calmer now, but in that annoying way she had when she wanted me to figure it out for myself. "You're a Protector of Souls, Stephanie. You know your path better than I do. Go with what you feel is best, as you know it will be the right way."

So, the usual little to no help, how awesome.

"Fine," I said again, as it seemed the only word I could manage without adding some more colourful ones to the sentence. "Unless I need a change of clothes from possessed-person spew splash-back, I'll come right to the temple once I'm done." I hung up and stared dumbly at my tea for a moment as if begging it to bring back my calm.

"I'm fairly certain he was only popping his cookies as he was on holy ground," Trishna announced as a way to bring me back to the matter at hand. "He should have dried up by now at that park, but best not to wear any religious symbols or such, just in case."

I gave him my best squinty-eyed look as I tried to figure out if he was attempting humour or truly offering me helpful advice. I sighed heavily as I realised it was the latter.

"Fine," I said, sticking to a nice safe word, before rising to my feet to go grab my gloves, bag and keys. It was time to go for a walk in the park to meet a man who helped ruin my life. Couldn't someone from my past who I actually *liked* come to me asking for help? Seriously?

# Chapter 5

I'D NOT yet learned why meetings with those referred to me from the Temple of Isis happened in parks, but I'd used Shortens for a few 'Protector of Souls' consultations before. It was small, tidy, and rarely used by people other than dog walkers and the odd cyclist. I knew for a fact that there was a large square patch of bare earth at the middle, with an old oak tree at its centre. The outside of this square patch of earth was lined with park benches, and this was where we found Simon.

I approached him from the far end, keeping to the shadow of the oak as much as possible as I wanted to assess the situation before he knew I was there. From this distance he just looked worse for wear after a night out on the town. Rumpled and stained clothes, stubble, messed up hair, and bleary-eyed. I'd spent a lot of my days courting Theo waking up to find such a sight sitting on my couch. Love had obviously made me stupid to not see it as a bad sign of things to come. Oh well, best not dwell on old business when it was new business I was here to attend to. I had to admit, that besides his rubbish appearance, there was a feeling I was getting from him that was new, and not very nice at all.

"Lovely day for it, Stephanie."

I groaned, and turned to find Mr Vontant standing under the tree.

"Seriously?" I asked him in exasperation, ignoring Trishna's sudden look of concern. "You choose *now* to come and protect me from a bad guy? I'm about to deal with something else and now I have to keep an eye out for flaming balls of hate or something?"

"Actually, I'd say he's here *because* he has to keep his part of the deal while you talk to Simon," Trishna said uneasily. "I've been trying to tell you, this is bad."

"Why it's the ghostly monk in a new suit of flesh and bone, how marvellous!" announced Mr Vontant as if describing something rather unpleasant. "Can't keep a good man, or even you, down I see?"

"Well if it isn't Satan's little helper. Stolen anyone's lunch money today you midget?" Trishna sneered. I don't know what surprised me more, his attitude or his lack of uncouth words.

"I'd be careful if I was you *monk*-ey man, as I'm sure there's a loop-hole to her deal that would allow me to make you a smear in the gravel," Mr Vontant bridled, and I felt a need to stop gawping at them and actually step in to sort it all out.

"I assure you I am fond of and wouldn't like this man here, who's letting me call him Trishna, hurt in any way," I told Mr Vontant, moving next to Trishna and placing my hand on his chest to indicate he was who I was referring to. "So back off before I call up another demon who owes me a favour to kick your arse back to the 'World Down Below' for me."

"I always knew you cared," Trishna grinned at me, before giving Mr Vontant a smug look.

"And you can stop tormenting the demon help!" I snapped at Trishna, quickly removing my hand due to the tingle I was getting from the touch. "I try and treat them with as much respect as one can give to evil little so-and-sos, and I'd like you to do the same please."

Despite the name calling, it was now Mr Vontant's turn to look smugly at Trishna. Seriously, it was as bad as being back in school.

"Just stop it now, both of you and can *one* of you explain why, exact-ly, Simon is now such a scary thing that I need a demon bodyguard when I talk to him?" Exasperated wasn't nearly good enough to de-scribe how I felt.

"This is why," Mr Vontant told me and, as a cloud covered the sun and threw the park into shadow, he waved his hands over my eyes. I really hated when he did that, even if it was the only way he could let me see things I usually, thankfully, couldn't.

Simon still sat on the bench, looking dishevelled and miserable, but there was now this black, shadowy little figure riding him piggyback, its mouth attached to the side of his neck, obviously sucking *something* out of him. I shuddered at the sight and, just before it faded, the creature lifted its head and looked straight at me, its bugged out eyes glaring, its wispy, smoke like hair floating about it and its jagged teeth set in a snarl. I half expected it to croon 'My precious' from how it looked, but then the sun came out and the creature faded back into the level of existence I couldn't see.

"Isis protect me," I breathed. I was not usually one for such statements, but I felt a certain need right then to remind the motherly Goddess of my existence. It had seemed better than 'Isis? A little help?'

I don't know if that creature, whatever it was, had alerted Simon to our presence, or if he suddenly realised there were three people under a nearby tree staring at him — one of them a man in a suit, another a man in jeans and a scruffy leather jacket and me in my near accountant uniform with gloves — but he suddenly looked my way and raised a hand in greeting.

"Before I go over there and risk him touching me, or shaking my hand or something, can one of you truthfully promise me that *thing* can't suddenly get on to me?" I asked shakily, raising my own hand in return.

"That *thing*, as you put it, is what your people call a wraith-like creature known as wroth," Mr Vontant replied calmly. "And no, transference and possession like this cannot happen without you expressly giving your permission to Wroth to take you and your life force."

"Wait a minute, wroth are a type of creature? I thought it was an evil God or something?" Yes, *that* was what I took from his answer. My mind skipped over why in the hell anyone would want to give themselves freely to a 'wraith-like creature'.

"Oh no, she's got that look on her face again," Trishna muttered, and I wondered how many restitution points I'd lose for elbowing him in the ribs.

"Wroth *is* a singular... person," Trishna explained. "But his minions are also called wroth as they belong to him, um, it... I think. It's something I really think we can discuss when there isn't a guy possessed by wroth wondering why you're not going closer to him now he knows you're here."

"And the Birdfolk bit?" I had to ask. I mean, these guys wore *nothing but feathers*! What was up with that?

"Less talking to us, more talking to him," Trishna hissed, pushing me forward. "You're perfectly safe, I mean you've got Mr Vontant here and all that."

Why then, did I feel far from safe as I slowly stepped forward to talk to Simon?

\*\*\*

"Stephanie, hi," Simon said, standing up and giving me a weak smile as I approached. Awkwardly he held out his hand for me to shake, but I instead crossed my arms to show I had no intention of doing any such thing.

"He probably doesn't know it's there and it can't just jump you without permission," Trishna hissed in my ear.

"Yeah, no. . . gloves or no gloves, there are far more reasons why I don't want to shake this bastard's hand," I said loudly and coldly enough for all around me to hear. For the moment, in the bright sunshine, I was ignoring the invisible wraith-like creature around Simon's neck and just focusing on what a turd he'd been in my past.

"Ah, still not over that misunderstanding." Simon tried to sound light hearted and mildly embarrassed as he spoke, but he wasn't fooling me. I'd insulted him to his face and he was still willing to speak to me? That in itself showed how desperate he was for my help. "Brought your posse along to beat me up if I say the wrong thing then?" he added in the snide tones of the Simon I knew and loathed.

"Simon, this is my friend Trishna, not here to beat you up, more for moral support," I replied by way of introducing them. "And this is Mr Vontant, and he won't be beating you up just yet either. . ."

"Unless you instigate it, of course," Mr Vontant said smiling and leaning forward to shake Simon by the hand.

A wary looked crossed Simon's face, as I'd hoped it would, before he ran his fingers through his hair and sat down shakily.

"Man Stephanie, I'd heard you'd taken up with some weird people, but I'd never expected *this*." Simon waved a dismissing hand at my two 'men', and their varied wardrobe, before turning his troubled expression back to me and staring a little too long for comfort at my elbow length gloves.

"And I didn't expect to see you back in my life until the day I got to dance on your grave. So I guess it proves we don't always get what we want," I told him with sugar coated sarcasm, ignoring Trishna's groan and face palm. Look, I'd said I'd meet him, not that I'd be *nice*.

"And speaking about what people want, Simon," I said in a brittle tone, "What *exactly* is it you want from me?"

"I. . ." he started and then seemed to get confused and shook his head as if to clear it. I subtly moved back a step, hopefully out of projectile vomit range. . . just in case.

"I need your help," he blurted out as though trying to tell me something before someone interrupted him. "I met this wild chick all in feathers, she took me to this club and all this weird shit went down. I thought I was in for a good night and all I can remember now is drinking a lot of some really potent booze and feeling like crap ever since."

Okay, so nothing had really changed in Simon's life then as, from memory, that sounded like a typical night out for him.

"And when was this?" asked Trishna, making me realise I should be focusing on the here and now Other World stuff, not my past, personal hatred of someone who was clearly a reject from the human gene pool.

"A week ago," Simon replied, eyeing Trishna warily. What? It's not as if he was still dressed as a monk or anything. The jeans, dark t-shirt and well-worn leather jacket actually suited his new form quite well. Not that now was the time to think such things.

"I woke with little memory of the previous night, one hell of a hangover, and the biggest hickey on my neck I'd ever seen," Simon continued.

"So, just a typical Saturday night for you then?" I said, unable to help myself.

"Something like that," Simon replied with a half-smile so like his old self my fists began to clench. "But the feeling just hasn't gone away and. . ." here he faltered and looked scared, "I hear things, see things, *feel* things that just aren't quite right."

"Possessions in most forms have these after effects for the first seven days as the carrier settles into its new host," Mr Vontant announced casually, not usually one to offer free information. Noticing my startled look he shrugged. "Everyone has to have a hobby you know."

O-kay, from his remarks, Trishna's visible embarrassment, and the horror dawning on Simon's face, this was just all going oh so well.

"Possession?" queried Simon, looking to me for a straight answer, "Come on Steph, that weirdo church was bad enough but what is he trying to tell me?"

I studied Simon for a moment, really not knowing the best way to proceed, then took a deep breath.

"Simon, remember my sister Estella? Well she joined that 'weirdo church' and became a Priestess of Isis. They tend to try and rid the world of those who walk in Darkness, like Mr Vontant here, who's a demon." What the hell, boots and all sounded a good enough approach to me.

"Unfortunately Estella got caught in a blood crossfire while she and her fellow priestesses were slaying a vampire. She got infected, became undead, and needed to be rescued before her soul ended up in purgatory. I did this, and was chosen by Isis herself to become a Protector of Souls. You know. . . Isis, the Goddess? She's moved with the times and is pretty awesome, not just some old Egyptian fogey. Anyhow, now it's my daily job to help those, under her guidance, who stray from the Light and are in trouble within the Darkness." Time to end on a high here people.

"Which is why I am now standing here, Simon. You've been possessed by some sort of wraith-like critter and I need to fix it before you end up in Hell."

Finished with my rant I stood back, and waited for the ridicule I was sure would follow.

"Actually, his soul will end up in Hell within the next day or so, replaced by the wroth possessing him," Mr Vontant apologised. "So unless you plan on doing something quickly, this is just lip service to make it look like you tried to do something useful, and cover your arse as Protector of Souls."

I glanced over to the neat freak demon and was about to say. . . something. . . when Simon caught my whole attention by leaping up onto the park bench and taking a swipe at me, only to have it deflected by Mr Vontant.

"Filthy little Protector who walks in the Light," came a strangled, growling voice from Simon's distorted face. "This body is now *mine*! Its soul is to be nested in among other souls of the damned down below. Do not try to stop me!" then, with a scream of rage like pain Simon threw himself down onto the ground in front of me, cowering with his hands over his head.

"Oh God make it stop, make it stop, *make it stop!*" he burbled in near hysteria.

Heck, I'm fairly certain I would have too if I was fighting something sucking the life out of me. As it was all I could do was stand there, open mouthed with shock at it all and expecting my subconscious to take over and fill in the blanks like it usually did. Nothing happened. Mr Vontant, however, bent down and picked Simon up off the ground, dusted him off and promptly handcuffed his hands behind his back. I didn't even know he carried handcuffs!

"There!" Mr Vontant said smugly. "Dark forces attacked you, I protected you, and I've now restrained your enemy. Be seeing you. . ."

"Hang on a minute!" I exclaimed as he turned to go, "How the hell am I meant to handle this now?"

Mr Vontant straightened his suit with visible irritation and gave me a withering look. "You do remember that answering your dim-witted questions isn't part of our deal, don't you?" he pointed out tiredly.

"You can't just handcuff someone and walk away," I insisted, trying to ignore the look of confused terror on Simon's face. "I mean, what if I need to take the cuffs off?"

"I can assure you that if he's been possessed for seven days you won't want to take those cuffs off him," Mr Vontant said. "Unless you want me to turn up again to slap another pair on him."

"Please help me," Simon whispered, staring straight at me. He was terrified, and who wouldn't be with that withered little nasty attached to your neck, slowly taking you over.

"Yeah, trying to do that right now Simon, just shush and let the grown-ups have a minute to sort this out," I said turning back to Mr Vontant. Yep, tact wasn't part of my job description either. "Mr Vontant, I need to know what to do to him to help."

The neat little demon frowned at me and took a step back to turn away. I mean, he'd been all info plus on the possession just a moment ago.

"I may have shared a bit of my hobby with you, but free information on how to *undo* a possession is not part of the deal Stephanie and I won't negotiate with you again. . . not after the last time. You have two choices, release him back to the chaps in the feathers or kill him. It's all that can be done for him now. There's no going back once this process has started." And before I could even splutter a protest, Mr Vontant had vanished.

"Oh God, oh God, oh God. . ." whined Simon, sinking to his knees, after witnessing the demon's departure. For once I was prepared to cut him some slack, after all it's not every day someone handcuffs you then vanishes into thin air in front of you.

"Calm down Simon, you're going to be okay," I said giving Trishna a pointed look, as I just *knew* he was about to correct me. Yeah, so I knew Simon was *not* going to be okay, but this was my thing now, trying to protect people's souls.

"How exactly am I going to be *okay?*" spat Simon still in near hysteria as he scrabbled away from me in the dirt, hands still cuffed behind his back. "I've been handcuffed by a guy you say is a demon who just told me I was being possessed, and then disappears into thin air. And there is this damned voice in my head telling me to kill you both and get back to Clarissa."

"Clarissa?" I had to ask to stop myself from slapping him, I mean yes his near hysteria was almost a good enough excuse to, but still.

"The woman all in feathers," he hissed, gritting his teeth and straining against the cuffs.

I looked to Trishna for advice and he just shrugged, I knew he wanted to tell me exactly what he knew and that it was truthfully not the best news for Simon but his new found form obviously held enough tact for him to keep it to himself while in Simon's earshot. The thing was, I couldn't believe there were just the two choices — full possession or death. Something deep inside me told me there was another option still open to me and I just had to find it.

"Oh God, oh God, oh God!" Simon's voice was getting louder as he fought against the cuffs and as quiet as this park was, someone was going to notice us soon and call the police. And so far I'd avoided enough tricky questions from them when spotted going about my business. They weren't really the type to believe in the Other World that easily, not when they'd seen enough of what the *normal* world could do to itself on a daily basis.

"Okay, time to go," I announced, grabbing Simon by an arm, hefting him to his feet, and dragging him off toward my house. As it was only a few blocks away we had walked. I didn't really want to take him to my house — for many reasons and not just because I really didn't want him to know where I lived — but I couldn't just stand around the park all day.

"Are you sure this is wise?" Trishna asked. I gave him a look that pretty much said it all, I mean me, wise? Puh-lease!

"Okay, let me reword that," Trishna grinned nervously, "Are you sure you shouldn't just let him go be one with the Birdfolk?"

"No!" snapped Simon before I got to answer. "Despite what this damned voice is telling me, I do *not* want to be a part of that freak show!"

"Hey you're the one who agreed to it," Trishna told him without compassion.

"I was tricked," Simon spat, "I was drunk and could have agreed to anything I was that off my face."

"Ain't that the truth," I snorted, unable to help it. Then I got that usual tingling feeling I got when my Other World spidey sense was on to something.

"Can such a thing be legally binding if it's agreed to by someone not of sound mind?" I asked Trishna over Simon's head.

He shrugged, then thought about it. "Wraiths aren't into the legalities of it all, like demons, and it would be a struggle to say drunk was the same as insane."

"Oh, I don't know. . ." I replied thinking hard, "I've seen Simon when he's really drunk and only someone crazy would do half the stuff he's done."

"Gee thanks," Simon snapped, obviously trying to keep it all together as I frog marched him home. I had to say, even for a jerk, he was taking this all reasonably well. "I may get a little out of hand when I've had a few, but this is wrong." He began to writhe so hard he wrenched my grip on his arm.

I stood back warily until I realised he wasn't fighting against me, but against the wroth around his neck.

"Just keep fighting it Simon," I said, astounded by the concerned tenderness in my voice. "Where there is a will there is a way. And if you can keep a hold of your own will, I promise you I will do what I can to find a way to free you."

Oh great, what a time for my subconscious to step in and fill in the blanks.

# Chapter 6

"SO, YOU'RE just going to keep him locked in one of your guest bedrooms, in an induced coma, until further notice?" Trishna said as I bid goodbye to the Temple of Isis' Apothecary at my front door.

"Pretty much!" I replied in as light and airy a tone as I could, after I'd shut and bolted the door and turned to face him. "It's not as if I can keep him in the Inner Sanctum and it's also not as if I expect you to help me look after him." I headed down the corridor to where the bedrooms were located.

"You can't save him you know," Trishna sounded frustrated, but at least he wasn't swearing. "By keeping that puss riddled septic ulcer of a dog alive, you're just prolonging his pain." Oh well, so much for no swearing.

"There is a way!" I said, losing my cool and getting snappy. Restitution my arse — *he* started it. "I can feel there is a way and I'm going to do my best to find it."

"I don't believe it," Trishna replied. I frowned uncertainly, he actually seemed pleased I was angry at him. "And I would be doing something about it if Roxanna didn't believe you for some reason. I mean, to keep him imprisoned and in torment doesn't exactly work with the 'walking in the Light' side of things."

"Yes, if it wasn't for Roxanna's blessing, you'd think I was just having my revenge, blah de blah de blah de blah," I replied coming to a stop outside the door to the bedroom Simon was in. We had reached the part of the conversation we'd already been at several times and I was tired of it.

"Trishna, I am not the total newb I was when we last met," I said calmly. "I've learned a lot in the last six months. And one of the biggest things I've learned is to trust my instincts. Something within me tells me there is a way I can save Simon. And if I learn what exactly that is, who knows who else can be saved?" I watched his annoyed expression as this all sunk in.

"I would much rather just walk away from that toad of a man — and I mean Simon here and not the wroth around his neck — but I can't fight my instincts." And on that note I slipped into the room and closed the door between us. Leaning against the door I took a deep breath as my instincts and I needed that break from who I'd just left on the other side, as well as a breather from who I was about to face.

Simon lay on the bed before me. He was in a deep sleep induced by whatever it was the Apothecary had given me to dose him with — she and any other priestesses being unable to get near him without a mess — and he finally looked calm and peaceful. Well, if you ignored the chains and manacles attaching his wrists and ankles to the rings in the ceiling. I couldn't leave him in the uncomfortable position of being handcuffed behind his back. . . but I didn't want Mr Vontant dropping by every time he woke either. I had often wondered why there were hooks and metal rings in the sturdy beams of this room, and had hoped it had been more to do with some unknown old-style childbirth. Now I was guessing it wasn't, because from the way the priestesses had manhandled Simon — once knocked out — onto the bed. I got a strong feeling they'd done it before. . . often.

Leaving Simon sleeping I slipped back into the corridor. Trishna was not there to greet me, but from the noises from the far end of the house it sounded like he was in the kitchen boiling the kettle. Yes, even now he still had a tea habit. I guess there were worse things to be addicted to when you've been carrying around someone else's memories all your life. I winced at that thought and decided to avoid the guilt involved for the time being. I was more a 'one problem at a time' sort of person and right now I felt Simon had slightly more priority.

"I'm in the study if you need me," I shouted to Trishna, fairly certain loud voices wouldn't be able to wake Simon, then turned on my heel and headed to the room in question.

***

The study had probably been the cottage's original box room. It was a small, pokey, windowless room with walls covered with floor to ceiling bookshelves, except for the small spot left clear for an old-style roll-top writing desk. Besides the naked light bulb hanging from the ceiling, modern technology hadn't made much of an impact on the room. Yes there was my laptop stashed in the roll-top desk, but I rarely used it as a piece of paper quickly scrawled with the required ritual fitted into my pocket far easier. Plus, paper was easier to dispose of if needed in the flame that burned continuously at the Temple. Something about certain things should only ever be written down for their purpose and then destroyed? I don't know, but it felt right too.

Also, in some of the situations I'd learned to deal with, anything with a power source became not only useless but dangerous, as the energy could be drained and used against me. Heck, I'd even taken to writing with old-style 'lead' pencils, or a quill and ink as it just seemed to fit better with what I was doing. We won't even go into the incident involving my first laptop, purified water, and some rather angry black witches. Technology just didn't tie in well with my new job. Except for my phone. . . so far it hadn't held enough energy to be used against me, had survived most soakings in my pants pocket and barely had a crack on its screen. It was also Roxanna's main way to contact me so if she thought it was okay to use, I was okay with using it too.

I sat down in my little wooden chair on wheels and surveyed the overflowing bookshelves. It only looked a mess, I pretty much knew where everything was, even if I'd not yet read all of it.

I sighed as I realised the order would now have to be changed as I had wraiths over in my section on references to 'creatures and beasts of the Other World' while the Birdfolk of Wroth were over in the 'occult groups of Darkness' section. Hopefully cross-referencing them on my laptop's database would be enough? See, I said I still had a use for it. I pushed the roller top of my desk up and pulled the said device toward me, as well as a notepad and pencil. Booting the laptop up and opening my rather high-tech homemade database I first searched for Wroth, wrote down all books I'd so far discovered referencing him, her, it? I then did a search on wraiths and listed all those references too before turning my laptop off and gathering the required items from the shelves. It was a small pile of books and parchments, but I still hoped it would contain something of use. Once I'd made myself as comfortable as I could — leaning back on my chair, writing arm resting on my desk, and feet on one of the nearby bookshelves — I started going through it all. Look, if I had to learn this stuff then I found it easier if I was comfy, my professional persona was left at the door with my gloves.

***

I emerged two hours later with a sore arm, cricked neck, and a handful of notes scrawled onto my bright yellow writing pad. It was a start and something I felt I could happily take to Roxanna to seek further advice on. I knew she had a few reference books of her own and at times let even non-priestess types near them. . . if we'd washed our hands and were wearing white cotton gloves.

"Anything of use?" asked Trishna when I found him at my kitchen table reading a Chinese newspaper. How had he got that?

"A bit," I replied tiredly as I sat down myself and took out my phone. "I have a few ideas to run by Roxanna before I give up." I typed out a quick text message to her and dropped my phone on top of my notes on the table.

"I better go check on our guest, I suppose," I said, heaving myself to my feet and wandering back down the hall. According to the Temple's Apothecary he should be out for another four hours, but I felt it best to check as I was pretty sure that estimation was given to a non-possessed person.

He appeared asleep, still breathing deeply and his pupils reacted appropriately when I cracked a lid and flashed the pen light left by the Apothecary. But I'd been advised to always double check with him and so took a solid silver pin out of an apparently purified pin cushion situated by the door and pricked him in the sole of the foot. Who would have thought that was how you checked whether a possessed person was faking a drug induced sleep, oh the modern methods we used! Still, the reaction was nil. I did it once more for good measure then had to restrain myself before I got a little too carried away. He was still out of it, I was certain of that as I wiped the blood from his foot and absently burned the tissue in the sacred flame, lit from the one at the temple - sitting in a lamp by the pin cushion, before leaving the room. Yes, gone were the days I idly just left someone's blood lying about, even within my own home.

"Still out of it?" Trishna asked upon my return to the kitchen, I nodded as I sat down and checked my phone for a reply.

"I even pricked his foot for good measure," I said, feeling a sudden need to reinforce I knew what I was doing these days.

"Oh lookee," I said, after scanning Roxanna's reply, "we've got ourselves a dinner date at the Temple to discuss the situation."

I was actually relieved at being able to avoid another night alone with Trishna. We'd talked a lot the evening before, but I really didn't feel like doing that every night. I mean, he knew some of my deepest, darkest secrets and what they felt like. . . it wasn't as if we needed to rehash them daily.

"Learned anything you want to discuss before we go over there tonight?" Trishna casually asked.

I gave him a squinty-eyed, suspicious look.

"I mean, so I can be a sounding board for your ideas!" he added defensively.

I bit my tongue rather than reply with 'you mean to check I *do* actually know what I'm talking about?' I was trying to find restitution with him and all that so why start a fight over nearly every topic?

"Well, it's not much," I answered instead, picking up my notes and shuffling through them. "Just stuff on wraiths being the spirit, not ghost mind you, of someone who feels they were unjustly put to death. That they're old spirits too, like *really* old. Centuries of hate and plots for revenge stewing around in an unfettered soul."

"Why do you say wraiths aren't ghosts?" asked Trishna curiously, as if I was touching on something new to him.

"Because, from what I've gathered, ghosts are the souls of people trapped between our world and the next by dark ritual," I replied. I glanced up at him from over my notes and hoped I wasn't touching a nerve. "All that chain clanking, white-sheet stuff the normal world thinks of as ghosts isn't true. If such things do really exist I'm guessing they're a different form of spirit again. But no, a ghost is just a trapped soul, an energy force bound to an item of their creation in this world and used as an extension of someone else's power. Wraiths are different." I was worried by the look on Trishna's face as he sat back in his chair as if I'd just stunned him.

"You really *have* been doing your homework, haven't you?" he said with something like awe in his voice. I shrugged, not really knowing what to say, then realised with Trishna I could pretty much say anything.

"When you live alone, have no social life, and deal with situations daily that can cause harm and death to those who don't know what they're doing. . . let's just say it's been a steep learning curve and an interesting six months since I laid you to rest." That said it all really.

"And now you have my *full* attention," Trishna said. He leaned forward, elbows on the table, chin cradled in his hands, to prove it.

I supressed the sigh I wanted to give and turned back to my notes.

"So, anyway, wraiths are malignant spirits who have been dwelling in their own spite and anger for centuries. They're not bound to anyone or anything and, from what I can tell, mostly exist in this world. Though I did find some references to them heading 'down below' to make deals with the demons. . . Though I do have to point out that those facts are a little sketchy, even for Other World record keeping." I flicked to another page and continued.

"Wraiths in general have no corporeal body and, being unbound to anyone as they are, have no ability to possess a person, even if that person freely gives them permission to do so. So a bit of a sticking point in regards to Wroth the wraith there." I paused, underlining that point in my notes and casually glanced up to see if Trishna felt as uneasy about those facts as I did. How could Wroth control so many if wraiths can't possess someone? Trishna merely nodded so I continued slowly.

"Yes wraiths are nasty and can cause harm when their tainted life force builds up to the extent they can use the energy to go a little poltergeist on you — totally different spirit there too by the way — but they really have no real control over the solid world. And so their desperate need for revenge tends to go unanswered." I glanced at Trishna but he really seemed fascinated at what I was telling him and not about to interrupt and correct me. Damn.

"Which brings us to Wroth and *his* Birdfolk." It was time to plunge into the big issue as I saw it. "See, I wasn't too sure if a wraith can have a gender so there you go." I ignored Trishna's snicker to my quick aside. Yes I was still learning something new every day.

"From the texts I've read, Wroth is *really* old, even for wraiths. I mean, possibly back to the Stone Age and blood sacrifice era of things. One researcher on the ancient evils of our world suggested he was originally an Aztec priest, and it's where his thing about dressing his victims all in feathers is all about. Though I actually find that a little too silly. . . even for Other World theories."

"You cynic you," Trishna smiled, seemingly absorbed in what I was saying. I rolled my eyes at him, that couldn't count against restitution could it?

"So anyway, as mentioned, the only way a wraith can become con- nected to this world and able to inflict its anger upon anyone is it builds up enough energy. It can't simply ask a living person to give it permission to 'join' them. And yet somehow Wroth has managed to do this. And not just once but many times. And I can't tell how long he's been doing this either as there was nothing in the records. But, saying that, he *has* done it. And now seems to have great power in the Other World through both the living and the dead."

"Hang on a sec.," Trishna said. "I know multiple ghosts can be bound to someone but for a wraith to be able to bind itself to more than one host. . . that sounds a bit off. I was led to believe Wroth was wraith-*like*. . . *not* a wraith."

I relaxed, relieved he seemed to be getting the same vibe about it as me. "I agree. Despite a lot of the texts I read telling me Wroth is really just a mean, old wraith I can't believe it completely. The fact he can do what he can is more than a *little* off. But then that wroth creature on Simon mentioned a 'nest of souls down below' and it got me thinking he's either not really a wraith. . . or that the texts are right and that maybe he made a deal with a demon, a trade of power for souls?" It was a long shot, but I was no longer as green as I was cabbage looking and it just made sense.

"Well if that doesn't just prove the best whore in the house has the pox!" Trishna said, leaning back in his chair.

I winced. I had been hoping his new persona had come with a better turn of phrase, obviously I was wrong. Suddenly I realised what he'd said meant I'd surprised him. "What?" I asked, trying not to sound too dumb, "And please keep the explanation to a G rating level." You could never be too careful.

"I would never have considered a wraith and a demon working together. . . boggles the mind!" Trishna answered, obviously struggling to keep his words clean. "It all almost makes sense now, but there's still something missing. And not just wanting to know what a demon would get out of the deal."

He had a point, there did seem to be something missing. Although the demon side of it did seem obvious.

I shrugged. "So what happens to the souls of those possessed, assuming a wraith *could* somehow do it?"

"As with any possession, purgatory. Mostly to pay for the sins their possessor undertook while in control of their body."

"And where do demons get their power and standing from?" I asked, waiting to see if he could see where I was taking the conversation.

The look on his face proved he'd figured it out too.

"From the remaining life force sucked out of the souls they capture and carry to purgatory," he said in disbelief. "But that only works if the soul they get has made a deal with *them*. They can't just grab a soul away from a possession by someone else. Dark Nature states any deals made with a demon are void if the person making the deal is possessed."

"Yes, but what if the deal is between the possessor and the demon?" Despite the disturbing subject of our conversation I actually smiled as Trishna finally worked through the enormity of what I was proposing.

"Of all the slippery nippled little whores and their pox riddled owner!" he gasped. "By Isis you've turned out to be one clever little bint!"

I ignored the backhanded compliment hidden in the filth and took a shaky breath.

"So you think my theory might be correct?" I asked. I hadn't realised he could look even more surprised.

"This is just a theory?" Trishna said in disbelief. "Stephanie, I think you've hit the nail right on the head with this stuff. That is some scary, clever smarts you have there."

Okay, that was a little unsettling to hear, I mean who else wouldn't have put two and two together when they'd looked at this issue from all angles. Hadn't anyone who studied the Birdfolk of Wroth *wondered* how he could be a wraith and have so many people under his possession? Hadn't anyone questioned whether it really *was* a wraith at work, and one going solo to do it too? I mean, I had a feeling binding someone to your soul and will was pretty similar to possession and having done that myself and remembering how hard it had been to be in control of someone else. . .

My gut twisted at the memory of it all. How many people had the ability to do what I'd done? And to a demon no less. Possibly *that* was why all these academics who walked in the Light hadn't made the connection. It's not as if they'd have had as much exposure to demons — and lived to tell about it — as I had.

"You've got that sour lemon face going again Steph, the one you tend to get when you don't like what your inner monologue is telling you." Trishna's voice broke through my thoughts and I blinked at him a few times to control my urge to throw up.

"People who walk in the Light don't know what it is like to possess someone, do they?" It was a dumb question and it deserved the snort of amusement it got.

"Not if they want to keep walking in the Light they don't," he replied, studying me carefully.

"Then that's why they don't know half the stuff that's going on around here!" I exclaimed, surprised at how frustrated that made me. "If they only knew of the deals with demons, and the depths into which the Darkness actually plunged, they'd have figured this all out years ago and I wouldn't have Simon drooling on a pillow in my spare room right now!"

"Everything has a cause and effect Steph." Trishna sounded as though he actually was trying to soothe me, rather than agree with me. "We need a clear definition of what is Darkness and what is Light to ensure a balance of both in the world for it to develop the way it does. Conflict causes death, but it can also cause progress." I boggled at him, I really did.

"You mean some of those in the Light probably *do* know and don't do anything about it?" Please tell me I was wrong on this one. Trishna just shrugged at me apologetically.

"There are people in the Other World whose sole job is to keep the Light pure and the Darkness impure. To keep them as two clear, but separate, entities. Balanced — as it should be. But they can't be everywhere or control the actions everyone. People still need to have free will, or there would be no difference between the good guys and the bad guys." I was amazed he was able to explain it so clearly without a single swear word.

"So you're telling me wraiths and demons can make deals to suck people's souls into purgatory. . . and that's *okay*?" I was angry. I could see his point about people needing to have free will to do and make their own decisions. . . but standing back to just *let* them get possessed? Claiming they were good people, while knowing about and *allowing* bad things to happen!

"If the people of the Light held all the power Stephanie, the Light would become sullied and soon fade to Darkness. Power over all isn't the answer. This is why there is no *one* body in charge of running everything. Just a group of people wanting to help keep the Darkness and Light separated. As long as the line between them is clear, the rest is up to either side to sort out who does what. This is where people like you come into it. You help keep the balance and not just allow the Darkness to take over."

I could see his point, power corrupts and all that. But I scowled at him all the same.

Whenever I looked at the big picture of the Other World like that I got a headache. I just couldn't understand its simple black and white approach. As a result I found it easier simply to focus on just my little part of it where I *definitely* walked in the Light and saved people. Because that's what we good guys did. It's just that real life wasn't so black and white. There was a whole rainbow of what ifs out there that couldn't be controlled by a simple 'Walk in Light' or 'Dwell in Darkness' attitude — right?

"Okay, if you keep that lemon face up the wind will change and you'll stay that way," Trishna said.

I could tell that while he sympathised with my frustration he just couldn't see it the same way that I did.

"If wroth-boy to be is out for the count, let's go for a walk to clear the air before heading over to the Temple for dinner," he said, obviously trying to make things better, even if it was just so I wasn't in a mood when we visited the priestesses.

I did my best not to scowl at him, unfortunately this wasn't something I could let go easily.

Trishna reached across the small table and placed his hand on mine. I found my eyes closing in response to the soothing sensation he delivered to me. Darjeeling to the soul, almost. I counted back from ten slowly and then opened my eyes again, giving his smug look my best half-amused squinty-eye.

"Let me just call them first," I replied, trying to push the feeling of disappointment at the world away with his hand, while savouring what it was he had replaced it with. "Someone is meant to be here at all times while I have a possessed man chained to my bed. It's in the cottage's rule book. Go figure."

He smiled at my attempt at humour and leaned across the table to give my shoulder a squeeze, sending a different tingle of energy through my body.

"You are a good person Steph," he said sincerely. "This world is full of putrid, evil, slimy bastards and you should be proud that you don't just accept that but try to do something about them."

Even though I smiled at this, I suddenly felt wretched. Wasn't *I* meant to be the one making *him* feel better?

"Thanks Trishna," I said with a weak smile, before grabbing my phone and dialling the Temple's number. He'd given me an answer as to why the Other World was the way it was and I accepted it. . . for now. But if I had any say in it, things *were* going to change.

***

The walk that afternoon helped and I was able to pile my plate high and sit down with the priestesses at a comfortable meal that evening without coming across as too bitchy.

"I just want to know why you ladies go out chopping off the heads of vampires possessing people but don't do the same for wraiths." I realised I was pointing my fork aggressively at Sophia, one of the second-level priestesses at the table and quickly lowered it.

"Because wraiths can't be killed, nor can they technically possess a person," Sophia replied calmly, appearing to take no offence at the fork pointing. "As for a Dark Force possessing a person, all we can do is simply destroy the host they are possessing. Which, in Wroth's case, would be a bloodbath as the Birdfolk mass in their hundreds."

"And while the deal you believe Wroth has made with a demon stands, there will always be new victims." This was Roxanna, her voice holding the stern, motherly tone she knew got through to me when I was in this mood. "We can't simply kill everyone to stop them becoming possessed Stephanie. All we can do is try and warn them against the dangers of walking in the Darkness. To do otherwise would be killing the innocent, meaning we would be no better than those already *in* the Darkness."

I did my best not to pout because I could see her point. Trishna snickered beside me as the pout appeared. The elbow that wanted to dig itself into his ribs was kept firmly at my side. Elbow jabs would count against restitution, even I could see that.

"And it's hard keeping the world safe when most of it doesn't even recognise there is an Other World, particularly when the Light and the Darkness tend to balance each other, allowing the world to go on around them blissfully shielded to it all," I said, dropping my cutlery and pushing my plate away, no longer hungry.

"Precisely," Roxanna sympathised with me across the table. Discussions on the Light and Darkness were one of our main topics when I came to see her, as it's pretty much what I did for a living now. Fought one while stating I belonged to the other.

"So to destroy Wroth's power I would need to cancel the deal with the demon before I could stop the possessions," I mused out loud. How hard could that be?

"I sometimes worry about your affinity with demons and their deals," Roxanna sighed. She gave me a look that reminded both of us of the little black book in my pocket that contained all the deals I currently had with demons. She liked to pretend she didn't know about it, but was always quick to remind me it was there.

"Sadly it comes with the job description," I replied, trying to justify it all. I mean, it's not as if I *chose* to deal with demons. . . it's just that occasionally my work meant I had to deal with them as well as the souls I was trying to save. And as a demon is more than happy to make a deal to get itself out of any situation it didn't want to be in, and I wanted to get rid of them, these deals just seemed to happen. I had never once used a deal to perform dark acts of my own, so it's not as if I really *dabbled* in the bad stuff or anything, right? Wouldn't Isis fire me if she thought I wasn't doing my job right? Goddesses see and know all, or so I was told.

"I doubt you could make a deal with this one though," Trishna put in, unaware of Roxanna and my secret looks.

"How come?" I asked, shifting my gaze to him to avoid any further reproachful looks from the High Priestess.

"Well, I'm guessing it would keep to the world down below if it had so many souls to look after. As mentioned, Birdfolk of Wroth number in their hundreds."

"What makes you think it would be guarding the souls?" I asked, interested. "I mean, they technically don't belong to the demon until Wroth hands them over on the point of the possessed body's death. Well, I'm guessing that's the deal."

"True, but you can't just have a collection of souls sitting around unprotected like that. What if part of the original deal was to guard them until they're ripe for picking?" As much as Trishna had a point with this, I winced at the term and then glanced around the table at the priestesses with us. From their looks of distaste I could guess we'd overstepped the mark of polite conversation that should be discussed at the dinner table.

"Later," I told Trishna and gave him a warning look. He glanced around the table then nodded, looking down at his near-empty plate as if it would give him a clue as to what a better conversation topic would be.

"I don't suppose there's a chance one of you frilly curtain clad ladies could find me a decent cup of tea? Rather than the floor sweeping shit I noticed on the way in?"

I buried my face in my hands to supress the groan more than the grin that I found creeping onto my face. When all else fails, let's talk tea. . . obviously!

# Chapter 7

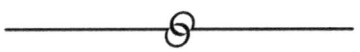

NOW I know I've mentioned my dislike for being woken in the morning before I'm ready to be. It's a *small* pet hate, especially when you compare it to being woken in the middle of the night by someone climbing on top of you while you're asleep in bed.

"Trishna, we talked about this. . ." I mumbled, struggling to sit up only to find myself knocked back down into the pillows.

"Silence," a voice hissed as rough hands started to fumble me all over.

"Trishna?" I gasped, smacking the hands away, only to receive a hard smack across the face.

"Not Trishna," said a second voice from over by the door as I struggled against the hands holding me down.

"Mr Vontant?" I gasped at this second voice, before realising if he was in my bedroom then things might not end well. And I'd only just put clean sheets on the bed too.

I suddenly realised that the rough handed treatment I was receiving wasn't to cop a grope but was someone trying to find something. As I squirmed to get away from whoever it was trying to pin me down and search me — one handed — in the pitch black room.

"*Mr Vontant!*" I said with more feeling, we had a deal here.

"Oh come on, it's just been a little slap so far, nothing that is particularly a threat of Dark Force proportions. I'm curious to see where this goes," came the neat and precise voice from the darkness.

"Why does it sound like there's an orgy in here and I wasn't invited?" That half-asleep voice was Trishna's as my door opened. He was just turning on the light when I decided I'd had enough of all this and raised a knee neatly between the legs of my assailant. It was a move I used more often than I'd like to remember. The muffled whimper and easing of pressure as the obvious male toppled off me gave me some satisfaction.

Sitting up, blinking as my eyes grew accustomed to the bright light overhead, I tried to take in the scene. Mr Vontant stood at the foot of my bed, hands folded neatly in front of himself, a slightly disappointed look on his face. Beside him in the doorway, in barely any clothes save some tight cotton briefs, stood a bleary-eyed Trishna trying to focus on what was going on. Turning to the other side of the room I caught sight of the figure of a young man, suited up similar to Mr Vontant, as he unwound himself from the fetal position I'd put him in with a hard, pointy knee.

"Oh, so *I'm* not allowed to share your bed but any old demon will do?" asked Trishna in an amused tone. "What did I miss this time frizz-head?" I turned to scowl at him but just caught a glimmer of movement as the man on the floor suddenly leaped to his feet and came at me with a knife.

"That is enough, Benjamin," Mr Vontant said calmly, suddenly appearing on the same side of the bed as my knife-wielding assailant. There was a sickening sound as he coat hangered the youth with a well-placed arm in front of his neck and 'Benjamin' was on the ground again, Mr Vontant kicking his knife out of the way.

I scrambled up into a crouching position in my bed, no longer bemused over it all.

"Benjamin? Should I be suspicious you know the name of my attacker Mr Vontant, or the fact you *let* him attack me?"

"He was initially merely searching you and therefore not a danger," Mr Vontant sniffed, as he straightened out a crease on his sleeve. "I was curious to see what else he had in mind. No harm in that."

I felt my left cheek, still stinging from the slap, and did my best to control my anger.

"You really shouldn't piss her off in the middle of the night," Trishna said, as he sat down next to me on the bed, almost taking up our protection stance of old. "I mean, she keeps a bottle of purified water under her pillow. Do you *really* want to know what it's like to feel her controlling *you* — body and soul?"

Mr Vontant's annoyed expression was replaced for a moment by a flash of sheer panic. "Fair point," he admitted. "I am extremely sorry to have inconvenienced you Stephanie, I was simply curious as to what he was searching for."

"And you know who *he* is because?" I asked, glaring at the young man now sitting on the floor glowering up at me.

"Because he's a demon," Trishna answered for him. "You can smell the brimstone on his breath from here." He gave Mr Vontant an angry look. "And the reason Mr Vontant here was waiting was because there's always the chance of a new deal to be struck. Say. . . by knowing the location of whatever it was Benjamin here was searching for."

This was all too much for me after being woken so rudely and so I swung out of bed, lurched to snatch the bottle of purified water from underneath my pillow, and gave my best pissed off look to both the demons.

"Now you're in trouble," Trishna grinned, also rising. But as my bedroom wasn't big enough for us all to be on one side of the bed he just eased himself to the end of it, as close to me as he could.

"On your feet!" I snapped at the younger-looking demon, ignoring Trishna's barb. Benjamin — and come on! What sort of name is that for a frickin demon? — ignored me and just glared.

"Obviously you're a new kid on the block around here," I snarled at the seated demon. "When I tell you scum to get to your feet, *you do it.*"

Even Mr Vontant backed away at that tone. Seriously, I am *not* a morning person and there is no way I ever like to be woken before I get my much needed eight hours.

"Burn in the deepest pit of underworld and weep puss from your fetid mildewed mouth you whore of the seventh order!" Benjamin spat. Was that the best he could do?

I leaned down and grabbed him by the front of his shirt and hauled him up, surprising myself again at how strong I got when *that* angry.

"The name is Stephanie Muriel Anders," I hissed at him and he gave a scared glance to Mr Vontant standing next to me. "And if you don't want it scrawled over your forehead, while I make you bitch slap yourself silly, I suggest you start doing what I say."

"Ani?" Benjamin said in almost a meep, addressing Mr Vontant imploringly.

"You really should read the fine print when accepting a contract like this," sighed Mr Vontant, obviously disappointed in the younger-looking demon.

"Now Stephanie, how about you put the silly little demon down and count to ten before we get to the bottom of all this?"

I flicked my glare to him and sighed. Mr Vontant was right, I was pretty sure binding myself to every demon that pissed me off would soon see me kicked out of the 'walking in the Light' gang. Plus, if I did that, how would I find out what the hell was going on? The very thought of interrogating the demon from the inside out was sickening.

With a disgusted grunt I pushed Benjamin away from me and against the bedroom wall, and then bent down to collect the knife he had been threatening me with. Another trophy for the Inner Sanctum.

"That's my girl," Trishna said, smiling as I handed the knife over to him.

I had meant to stash it on myself. . . then realised I was only wearing a baggy t-shirt and underpants. Not that many places to stash a demon's knife safely. I blushed at the realisation I was in a room full of men and had barely anything on.

"And she's back," Trishna laughed, catching my unease, still oblivious to his own near nakedness. Heck, it was one way to calm me down in a hurry.

"What the hell are you doing in my room?" I decided to get some of that anger back and turned a good glare onto Benjamin.

He cowered slightly against the wall but tried to give me a defiant look. "I don't have to tell you a thing!" he hissed, then went cross-eyed as he tried to vanish and realised he couldn't. Mr Vontant sighed again, turning it into almost an embarrassed cough.

"This is a house of Isis," Mr Vontant pointed out. "It has an inward clasp of the moon entwined into its very foundations, you fool. Didn't you research *anything* before popping in?"

"A *what*?" I couldn't help it. There were still some things I had to learn and I'd not heard of that one before. And it was my house so I was fairly sure it was something I should know.

Mr Vontant gave me a withering look. "We are not open to having a Q and A, Ms Anders. Look it up in our contract."

"It's a protecting rune carved into the essential corner stones of a building when it's built," Trishna explained. "It means entities can enter at will, but need to be given permission before they can leave. Something to do with spirits, Gods, unwelcome visitors, that sort of thing."

Damn, he'd need to tell me that again later on when I had a pen and paper so I could write it all down. Though it did explain why Mr Vontant rarely came inside and when he did he stood by my front door coughing loudly, not-too subtly suggesting I open it. Like some giant disgruntled house cat in a suit needing to use the world as its litter box.

"Anyhoo," I tried to brush this titbit of information aside, "What the hell are you doing in my house?" I said, turning back to a rather sullen looking Benjamin.

"I was carrying out a contract," he said, glancing at the purified water I still held in my right hand.

"And that contract was to?" I prompted, knowing I probably wasn't going to get an answer.

"To release the acolyte of Wroth," Benjamin mumbled, surprising everyone else in the room by doing so. He, as far as I could tell, was under no obligation to actually give me information freely. But hey, maybe I'd scared him enough to get it out of him.

"Who sent you?" I decided if he was going to answer, I was going to keep on questioning.

"The person who assigned me the contract," Benjamin answered, a touch of smugness in his voice. Oh well, you couldn't win them all.

"If you were here for Simon, what were you doing in Stephanie's room?" Trishna asked, a suspicious glint in his eye. Benjamin looked a little shifty at this one and I just happened to rub my still red cheek with the cold glass bottle of purified water while giving him a thoughtful look.

"I was searching for the key to unchain him!" Benjamin burst out.

"Well thank hell for that," Mr Vontant grimaced. "For a moment I thought you were going to say you got the wrong room."

A look of panic flashed across Benjamin's face.

"Oh damnation of the innocents, you *did* get the wrong room!" Mr Vontant spat, the vile creature he truly was showing briefly from beneath his smart suit. "What are they teaching you wastes of meat these days?"

I nearly felt like joining Trishna as he sniggered at this revelation, I mean seriously? *This* was the sort of demon now being sent after me?

"What if I did, as the acolytes captor, I felt it best to search her for the key to unchain him before I discovered where he was."

"And how do you know I've chained him up somewhere?" I asked, suddenly realising that if Benjamin hadn't even found Simon yet, how did he know I had him trussed like a turkey?

"Lucky guess," was all Benjamin would say, starting to show all the signs of being about to clam up. And as much as I dislike my sleep being disturbed, once it was I needed a pretty damned good reason as to *why*. So I was not about to let him go silent now.

"Trishna," I barked, handing him the purified water and advanced on the younger-looking demon. Grabbing him by the ear I gave it a good twist.

"You festered pustule on a. . ." he began, ending in a scream as I twisted harder.

"It's time for a talk buddy," I hissed, dragging him to the door of my room with a confused looking Mr Vontant following, obviously curious to see what I was up to.

"Where are you taking him?" Trishna asked, stepping out into the hallway first to get out of my road.

"There is a containment circle out on the back verandah etched into the decking. When the bad guys try and give me the silent treatment I'm to seal them in until I get the answer I'm after," I grunted, hauling the now squealing demon down the hallway.

"Vontant!" Benjamin squeaked, catching the eye of the fussy little demon as he followed behind.

"Trust me, it only hurts more when you struggle," Mr Vontant replied, some of his usual calm slipping and a look of discomfort on his face. I don't know *why*, it's not as if he'd ever ended up in the circle. I mean — not wanting to give anything away — but I've never actually had to use it. Simply had its function explained to me when I was being taught the ins and outs of the place.

"I don't want to be contained! I will tell you everything you want to know about my contract!" squealed Benjamin, proving exactly why I'd never had to use the circle. Suckers.

Then again, I wouldn't want to be put into a containment circle either. It was as close to being bound to someone as it gets. Meaning I'd pretty much have control over him to tell me anything I wanted to know, or have him sworn to a contract. . . pretty much like he was already.

We had made it to the dining area and I tried to kick out one of the large solid wooden chairs at the table, to sit him in, winced and swore at the pain caused from kicking solid wood with a bare foot and ended up releasing Benjamin as I hobbled back a few steps.

"Newb," Trishna grinned, now bringing up the rear as he'd stopped in his bedroom to, thankfully, put a robe on. Dark grey silk, nice.

I turned my attention back to Benjamin, who was now seething angrily nearby, wanting to pounce on me, but deciding not to after catching the steely gaze of Mr Vontant.

"Make it worth my while boy and she's all yours," hissed Mr Vontant. "Otherwise I suggest you sit yourself down and answer her questions. As I'm pretty sure neither of us is going to be allowed to leave until you do."

I blinked at Mr Vontant a few times for his offer. We had a deal, and a bloody good one too. But demons will be demons and there is always the hope of a better deal to be made. His last sentence then sank in and I remembered the seal on the house. Of course! Mr Vontant couldn't leave either.

"Sit!" I snapped at Benjamin as he continued to glare at me, seething. "As you're *so* not leaving here until I have my answers. One way or the other, and I do mean *both* of you."

I pulled the chair out from under the table a little more to indicate where I wanted him to be before I moved over to a pile of books stacked on the kitchen bench. When I turned back around it was to see Mr Vontant roughly pushing Benjamin into the seat. I knew he wasn't doing it as part of our deal, but had simply realised what I'd meant about neither of them leaving until I got what I wanted. No deal, simply a bit of innocent blackmail.

"Now," I said, approaching Benjamin with the item I had taken from within the books. "You're going to tell me who sent you, how they knew Simon was chained up and why the hell they want him so badly." We exchanged glares for a moment, as Benjamin readjusted his sitting position to a more 'casually lounging' look. He had said he was going to talk. What a good thing I had expected him to now act as he was. "Right, if that's how you want it!"

I grabbed one of his hands and wrestled it onto the table in front of him. Then before he could remove it I stabbed the silver dagger, I'd been holding through his hand, pinning him to the table. Man I'm glad my little cottage was so sound proof.

"Holy shit, Steph!" Trishna gasped, shocked at what I'd done.

Come on people, was no one watching as I took the dagger from the spine of one of my books and walked over with it?

"That is a dagger of enforcement," I told Benjamin, ignoring Trishna. I'd been dealing with demons for six months now without him, they weren't the sort you played nice with.

"I do hope you cleaned it after our run in with the Black Cat Cult the other week," Mr Vontant sniffed.

Trust Mr Vontant to have noticed me playing with sharp objects.

"Cleaned, purified, and good to go," I told him, not happy to be using the knife in such a way. . . especially not on the good dining table. And I'd only just polished it with beeswax last week too. But talking to a demon sometimes meant having to spill a little blood, and not always mine.

"You go around stabbing people these days?" This was Trishna again as he approached Mr Vontant and myself as we stood over Benjamin waiting for him to recover a little.

"You whore with a thousand syphilitic lesions —" Benjamin managed before catching the determined look in my eye.

"Don't make me ruin the wood any further by having to twist the dagger a little more," I sighed, moving forward to place a cloth under the table where he was starting to drip blood onto the rug. Seriously I had thought this a good idea at the time. . . now I wasn't so sure.

I straightened from fussing over the floor as Mr Vontant restrained Benjamin's free hand from taking a swipe at me.

"Make it quick Ms Anders," the older looking demon hissed, never having been one to want to hang around with me for too long. Never could quite understand that.

"Okay, demon known tonight as Benjamin I have impaled you with a dagger of enforcement into old oak. This means you're now going to answer me true, or face the consequences."

"Oh, silver enforcement dagger into *oak*! If he tells any fibs he's going to burn from the inside out. Now I'm with you," Trishna said finally getting over the shock of me stabbing a demon to my table. "One of the best ways to get a demon to talk without binding them. You really have picked up a trick or two in my absence." Although he was still looking a little shocked from my actions, Trishna had taken up 'the stance' just behind my shoulder. With all the energy now buzzing around the room from the enforcing I felt a little uncomfortable about this move, as he was no longer a tool to extend and strengthen my life force, but an equal. Still, at least that meant he had my back, right?

"Rot in hell you —" Benjamin began, but I seriously didn't have time for the twelve word insults. If at all possible, I wanted to be back in bed before dawn.

"Oh just shut *up*! That is the one thing that really annoys me with you demons and Other World types. Must every conversation boil down to some diseased bodily function and a prostitute or dog?" Okay, so losing my train of thought there a little. I focused on the questions I wanted answered and how to word them in such a way there shouldn't be any loopholes.

"Who sent you here tonight?" I began my questions. "Remember I have commanded you to answer me true."

"The person who assigned me the contract," Benjamin replied tersely. We'd been over this bit already.

"And what is the name of the person who assigned you the contract?" Yes, it was 'twenty questions for dummies' time.

"I didn't catch their name," Benjamin said smugly, then hunched over with pain from the attempt to lie.

"Obviously not been impaled to oak with an enforcement dagger before," Mr Vontant tutted in false sympathy as Benjamin straightened in his seat with a look of fear on his face. "You lie in answer to her questions and the dormant, centuries old, sacred wood is going to suck your life force out. It stores it for other purposes. . . and really does sting like a bitch."

"For the second time, what is the name of the person who assigned you the contract?" I said, making it clear that I could go on like this all night.

"Seth," Benjamin spat, as if the word tasted bad.

"And who exactly is this Seth, who assigned you this contract?" Okay, time to spoon feed the questions.

"Leader of the northern flock of the Birdfolk of Wroth."

"Well, that would explain their interest in Simon," I said as an aside to Trishna, who nodded.

"How did you know he was chained up here?" I asked Benjamin.

"What else would you do with a captive?" hissed the younger-looking demon, wincing a little as the oak tugged at his life force. It hadn't been a lie, but the ancient wood had sensed it wasn't exactly the truth either.

"How. Did. They. Know?" I asked through gritted teeth. This question was important as I had a fear the Birdfolk had somehow got into my home and had scoped the place out.

"It is standard practice of the Priestesses of Isis to chain a captive of Darkness in this house," Benjamin growled. "Or so I was told when accepting the contract."

As he didn't flinch or writhe in pain it was safe to assume he'd told the truth. So everyone but me knew the common practices of the Priestesses of Isis. . . and they were known to chain bad guys to beds in my house. O-kay!

"Why are the Birdfolk so keen to get Simon back?" I knew I was shifting away from the official questions, but I was curious.

"He is a sworn acolyte. He freely gave Wroth permission to take his soul and add him to his legions. He belongs with them and they have a right to take him back." The way Benjamin said that it was obvious he was reciting something he'd been told.

"Look, the idiot was drunk when he did that and I seriously don't think it should count. Plus he's not fully possessed yet and has asked for my help so Wroth and his legions can go flock off."

Benjamin gave me a slightly startled look. What, as if Wroth was the first creature I had been disrespectful about?

"Simon has agreed to join Wroth and my contract is to take him back to them, no matter the consequences." Benjamin sounded uncertain here, as if wondering where I was going.

I decided to get back on track.

"So what exactly is Wroth's deal? Does he live in Hell with his collection of souls, and if so, what about all these soulless folk now dressed in feathers? How can one wraith possess so many?"

Here Benjamin looked uncertain and Mr Vontant shifted uneasily next to him.

"Stephanie, he said he would answer all questions relating to the contract, don't you think you've stepped out of that line of questioning now?" Mr Vontant didn't seem that happy to be drawing my attention to himself. Especially after I put my head to one side and gave him a thoughtful look.

"Ah, but you see, I never *promised* where my questioning would go. Just that he had to answer me true." I smiled sweetly at both demons before me. "And as you're both my house guests, until I say otherwise, I thought it best to get some of the grey areas of this situation coloured in."

"That was *not* part of the deal!" Benjamin hissed angrily.

"And when did I actually agree to any deal?" I asked him, all wide-eyed and innocent. Mr Vontant ground his teeth at this and moved to remove the knife from Benjamin and free him.

"Ah ah!" I warned the neat little demon. "Releasing Benjamin would be putting me in harm's way of dark forces Mr Vontant. Now *that* is a deal I remember quite well."

The neat little demon stepped back a bit and gave me a calculating look. "Well played Ms Anders, I keep forgetting how clever you can be sometimes."

"Yes she hides it well, doesn't she?" Trishna grinned from behind me.

Ignoring all this I went back to my questioning of a rather peeved looking Benjamin.

"Benjamin, bound to answer me true by being impaled by an enforcement dagger into oak, what is the deal with Wroth? Where does he reside and how can he possess so many people at once?"

"Meet me in Hell where I will show you what it's really like to be impaled by sharp objects," Benjamin hissed.

"Don't make me twist that knife," I warned him wearily. I really didn't want to have to explain the existing damage to the Temple of Isis' chief carpenter as it was.

"I will not answer!" Benjamin stated, and then held it together quite well as the oak table tugged at his life force a little. He might not be lying, but he wasn't answering my questions and the oak somehow knew this. Scary, I know. And to think I often ate off it.

"Where does Wroth reside, and how can one wraith have control over so many people?" I asked again, determined to get an answer. I was getting a mild feeling I was over stepping my place in the Light, but it's not as if I'd jumped boots and all into the Darkness by wanting the answers. All the same, I was treading a fine line between getting answers under duress and actually torturing the demon I'd knifed to the table.

"Stephanie, don't make me into a snitch by having to tell the Priestesses of Isis what you're doing." Mr Vontant sounded agitated now, even though he wasn't the demon I was questioning. It seemed in their nature to not give up any information without there being a deal in place.

"And how the hell are you going to manage to tell them that Mr Vontant?" I asked sharply, as the more he interrupted the longer this was going to take. "As you're going to have to wait till I let you out of here before you can do it."

The small, neat looking man fumed at me for a few moments before looking down at the younger demon clearly in a lot of pain. Benjamin's hair was also starting to turn grey at the temples, and I put it down to exactly how much life force he was losing here. And as much as I could possibly get away with a knife hole in the table, I really didn't think the priestesses would be too happy to find a dead demon attached to it with said knife.

"How much life force does a demon have exactly?" I asked the room in general. "And can you actually kill a demon by draining it of its life force? Please tell me you don't then end up with a demon ghost as I can tell you a Buddhist's ghost was unbelievable enough!"

"The places your mind goes when the shit hits the fan," Trishna said, shaking his head. "How about we just focus on the situation here and now before it gets that far?" Despite his amusement, Trishna's tone was starting to sound a little strained too, obviously knowing exactly how fine a line I was now walking. "I really don't think you're going to get the answers you want here tonight Steph, so let's just get rid of them."

He turned me to face him, a serious look on his face. "Come on, we're stepping over the line here, even for demon wrangling. Let's finish it now."

That unsettled me more than I thought it should. In the past I'd felt Trishna was almost a part of my subconsciousness, saying out loud the things I thought, but would never dream of voicing. So to have him express my feeling of unease about moving out of the Light meant I seriously needed to set my priorities of what I wanted out of this evening's discussion. And then end it as peacefully as possible.

"He's right Stephanie," Mr Vontant said, breaking into my thoughts and drawing my attention back to the demons in the room. "Just banish me with the proviso of taking Benjamin away at the same time in a way that breaks his contract and stops him coming back. Let's not start dabbling in things that we shouldn't be."

As much as Mr Vontant had a point, he also had a certain look in his eye that I'd grown to know. It meant I was on the cusp of knowing or doing something he really wished I wasn't able to do. This didn't fill me with any confidence as I was fairly certain it meant stepping further away from the Light.

"Fine," I said, ignoring the sighs of relief from the others. "My banishment deal tonight, Mr Vontant, is you tell me where Wroth is and *why* a wraith can control so many. For that I will banish you both back to the Below World of Darkness and give you Benjamin's full powers down there for six lunar months."

The breaths that had just been so slowly released were now sharply drawn back in. I refused to look at the expression on Trishna's face, as I was fairly certain he was disappointed in me. Benjamin wore a look of pure disgust, but it was Mr Vontant's look of calculated greed that had my full attention.

"He is but a lowly second class demon," mused Mr Vontant, obviously trying to work out a better deal rather quickly. "Six months of his power wouldn't be enough for me to take him away without that added ugly bonus you want."

"I could just banish you as is and deal with Benjamin by myself," I said with a shrug. "It's not as if I've agreed to remove him from the dagger yet. If I banish you first without giving you his powers, you'd simply have to come back to protect me from his dark forces, as per our original deal. Well, whatever dark forces are left once I'm done with him."

Mr Vontant's expression took on an unsettling look of desire as he realised I'd negotiated him into a corner.

"You are wasted on the Light Stephanie my dear. I know I have said this many times before, but this time I *really* mean it. The things we could do together if you just let me. . ."

Trishna cut him off by coming to stand between the two of us, I'd not realised until then exactly how close Mr Vontant and I had suddenly been standing. Oh Isis, that wasn't a good thing, caught in the Glamour of a demon I was dealing with. I wasn't usually that easily distracted, obviously I was getting too comfortable around Mr Vontant's presence, and didn't that just make my skin crawl!

"Focus Stephanie," Trishna warned me. "I know you're determined to get the answers you want about Wroth, but just remember who you're dealing with to get them."

"Do we have a deal?" was all I said, still focused on Mr Vontant, but this time with my mental barriers up higher. "You tell me what I want to know about Wroth and I give you Benjamin as a chew toy for six lunar months?"

"I wish you to define exactly what it is you want to know about Wroth," Mr Vontant said patiently. "As, from what I've seen tonight, you seem to have mastered the 'Words are important' game at last."

"I want to know where Wroth resides, is it up here or down in Hell. And I want to know how one wraith can control so many people.

Possession stretches the life force pretty thin at the best of times, so obviously there's something else happening besides a mere soul stealing wraith. So what exactly *is* Wroth? And I want you to ensure you answer me true on *all* of it."

"And for answering you this, I am banished, taking Benjamin with me and I get full control of his powers in the Below World of Darkness for six lunar months?"

"Correct. Starting from the time we make this deal, but after I have released Benjamin. And I want my answers on Wroth *before* I agree to do any demon releasing."

Mr Vontant still didn't look too happy about the whole situation as I knew I was asking for a lot of insider secrets from the Darkness. But he also knew I was more than prepared to just banish him with no new deal, knowing he would have to come back and help me anyhow and get nothing out of this situation.

"As much as I regret having to do this, I do want to get *something* useful out of tonight, so — deal," and Mr Vontant raised his hand to shake mine.

For a moment I mentally went over everything we had said to ensure I'd got what I wanted, then I shook his hand. The deal was set.

"Well played Ms Anders," Mr Vontant said coldly, and I knew he was really annoyed with me as he only ever called me that when I'd *really* put his nose out of joint.

"My answers please Mr Vontant," was all I said in response, not wanting to lose the tension I'd built up to keep control of the situation.

"You will fry in the deepest canyons of pain and despair before he answers," Benjamin hissed, obviously in pain but showing that good old demon fighting spirit.

Mr Vontant gave him a look of impatience before stepping forward, with his right arm swinging, and punched Benjamin so hard he fell off the chair and ended up dangling, unconscious, from his skewered hand. Then, before I could even say or do anything about it, Mr Vontant made a tsking sound and hauled the younger demon's limp body back onto the chair and propped him up in such a way that he then stayed there.

"Your answers, Ms Anders," Mr Vontant announced, stepping away from Benjamin and straightening his suit while giving the other demon a final look of disgust. "I will answer them in the way they were given, but if you're going to take notes you better move quickly as I won't stop to answer anything more once I've started." Given this not-too subtle hint, and knowing Mr Vontant didn't enjoy giving away information for free, I scrambled back to the kitchen island, snatched the pad of paper and pencil I'd left there earlier in the day, flipped to a clean page and then pulled up a chair next to Benjamin. Mr Vontant seemed to sniff at my eagerness while Trishna was strangely silent. I really did get the feeling he hadn't liked how I'd handled tonight or how eager I was to gain information from a demon, but I would deal with all that later. I walked in the Light, but when dealing with demons I'd learned you had to mean what you said, by force, threats and violence if necessary.

"Wroth resides, if you can use that word on such a creature, in the Dark World Down Below. He does, however, have free and easy access to either realm, as does any of his kind when on duty."

Mr Vontant glared at me as my mouth opened in question and shook his head slightly before going on. It was obvious he wasn't going to expand on any of his answers.

"I don't care what those texts of yours say, wraiths are simply the angry, tormented after image of a soul trapped in this plane of existence and *can't* possess anyone. So your assumption they are not being possessed by a wraith is correct. . . as much as that pains me to say. I will even be so generous to add that, technically, they're not being possessed at all."

I gaped; I stopped writing and just gaped. I was obviously in for a doozy when it came to my last question.

"And finally, and please write down that this is against my better judgement and given because I feel it's the only way I can escape your clutches, all texts and scrolls stating Wroth is a wraith or wraith-like are incorrect," Mr Vontant paused here for effect. "Back in the past when scribes from the Light came up with these theories that Wroth was an ancient wraith-like creature that possessed souls and added them to his feathered nest — they were wrong. Those of us who know the truth dwell in Darkness and obviously have never bothered to actually correct these theories."

I started to open my mouth again and Mr Vontant raised a hand. "Not everyone who has dealt with demons and written down the answers realised they must emphasise that we 'answer them true' with everything we say. And so the legend of Wroth has happily been deflected in this manner for a century or so."

"So what exactly *is* Wroth?" I asked, unable to keep quiet any longer. "And don't go giving me that look, it was part of the original set of questions."

Mr Vontant and I glared at each other for a few moments before he sighed and straightened his suit in agitation. "Wroth is an abomination," he sniffed.

"Nice try brimstone breath, but that won't cover the answer," Trishna said, causing me to glance up at him where he stood by my shoulder in his usual position.

"Fine," Mr Vontant snapped tetchily. "Wroth is an ankou. There, I said it and I have now answered all your questions." He made a move to grab Benjamin to get the banishment side done.

"Hold on a sec," I said, writing it all down while also thinking through all I knew on the ankou.

"Celtic creature that is a type of a grim reaper," Trishna said.

Gee *thank you*, I thought. I had remembered *that* much myself.

"Yes," I said, sharing my glare between the two of them. "But usually they are the last man who died in a region for the year who was then charged with the duty of collecting the rest of the souls, on a person's death, for the next year." I *had* been doing my research after all.

"So how can Wroth have existed for centuries? And what is he doing with the souls of all these still living people?" Trishna asked.

We looked at each other with concern before I turned back to Mr Vontant to smack his hand away from the dagger pinning a still unconscious Benjamin to the table.

"Uh uh!" I warned Mr Vontant as he hissed angrily at me. "I asked you to tell me what *exactly* Wroth is. And you can't just say he is an ankou. He is obviously far more than that."

"Why you little festering . . ." Mr Vontant began before fully taking in the look in my eye. Yes, he was used to me and that look and knew it never ended well for him.

"Fine," Mr Vontant sighed. "But I really feel you are stretching the deal here Ms Anders. Wroth is an ankou who got to enjoy his job too much. He learned how to widen the region he collected from when one of his villagers travelled to the New World. He got a taste for this travel and for seeing it all. And so he found a way to collect souls from a body while keeping that body alive. While the body continued to live, his job was only half done, his duties still continue and will do so until the death of the last body he has trapped in such a way. By doing this he not only extended his life, but those of his victims. Some Birdfolk are now over a century old while still only looking in their sixties. As I said, Wroth is an abomination. He has failed to do his duty and has kept many souls from their rightful places. As the body still lives, the soul is not passed on to the new life and so can be used as a source of energy for Wroth within his 'nest' in Hell. Soul energy, I may add, that he does not have the right to possess."

"Meaning there are no doubt a few demons chaffing at the bit at the IOU he's given them," Trishna snickered. "If he is holding all those souls, he's got your dark powers by the short and curlies."

"Not all souls collected by an ankou are destined for Hell, so it is not just the Darkness he hoards them from. And I can assure you that very few know his true origin, even among demons. Even I don't fully understand how he is getting away with it," Mr Vontant snapped.

I was pretty sure a lot of demons would have liked to know exactly how he was doing it. They were obviously going to be rather pissed off by this creature hoarding souls when they themselves would rather be doing it. As that was how a demon got its power, through the amount of souls it had to torment before it had to give them up to their next life.

"How did Wroth do it? How did he change and extend his reign?" I regretted the question as soon as I'd said it as we all knew it wasn't part of the original deal.

"Tut tut," Mr Vontant said, and smiled evilly. "By asking a new question I will take it as a sign you're satisfied with my answers to the ones in our deal. And so it's time to send us on our way."

I stood up to protest, I knew I could wrangle a few more snippets of information out of Mr Vontant if I could just think up a new plan. I felt Trishna's hand on my shoulder, his calming influence bringing me back to our current situation.

"I really do think they've kept their part of the deal Steph, it's time to do our side." He turned me to look at him again, to see the concern on his face. "Tonight hasn't exactly been a Light versus Darkness deal, Steph, we've muddied the waters of the two enough so let's just let them go before. . ." here he broke off and just gave me a meaningful look.

I sighed, feeling the weight of what I'd done crushing me. Trishna was right damn it, I'd walked a little too close to crossing the line by threatening to imprison the demons if I didn't get my way. So it was best to keep the deal and end the early-morning's entertainment here and now.

"Fine," I muttered, turning back to the two demons at my table. "Get ready for this in case he's faking it." I took hold of the dagger. "Benjamin, demon sent here to do all sorts of annoying stuff, I release you from the binding of silver and oak and banish you to the Dark World Down Below where your powers will belong to Mr Vontant for six lunar months." I pulled the dagger out but when nothing happened Mr Vontant just shrugged and scooped the still unconscious demon up into his arms. It was quite a sight to see the smaller demon holding the bigger demon with such ease.

"Mr Vontant, as per our agreement here tonight I release you from the binding nature of this house and banish you back to the Dark World Down Below with not only your own powers fully intact, but with the powers of Benjamin for six lunar months, starting from now. You cannot return to this plane of existence unless summoned or are acting upon previous deals you may have made." Yeah, I'd banished Mr Vontant a few times now and we both knew the routine. Then realising I actually had to *release* him from the house, I wandered over to the glass back door and slid it open. I was drained but still felt reluctant to let him go. There was so much more I wanted to know and I was pretty sure I *could* have made him tell me.

"You are wasted here, Stephanie," Mr Vontant said to me again, stopping by the door to do so, before slipping through it and literally vanishing into the dawning light. I slid the glass door shut and locked it again, giving Trishna a wary look as I did so. He was still looking at me with concern, a look that left me feeling uncomfortable.

"I suppose all we can do now is put the kettle on for a pot of tea. Buddha's Tears seem in order," was all he said though, before turning away and moving into the kitchen.

I didn't really think that was what he actually wanted to say about what had just gone on, but I was glad tea had once more had the last word. Heck, when all else fails, make some tea. Right?

# Chapter 8

"YOU know you could just turn it off. If it keeps vibrating across the table like that it'll end up in the marmalade you spilled."

I gave Trishna a sharp look before glancing back at my phone as it skittered across the breakfast table, telling me a certain someone wanted to talk to me. He was right, but I didn't want to admit it. I was still too much into my 'not a morning person' phase after so little sleep that I didn't want to agree with, or talk to, anyone. I mean, wasn't it enough I was out of bed, showered and dressed? So what if Trishna had too, he was a morning person and it showed in his look of crisp new t-shirt, bare feet and jeans as he sat there goading me. Even what he wore seemed to be goading me in comparison to my rumpled blouse and yoga pants.

"Does she send the white-laced goon squad over if you don't answer after the tenth attempt?" he remarked, casually taking a napkin from the holder on the table and wiping up the marmalade as my phone buzzed back into life and started moving again.

"Not always," I replied, though I was pretty sure that Roxanna herself would be over in ten minutes or so if I didn't pick up. What with Simon still zonked out with what would appear to be a misbehaving ankou wrapped around his neck, I was pretty sure the High Priestess was looking for hourly updates.

My phone buzzed again and I just stared at the crumbs on my plate as if they were simply the most fascinating thing in the world. With a sigh, and a muttered bad word, Trishna grabbed my phone off the table before I could stop him.

"This is the phone of Stephanie Anders, Protector of Souls. She can't answer right now as she's too busy nursing a guilty conscience over dealings with demons last night. How can I direct your call?" He spoke quickly, leaping up from the table as I tried to swat the phone away. We were both aware it was Roxanna who was calling me. Damn it, if I felt comfortable to swear at an Other World level, boy he would have got an earful!

As he danced away from my further failed attempts to get the phone, Trishna made some agreeing noises into the phone and then hung up, tossing it back at me.

"She's on her way over with the Apothecary. I suggest you change into something more presentable before they arrive." He eyed me over in a way that left me feeling uncomfortable. "Though if you *do* plan on doing some yoga while in those pants, I'd be happy to stay and watch." He grinned and dashed off to his own room, avoiding my lunge, to obviously finish getting dressed himself.

Helping him find restitution was going to be hard. How are you meant to help someone find peace when they kept giving you the urge to hit them?

***

"Stephanie, you are aware of my opinion of your dealings with demons." Roxanna may have sounded calm as she said this, but there was that edge to her voice that always made me squirm, leaving me no doubt I was in trouble with the head teacher. . . again.

"It's not as if I made a deal with any *new* demon. Just made a new deal with one I already had deals with."

Yeah, no. . . that wasn't as good out loud as it had been inside my head.

"And do you realise what the chief carpenter is going to need to do to this table before it can be used again? Demon's blood and energy infused into the very fibres of the oak. Not a good thing." Well, when she put it like that. . .

"I'm not going to apologise," I replied defiantly, then immediately wilted a little under her look of disappointment. "You're the one who keeps telling me to go with my gut and do what I feel is best done. And I did. How am I in trouble for this? I even discovered that those who have walked in the Light before me were mistaken about Wroth. Just think of what we can do with that sort of information."

"I will agree that I do indeed encourage you to go with your instincts," Roxanna admitted patiently. "But if you want to keep walking in the Light so confidently, you may want to start thinking a few things through before acting on them."

I refused to give the sigh that these sorts of comments seemed to induce in me. Instead I turned my attention to Trishna as he served the tea. We were in the front sitting room of my cottage catching up on last night's events while the Apothecary assessed Simon.

Roxanna thanked Trishna for the tea he handed her, in the best chintz china I had too, before turning back to me with one of her studying looks. She then surprised me by being the one to sigh.

"There is just something about you Stephanie, something I feel I am missing. You are right. You did your best, gathered some valuable information and dealt with two demons without bloodshed. . ."

"If you don't include the stuff on the table," muttered Trishna as he sat down next to me with his own cup of tea after giving me mine. I didn't elbow him in the ribs. See, working on restitution here.

"Yes, ignoring that," Roxanna went on with one of her cat and mouse glints in her eyes. "All I can say Stephanie is tread carefully. You are the Protector of Souls, blessed by Isis and belong in the Light. Please ensure your path stays true. Yes you got some valuable information out of those demons. . . but at what cost to yourself and your true path with Isis?"

I nodded, what else was there to say or do? It was so rare I needed this type of pep talk these days, as I felt justified in my actions. It's not as if I was out burning kittens or beheading non-believers on my days off. I walked in the Light and it was going to take something pretty big to stop me from believing that what I did was against the Goddess's will.

"What if I said. . ." I started, but was cut off by a politely raised hand by Roxanna.

"As I've told you before Stephanie, justifying your actions by saying you were doing it for charity does not suddenly make a bad thing good."

Trishna snorted next to me, obviously amused at my current work around excuse. I mean, had the High Priestess *looked* at social media of late? Everyone else seemed to think saying some reckless stunt was done in the name of charity justified their actions. Oh wait, maybe being part of the Other World and walking in the Light meant I was supposed to have better morals and principles than those wanting to be viewed by millions online. Got it.

Before anything else could be said the Apothecary entered the room. I would have liked to have named her, but never having had her introduced as anything *but* 'the Apothecary' meant I was out of luck.

"He sleeps but the Darkness binding him grows stronger," the Apothecary announced, declining Trishna's offered cup of tea with a polite shake of her head. "There is little more that I can do for him now so, with your permission High Priestess, I will check on my work in the garden here before returning to the Temple."

"Of course," Roxanna thanked her.

"So, where was I?" I asked when the Apothecary had left, not wanting to fill the sudden silence but wanting to get on with my day. "Oh, that's right, Layman Smith will be expecting me for today's lesson."

"That is true," Roxanna said as she gracefully got to her feet. "And while you follow your daily duties, remember to keep in mind my warning Stephanie. Tread carefully, as getting too close to the edge of anything may cause you to fall."

We all knew what she was talking about and that my not so subtle attempt to drop the subject hadn't worked. Still, she didn't press me further and, after the brief hug she always seemed to need to give her friends, Roxanna left quietly.

"Layman Smith?" Trishna asked as we took the tea things back into the kitchen to clean them and put them away. Yes, I *was* a clean freak. Order out of chaos and all that.

"He's just this guy helping me learn a few things," I replied casually, "You know, boring stuff. You may as well stick around here and keep an eye on Simon and watch TV."

From Trishna's sudden focused look on my expression I knew he hadn't fallen for it. Damn.

"There is already a priestess in with Simon, she came with the Apothecary," he mused. "I had wondered at the time, but they obviously knew about this 'daily duty' you need to go do. So, spill, what you doing?"

I wanted to sigh, I didn't. I fussed over straightening my already straight tea towels instead.

"It's nothing. I see Layman Smith every few days and he helps me out with learning some of the more. . . physical aspects of being the Protector of Souls."

"Physical? What, like how to flee a Black Witch coven with their ghost familiars and *not* pull a hammy," he was smirking at me now and I knew he wasn't about to let it drop. . . or let me go alone.

"Fine!" I snapped — still no sigh I swear. "He is my weapon's instructor. It's not as if carrying a sword means you can use it without hurting yourself in the process."

The smirk turned to a snort of laughter and I restrained myself from giving him a dead arm. Stupid restitution.

"Was this a mandatory part of being the Protector of Souls?" Trishna asked through his amusement. "Or is there a simply fantastic story I need to hear as to how you came to this conclusion?"

I refused to answer his questions as I not only didn't want to incriminate myself, I didn't want him laughing about the whole thing for days to come. So swinging a sword wasn't as easy as it sounds. We all make mistakes.

"I need to get changed or I'm going to be late and Layman Smith *hates* it when I'm late," was all I actually said. I'm pretty sure my damn expression gave me away, however, no matter how hard I'd tried to hide it, as Trishna's laughter could be heard all the way to my room.

*****

I will state here and now I've never been one for all the technical jargon and official names for things. Which is possibly why it's taken me so long to realise how important the right words can be in the Other World.

And despite Layman Smith's best efforts I still fought more from instinct than practising to his shouted commands. There was none of this 'deflect, edge, fade, guard' nonsense when I fought him. More 'left, right, dodge, whack, and duck'.

Yeah, Layman Smith and I weren't on the best terms because of this, but it was his duty to teach me and mine to learn so we were stuck together.

"Fade damn it!" he yelled as he came at me with a bamboo practice stick. I think I did a 'pass back' by mistake and got a new bruise in the ribs for it.

"Screw you!" I spat back and thwacked at him with my own bamboo sword. He parried it. . . or whatever. . . and jarred my arms so hard I nearly dropped my weapon. Layman Smith seemed to be in a grumpier mood than normal and it was starting to rub off on me.

"Move back to guard, and then I want to see you move to stance and try again," Layman Smith announced sternly. He was in his mid to late fifties and had the appearance of a person who had worked with, and made, weapons all his life. I guess the name of Smith was a bit of a giveaway too. He was a short, stout, stern man who really put my teeth on edge every time I saw him. Not because he was evil or walked in Darkness, but simply because his dislike of me emanated from him more than his BO did.

"From stance I want to see you pass forward and when we connect, attempt to shed my blade," he grunted, and moved back into the stance I called 'lazy enguard'.

"He wants to you take one step forward and then, when his sword hits yours, slide yours down his blade as a way to deflect him," Trishna called from his seat in the corner, my 'Sword fighting for Dummies' self-made notes in his lap. Yes, he had come and was now enjoying himself immensely as he watched Layman Smith chase me from one end of his work out weapon's room to the other.

"Shut. Up," I snarled at Trishna, forgetting restitution for a moment, and tried to take up the stance I was expected to do.

"Sure my two hours isn't up by now?" I asked Layman Smith, doing the best to keep the whine out of my voice.

"Barely started," the older man grunted back. "Besides, if you ever get yourself caught in a melee, you can't just call time after two hours and go sit down for a breather."

"I just don't see the point to grown people hitting each other with bits of wood and how it is the same as sword fighting." Yep, still no whine in my voice, just.

"And you think I would let you use a *real* sword on me? Am I that dumb looking?" Layman Smith then nodded to show we were to begin again.

"At least when I hold my sword it feels real and not just me trying to smack you in the head with a stupid stick!" I grunted before going through the motions he'd asked of me. I took a step forward, our sticks connected and I tried to let mine slide down his blade in a way to deflect it away. It didn't end well and his sword ducked under mine and I got another very hard poke in the ribs as I lost my balance and stumbled. The bastard.

"What in the hell is your problem?!" I yelled at him, rubbing my ribs hard after his last attack. I mean, damn it, he's meant to be teaching me here, not damaging me. We had been doing this now for four months and every lesson seemed to get rougher while I seemed to learn nothing from it.

"How in Isis you're meant to be a Protector of yourself, let alone the innocents who need you, I'll never know," Layman Smith sneered as we returned to our guard stance. "You're meant to be blessed by our beloved Goddess and be here to protect others and yet you don't seem to be able to do a damned thing without summoning creatures of Darkness to do your bidding."

Ah, so he'd heard of last night's adventures too.

"They don't do my bidding," I snapped back, finally glad we were actually venting the months of built up anger in a verbal manner rather than just hitting each other. "They keep their side of the damned deals we make. There is a difference you know!" Was there? Of course there was, there *had* to be. Demons did *not* do my bidding and I didn't need them to kick arse. . . did I?

"I think you've touched a nerve there Layman Smith," Trishna called, the smile and amused tone barely masking a wariness creeping into his voice as he read my expression. "I really don't think you should push her buttons too much. Just saying."

"What's she going to do, beat me into submission with her canny wit and blunt sarcasm?" snorted Layman Smith, obviously amused to have an audience.

"Screw you metal maker," I bit back, happy to express my pent-up tension in this way. Wow, I'd never thought these lessons would be *so* useful. "It's okay for those who get to sit by the fire making things to make judgement calls on those of us actually out there *saving* people." Oh, he didn't like that *at all*. The usual look of dislike on Layman Smith's face contorted into one of pure hatred. . . if only for a split second.

"If I wasn't sworn to help you as part of my devotion to the great Goddess, I would show you just exactly what I can do with the metal I make," he hissed. "As far as I'm concerned you're an imposter. You don't walk in the Light, merely pretend to. And at least if I teach you to fight I will know how to defend the Temple against you when you finally show your true colours."

I don't know exactly happened next, but his goading and aggression pressed all the right buttons and I suddenly dropped the stupid bamboo sword he'd been making me use all these months and walked over to

Trishna and unsheathed my own sword. The one I brought with me every lesson and had never been allowed to use.

"Okay wise arse, prove it. Prove you're the good guy in this situation while I am the useless baddie."

Trishna started to stand to support me but I gave him a look that had him sit back down. If there was going to be a fight, it was going to be mine. Alone.

"I walk in the frickin' *Light*. I was blessed by Isis herself and I'm pretty damned sure She knew what She was doing, being a Goddess and all that. And if I am an imposter She's the one to come and tell me. Take me on as I am with my true weapon. If you kick my arse, I'll stop complaining and deal with your gloating."

"Stephanie. . ." Trishna's tone held that warning note it always got when he felt what I was doing probably wasn't the best idea.

"Stupid girl, I would lose my home and job if I succumbed to such a temptation. Not all of us can just jump from Lightness to Darkness when it suits us."

The. Bastard. I walked in the Light, *everyone* knew that. So I dabbled with demons, how the hell else was I meant to save so many souls? "Fine, no sword, just fists."

I dropped my sword, and before he'd had a chance to answer, or for Trishna to stop me, I shoulder charged him, knocking him back a few steps.

"Come on then *little* man." I emphasised his height, pretty sure he suffered from short man's syndrome among everything else. And the rest is pretty much history as he clenched his fist and came at me. A man who had swung heavy hammers all of his life and had the strength of men half his age and twice his height. . . against me in a *really* bad mood and wanting a way to vent it. I walked in the Light and wouldn't let anyone tell me otherwise.

Hey, he started it.

# Chapter 9

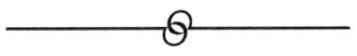

"HE WILL be out of surgery soon but will need to have his jaw wired closed for at least two months," the Apothecary explained to Roxanna as I stood before her, head bowed and definitely feeling like a naughty school girl this time. "His ribs are merely fractured, not broken. He has lost two back molars on the right side and had three dislocated fingers on his left hand."

Look, it wasn't if I hadn't got hurt either you know.

"And her?" came Roxanna's crisp tone, I flinched a little at it, but didn't look up to meet her eye.

"Cracked rib, major bruising to the face and upper torso, twisted ankle and split lip."

Well, when she compared our injuries like that, of course his sounded bad.

"And it appears Trishna's nose is thankfully *not* broken, despite the blood and swelling," the Apothecary ended with. "We're pretty sure it was her elbow that did it when he tried to pull her off the unconscious Layman Smith."

Ooops.

As Roxanna dismissed the Apothecary with her thanks the room suddenly grew a lot more foreboding with just the two of us in it. Roxanna's private chamber was never that big to start with, but today it suddenly seemed a *lot* smaller.

"Well?" No offers for me to sit down and rest my throbbing ankle, no offer of a drink, just an icy question.

"He refused to believe I walk in the Light or could fight my own battles without the aid of a demon or two." I hadn't meant it to sound so pathetic. . . but hey.

"So you beat him into submission, broke his jaw and sent him to hospital?" Still icy.

"He was meant to be the better fighter than me!" I protested to the floor, still rather pathetically. "He's been goading me for months and just chasing me about the room while hitting me with a stupid stick. I mean, it's not as if hand to hand combat *wasn't* on our curriculum."

There was a long pause and finally a sigh, but from Roxanna, not me.

"You may sit and rest your ankle Stephanie," she finally said, her tone mildly thawed and sounding more disappointed than angry.

I stood for a moment longer, wanting to rebel and stay repentant on my feet, but my ankle seriously did hurt and demanded I take my weight off of it. And so I sat, hands clasped demurely on my lap — hiding most of the grazed knuckles — and head still bowed. What had I done? He had just goaded me and that damn stupid anger of mine had taken over. None of it was meant to have happened, the fight, let alone me beating the snot out of him. I guess some of his training had rubbed off on me after all.

"I blame myself for this you know," Roxanna said, still sounding angry, but not necessarily at me. My head snapped up and I gave her my best squinty-eye. Easy to do when the eye in question was half swollen shut from a rather good punch from Layman Smith.

"You? You're not the one who let the little sod get to you until you lost your temper and gave him a good thump," I exclaimed, wincing at how hard it was to say certain words with a split lip.

"No, but it was I who decided to pair you up with Layman Smith, knowing his opinion of you all those months ago." She still sounded disappointed but her tone was visibly thawing. "At the time, I had felt it would add a nice level of friction for you to use that passion of yours when learning to fight."

"And instead I played nice and kept my manners until I got tired of the little runt smacking me with a stick and beat him up." I had meant to sound remorseful as I said this, and hoped she hadn't heard the tinge of pride. Look, he'd *deserved* it! Saying I didn't walk in the Light and all that. Shying away from the studied look Roxanna was piercing me with, I tried to put my sore ankle up on my other knee, only to have my cracked rib remind me it was there and cause me to just wriggle about in my seat and whimper.

"Every pain from those injuries you now suffer, you deserve," Roxanna went on to say in her stern motherly tone. "And may you be truly repentant and aware of that as they heal — without the aid of Isis' Light I may add."

I just nodded dumbly, unable to even pout due to the split lip.

"And I promise to send Layman Smith a big bunch of fruit, chocolate or something as the beginning of my apology." I eyed the High Priestess carefully, hoping to see her finally finish thawing.

"Not exactly the perfect gift for a man whose jaw you broke and that will need to be wired shut for some time," she pointed out in a tone laced with irony. Damn, I'd forgotten about that.

"Flowers?" I mean, what did one get a Weapons' Smith after you well and truly kicked their arse and put them in hospital.

"I feel a heartfelt letter of apology, which I will help you write mind you, will be enough." There was a cautious amusement to her tone. Yes I know I'd done wrong here, but she had just admitted it was possibly her fault.

"Ah yes, words being important and all, the written word especially so," I conceded just as the door opened and Trishna shuffled in. Damn, how many karma points did I lose for whacking him like that? His nose was twice its normal size and both eyes were black.

"Oh Trishna, I'm *so sorry!*" I exclaimed getting to my feet, trying to hobble over to help him into a chair, hurting my ankle even more and falling heavily against him and almost knocking his head into the still open door.

"Damn woman, I hope you're better at soul protecting than you are restitution," Trishna said, as he gathered me into his arms to steady me, then helped me back into a chair.

"Thankfully she is," Roxanna answered for me, and finally there was some real warmth in her voice.

I kept my eyes firmly on my hands in my lap, not wanting to scare away the beginning of Roxanna's good mood, or catch the glint of amusement that was no doubt in Trishna's eye as he eased into the chair next to me.

"And as you're going to be out of action for a few days Stephanie, I am going to assume you're going to put that time to good use?"

I raised my eyes again to meet Roxanna's as her gaze played the old cat and mouse game.

"Well, I won't be sitting around," I said bluntly, brushing past the situation that had brought me to her office, possibly kicking and screaming, an hour earlier. She quirked a questioning eyebrow to this statement.

"Look, I'm sorry I lost my temper with Layman Smith, and I'm sorry I got us a little roughed up." I ignored Trishna's attempted snort and consequent groan of pain. "But I really don't think Simon *has* days. If I'm going to try and save him from this ankou, I need to act now."

Roxanna sat back a little as she pondered what I'd said, clearly thrown by the fact my focus was still on helping Simon, despite everything else.

"And how exactly do you plan on getting the ankou to let him go and return his soul?" she asked, interested but cautious.

"Firstly I'm going to try and talk to the ankou while we have it still connected to Simon."

"I'll get some drop sheets and plastic matting ready for that fun interview," Trishna said, slightly nasally.

But seriously, what else did they expect me to do? It's not as if I was going to have weapon's training any time again soon. . . and I didn't want Simon in residence longer than I had to.

"On one condition," Roxanna warned, rising to show our meeting was almost at an end. "You ensure you stay in the Light and allow no demons into your home. It is a place of Isis after all."

"Agreed," I replied, also struggling to my feet. "That is aside from those who pop up uninvited thanks to deals they have with others. . . or those that pop up uninvited due to existing deals with me."

Roxanna shot me a look of sheer exasperation as Trishna got up and helped me from her office. But come on, what did she really expect? I was keeping my promise to her as much as I could, wasn't I?

# Chapter 10

"SO TELL me again how you plan on communicating with the ankou wrapped around idiot boy's neck?" asked Trishna in a muffled voice when we were back in my kitchen. He had an ice pack on his nose to help with the swelling, while I had my foot up on a chair with another ice pack for the same reason. We were sitting at my little table. The larger table had been cordoned off and the Head Carpenter had been rather stern with me about touching it, let alone *using* it again until after he'd had a chance to truly cleanse it.

"If we want to be technical about it. . ." I mused, reefing through the piles of notes, books and parchment cluttering the smaller table, "I can't talk to it."

"That's helpful." Trishna moved his cup of Darjeeling from where it was being threatened by an avalanche of hand written notes. "I can see this is therefore going to be a long night. How *are* you going to talk to it then?"

"Well, I want to keep Simon doped to restrain the ankou and stop it from using him. Unfortunately that also means it can't use him to talk to us, like it did yesterday," I explained, ignoring his sarcasm as it was far less superior to my own. "So I will need someone who can see into the spirit world. You know, like an undead, ghost, demon. . ." I gave Trishna my best innocent look, marred by the bruising to my face, and he shifted uneasily in his seat.

"You promised Roxanna you'd not call on the services of a demon to do this," he warned me.

"Yes, and I will keep that promise," I said patiently. "But I got the feeling yesterday that someone who remembered being a ghost also seemed to remember how to see with spirit-sight."

I won't repeat the words that flowed from Trishna's mouth as he threw the ice pack onto the floor. I could almost smell the memory of burned tea, I really could.

"I'll take that as a 'Why yes Stephanie, I can indeed still use spirit-sight and would be delighted to help you out with this' shall I?" I said with false casualness as I straightened one of the piles of notes on the table. I couldn't look him full on but glanced at him out of the corner of my eye. He was just sitting there arms folded and looking grumpy. So not much had really changed in this incarnation.

"You do know that asking me to see and talk to a soul collector isn't really part of the 'finding restitution' thing you and I have going on," Trishna said finally.

"Yes, but it's not as if it's going to *harm* the whole restitution thing, is it?" I asked, trying to hide my relief, as my other option had been to call on Mr Vontant. "I mean, you and me, facing the powers of Darkness, righting the world and opening it up to more Light. Surely that's got to count for some restitution points?"

He snorted, which sounded nicer than his verbal tirade had been, despite the wince it caused him to make.

"And when we're all done and Simon is sorted and out of our hair, I promise to spend far more time seeking restitution with you. You know, breakfast in bed, Buddha's Tears, and the last Tim Tam, I'll even let you be in control of the remote. . . when I'm not watching TV." My over the top look of faux innocence finally broke through Trishna's grumpiness and his second snort was one of laughter, followed by a heartfelt smile.

"Do you join me in the bed for this breakfast at least?" he asked cheekily, knowing full well what my answer would be.

"Uh, no," was the actual polite version of what I wanted to say, "And that image is now going to stay with me each time I reach for the cornflakes." But I smiled to show him that I wasn't that grossed out by the thought. I mean, he *knew* I saw him as almost a brother, right? This was just the new level of Trishna banter that didn't resort to too much swearing.

"Fine then," he said, still smiling. "When do you want to try talking to old skin and bones features?"

"Well, I'm not doing anything right now," I replied with a grin of my own before staggering to my feet, rib and ankle still being painful, grabbed a pen and paper and headed toward the hall.

The words Trishna used as he got up to follow me made me wonder if I'd ever forget the smell of burned tea around him. I seriously doubted it.

\*\*\*

We entered the room to find the Priestess Imelda in silent vigil in the corner of the room. Part of me had forgotten she was there, but then again with me having to go in and out all day on 'Protector of Souls' duty, it made sense to have someone here watching over Simon.

"Priestess, how's he doing?" I said with a smile, thinking he looked like crap. There was none of that look of peaceful innocence on his face. There was actually a slightly pained look, but the deep, slow breaths told me at least that he was knocked out good and proper.

"He is due for his next sedative in an hour," Imelda replied, shifting slightly to show sitting around all day wasn't something she was used to, or found comfortable.

"And you," I went on to ask, gratefully accepting the chair Trishna had thought to bring in for me. "Is there anything you require? We're going to be here for a few minutes if you feel the need to stretch your legs or whatever."

The priestess gave me a slightly wary look. "Thank you Protector, but my needs have been met right now. I take it you are going to try and communicate with the creature of Darkness possessing this man?"

Boy, the Isis grapevine worked quickly around here! We'd only left Roxanna's rooms an hour or so ago. Obviously Imelda had a phone hidden away under her many layers of white curtain-like lace as she hadn't even seemed surprised to see how beaten up we were either.

"Trishna is going to try and talk to the. . . uh. . . wroth thing. I'm here to take notes." I told her, trying to sound more casual than annoyed she was obviously going to stay for the interview. Why did I get the feeling Roxanna hadn't trusted me with the whole demon thing?

"And I wish you good luck with that and will remain here to help you to clean up any mess this may cause the host to produce," Imelda replied sweetly, giving me a look that said she wasn't about to budge unless Isis herself walked in and asked her to. Damn. And what was that about mess? No one told me you could projectile barf while comatose. Don't tell me I now needed to start on a new book 'The possessed and what is best to wear when addressing them'. Urgh.

"Quit your sour-faced inner-monologue look and let's get this sorted," Trishna muttered, fidgeting where he stood at the end of the bed.

"Wroth knows we're here and has been watching the whole situation with a rather nasty look on his face."

Oh, I hadn't thought of that. The whole 'out of sight out of mind' thing seemed to make sense now as I stared at the head of the bed and did my best to see something that was there, but invisible to me.

"And where is he exactly, you know, so I know where I'm looking?" I asked casually, trying to sound professional and obviously failing in Trishna's eyes.

"He's still sitting on Simon's right shoulder, arm around his neck. And, if you must know, flipping you the bird."

Priestess Imelda shifted uneasily next to me. Was it because she hadn't known there was an invisible creature in here with her? That the living, breathing version of Trishna still had the ability to see it? Or that it was now giving us the customary Darkness greeting?

"Hi Wroth," I called, waving at someone I couldn't see. "I can assure you that if I *could* see that finger of yours I'd have broken it by now so put it away." Yeah, I was a professional, anyone could see that.

"Do you want me to tell you *everything* he is saying? Or just pick out the parts that aren't a profanity or suggestions to do with diseased parts of the human anatomy?" Trishna asked all innocence as he watched and listened to the creature. "Gosh Wroth, I really don't think Stephanie even knows how to *spell* that, let alone knows where it's located on a dog." Yes, he was enjoying himself, despite being asked to do something that reminded him of his less happy days as a ghost and tool of a vampire.

"Just the stuff I need to know about the possession and how to stop it, please."

"Apparently that's not something you're going to find out until the moon crashes into the earth and splits it open. . . and then something about the Dark World Down Below having a. . . naked party. . . at your mother's house." I tried to purse my lip, was reminded of my recently split lip and so scowled instead. Why had this all seemed so easy when I'd come up with it out in the kitchen?

"Great, so now I need to go and find the best way to threaten an ankou to make this little bugger talk to me." I sighed, wanting to throw my pen and paper down in disgust.

"Well that bit is interesting to know," Trishna mused, still listening. "I don't think he meant to tell us that. . . but it appears this little chap isn't actually an ankou, merely its partner in crime."

My eyebrows rose in surprise, until the pain reminded me of my swollen eye. We had known Wroth wasn't a wraith, and had done a deal with something to extend its powers and all that. But we'd not known what or how.

"Do go on. . ." I urged, making a quick note of this while glancing back at Trishna and the concentrated scowl on his face.

"That's about it, I think." Trishna looked over to me apologetically. "I don't think it meant to even say that much. Just that Wroth wasn't here yet and that we would be sorry when he arrived. . . along with more dog anatomy and prostitute's diseases."

"Why is Wroth coming here I wonder?" I mused, tapping my pen against the pad of paper.

Imelda coughed. "Well, it would appear safe to assume that this creature was able to extract Simon's soul before possessing his body. And now Wroth is coming to get it for his nest. . . assuming *he* is an ankou."

I looked at her surprised. Damn, those white-lacy curtain-like robes still threw me and made me forget the wearer was often an incredibly intelligent individual with absolutely no fashion sense.

"Of course!" I exclaimed, wanting to give her a high five but concerned that she wouldn't know what it meant, or alternatively think I was about to slap her. "Simon freely, but while incredibly drunk and therefore it shouldn't count, agreed to give his soul to Wroth. We don't know why, but all the Birdfolk seem to do it. This little wart on a hippo's bum somehow has the ability to take the soul and keep the person alive. Wroth will then come and collect it to store in his nest and this guy will then keep doing whatever it is he does best up here with Simon!" I looked at the other two so pleased with that epiphany. Priestess Imelda grinned back, obviously pleased to be of some help while Trishna was obviously listening to two conversations at once.

"And why shouldn't she call you that?" he snapped at the head of the bed. "You said she was a lot worse and a lot dirtier parts of uglier animals, get over it." He gave me a wink, obviously enjoying himself when dealing with a fellow Other World potty-mouth. "I think you've hit the nail on the head with that one Steph, this little guy is not a happy chappie."

I felt a sudden chill and found myself standing up quickly.

"He still can't, you know, *jump* onto me without my permission can he?" I asked as goosebumps rippled up my arms.

"No. . ." Imelda breathed, also slowly standing and cocking her head slightly as if listening for something, "I can feel it too. We have another guest."

"Uh?" It was the best I could come up with as I exchanged looks with her and Trishna. He had stood up straighter too, but his attention was still focused on where Simon's head rested. Imelda was now looking toward the door with one hand reaching up to the vial of salted water hidden at her chest. Me, heck I didn't know *what* I felt. All I'd got was that tingle down my spine and goosebumps. It didn't feel like anyone had come into the house and there was no evil presence that I could feel.

"Are you sure?" I tried again, wanting one of them to respond.

"Oh yeah, pretty sure," Trishna said as he started tracking something, or someone, invisible as they entered the room and moved toward the bed.

"Wroth?" I asked, trying to sound calm and professional and not as if I wanted to wet myself. Why couldn't I *see* it.

"He says. . ." began Trishna.

"That I am indeed Wroth," came a whispery voice as a tall, old, gaunt man dressed in a dusty old frock coat, breeches, stockings and buckled shoes, his long white hair tied in a ponytail suddenly appeared at the head of the bed. He didn't look over at me or acknowledge our presence, merely bent over the still slumbering Simon to listen to the still invisible creature on his shoulder.

"Oh Isis preserve us," gasped Imelda, and shut her eyes. Despite my injuries I found myself standing between her and Wroth as she cowered behind me. I could see the logic in closing your eyes because if the ankou couldn't see you, it couldn't hurt you. . . but I was a stubborn sod and was fully aware I'd seen him. Plus, Mr Vontant wasn't currently leaning in the doorway with some pithy remark so I was pretty sure I was in no immediate danger. Yes, that line of logic was going to bite me in the arse one day, I was aware of that. Here's hoping that today wasn't that particular day.

"What have you done to this new disciple of Wroth?" came the raspy tones of the ankou. The old man threw me a mild questioning look. "Do you really think enforcing sleep is going to stop us? I know your sort, not even you can stop us once the deal has been made."

"I wouldn't be too sure of that buddy," I snapped, hopefully sounding bolder than I felt. I had a sudden longing for my sword, still at

Layman Smith's no doubt. At the same time I tried wracking my brain for the answer to how one killed a reaper.

The old man wheezed a laugh at me and turned his attention back to Simon as Trishna came to stand with me.

"Be careful, Stephanie," Trishna warned me. "Pissing off an ankou tends to mean you wake up dead the following day."

I clenched my teeth at this remark, not only to swallow my fear but to bite back what I wanted to say. Unfortunately I'd read the same tales and they did indeed scare the willies out of me.

"You stay and protect our new follower of Wroth my pretty. He is your body to play in now," the old man wheezed at the invisible creature, patting the air where its head probably was. Wroth then extended both his long, bony hands toward Simon's head and. . . took it off.

Which was weird, as Simon's head was still clearly attached to his body. But a ghostly cloudy-green coloured copy of it was raised by Wroth before being tucked carefully into a large leather bag the old man had slung over his shoulder. Then Wroth turned his pit-like eyes back on to me.

"I feel the protection spell holding me to this house. I recommend you allow me to leave now — otherwise there is still room for more than one soul in my bag." He advanced on us slowly, "I am sure I remember how to take one and still kill the host. Not everyone I touch lives to see another day."

The look Wroth gave me reminded me of how badly I needed to pee. And yet. . . I so wasn't about to let this guy just waltz on out with Simon's soul in his bag.

"You're not leaving here until you return Simon's soul to him. It has been taken as part of an agreement made while one party didn't have the *capacity to contract*." I don't know what I found more amazing, that I actually *said* that to a reaper, or that I'd remembered some of my studies in contract law from decades ago. Unfortunately this got Wroth's full attention as he turned to me and raised a questioning eyebrow.

"A protector of souls wise in the ways of the lawmakers? How very interesting," Wroth said in his whispered tones. "On what grounds do you make this accusation?"

"Stephanie. . ." warned Trishna by my side, but I simply brushed his hand off my shoulder and focused on Wroth.

"Simon was drunk at the time he agreed to give you his soul. Therefore the agreement is not valid as he was incapable of truly understanding what he was agreeing to," I said, after clearing my throat and wishing I sounded more certain about it than I felt. Wroth snorted and slowly shook his head at me.

"The supplicant was made aware that what my followers were offering him to drink was alcoholic. He still drank it. It wasn't my follower's intention to get him drunk, that was his choice," Wroth explained patiently, almost as if this was something he'd had to explain before many times. "When he was offered the extension of his life, strength and abilities in exchange for his soul and will, he agreed voluntarily. We have kept our side of the contract by installing my Impa Shilup into your friend once his soul had been removed. The contract is sound."

"He was drunk, I say it wasn't," I snapped, unwilling to let this go. Surely that had to count for something?

"You doubt the validity of the contract?" asked Wroth, showing more interest in me than I was comfortable with. "Do you wish to take me before the Arbiters to resolve?"

"No!" exclaimed Imelda from behind me at the same time as Trishna.

"We believe you'd understand the laws of possession and soul collecting better than anyone," Trishna assured Wroth. "There's no need to call upon the Arbiters."

Who the hell were the Arbiters? I was yet to find them in *any* of my notes. And yet they were obviously not someone I wanted to meet in a hurry, judging from the reactions from both Imelda and Trishna.

"It is the Protector of Souls I speak to," Wroth replied with a warning tone. "If she feels this soul is not mine to rightly take, I will willingly seek the counsel of the Arbiters." The ankou watched me, curious as to whether I was going to protest further or give in to his threats.

"You're going to have to find a way out of my house before you can do that." Did I actually just say that? "You may have Simon's soul, as part of your agreement with him. . . but I'm pretty sure nowhere in that agreement does it say *I* have to help you get it back to Hell. While you're in my house, so is his soul. Being protected by, me *Ani*." The cold fierceness in that last sentence frightened even me.

This caused a mixed reaction by those in the room. Imelda the priestess whimpered, and drew away from me. Trishna muttered things under his breath I'm pretty sure I was glad I couldn't hear. As for

Wroth, he stared at me for a moment longer then snarled and stalked out of the bedroom, becoming invisible again as he did so.

"Stephanie, you do realise Isis' protection doesn't make you immortal and that there is never a good time to piss off a flipping *reaper*!" Trishna finally said as I stood there shaking with a combination of fear and the release of adrenaline.

"It's fine, he can go when I say he can. And I'll say he can go when he returns Simon's soul to him." I tried to steady the quaver in my voice. "He can't do anything to us, he just bluffs a lot. We're fine, just fine."

"Of the most selfish and inconvenient times for you to need me to fulfil my side of a deal!" growled Mr Vontant as he appeared before me in the doorway. "What in the cesspits of the Dark World is it now?"

Okay, so maybe things weren't going to be as fine as I had thought. Damn.

# Chapter 11

"HOW is it *my* fault? It's not as if I agreed to let the damn thing in!" Yes I probably sounded a bit strung-out as I said this, but I happened to be hobbling on my sore ankle around the inside circumference of a salt circle in the middle of my kitchen floor at the time. Trishna had drawn and sealed it on Mr Vontant's instruction, while the demon himself stood by the back door arguing with the now invisible Wroth.

"Reaper's never need your permission to enter a house Stephanie," Mr Vontant sighed wearily, obviously only half listening to whatever the ankou was saying. "And, generally, they can leave again without permission too. Just not in this house."

"He can leave as soon as he gives Simon back his soul," I hissed angrily. And yes I was angry at the whole stupid situation and at my stubbornness, but I'm pretty sure that anger was mainly being fuelled by the fear I felt for getting into such a situation. I mean, yes I know I'm the Protector of Souls, but this was *Simon* we were talking about. And if the ankou's contract was as sound as he said it was, who was I to stop him?

Oh, that's right. I was the protector of *all* souls, not just the ones I chose to save. And that meant I at least had to try and keep Simon and his soul together, even if that meant royally pissing off a reaper who was now perfectly within its rights to take my soul as retribution.

"In case you missed it, Wroth is just pointing out that the circle can only protect you during daylight hours. The night's Darkness is his domain and he gains more power then." This was Trishna, not being at all helpful. "Oh, and with this whole legal precedent of an ankou being able to kill anyone who pisses them off, I've decided to go fully impartial in the hopes I just get out of this with white hair. So when he really gets pissed off, I'll be opening that door without notice. Just so you know, when it comes down to it."

"That is *not* helping Trishna!" I growled at him.

From the look he gave me it was obvious he already knew this but was torn between standing by my side, and saving his own skin.

"If only you would let me contact the High Priestess!" Imelda said, standing just inside the kitchen, apparently afraid to be away from her duties watching Simon, but also needing to know what was going on while there was still a reaper and demon in the house.

"And she will come charging over to take control, and as soon as she opens the door to come to the rescue Wroth will high tail it out of here and be on his way."

I hadn't meant to snap, I really hadn't, but from the look Imelda gave me you'd think I'd just slapped her.

"Priestess Imelda, please. . . I'm sorry!" I tried, but she turned in a flurry of lacy curtain-like clothes and hurried back to Simon's room.

"Why don't we just let him go?" Trishna broke through my anguished thoughts about the size of the apology Roxanna would now expect.

"What?" I turned back to him with a look of angry bewilderment. "Have you only just stepped into this conversation? We're trying to *save* Simon's soul here by *not* letting the ankou loose, when he will immediately take it away to Hell."

I felt the silent 'dumbarse' I mentally added to the end of what I said was something he also heard, but that it wouldn't go against my restitution attempts as I technically hadn't said it.

"Yes oh queen of patience and tact. But it's not as if we don't know where he's going to be heading with this soul now is it? He's not about to swan about all over town with it."

I stopped and actually blinked a few times to see if it would help my brain catch up with the obvious.

"I have a feeling I know where this is going, and I can assure you here and now that *none* of your existing deals with any demon covers them chasing an ankou around Hell until they can pinch a soul back," Mr Vontant pointed out from over by the door. He turned an impatient look back to where I assumed Wroth was.

"My good man, if you want her to know that, I suggest you simply slip back into her reality and tell her yourself. I am *not* your lackey." Mr Vontant's manner may have been polite but his tone, when addressing Wroth, was glacial. Meaning he respected the creature for what it was, but believed himself to be the more superior being. And as ankou originated to deliver the souls of the freshly dead down to Hell. . . I was pretty certain that made demons Wroth's boss.

And so Wroth reappeared in my reality and stalked angrily over to where I stood inside the protective circle.

"What I said was I don't care *who* you are or *what* the rumours of this Ani person might be. You wouldn't dare step foot in Hell. No one is that stupid or stubborn."

"Well. . ." started Trishna but I shot him a warning glance that would peel paint.

"I am the Protector of Souls," I growled at Wroth through clenched teeth. "And as much as I think Simon is a turd on toast I'd more than happily see you eat for breakfast, I promised him I would save him. It's my job. If that means I find a way into Hell, I will!"

Wroth simply snorted at this before he turned and walked back to the door.

"Then prove it," he almost spat. "Release me, and I look forward to you coming to find me in Hell. Then and only then will I give it to you and allow it to be returned to its body."

Oh game on reaper man!

"Get me out of the circle," I snapped at Trishna. I was unable to break it myself, being as it was connected to him and not me. "Get me out of this damned circle now and I will show this ancient bag of bones exactly what I will do to him when I find his nest."

Warily Trishna did as I asked, then grabbed me by the arm to stop me storming over to where Mr Vontant and Wroth were standing.

"Carefully Stephanie," he warned me. "I don't care how powerful you are up here, you are a nothing in the Dark World Down Below."

Gently pulling myself free I continued over to the door. Hobbling a little on my sore ankle, I stepped between the demon and the reaper, to prove neither of them scared me, and opened the door.

"Be gone denizens of Darkness and the Dark World Down Below."

As Wroth stepped through the door he turned back to give me a final studying look.

"See you in Hell, old man," I growled.

Wroth almost looked taken aback for a moment. He then turned away and vanished from my sight as he crossed the threshold.

"Stephanie, Stephanie, Stephanie," tsked Mr Vontant as he took his turn to leave.

"I do hope you realise our existing deal doesn't include me helping you get to Hell in your current, living, form?"

"I do," I replied wearily. "And you can be assured I'm not about to make a new deal with you to get me there either."

"Then, may I ask how?" Mr Vontant seemed genuinely curious about this.

I tried to quirk my eyebrow as much as my swollen eye would allow. "Funny Mr Vontant, I don't remember our current deal having an open question and answer session either. Something you're often reminding me of."

The neat little demon smiled with genuine amusement as he stepped through the door. "Touché Ms Anders. Well played again. I do hope we meet again on this plane of existence. I will miss your repartee." And then he was gone before I could respond.

I snicked the door shut and locked it before turning back and realising not only Trishna, but Imelda was standing there watching me.

"You let them go without making a new deal," Imelda said in amazement, as if this was something I was unable to do.

"You let them go without bullying one of them into telling you how to get to Hell," Trishna said in an equally amazed voice.

"Oh, I know how to get to Hell," I said lightly, trying to ignore their shocked looks as I walked to my study. "And now to find my little black book of demon deals and find the best candidate for calling in the right favour."

Did I know how to leave people gaping at me in disbelief, or did I know how to leave people gaping at me in disbelief?

# Chapter 12

"HELLO Tathal, fancy meeting you here." My tone had been casual and quiet, but the demon I addressed flinched away so badly he fell off the bar stool he had been lounging on.

"Ani," he squeaked as I helped him to his feet, my elbow length black leather gloves actually complementing the tailored pants and sequin blouse I was wearing — along with the most supportive running shoes my injured ankle could fit in — and suiting our surroundings well. It was one of the less seedy nightclubs I knew certain Darkness followers hung out in.

"I hadn't expected to see you again so soon," he added, looking over my shoulder at Trishna, who despite his black eyes and swollen nose, scrubbed up well in a suit.

We won't go into how ghastly I looked with my bruises and bumps. I mean, I'd only been beaten up just that morning after all. There was no amount of concealer that could truly hide it all, despite my best efforts. Still, the long, black leather gloves did go well with the outfit all the same and so I didn't look as beaten up and out of place as I would have if I'd turned up in my usual 'Protector' attire. I deliberately didn't introduce Trishna, words and names *were* important in the Other World after all, and it was up to the individual as to whether they wanted to let someone else know their name.

"I thought you promised not to lurk around this place trying to pick up drunk and horny teens," I replied, still trying to sound casual. "I mean, buying under-aged people alcohol is one thing, but convincing them to sell you their souls in trade for a little sexual charisma — we talked about that Tathal."

"I never said I wouldn't come back, just that I promised to check their ID first," Tathal sniffed with disdain, trying to get some of his demon superiority back. But he was a fairly young looking demon and I'd found that the younger they looked, the worse they were at their job.

Benjamin hadn't been my first failed demon attacker. They had to start somewhere after all, deals and souls were the only ways they would get anywhere in the Darkness down below.

"Just see that you do. And no more under-aged witchcraft either."

I smirked at the blush my statement caused before turning to Trishna.

"I last caught up with Tathal here when he tried a bit of that old Demon Thrall on what he thought was a drunk seventeen year old at a party. Turned out she was indeed seventeen, but wasn't drunk. More demon hunting for her coven for an upcoming full moon ceremony." I tried to keep the laughter out of my voice, but it still was a funny memory when it was explained how the Lakeside coven had been collecting their demons. Just because a young looking demon was inexperienced didn't mean they didn't hold the right sort of powers for black ritual. But it did mean they were a little more gullible and willing to, say, dress up a little at their victim's request, if they thought it meant they would score their soul. He hadn't scored, on any level, and I'd ended up having to 'rescue' him from a circle. Which meant he now owed me a favour. . . also known as an existing deal yet to be finalised. So all above board if Roxanna asked.

"What do you want, Ani?" Tathal snapped, obviously still embarrassed over it all. "I'm not up to anything I'm not sanctioned to do up in this world." He eyed me over with disdain, "And do you really think you should be out in public with a face like that, you look like hell."

A smile broke out on my face, despite the split lip.

"Funny you should put it like that. Obviously I've managed to get my look just right for the occasion."

Next to me Trishna groaned, picking up that death wish tone in my voice. In front of me Tathal shot me a worried look and tried to vanish, going cross-eyed at the failed attempt.

"Sorry bud, slipped a bit of binding silver on you when I helped you up," I told him sweetly.

Tathal snarled and clawed at the left arm of his suit sleeve, revealing his wrist, now encircled with a thin band of silver. It was a little trick I'd picked up from one of the many rescues of Mr Vontant I'd had to do. It was a basic way to anchor a demon in our reality for a short period of time when you didn't want to summon and bind, or earth them. The bracelet was only thin, enchanted silver — a demon's sweat would corrode it away within half an hour or so, making it only a temporary restraint. It also wasn't that commonly done, as there weren't that many people powerful enough to deal with a pissed off demon once the silver broke away.

"You festering. . ." he began the usual Other World tirade until I held up a warning hand.

"Shush!" I warned him. "I don't have the time for your twelve word insults right now. We can either do this the easy way and discuss me calling in our existing deal, or we can wait for the bracelet to break and I then make the deal with Mr Vontant when he turns up to protect me. Your call."

Tathal seethed for a moment, actually being quite restrained for a demon.

"And let me just add that if I make the deal with Mr Vontant, he not only is going to get your limited powers for six lunar months, I'm going to get in *big* trouble with the High Priestess of Isis as I sort of promised to not make any new deals right now."

"Nice work around," Trishna said amused.

I shot him a warning look too. What can I say? I had promised I wouldn't make any *new* deals with demons to get me to Hell. However, I had also mentioned I couldn't promise not keeping to deals I'd already made. Yes I'd sort of hinted that was really just me and Mr Vontant, but when I'd rescued Tathal from the Lakeside coven I'd not really known what I wanted in the deal so had simply said I would call on him for a favour at some point. All perfectly legit and above board. . . sort of.

"Six lunar months? Of all the nasty little. . ." Tathal started again.

"Tick tock Tathal," I warned him, not interested in hearing even his G-rated tirade. I wanted to use our existing deal, not open a new one. "You either stop complaining and start listening, or I may as well just order myself a drink and wait for Mr Vontant." Even with a battered and bruised expression, I still had a good poker face.

"Fine. We will open negotiations into our existing deal," Tathal sighed and slumped back onto his stool.

Beside me Trishna visibly relaxed out of his protection stance at my side as I eased my sore and sorry self onto the stool next to Tathal.

"I want to go to Hell," I told him calmly. "And I want to go alive, in my current state with my current abilities."

I was expecting Tathal would boggle at me and the concept but instead he just snorted contempt.

"Yes, we've all heard about your pig-headed desire to chase an ankou all the way to Hell for just one stupid soul," Tathal said witheringly. "And I will say here and now that any deal I've made with you can only be fulfilled up here. If you wanted me to take you to Hell, not that I could under those criteria, we'd need to have a whole lot more to deal with before it could happen."

"Ah, but I never said I wanted *you* to take me to Hell, Tathal. What I want from you is an introduction to the *Ferryman*."

Cool, that got them both boggling at me. Obviously it was all about the timing.

\*\*\*

"If I find that little twerp has somehow screwed me over on this deal I am so going to kick his arse from one end of this reality to the other," I muttered, for about the fifth time, as we stood on the side of a freeway, in the middle of the night, in freezing cold drizzle. I mean, *why* did it have to be so damned cold? To make getting to Hell feel all the better? Like when you travel to the tropics midwinter to defrost your soul?

"Tell me again why I'm here," Trishna said. "I mean, where in our deal of my restitution does it say I have to freeze my balls off on a roadside and *then* go to Hell."

"Because we're a team, and you know you like having adventures with me. Think of it as a team building excursion that is part of the whole restitution experience."

I ignored the filthy look he shot me and instead looked up to the sodium lamps we were standing under. The near snow like rain swirled and danced within the light in a rather peaceful and pretty manner. Maybe if I focused on that a little more I could find some inner calm before it all kicked off.

"And I mean, seriously, a *handbasket*," Trishna said. "Must you embarrass me like this?"

Nope, no inner peace for me tonight.

"What is life if not for a little whimsy?" I asked him innocently. I'd had to stash my purified water somewhere and come on? I mean, this was probably the closest I'd ever get to being able to say that I'd actually gone to hell in a handbasket. 'In', 'with'; there's not that much difference. So my bucket list was a little different to the norm, sue me.

"Ah, I see you found the right spot," Tathal said, appearing out of nowhere as easily as if he'd just stepped out of the shadows.

"Not that we quite know what this spot is all about," I replied, trying to hold onto my temper. I was cold, standing on the side of a freeway in the middle of nowhere. And that 'nowhere', I will add, had *no water* nearby so how the hell was this getting us to the Ferryman? Thankfully, I was tactful enough not to say this all out loud.

"You wanted to meet Charon and get him to take you to Hell. This is where you have to be to hitch a ride tonight," Tathal told me coldly, who'd obviously heared all that stuff I'd not said out loud.

"Hang on," I butted in, seeing Trishna was about to speak. "Karen? The Ferryman's name is *Karen?*" Why did they both just sigh at me and roll their eyes? I'd looked the old bearded guy in the boat up before we'd headed out to the bar; *nowhere* had it mentioned his name was Karen.

"Charon you newb," Trishna muttered in my ear as Tathal looked at me with disdain. "C.H.A.R.O.N. The Ancient Greeks pronounced the 'ch' sound as a hard 'k'. Please stop embarrassing me here."

Ah, well that would explain the Karen part. . . but why were we still standing on this landlocked freeway? Where was the boat, and the water?

"Please don't call him Karen when he gets here," Tathal said wearily. "Not that I can promise it will be Him you see tonight. He makes so few personal visits these days, and rarely outside of the Mediterranean." I think my scowl spoke volumes as Tathal actually squirmed.

"Look," he pleaded, "I did my best. I called up my contacts, found where the closest soul collector was tonight and arranged for him to swing past and pick you up. What else can I do?"

"Well, there is keeping your side of the deal and all that," I said in the dead-calm voice that people who knew me knew meant I was becoming pissed off. "I have spare salt water right here if you want to see if I still remember how to bind a demon soul and will." Okay, pretty sure that last bit would tell even those who don't know me how pissed off I was right now. Tathal took a few steps back holding his hands out before him as if warding himself against such an act.

"The afterlife and ferrying of souls just isn't as simple as a single boatman and the river Styx anymore," Tathal tried to explain quickly. "What with population growth and global spread, the mixing of cultural beliefs and the whole economic crisis meaning not all souls have the right fares due to inflation. . . times are tough and you simply get what you get."

Wait, the Other World and *afterlife* were also affected by the economic crisis? Of all the horse pucky excuses I'd ever heard. . .

"You also have to remember Steph that times have changed and not everyone is going to be expecting an emaciated old man with a beard rocking up in a rickety old boat." This snippet of skewed logic came from Trishna.

"You mean you believe him?" I said, amazed.

"Honey, when you can remember snippets of all the lives and deaths for the past one hundred years or so you don't have any choice. And just to remind you, I do have a little experience in this area," Trishna added dryly. He didn't exactly point out whose fault it was he remembered them, but it was loud and clear in his expression. I would have said more at this point, possibly even apologised *again* but a change in Tathal's stance drew my attention back to him.

"He's coming," Tathal announced, almost looking like a hunting dog going on point.

I turned to look in the same direction he was focused on and waited.

I heard the van long before I saw it. The engine sounded pretty rough and there was the sound of metal being dragged mixed into it. Then, out of the swirling mists, there appeared. . . a beaten up white van. Actually it was more than beaten up, it looked like it had already been in a few accidents and had rolled over several times after impact. How it was still road worthy and working, I really didn't know. But it was a creepy sight all the same. The stuff of urban legend: a dark, stormy and lonely night in the middle of nowhere, a beaten up old van stopping, offering you a ride. Where the journey ended was anyone's guess. I got a rash of goosebumps just allowing my imagination to flit over these thoughts.

Tathal stepped out onto the freeway and held up a hand to wave the van to a stop. It was then, under the sodium lights, I saw that the driver also appeared to have been in the same amount of accidents. And from the way his head was sitting, free from the body, on the dashboard in front of the steering wheel, there was a good bet he'd not actually survived the last one himself. The grin on his rather mouldy looking face was rather eerie and my goosebumps increased — the term 'grinning from ear to ear' came to mind.

"Ooh, a dullahan!" Trishna said, almost sounding delighted. "They can have the most wicked sense of humour, despite being a Fae. Never give them your name though, as repeating it can have rather a fatal effect."

"Ankou, dullahan, that damned idiot in his Irish shop. . . I never realised this area was so Celtic." I mumbled, more for something to say that wasn't as rude as what I was thinking. Saying I found the whole situation suddenly rather unnerving was a *serious* understatement.

"You should see some of the folk who come and collect you for the afterlife in China," Trishna told me, noticing my mood and putting his arm around me for comfort. I swear that I only flinched because he hurt my cracked rib and for no other reason. However, he quickly removed his arm and flashed me a look I didn't quite understand, before moving over to where Tathal was talking to the dullahan through the broken driver's side window. Trying to find something else to focus on until I felt in control enough to go join them, I noticed that the licence plate of the van was 'Charon'. Well, I guess that meant we'd pulled over the correct undead vehicle. I wondered how many of these sorts of things were out there on our roads that we mere mortals just couldn't see. On a dark, cold and miserable night like tonight I could easily imagine vehicles and passengers alike from fatal accidents getting back on the road to seek souls and ignorant hitchhikers alike to collect. I gave a shudder, feeling I'd just about scared myself enough with *that* mental image and moved over to where the others were talking to the head on the dashboard. It, er, he? Turned his eyes toward me as I approached and his grin, decomposed look and, well, bodiless appearance caused me to shudder again. As much as I was getting used to the Other World, it was going to take me a little while longer to get used to the afterlife subculture. It may have been one of the Fae folk but they were also a mouldy old headless corpse. Not the sort of faerie anyone likes visiting their home after dark.

"As I was telling the driver, we don't give our names," Trishna explained as I came to stand beside him. "All we want to get to the other side. And there will be no payment until we are safely on the other side."

"It's a fair deal," the head on the dashboard replied. "I have two more stops tonight before we reach the ferry and then it's just the final voyage we've got to make before reaching journey's end by morning."

"Oh. . . good?" I answered, trying to sound like I really knew what they were talking about. I knew a dullahan was another type of soul collector, a dark faerie, but other than that and the whole headless bit, I was drawing a blank. And now I was a little confused there was actually going to be a ferry. I mean, where was the cart made of human bones? And if there was going to be a ferry was I wearing any gold, because if I was my journey would finish before it began? The only things I felt I was confident in knowing about a dullahan were they were Fae, could kill you just by saying your name, and have a severe aversion to gold.

"Here," Tathal told me. Taking one of my hands he opened a small leather drawstring purse and poured some ancient looking silver coins into it. "Danake to pay for your journey. Just to ensure I've fully kept to my side of the deal. It's the preferred payment choice of the Ferryman, even to this day." He smiled as he gave me the empty purse and I fumbled to put the coins back into it, my hands not just shaking from the cold.

"I don't suppose I can get you to keep quiet to the other demons about us going to Hell?" I asked, as I closed up the purse.

He snorted. "Oh fat chance of me dobbing myself in and being the one blamed for letting you in there. And when it comes down to it, I've *not* let you into Hell. I've merely pulled over a passing dullahan and given you some coins. We're nowhere near Hell right now. He's on his way to the ferry that will take you to the other side. Still not technically Hell until you pass through the gates. Best I can do."

I gave Tathal a studied look for a moment. Despite the pure evil emanating from him, there was just something about demons that made me wonder about their origin. Beside their depravity and dark nature, there was something else. . .

"But I can assure you that if I see you down there when I'm connected to my full powers. . . the things I'm going to do to you for *daring* to bind me in silver. . . they'll be picking you out of the scenery for millennia to come."

Then again, maybe they truly were all complete and utter evil personified and I'd just got the wrong end of the stick again.

"Okay, time to leave," Trishna announced as he opened the front passenger's door for me. I touched his shoulder for a moment and turned him to face me.

"Are you sure you want to come? Now is the time to tell me if you want to stay behind."

Trishna studied me for a moment and shrugged. "As if I'm leaving you to run around Hell alone," he replied with a half-smile and then indicated again I should get in. I took a look in at the dullahan and moved toward the back of the van. It had no windows, something I felt was a *good* thing, as I didn't particularly want to see where we were going.

"I might just take the back. . ." I announced and, despite Trishna trying to get there in time to stop me, I opened the back door. *Hundreds* of faces looked back out at me. Very old, very young, and a myriad mixture of those in between. Staring in at them all I just froze, even my lungs decided they were too shocked from the energy the souls emitted to keep working. Trishna gently closed the door again and took me by the shoulders, forcing me to focus on him until I stopped making choking, gasping sounds and my breathing had returned to normal.

"When the living travel to the afterlife, it's always best they call shot-gun," he told me gently, before leading me back to the front seat of the van. "How about I sit between you and the dullahan? He seems a little handsy and I'm pretty sure I'm not his type."

Oh that thought was so not helping, but as we climbed into the passenger front seat, at least it took my mind off what I'd just seen. And why wasn't I surprised the seatbelts didn't work? I mean, damn it, can you die when you're already on your way to the afterlife?

There was a cough from outside and I noticed Tathal was standing impatiently by my window and realised I'd not finished our deal.

"I decree you have completed your part in our deal Tathal and have granted me the requested favour. And as I completed my side by saving your sorry arse from those teen witches, our deal is now done and all ties severed." We frowned at each other a moment until I realised I'd forgotten the last bit. "Be gone oh foul beast of hell, never to darken my presence again."

Tathal's expression changed to one of relief and he blinked out of existence just as the dullahan pulled back out onto the freeway and we were finally on our way.

So, I was in a van, driven by a Fae man named Karen (I couldn't help but give him that name) and I was on my way to Hell. Okay, I was doing well, not even freaking out that badly. And, yes, I did indeed still have my handbasket. It's those little things, in stressful moments, that just help make it all work out, right?

# Chapter 13

I DON'T know if it was the foggy weather, the sensation of sitting in a dead man's van that contained hundreds of freshly departed souls, my stress levels, or the late hour. . . but I soon got disorientated and couldn't quite make out where we were anymore.

As mentioned by our driver, he made two more stops where he left his seat — tucking his head under his arm as he did so — before moving around to the back of the van, opening the doors for a moment and then closing them again. He would then climb back into the driver's seat, perch his head just in front of the steering wheel on the dash and continue on his way.

The weather seemed to get worse as the clouds descended and surrounded us in a real winter fog. We couldn't see more than a metre or so in front of us, nor did we seem to come across any other vehicles on the road. But as it was now the wee hours of the next day, I hadn't been expecting much traffic.

"Is it just me, or does travelling through the afterlife have an almost soporific effect on everyone?" Trishna asked beside me, stifling a yawn.

Of course! I finally realised why it was so cloudy around us, why I didn't recognise any of it, and why we hadn't seen anyone else on the road. We weren't in our world anymore. This was that veil thingy in between the two worlds. Why did I suddenly feel so claustrophobic about it?

"It might just be you mate," the head on the dashboard said, not helping my near hysterical mood change at all. "Then again I've always found night driving has that effect on me. That's how I meet a lot of the people I ferry around."

Okay, so small mercy there then that neither of the last two stops were to pick up souls from car wrecks. . . that I saw.

"I hate to butt in with a rather childish question, but are we nearly there yet?" I asked, not wanting to give an opinion on our current location as I felt the less I thought about it the less likely I was to freak out. Damn I was dedicated to my job to be doing this for Simon! He better be grateful at the end of it all or I might just give him back to Wroth. Was it still protecting a soul if you were the one allowing the ankou to take it? I mean, it wasn't a new deal or anything, more of a re-gifting of sorts.

"You know I really do wish I could read your mind when you get that expression," Trishna said, in what I thought might be an attempt to be comforting. "I'm sure there's all sorts of crazy going on in that brain of yours that would make me laugh myself sick to listen in on."

So glad he wasn't the one who was meant to be finding restitution as he'd have just failed miserably.

"I would say 'bite me' but I'm afraid you would," I sighed wearily. But he had a point. There *was* all levels of crazy going on in my head right now and if it hadn't been for his bluntness I might have already reached the hysterical stage.

"We're almost there," the dullahan's head grinned from the dashboard. "The ferry terminal should be coming into view any moment."

And he was right. A few minutes later the fog cleared enough to show shadowy buildings that had a harbour like theme. There was even a rather cynical looking seagull sitting on a bollard near the water's edge. There were seagulls in the veil? And obviously they didn't think much of the place, going on this one's expression. Then again, don't all seagulls look cynical, or is that just me?

I had been expecting the van to pull over and let us all out to form an orderly queue and await the old man in his little rowboat. So when it pulled up in a queue of other beaten up and crushed looking vans and buses to board one of those large car and passenger ferries they use to island hop with, I honestly had to make a deliberate attempt to *not* allow my jaw to drop. The scale of undead being shipped to the other side was astounding.

"Is this like a monthly trip or something?" I asked, as casually as I could, not wanting to sound as dumb as I felt. "There are so many vehicles."

"This is the nightly run, we collect the souls that have passed that day from the world over and take them all across in one go." The dullahan grinned at me. I know it wasn't his fault, as one of a dullahan's things is that inane death grin, but it did come across as rather inappropriate to seem so happy to see so many dead in one day.

"Look at it this way," Trishna said calmly, "There's over seven billion people on the planet right now. What with age, illness, war, famine and acts of stupidity a *lot* of people die every day and have to go somewhere."

Yeah, no, that didn't help. Especially as it had me thinking about certain people in my life who had recently passed.

"You also need to factor in those who believe all living things have a soul and they all need to get ferried across too," the dullahan added.

Well that, at least, explained the livestock and timber trucks I thought I'd seen through the swirling fog.

"But I thought people just died and. . . walked in the Light or whatever," I said lamely, knowing I sounded as stupid as I felt. I mean, I *had* been doing research since starting on my new career path, but it had centred around the living and undead I would come across in my daily duties. I'd not really touched on the *after* death stuff too much as I had just assumed the souls either went to heaven, hell or that eternal waiting room of pain and damnation known as purgatory. Catching my worried look Trishna gave me a sympathetic look.

"If guided by a God or Goddess from their point of death, the soul does indeed go straight into the Light. . . or the other places," he replied patiently. "But for the rest of us, we come to the ferry, cross over to the other side and get sorted out from there." The mental image I got of a load of deities standing at a ferry terminal holding up placards listing their faith and followers was a little unsettling, but at least it meant my sarcasm was awake and trying to keep me from the near hysteria I was feeling. I wonder if all souls felt this way when passing through the veil to the other side. Or was it just the ones that were doing it when still attached to their alive and kicking body? No, that thought wasn't helping me either.

Our van moved forward in the queue and we were soon aboard the ferry where other soul collectors were directing the vans to where they would be parked for the journey. Most seemed to be dullahan or ankou and I didn't know what was more unsettling: the dullahan swinging their heads around by the hair as a way to direct the traffic, or the ankou dressed as if attending some macabre New Year's Eve party — ankou being created from the last souls to die in the previous year. Someone's party obviously hadn't ended as expected.

"I thought ankou are only meant to collect the souls of their own village or land. Why are they here?" I asked, feeling I was on safer ground in asking that, as it wasn't as dumb a question as the others I'd ask.

"Surplus stock," the dullahan grinned. "Party bus crashed a few minutes before midnight and they all technically died at once. Had to go *somewhere* to fulfil their obligations."

Okay, maybe I should just stop asking questions for now as I wasn't enjoying any of the answers I was getting. I decided to just look out the window and keep quiet for the remainder of the trip. As the other vans and mini buses settled in around us I noticed other reapers among them. Most were of the more skeletal type but the robes often varied in colours from black, red, green and into white. Obviously death came in all shades around the world. I glanced at the black van parked next to us and saw its front seat was taken up by a group of women who I really wish I'd not looked at. I have no idea if they were pretty under all the blood on their faces, but the slip of a fang on one as she laughed at something another said, or the claw like hand waved at me by another when she saw me looking had me shiver and look quickly away.

"Keres?" I whispered to Trishna as he took a glance next door too.

He mused for a moment and then shrugged. "Probably, where there is a violent death in the Mediterranean you're going to get a truck load of Keres turn up for a bite to eat."

Damn, I was meant to stop asking questions, right?

"I'm guessing asking you guys to play eye spy to kill time as we journey over is out of the question?" the dullahan grinned, having its body pick up the head off the dashboard and sit it in its lap so it could look over at us, now we weren't driving.

"Uh, no," I replied as politely as I could. "I don't suppose we're allowed to get out and stretch our legs during the trip?" Suddenly I didn't want to be sitting so close to a mouldy man with his head in his lap in a van on a ferry on the way to Hell. The dullahan shrugged in reply, while grinning at us from his own lap.

"I wouldn't," Trishna warned, a worried look on his face. "We have an arrangement with this soul collector to get us to the other side safely. Pretty sure we're fair game to any of the others if we step out of the van before we get there. The living aren't exactly *encouraged* to make this trip after all."

"Yeah, and some are perfectly within their rights to kill you stone dead simply because they don't like the look of you," the dullahan added. "Only a few of us need to know your name to do that."

I was going to say more when I noticed a rather regal looking Chinese man dressed in the ancient attire of royalty approach the van and look in through the windscreen at Trishna with a raised eyebrow.

"Again?" the man asked in annoyed frustration.

"Just visiting this time," Trishna smiled back, seeming pleased to be annoying this specific reaper.

"Yanlou, how's it going?" the dullahan asked, lifting its head up to the side window as a form of greeting. Obviously not someone a dullahan can kill if he knew his name and used it.

"Fair," the regal Asian replied, unrolling a scroll he'd had tucked up his sleeve. "Please go over the list and confirm you have made all the right collections. Though I doubt two *living* people will be accounted for," he added snidely.

"What can I say," the dullahan answered, putting his head back in his lap and taking the scroll to hold it in front of its eyes to read. "I had a deal with a demon, she had a deal with a demon, it all sort of happened last minute."

Yanlou snorted at this and shook his head in my direction. "She the one to blame for your predicament?" he asked Trishna.

"Well, blame is such a strong word. . ." Trishna began, "But yes, yes she is."

"Hey!" I complained, then wilted under the regal man's glare.

"But she is working on the restitution as we speak so pretty sure it'll all be sorted out soon," Trishna went on quickly. It was pretty obvious he hoped I wouldn't open my mouth and say anything too offensive.

Yanlou snorted again and held his hand out for the scroll. "I can't see how bringing you, alive, back to the afterlife is a very good attempt at restitution."

I bit my tongue at Trishna's warning look.

"All present and correct in the back," the dullahan replied, with a grin.

Yanlou nodded the once and was on his way. After he had left, Trishna turned to me and muttered:

"You might want to study up on the Chinese culture if and when we get back home. Yanlou, Chinese God of death and ruler of our afterlife and all that. He's obviously got a big consignment coming in to be doing this stuff personally. But, from my previous experiences, he's always been a bit of a hands on sort of God."

I can't say I'd even heard of a God being hands on before. . . something to remember. I tried to make a mental note to look him up when we got home in case him spotting me bringing Trishna here just whacked me with a load of negative restitution points.

We then sat, mostly in silence, and I tried to not look at the various creatures walking about among the vehicles. Apparently they all had their own check lists and were moving from driver to driver to confirm their souls were where they were meant to be. So, it wasn't quite placards at the terminal like I'd imagined. But in some ways seeing the rulers of the dead moving through the crowd of vehicles was even more disturbing. Still, I guess it showed they were dedicated to their jobs. And so was I, which is why I was currently watching a skeleton dressed like a Catholic saint chatting to our semi-decomposed headless driver.

It almost became like bingo after a while. A game as to who could name the deity or soul collector first. After Santa Muerte (the well-dressed Mexican skeleton saint) there came an actual Angel of Death, wings and all. I didn't catch all their names, Trishna obviously being better at this game than I was and so he started quizzing me on each to see how far my knowledge stretched. It wasn't exactly *fun*, but it gave me something to do to try and take my mind off where I was, who I was with, and what I was about to try and do. Just when I thought I was really going to need to risk getting out of the van, as claustrophobia set in, the dullahan picked up his head and placed it back on the dash.

"We're here, time to roll," he grinned cheerfully.

I watched, with mild interest, as the other dullahan and ankou reappeared and started directing the vehicles off the ferry. I had to gape when it was our turn to get off and we drove out into — a bright, clear blue sky, fields of what looked to be rushes, and a shimmering desert on the horizon.

"Awesome!" announced the dullahan, a little more eagerly than I felt he should have, "It looks like you've turned up on Ancient Egyptian day! I do love it when they mix things up with theme days like this. Gives some of the older Gods and Goddess a chance to strut their stuff and show us how things used to be done."

There was so much I wanted to say to that, but I no longer had the energy or ability to respond. We moved over to one side of this boggy field, with the majority of the other vehicles, and parked.

As I got shakily out of the van and tried to ease the numbness out of my backside, without Trishna's help, I looked around at where we had ended up.

It was indeed a field of reeds, the ground was damp and muddy underfoot and I could just make out a river glittering in the distance behind us. No sign of the giant ferry we had just left, and I couldn't bring myself to ask where it had gone as I was sure the answer wouldn't help me feel any better.

We had parked in front of a huge stone building that looked like the entrance-way to some of the temples I'd seen in tourist brochures of Egypt. I may have been living my life until recently as a hermit, but I'd been a hermit who enjoyed living through the glossies and daydreaming. I must say, when the afterlife did themed days, they certainly didn't cut corners. Made the 'loud shirt days' where I used to work look even lamer than I'd thought they'd been at the time.

"Hall of Judgement?" I queried Trishna as we made our way to the front of the van. The dullahan had made his way to the back to let out his collected souls and I hadn't really wanted to see them again.

"I'd say so. . ." mused Trishna as we looked in through the Mastaba's entrance. The doors were wide open and there were some distinctly Egyptian looking deities wandering around just inside. "And lookee, it appears we're going for the hearing in front of forty-two Gods and Goddesses, before the guy in the Crocodile head gets out his scales and plops your heart in it to weigh it and pronounce final judgement. I do like things that follow a good old tradition like this."

Man he was a little too cheery about being here. . . then again exactly how many times had I sent him here, that he remembered, in the last one hundred years? Yeah, let's not go into that right now.

"Will we have to go through that?" I asked as souls, only partially visible in the bright sunlight, started to make their way into the Hall around us.

"Oh the gaggle of Gods and all that is just for the unclaimed souls," the dullahan answered, coming back to us now his shipment had been, uh, unloaded. "I'll take you in through the side door, see if we can just slip you in without the crowds." And gee, didn't *that* just sound so comforting?

And so we hiked through the mud to the side of the Mastaba. . . since when did houses of eternity have a side door? As the dullahan followed some of the other reapers inside, Trishna and I were close behind.

"Here you go, I've successfully got you into the afterlife and completed my end of the deal," the dullahan grinned, raising his head to shoulder height to look at us both. He held out his free hand in the universal sign of 'pay up now'. I handed over the small bag of coins Tathal had given me, and the dullahan's grin widened.

"Cheers for that. The gate into Hell itself is somewhere in the back rooms, I'm sure you'll be fine." And before I could do more than splutter, he was gone again.

Um, great? What were we supposed to do now? Unfortunately he really *had* completed his end of the deal and it was time I stopped expecting people to be there to show me what I was meant to be doing and start just *doing* it for myself. . . so I decided to take a look around.

I don't know why I'd expected it, but the inside was unsurprisingly a lot bigger than the outside. But when you're visiting the afterlife, and it happens to be hosting an Ancient Egyptian themed day just on a whim, do you really expect the laws of physics to actually be obeyed?

We really had entered at the side as well, and now stood halfway down a large, cold, marbled chamber, watching as thousands of souls came flitting in to stand before the now seated Gods and Goddesses. I frowned as I noticed more solid-looking figures moving through the mists of souls. They were in comfortable, but flowing clothes, Californian styled sandals, wore large, chunky jewellery, and carried clipboards. Actually, the more I looked at them, the more they reminded me of the many therapists I had been forced to see to help me struggle through my life up until now.

"Who are they?" I asked Trishna, doing my best to tone down the dumbness in my voice. "They seem to be talking to people and handing out pamphlets."

"Some people call them Guardian Angels, others think of them as spirit guides," Trishna murmured quietly in my ear, obviously not wanting to draw attention to ourselves. "I see them as a bit of a counsellor, you know? Hippy, dippy, therapy types? I try and avoid them where I can as they can be rather irritating and never listen to what you have to say because they think they know what you need to do, better than you do."

So, nothing like a therapist then? Oh sarcasm, I was so glad to see you'd survived the journey!

"But *what* are they doing here?" I asked, now using a voice as quiet as his.

"Well, in this Old Gods of Egypt set-up, the souls of the dead need to cite their reasons as to why they deserve to walk in the Light by reading passages from the Egyptian Book of the Dead. So those are being handed out and these. . . counsellors. . . are trying to explain it all to the poor, clueless souls. Most of them, I'm sure, were at least expecting clouds, gates and a bearded guy in a toga."

"Oh the pearly gates were last week dearie." One of the counsellors had spotted us and had come over, all smiles and smelling of patchouli and lavender. "Hi, I'm your guide to the afterlife today and hoping to help you in any way I can." She smiled rather insincerely and tried to hand me a pamphlet titled 'The Book of the Dead and how to use it'. I politely declined the offer, wondering if she actually realised we weren't, well, *dead*.

"No, you're probably right," she said as she gave us another smile, "I doubt the Gods will give you a chance to use this before striking you dead for turning up still alive. It's so rare that we get souls still attached to their bodies these days that few of us remember how to handle it properly."

I don't know if it was her likeness to a therapist I'd disliked but been sent to after my divorce regardless, or simply that she was an irritating person, but I really started to get annoyed by her.

"How about you go find an atheist to convert or something and we'll sort ourselves out, there's a dear," I said as politely as I could, ignoring Trishna's wince.

"Oh no honey, we don't get atheists in the afterlife," the counsellor said calmly, as if I'd not just told her to get lost. "This is a belief based level of existence and only works for those of us who truly believe there is, in fact, an afterlife. Atheist types just puff off into non-existence, and good luck to them too."

As she spoke I had been watching the crowd behind her where the souls were starting to solidify into people. . . and get paired off into groups. Seeing I was ignoring her, she followed my gaze and nodded approvingly.

"Excellent, see that large queue now forming? They're all lining up for their judgement with the Gods. That other group over there by the potted palms, they're waiting to be collected. Obviously they have some pre-existing deal going and are just waiting for their pick up."

Despite myself, I was fascinated by it all and was now actually listening to what she had to say.

"And what about that group over there that seem to be getting cornered by the rest of you counsellor folk?" I asked, trying my best not to sound rude.

"Oh, that'll be the agnostics," she said lightly, as if describing some playful little kitten getting up to no good. "We get a good whack of them these days." As she spoke, one of the souls in the agnostic group let out a yelp and tried to make a run for it. They were quickly brought down by a slightly thicker set counsellor.

"Oh dear, it appears we had another agnostic who felt they were an atheist. That little niggle of doubt they try and ignore gets them every time," our counsellor said. "I better go help the others with their sessions to help the poor souls decide whether they really believe in being here, or if they're about to puff off themselves."

I know I really wished someone a little too close to my personal space would puff off right about now, and it wasn't Trishna.

"Lovely to meet you before your time, I do hope you will be easier to deal with when you come back here officially." She gave us both a slightly off-centre smile and wandered over to the corralled agnostics. Faith was obviously taken *very* seriously around here and I decided that, when I got back home, I should spend a bit more time trying to figure out what exactly it was I believed in. Right now, if I popped my cork, I could see myself over in that gaggle of souls now being heavily counselled into submission as to what it was they actually believed. I really don't know what was scarier, realising I had better commit myself to a faith so I didn't end up like that. . . or ending up like that.

"You've got that look again," Trishna whispered in my ear. "You know, that shrew sucking a lemon one you always get when you don't like where your inner monologue is taking you."

I stilled the elbow that craved poking itself into his ribs. Instead I turned my full attention on him, leaving the souls to their queues, groups, and counsellor battering.

"Fine," I sighed, "time to look for the gates-to-hell." I glanced around wondering where to start. I mean, the 'back rooms' were probably behind the dais of deities, but could one really sneak passed so many Gods unnoticed? Weren't they meant to be omnipotent or something? And if they were, wouldn't that mean they already knew we were here and could have already stopped us? Damn, I wonder if I packed some aspirin in my handbasket.

As I rummaged, I suddenly felt a shiver run down me that wasn't as disturbing as one would have thought it should be. I looked up at Trishna with surprised annoyance and he gave me an innocent look back.

"Wasn't me," he told me with a grin, "I'm pretty sure if I could still do that to you I would have tried it on my first night in your house."

I rolled my eyes and was about to tell him what exactly I would have then done to him if he had, when he shushed me and pointed to the side group of souls. "Their rides have arrived."

I looked over and felt the shiver of delight again and realised the Gods and Goddesses of Light had arrived to pick up their specific souls and take them on their way.

"Oh, I hadn't realised old Priestess Aggie had passed." I pouted as I recognised Isis among the group, her mother like beauty almost drawing me to her side for another hug.

"I'm pretty sure it's a rather new thing to have happened," Trishna replied, "and one I'm sure we would have found out tomorrow. . . if we hadn't snuck into the afterlife to try and get into Hell without telling anyone."

He had a point there, and it was so sobering it stopped me from going over to Isis. I mean, did I *really* want her to know I was here and what I was up to? What if it meant she would unbless me or something?

The deities of the Light were now slowly leaving, and just before Isis and Priestess Aggie departed, the mother Goddess turned her smiling face to look over to me, looked me directly in the eye — and winked. Man that gave me goosebumps. But I was taking it as her consent and that the blessing was still sound. I think I also caught the pesky tears it caused in my eyes before Trishna saw them.

Shortly after those from the Light disappeared, the room took on a greasy, nasty feel as their counterparts arrived. There were one or two deities of Darkness among them, but the majority seemed to be demons. And who else would there be? I mean, the most common deal for your soul was made to a demon. It was their stock in trade, their bread and butter, their. . . oh look, hysteria had also made the trip with sarcasm.

"Come on, let's go," I whispered to Trishna, managing a *gentle* nudge in his ribs to get his attention.

"What? Where?" he asked as I started to make my way around the edges of the chamber to where the demons were collecting their souls.

"Well, duh!" I replied over my shoulder, "Where else would demons be taking their souls but down to Hell? We just tag along at a discreet distance and slip in when no one is watching."

"Sweet Isis and all her curtain clad ladies in white," Trishna sighed. "I am yet to see you *ever* be discreet, or able to go anywhere unnoticed." He did, however, follow me as I hid behind a potted palm closer to the collected souls. Some, unfortunately, just vanished along with their dark deity, but the good majority were slowly route marched out another side door. After a count of five hippopotamuses, we followed. We were either about to find the gate into Hell I sorely wanted, or discover the little souls room as they all stopped off for a pee break before reaching damnation. Either way, I'd be happy with the result as I needed to go to either place. That's a point, are their toilets in Hell? Or was that part of the whole Hell experience? What a time to realise I probably should have peed before I'd come on this journey. Ah well, best laid plans and all that.

# Chapter 14

———————⑤———————

HAVING read up on gateways to hell before embarking on this journey, I was expecting great stone archways guarded by three headed dogs, or at least a nasty-looking dolphin-type guy. An active volcano's open maw, or a sinkhole bubbling with blood red mud were even options. But all these came up empty. What I saw was... well, a shimmery, shiny bright and yet dark *slit* in reality. You could walk around it and it looked the same from all angles. It also filled me with dread, terror, revulsion, fear and all the other emotions I really didn't need right now if I was actually going to step through it and into what lay beyond.

"Is this it?" I asked Trishna, trying to keep the disappointment from my voice. I had been hoping for massive, stone carved arches guarded by something I could be pithy at, but run faster than. Despite the nasty sensation swirling around me, the whole 'gateway to hell' was rather anticlimactic.

"What sort of lives do you think I've led to be able to say for sure this is how we get into Hell?" Trishna asked me angrily. Though he did score brownie points for leaving prostitutes and their unfortunate health conditions out of it.

"Sorry!" I apologised quickly, not wanting to take my rising anger out on him. Heck, I was going to need a bit of anger to control the other emotions vying to be top dog inside me right now. "I thought maybe one of the theme days around here might have included a Cook's tour of the place." Oh look, sarcasm was still there too, bless it.

Trishna muttered something under his breath I thankfully didn't catch and went to step through the shimmering, nasty feeling slit in our reality. How chivalrous.

"No, I think on this occasion ladies first is the best option. Restitution points and all that," I said.

I grabbed his hand and decided to treat entering hell like removing a band aid. Once you've decided to do it, do it quickly and don't second guess yourself halfway through.

And so I stepped into Hell.

*** 

Actually, once you got used to the pounding noise, crushing heat, humidity, and red twilight darkness it wasn't so bad. Then I opened my eyes and retracted that statement and wished I could close my eyes again.

"Are my ears bleeding? Surely my ears are bleeding. What is that throbbing noise?" Trishna muttered next to me. How we'd ended up sprawled on the ground in a tangle of arms and legs, I don't know. But we were and it took us some time to untangle ourselves and get up.

"Actually, I'm pretty sure that's the sound of your heart beating. . ." I said loudly over the noise. At least that's what I hoped it was. I felt sick to my stomach from the constant pressure of the oppressively thick and hot air around us. I didn't really want to look too closely as to where we were, but it seemed to be some sort of cavern, dark, red around the edges and filled with the throbbing noise that almost seemed to be pulsating off my eyeballs as I tried to focus.

"Well, if it is my heart, it's good to know it's still beating," Trishna muttered seeking my free hand for comfort, and I felt unsettled enough to let him take it.

"So, Protector of Souls, you've made it to Hell with your handbasket. Now what?" he asked.

Yeah, I'd been hoping he wouldn't ask me that.

"Uh?" I thought about it a moment as I picked up the said basket and its contents, then pointed into the darkness that looked the same as any other darkness around us, "We go that way." Even in Hell you needed to start somewhere, right?

It was only when the salt crunched under my feet that I realised we had been inside a circle. Who the. . . heck. . . put a protective circle on the other side of a gateway to hell? And, speaking of gateways, where was it? I don't know what unsettled me more at that moment, the fact I'd just broken out of a circle, or that I'd just noticed the gateway we'd come through didn't appear to exist on this side?

The plus side was that breaking the circle seemed to lessen the pounding sound in my head. Heat and humidity were still a bitch, but you can't win everything.

"Well, well, well. What *do* we have here unannounced and free of the binding circle?" If the cocky tone of voice wasn't enough, the suit itself was a giveaway.

"I'd say some lesser demon stuck on gate duty as he doesn't have enough power to do much else, judging by the poor cut of his coat," I replied in not the most pleasant of tones myself.

Next to me Trishna groaned and I caught him face palming as he muttered: "Really? To an *actual* demon in its native habitat?"

"I'm pretty sure he'd have to be clad in Armani before I'm willing to be afraid of him," I replied, releasing Trishna's other hand from my grip and moving closer to the foul-creature-from-hell in what looked to be a very cheap and shabby suit.

"Oh, you're not the hero type come to rescue a loved one from the deepest pits of Hell are you? That's so two millennia ago," the demon retorted. He was obviously trying to cover up how much my total lack of respect or fear had unsettled him. "Name?" he demanded.

"Yeah, no I don't think so buddy," I replied, stepping closer. "No names, no loved ones to rescue and *so* not a hero."

The demon glared at me, but I'd caught his initial look of worry before he'd done so.

"Just here for a postcard and a couple of 'my friend went to hell and all I got was this t-shirt' souvenirs are we?" he sneered at me, showing he lacked the ability to make sarcasm really work.

"Actually I'm here to take back a soul some dumb ankou thinks is his, when said ankou is so obviously wrong," I answered, going for a casual tone when proving my sarcasm more superior. "I know it's not best to give in to a dare and all that, but what is life without a little whimsy?"

"Visiting Hell is whimsical?" stuttered the young demon before suddenly blinking out of existence.

"Great, now you've upset him enough he's gone off to get some back up," Trishna snapped. "I'd say we have a minute tops before we get demon gang raped. Seriously Steph, I don't think you're taking this situation seriously enough. This is *Hell*. Things will be different here than back in our own reality."

He had a point, but I'd also been trying to ignore that point ever since I'd got here. If I entered the situation feeling helpless and having lost before I'd even started, I'd not have bothered in the first place.

"Then I strongly suggest we run," I said smiling at him. I grabbed a hand, and ignoring my still sore ankle raced for what I hoped was a distant wall containing a door and a way out. A map to Wroth's place would have also been useful, but a girl can't expect to get everything her own way when she visits Hell for the first time.

*** 

I must say I found running in Hell a difficult experience. The whole world around me seemed to keep changing from moment to moment. First it seemed the dark, oppressive caves and cavern. Then it was like an open inferno where I had to keep my eyes on my running feet to avoid peering into the many pits around me and seeing was happening to people within them. The next moment it was an icy plain covered in snow drifts I had to struggle through before tumbling down into a desert where the sand seemed to be alive with all the creepy crawlies I've never really liked, and had never had a big enough can of bug spray to remove.

"So glad this place is living up to its reputation," I gasped as we stopped for a breather after reaching more tunnel like areas. We hunched down in the dark, claustrophobic heat and breathed heavily. I guess I should have been thankful there was at least air down here for me to be breathing. It didn't always have the nicest smell — or taste — to it, but it was clean enough to breathe without coughing up half a lung. Small mercies, and all that.

"It's almost as if the place can't make up its mind as to which representation of hell it wants to be, so it's trying them all out at once," Trishna panted next to me. "I guess it's a small mercy we've not got stuck in some Government style queue or a party with Jean-Paul Sartre yet."

"That last one would only work on me if I actually had friends," I replied, easing myself back up to a standing position while cradling my ribs as they reminded me I'd been in a fight just the day before.

"We could always put you in a room with some of *my* friends to see if the theory was still sound," a cocky voice from behind us said.

I groaned as I turned around, as the voice was one I actually recognised.

"Hi Jamal, fancy meeting you here," I said wearily, eyeing the demon over while doing a bit of maths in my head. Yeah, he had his full powers back by now — damn.

"It wasn't hard to guess who it was after Timpsk came whimpering to me about some smart mouthed woman with a wreck of a hairdo walking into Hell as if she owned the place," Jamal snorted. I could tell he'd remembered our last deal and was just raring to get a bit of payback happening. Timpsk, the demon in question, nervously hovered just behind him.

"And once I thought long and hard as to where you would be, you weren't too hard to pin down," Jamal went on. Why was I not surprised he was your monologuing type? "Well, not hard for someone of my level of power, freshly returned may I remind you, to find."

At this point I was almost ready to just tell him to shut up and get on with whatever it was he had planned. But then I remembered some of the things demons have told me they had planned for me once they caught me. . . and kept schtum. And there was always Mr Vontant right? So far all we had was greasy Jamal and the timid Timpsk. If I was really in danger from them Mr Vontant would be here by now.

Jamal must have caught onto some of what I was thinking as he theatrically looked around the tunnels we were in and then turned back to me with a nasty-looking smile.

"What, no Mr Vontant?" he sneered. "Just you and your ghost in a new flesh suit? Oh, that's right! Your deals with demons are only valid in *your* reality. Down here they're worth less than the little black book you have them written down in."

I really didn't like where this conversation was heading. He'd just confirmed one of my biggest fears on entering Hell, and was about to make me forget it all by scaring me a whole lot more.

"Don't make me write my name on your forehead again," I warned Jamal, summoning the last of my false bravado to do so.

"Yes, speaking of that. . ." mused Jamal smarming his way closer to me, "Basket, now."

I really didn't like the way he made this demand, especially as it seemed to bypass my brain and go straight to the hand holding my handbasket. With a feeling like paper cuts all over said arm, it extended toward the demon, offering him the basket and all it contained.

"I mean, really Stephanie. Bringing purified water into Hell? What sort of crazy person *does* that?" Jamal sneered, taking the basket from me and smashing it into the floor. . . where it promptly burst into flames, with a little demon trickery no doubt.

"And the other one," Jamal demanded.

I did my best to give him a doe-eyed look of innocence. It didn't work.

"I am more than willing to come and get it off you myself," he warned. "But it might not be the only thing I then rip from you piece by piece."

I tried not to remember how much I needed the loo while his look scared me so much I nearly wet myself. I glanced to Trishna, at my side in his usual protective stance looking scarily like a demon himself still in the suit he'd worn to the night club. The look in his eye told me all I needed to know about how screwed we currently were.

"Fine," I sighed and fished a vial of purified water out from my cleavage. Old habits die hard and I almost always had one down there these days. I handed it over as politely as I could, but I was pretty sure both Jamal and I knew where I really wanted to stick it.

"Oh baby!" Jamal winked sleazily. "Maybe once I enforce my thrall on you we can both take turns doing that to each other."

Urgh, my brain needed a shower after *those* mental images. Hang about, was it me or did Jamal seem to be able to know what I was thinking? I'd not wanted him to take my purified water and I had wanted to be rather rude with that vial. I wondered if I could control what he did? So I put another thought out there.

"But before I unwrap this little present, Timpsk search her first as I'd hate to think what other little surprises she might have."

I tried to hide my smile at that one, as I'd just been thinking along similar lines myself. It was then that I remembered the secret vial of purified water I had strapped to my calf. Damn. Before I could do or say anything about it though, I found myself being spun around against the tunnel wall and patted down in a rather too handsy sort of way. I mean, how many vials did they think I could keep in my bra?

I turned back and eyed both demons warily once the younger-looking, cheaply dressed demon stepped away to frisk Trishna. Timpsk had patted me down to my toes, he *should* have felt the second vial on my left calf. I tried to hide all thoughts on it as he stepped back to Jamal's side, but I'm pretty sure I saw, for an instant, a look in his eye that let me know it might just be possible to do a deal with a demon in Hell.

"Why did I get a pat down?" complained Trishna, re-adjusting his own suit after it had been thoroughly patted. Actually, him in a suit down here was getting a little too unsettling as it made him blend in with the crowd and look as if he had joined the demon crew.

"Because she seeded a little thought in my head that you were hiding some water too," Jamal replied smugly. "Obviously she was just testing exactly how much control her old scars of binding have on me." The slimy, not so little any more, demon then turned his full attention to me. "And trust me sweetheart, those scars work both ways and I'm enjoying the open book tour of your mind too." He then stepped a little too close into my personal space and licked me on the cheek. And I mean *licked* me. One long, gross stroke from chin to eyebrow. Would there ever be enough sandpaper in the world to scrub away that memory.

"Leave her," Trishna warned him, trying to step between Jamal and myself to shield me. But the look in Jamal's eyes scared me enough without him also taking it out on Trishna.

"Don't," I cautioned him, gently tugging him away from Jamal. "I appreciate the thought, but please don't end up as a smear on this tunnel wall because of me."

"I think you should have told him that *before* you brought him along to Hell as your sidekick," Jamal sneered.

"At least *my* sidekick has a decent bloody suit on!" I snapped back, using what little courage I had left to distract the demon's attention away from Trishna. I was really starting to regret having brought him down here as I was never going to earn enough restitution points if something bad happened to him on my watch.

"Actually, down here we like to call them lackeys or *flunkies*," Jamal smarmed, moving too close into my personal space again. "A sign of a demon's power comes from how many we have too. I'd show you all of mine, but there are far more interesting things I plan on showing you first. And it's not just going to be my will you're going to feel *deep* inside you."

Okay, I didn't need to pee anymore. No, nothing that embarrassing, it's just the overwhelming desire to be sick at what he was suggesting overwrote my nagging bladder's signals. Though it was a close run thing.

"Time, I think, to slip into something more. . . comfortable," Jamal crooned, still a little too close for comfort. He stepped back and looked at our surroundings. "I really don't like your version of Hell Stephanie, lacks quite a bit colour, style and *smell*." And with this our surroundings shimmered and changed, morphing back into more of a Hieronymus Bosch's style of hell, with the added *delights* of wailing and the smell of sulphur and even less pleasant things. Hell changed depending on how you interpreted it?

"Oh yes, and in the best possible ways does it change to suit our needs. The afterlife is all belief based after all," Jamal said, giving me another oily smile as he moved closer again. We were now standing on some kind of rocky pinnacle, pits of all sorts of torment and debauchery happening below us on all sides. The whole scene was flames, heat, and some rather nasty things being done to some rather miserable looking, naked souls.

"Stop reading my thoughts!" I snapped, side stepping him as much as I could on the narrow platform of stone. I flashed Trishna a warning look as he tried to follow, to stay by my side. I really didn't want him involved in this any more than he already was. Heck, part of my brain was still hoping to find one of those dumb luck options to get us out of it all.

"You have yourself to thank for that little loop hole," Jamal sneered, again coming closer. All the running my sprained ankle had just been put through suddenly caught up with me and it decided now was the time to buckle under my own weight and down I went, flat on my back and winded. Jamal swiftly following to pin me to the ground with his own body.

"You have *no idea* how much pleasure I'm going to take from hurting you as much as I can," he hissed.

Unfortunately I could feel how much pleasure he was already feeling from the way he rubbed himself against me. As he peeled off my gloves and threw them into the fire below, despite still wearing the rest of my smart night club clothes, I suddenly felt very naked and extremely vulnerable. Words and thoughts started to fail me as panic shut my brain down. This was seriously about to happen, rape being the least of my problems. I let out a sob of sheer panic and frustration at not knowing how to fight him off when I suddenly felt a different sensation, a pins and needles like feeling starting in my ankles and building up through me. Exactly like I had done the last time a bad guy had pinned me down. Trishna?

I couldn't see him over Jamal's shoulder as the demon started to slowly bite off the buttons of my blouse. But I could see Timpsk hovering just behind him and, for a demon, he didn't look too comfortable to be in this situation. He did, however, keep glancing down toward my feet and then shooting death glances back at Jamal. What was going on here?

"Hell is belief based," Timpsk suddenly blurted out to the world in general. "He who has the greater will controls what it is like. He who can control what it is like, can control what happens."

Jamal was off me in a second, leaping up at Timpsk with a snarl. It was then I saw Trishna. He had indeed been feeding me his life energy, and while that might work for a ghost where all they have is energy, it should never be done by a living thing. The sunken eyes and new grey hairs threaded through the dark locks at Trishna's temple were proof of that. Not knowing exactly what I was doing I rolled away just as Jamal was about to throw Timpsk off our platform and into one of the volcanic like pits of torment below, I thought hard as to what I really felt Hell should be like.

Timpsk's yell of despair was short lived as he thumped into the floor of the corridor as the cave like tunnels once more sprung up around us. I was pretty sure I'd even been able to turn the temperature down a bit too.

"No!" snarled Jamal fiercely as he turned back to me. "This is *not* how it should be."

I could feel the world around us try to shimmer and morph again as Jamal and I locked gazes, but I was determined to not let the slimy little git win. Even as Jamal approached to try and tower over me, Trishna was now by my side, helping me up, using his touch to feed me energy.

"Trishna stop, it's killing you," I breathed, worried about taking his life force, and trying not to lose my control over our surroundings.

I felt the prickling sensation ease, but still found great comfort in his physical support.

Jamal showed his anger with another snarl as the world around us stayed a nice, solid stone tunnel. He tried to take a swipe at me but found his arm restrained by Timpsk.

"Sword," Timpsk said, looking me in the eye. He wrestled Jamal's arms behind his back and demanded it more urgently. "Sword!"

I really hadn't a clue as to what he was trying to tell me, but found myself focusing on his outstretched hand and imagining a sword in it.

"He who has the stronger will, can control what happens," Timpsk said smugly as a rather large and nasty sword materialised in his hand. It was nothing like the one I'd imagined, but I was pretty sure some of Timpsk's own belief had gone into the final touches.

Jamal stopped struggling when he felt the cold steel pressed against his neck.

"You wretched little slime-filled. . ." Jamal began, but never got to finish exactly which one of us he was talking about, nor exactly what part of an animal's anatomy was diseased as Timpsk pressed the sword deep enough into his neck to show blood.

"I won't be able to hold him once you and your will are gone," Timpsk said, obviously already struggling with the larger demon. "Just acknowledge you owe me one mother of a deal and then get your skinny little arse out of here."

"But, why. . .?" I know I really didn't have the time to ask the really stupid questions, but I really wanted to know exactly what little demonic tendency had caused this rebellion.

"I don't want to be another demon's *lackey* for millennia until I gain enough power to set myself up as an independent," Timpsk hissed, some of his true demon greed and evil starting to show. "You are Ani, stronger, smarter and more cunning than my current master Jamal. Now that I've done you a favour, the one I get in return better be worth it."

Sweet Isis, I had just been saved from rape and who knows what else, simply because someone wanted help to get a little higher up the demon totem pole? Was this also why Timpsk had kept quiet about the purified water I had strapped to my leg?

"You wretched little. . ." snarled Jamal twisting himself away from Timpsk, a sword of his own appearing from nowhere as he turned. But he was too late as, with a sickening sound and a thump, Jamal's arm, sword and all, was removed from his body with a graceful movement from the younger-looking demon.

"You have about five minutes before more lackeys turn up," Timpsk warned me, his sword pinning Jamal to the ground between the shoulder blades. "You owe me," he said again, his eyes boring into me.

And seeing I was pretty sure he was going to get one heck of a beating when the other flunkies turned up I nodded. "I will repay you in the best way I can while still being one who walks in the Light," I said as calmly as the whole scary situation would allow.

Timpsk winced. "I had been hoping for a better favour than that, but it will have to do. I can't promise being of much help the next time we meet."

I nodded too and turned to flee with Trishna before a thought occurred and I turned back. "I don't suppose you know where Wroth keeps his souls do you?"

I won't repeat the twelve string set of words Timpsk used, but I got the message — that was one favour too far.

Trying to protect my sprained ankle, we limped off at as fast a jog as I could manage. I felt it best we try and get as much distance between us and Jamal as possible before stopping again and trying to figure out how to find the ankou, his nest, and Simon's soul.

***

I don't know how long we ran, I'm pretty sure it was more than the stated five minutes. I also know we must have come near some pretty strong willed creatures while we did as the world around us sometimes changed. When it did I didn't try to stop it, in case it made me easier to follow. Some of the versions of Hell were the typical ones we'd already seen and some were downright weird. And that's actually saying a lot when you think of the ones we did see as being sane in comparison. I'm talking severed body parts floating in pools of luminescent green goo while Death Metal Opera was blasting my ears weird. My brain was going to need a good scouring if and when I got out of there.

All the time we scurried, quite frankly it was the best I could do with my ankle, I buried Jamal as deep down in my subconscious as I could. If he could find me, feel my thoughts and know where I was due to the mental scarring I had left behind by possessing him all those months ago, what was the point of running? So, instead, I thought of him down a great big hole, the very bottom of a well, chained to a very heavy rock and unable to get to me. I have no idea if this was going to work or not, but so far so good.

It was Trishna who finally said we had to stop and, looking him over I could see why. He looked like. . . hell. He had drained his energy, his very life essence to give me the strength to fight Jamal. Idiot retribution points be damned.

And so we stopped and I changed the world around us again so that there was a nice solid wall between us and the way we had just come. I couldn't face closing off the tunnel ahead of us too as I didn't want us to somehow get trapped like that.

"Never, ever share your life force with me again," I chided Trishna as I helped him to a boulder I created for us to sit on. "It was appreciated when you were a ghost, but you need that stuff for your own life right now."

And boy did he ever need that energy. Sallow cheeks, sunken eyes and those grey hairs. What made it worse was that I actually felt better than I had before he had given it to me. My ribs didn't ache as much and my eye was no longer swollen. His life, his energy, healing me.

"So, next time, I just let the demon rape you in front of me then?" Trishna snapped back angrily. I knew the anger was more at the situation than at my seeming selfish response. At least, I hoped it was.

"If it annoys you so much that I gave you some of my life, then give it back," he said, not exactly as angrily, but not exactly nicely either. Obviously he was going to be one of those grumpy old men when the time really did come.

"I can do that?" I asked, doing my best to keep stupid from my tone again. "I thought it was just something you remembered how to do from when you were a ghost."

"We're still linked, which is how I can do it at all," Trishna explained, cooling off a little more. "And I'm pretty sure it can go both ways, if you want it to."

I sat down on the boulder next to Trishna and thought this over. I really did want to give him his energy back — I just didn't know how. Then, without thinking, I leaned forward and, cupping his head in my hands, rested my forehead against his.

"Thank you for trying to rescue me," I whispered, feeling that familiar pins and needle sensation prickle up between us again. "And thank you for coming with me in this whole stupid mess." The sensation increased and started to feel quite comforting. The relaxed sigh from Trishna had me pull away, suddenly acutely aware of how much personal space we were sharing and how easily he could make it go somewhere I didn't want it to.

I studied him carefully and was pleased with what I saw. The grey in his hair had lessened and there was more colour to his face than there had been before. We stared at each other a little too long for comfort and I realised I was still cupping his head in my hands. I wanted to leap to my feet, wanted to put as much polite distance as I could between us, but I didn't want to offend him again and so stayed where I was. I felt the sudden rigidity in my pose as my hands fell into my lap, and the fact I suddenly found my shoes amazingly interesting, gave Trishna the message all the same as he sighed again and was the one who got up and moved away. Not my fault, his choice.

"So what are your plans now we're here?" Trishna asked to break the silence. "I could be wrong, but I'm pretty sure there isn't like an information kiosk or something that we can just wander up to and get directions from."

"Next you're going to tell me there are no phone booths with phone books we can find Wroth in either." My attempted humour raised a small smirk from him but that was about it.

"Not unless you think you can imagine one up for us and get all the details correct."

Thankfully he came back and sat down next to me on the boulder.

"I don't think I can imagine up actual facts without knowing them already, if that makes sense?" I replied, my brow wrinkling as I thought this over. "I think I need to know something to believe in it enough to make it happen."

I gave Trishna a startled look. "Hey, how come you can't make things happen around here? I can't see you being some weak willed sod with little to no imagination."

He snorted amusement at this comment, and I'd not even tried to be funny.

"He, or in your case *she,* with the stronger will wins out. No offence Steph, I know I'm a pig-headed and stubborn sort, but you're the queen of it. The demon possession on your third day on the job was a bit of a giveaway to that. It's why you were able to beat Jamal down here too."

"I still can't believe I did that," I said wearily. "I mean, doesn't he have more powers down here or something? Being a demon in Hell and all?"

"When he was stuck Up Above, and you released him last year, he had all his powers. He just couldn't come back here with it until the correct ritual took place. Just because it was Up Above doesn't make a difference. Power is power."

"But his. . . lackeys. Wouldn't they add to his power down here?" Was I trying to find an excuse as to why I could do this, or did I really want to know?

"Power is power. Pretty sure he still had his lackey's powers up there, even if he had been earthed to the walking orange hairball for thirty years." Trishna shrugged as he said this and then gave me a comforting look as my expression over the memory of the creature in question must have told him exactly how sick it made me feel. Today wasn't the first time one of the bad guys had thought to hump me for the hell of it.

"I suppose it's just one of those rather creepy things I need to accept in life," I said glumly, refusing to give into the sigh I wanted to give.

"What? Look doable to bad guys? Pretty sure some of the good guys feel the same way but are too polite to try it when first meeting you." There was a glint of humour back in Trishna's eye as he goaded me. I feel my restitution points were safe as I gave him the gentle thwack he so deserved for the comment.

"No," I replied with a slight grin of my own. "I meant how I can do things I not only didn't know I could do. . . but barely even realised a person *could* do. Even after this rather steep learning curve over the last six months, I'm finding it hard to believe I can do half the stuff I can actually do. And it's rather creepy knowing I can take a demon on, one on one, in their own world."

"I guess stubborn travels well," Trishna answered, I could tell he was about to say more, but I suddenly swore I heard something in the tunnel up ahead so I shushed him in to silence and pointed in that direction.

The tunnel I'd imagined up was the usual rock hewn walls and stony floor I'd decided I wanted Hell to be. But in the distance the tunnel had changed, it had become more like a brick archway and reminded me of pictures I'd seen of the sewers of places like France and London. Places where Victorian era brickwork was at its finest. If the change of appearance to our surroundings wasn't enough to let us know someone was coming, the glow of light now travelling along that far distant wall certainly confirmed it.

Although I'd not decided how the tunnel continued on beyond our resting spot, it appeared it now ended in a sort of T junction. Where we were sitting was in the tail part of the 'T' and whoever was approaching was travelling toward us from the left side of the top. I tried to stay calm and let their will take over, in the vain hope they'd not notice us, but as the light came closer the shadows it threw against the wall had me feeling unnerved. The light was a near blinding white now, which made the shadows on the wall ahead of it all the darker. As they approached, the archway grew into a cathedral sized opening, and we could now hear the shuffling, scraping sounds that accompanied its approach. My skin prickled uneasily as, walking toward us, judging by the shadow, was a great winged man, his long, slender body stretching along the wall toward us from the darker shadows. One wing was held erect, its feather-like patterning clearly defined in the shadow. The other wing, however, appeared broken and dragged along as the person approached. You could hear the scrape of it against the brick pathway alongside the shuffling of the feet.

I wanted to speak, wanted to voice my doubt and incredulity as to what I swore I was seeing. But I didn't want to alert this creature to my presence, especially after a warning look from Trishna. But. . . there was a frickin *angel* down in Hell! I almost wanted to shout out about it. I mean, how messed up was that? I had thought a Buddhist monk being turned into a ghost was bad enough, but an angel? An obviously injured, damaged angel! Surely I should offer to help this fellow person of the Light?

I gave Trishna a questioning glance as he placed a restraining hand upon my shoulder, strongly urging me to stay seated and stay quiet. What did he know that he wasn't telling me?

I found myself holding my breath as the creature — the angel — neared the entrance to our part of the tunnel. I was nervous as to what to do, as to what it would expect of me. Should I kneel? Should I raise a casual hand and say 'yo heaven dude'? Oh hysteria, I really do wish you'd stayed topside.

Our surroundings swirled as much as my emotions and I felt my lungs about to burst from holding my breath. And then two things happened. Firstly, my will reasserted itself and we were back in a stone hewn tunnel. Secondly, Mr Vontant stepped around the corner and stopped short at the sight of us with a frown. He straightened his suit as I let my breath go in a near sigh of relief. What the hell was going on here? Where was the angel?

"Ah, Ms Anders," Mr Vontant said in the prim and proper tone he used when he was annoyed at me, "There was a rumour you had managed to sneak in while Jamal was on gate duty. Such a perfect example as to why one should never leave one of the lesser demons in charge of the main gate."

I rose to my feet as Mr Vontant approached, but couldn't help but blink stupidly a few times as my brain adjusted to it being him who had come around the corner, rather than the angelic hunk I had been expecting.

"The. . . angel?" I asked dumbly. I realised I'd said the wrong thing as soon as I said it from the withering look Mr Vontant gave me. Trishna did his usual face palm just in the corner of my vision.

"Seriously?" Mr Vontant asked in near exasperation. "What on earth is it you've been studying over the last six months if you don't even know the fundamentals of demons?"

"Demons are angels?" I asked dumbly before mentally slapping that part of myself into silence as I remembered a basic line from the Christian New Testament — Satan was an angel cast out. An angel that was then supposed to have ruled over. . . Oh hell no! I had thought that was an inaccurate interpretation of an earlier text. There were no fallen angels as evil simply existed to balance good. Dark versus Light and all that. Right?

"Demons are fallen angels?" Okaaay, so my tone hadn't really changed from dumb, no matter how hard I'd tried.

"Only the better class of demon," sniffed Mr Vontant, giving Trishna a look that nearly screamed 'we can't take her anywhere can we?'

Oh screw that!

"Well if the Christian God saw a need to cast you out of the Light and into the Darkness you probably deserved it. Going on your attitude and the sorts of things you get up to," I snapped. I refused to be the butt of some demon and sidekick joke.

"Oh yes, heinous crimes they were too," Mr Vontant replied with a tinge of sarcasm. "We brought medicines to mankind and taught them how to heal themselves, rather than having to rely on their faith in their God and his will to decide who got to live or die. Though I do know of some who simply came down for the sex."

"Then there are those who brought fire and weapons and encouraged war as the way to resolve difficulties," Trishna added wryly, "And those who came to earth to teach man the joys of sin."

"Yes, but most of that was covered in the sex and interbreeding," Mr Vontant replied, obviously not that repentant for any of it. "And quite a bit of that teaching sin came about after we were refused entrance back into heaven. We were bored, it happens."

I did my best not to gawp at him as he said this. Some demons — *this* demon — were angels who got kicked out of heaven for some dodgy dealing and so decided to get up to all sorts of nasties as a payback? How could a good guy *do* such a thing?

"Oh don't give me that look Ms Anders," Mr Vontant said dismissively. "What can I say? Corrupting souls with deliciously sinful and painful acts. . . it helped to while away the centuries, take my mind off being abandoned and I also discovered it was *fun!* Don't knock it till you try it."

Even as I shuddered from the skin crawling reaction his statement had caused, I had a strong urge to punch Mr Vontant on the nose. There were good guys and there were bad guys. I know it's possible to go from being one to the other, but it just didn't seem right to me. An angel *shouldn't* still be an angel after millennia of sinning. No wonder one of his wings was broken.

"You said only some demons are former angels, what are the others?" I asked as my insatiable curiosity took over and the questions started to build-up.

"Tut tut Ms Anders," Mr Vontant replied in an amused tone. "I don't remember us making a deal for there to be a question and answer time. What's in it for me? And I can assure you that down here my prices are *very* steep."

"Oh come on, you started the dialogue," I snapped. "I mean, why go on about it if you're not willing to answer my questions? Anyway, why else would you be here? I'm pretty sure it's not to help me."

"Oh dear Dark Lord no," Mr Vontant agreed. "I'm certainly not here to help you. Merely passing and stopped by to say hi."

"Uh, Stephanie," Trishna tugged on my sleeve but I ignored him as I focused on Mr Vontant.

"To talk huh? Just happened to be shuffling your broken angel butt past our section of Hell and decided to stop and pass the time of day?"

"Steph. . ." Trishna tried again and I shook him off so I could make my 'annoyed with hands on hip' stance at Mr Vontant. The demon simply smiled slightly and straightened his sleeves.

"Oh dear, you've seen right through me," Mr Vontant replied innocently. "You're right. I didn't just stop to pass the time."

"No, he was the bloody distraction," Trishna muttered and I suddenly realised that behind me had become rather draughty. . . as if the dead end had turned back into a passage.

My expression obviously changed to one of worry as I realised this, because the smile on Mr Vontant's face grew wider. Trying to remain as calm and collected as I could, I slowly turned around to see who it was who had snuck up behind us. And, um, well. . . there were just a *few* demons now standing there. Besides Timpsk and Jamal I could see at least a few-dozen suited-men filling the tunnel behind them. I was pretty sure there were even more than that, but I simply couldn't see that far back over their looming shoulders and grim expressions.

"You bastard!" I growled at Mr Vontant, shooting him a death look over my shoulder.

He simply shrugged and smiled again. "Admittedly not one of my guilty pleasures, being a son of God and all that," he said happily. "But it does give me a great deal of pleasure to be able to hand you over to the Dark Forces, rather than always protecting you from them."

I suddenly felt as if my stomach was full of lead and my rather full bladder reminded me of its existence. This was *so* not how it was meant to be. I was meant to get to Hell, skim past all the demons, confront Wroth and get Simon's soul back. Why the hell weren't things going my way?

"Well, the fact you're *in* Hell would be a bit of a giveaway," Jamal sneered, obviously breaking through my mental wall of defence while I was panicking here. Not knowing why I even attempted it, I tried making a stone wall appear between us and the horde of demons. Trishna caught me as I reeled back with one mother of an ice pick style headache over my left eye.

"The power of belief even in you isn't strong enough against a league of demons," Timpsk said, almost apologetically, as I straightened myself out. So, power in numbers huh?

"Too chicken to take me on alone again, Jamal?" I tried with as much bravado as I could summon. I then realised he had two arms again. How could he have put himself back together again so quickly?

"It's amazing what a good seamstress can do given a few minutes," Jamal jeered, once more picking up my train of thought. "What with the amount of times we enjoy pulling people apart and then putting them back together again so we can rip into them once more."

Urgh, that was just sick. Even for Hell that wasn't a pretty thought. Especially after the amount of severed limbs and carnage I'd seen today already.

"But why skip ahead to what we have planned for you, when we haven't even started the initial fun here and now." Jamal smiled moving in too close into my personal space so I found myself stepping away from him. . . and that's when I found that the rock wall which had gone missing was back again.

"Mr Vontant?" I asked, I don't know why, but I wanted to know if he was still close by.

"Over here," the dapper little demon said from a place at the front of the crowd. "You don't think I'd want to miss this?" I really didn't like that smug smile of his.

"Bringing new meaning to innocent bystander," Jamal sneered, as he forced me back against the wall. There were a few muted laughs from the crowd of demons at this comment, but I failed to pay it much attention. I felt a hand in my own and realised Trishna was still with me, always at my side. . . even when I was about to have us used in who knows what sort of demon orgy. This was so not fair. What right did they have to be doing this? Yes they were demons, yes we just happened to be in Hell but our beef wasn't with them, I was here to deal with a soul stealing ankou. How dare they treat us like this! It wasn't as if I gave them such a bad time when they were up in my world. Well, most of the time I didn't. So what if I did a deal or two with the odd demon before I offered to help out? Even those who walk in the Light don't do something for nothing, right? How was a demon meant to respect you if you didn't deal with them first? My inner monologing had started as a pity party but with each question came the anger I needed to help me keep my fear at bay and to think more clearly.

"Back off!" I was not only surprised those two words came out of my mouth so harshly, but that they were the two words that had come out. I mean, 'off' had been a strong contender but the word ending in 'ck' that I'd been thinking of was a tad different.

Jamal looked a little taken aback and the demons pressing in behind him also seemed to pause mid-sneers.

"Excuse me?"

"I said back off," I told him. I summoned up as much of my anger as I could to mask my fear. "I didn't come down here to spend my time wrestling demons, so the lot of you can just clear out of here and let me get on with it. I have an ankou to find and sort out."

Some of the demons actually laughed at this and I gave them my best squinty-eye look.

"You, a person blessed by a Goddess of Light, a person who says she walks deep in the Light, a person who makes deals with demons and chases an ankou back to Hell simply because he had the last word. . . *You* don't think we have the right to be stopping you?" asked Jamal in a mocking tone. "You can't just waltz on into the Dark World Down Below as if you own it and expect to get your own way. We are the denizens of Hell and make the rules around here."

"Oh look, if I'd known it was going to cause you to start monologing again I would have just told you where you can stick your threats and walked off by now," I snapped back, frustrated at the situation and my seeming inability to get out of it.

There was more laughter from the league of demons behind Jamal, though this time they seemed to be laughing at him, rather than me. Obviously Jamal didn't have many friends among his own kind. Oh dear, he seemed to realise this and didn't look happy.

"Enough of your smart mouth!" Jamal snapped, slapping me hard across the face and forcing me back up against the wall again.

"Leave her be!" Trishna yelled, trying to put himself in front of me, but I wouldn't let him. I shook my head to clear it and then pulled Trishna back to my side.

"I'm meant to be the one doing the protecting this time round," I hissed at him, trying to ignore the look of wounded pride this caused.

"If he touches you again I'll rip his testicle off," Trishna muttered.

"Careful, he might enjoy that," a demon called from the crowd.

"Especially getting them sewn back on by the Mistress Seamstress," jeered another, and more laughter at Jamal's expense broke out.

I braced myself for a new assault.

"I've had just about enough of this," Jamal growled as he cast a dark look over the crowd. "They entered our Dark World under my watch and so they are mine to claim. So be it." He turned back to us with a rather unpleasant look on his face and drew a rather ornamental looking knife from up his right sleeve.

Before Trishna or I knew what was happening, or could stop him, Jamal lashed out and gave us each a quick slash across the right cheek. It stung like a bitch and I suddenly guessed what he was trying to do.

"Oh no you don't," I told him, "Our blood has to be given of our free will before you can possess us." More laughter, what the —?

"That is only a subclause to possession when we're up in your world Stephanie," Mr Vontant explained from the front of the crowd. "Here in Hell, in the home of those whose evil power emanates from their ability to possess one's soul. . . we tend to be able to bypass that bit".

Damn it, another update needed to my books when I got home. . . *if* I got home.

Jamal moved to take some of the blood now weeping from the cuts and I smacked his hand away.

"Don't even think about it!" I warned him again and reached for my spare vial of purified water. "We're not yours, and never will be."

There was a hiss of concern from the crowds as they realised I still had purified water and Jamal shot Timpsk a murderous look.

"You little rat fink bastard!" he said, and leaped on the smaller demon and started throttling him. "You let me near her knowing she still had that?"

There was a scuffle among the demons as some tried to encourage the violence while others tried to break it up so they could get on with the task at hand.

"Trishna, I have a plan," I hissed at the former monk at my side.

"Don't even think about it," he warned me as quietly as he could. "You can't go around possessing people and still claim to be one who walks in the Light. It doesn't work that way."

"Well it should do if I'm possessing someone to stop them being possessed by a bunch of demons!" I snapped back.

In front of us the demons were still scuffling and none were really paying us any attention. That is, pretty much all of them besides Mr Vontant. Even as further fights broke out around him as those trying to stop the fight started hitting those who were encouraging it, Mr Vontant's clear gaze pierced me through the crowd, eagerly watching to see what I would do.

I tried to ignore him as I turned back to Trishna.

"Stephanie please," Trishna almost begged. "Don't do this. It's going to being exceedingly unpleasant for me and really not that good for you either."

But what else could I do? Either I possessed his soul and will to protect him, or the demons would. Hang on, what would happen when they then possessed me? They'd still get Trishna. Damn it this sucked.

I then had one of those scarily lucid moments where I felt I knew what to do, but by doing it I was doing one of those things that really shouldn't be done. I wiped some of my own blood from the cut on my right cheek and smeared it on my left.

"I give my blood to myself freely," I whispered. I was amazed at how all the demon fighting around us suddenly stopped as I felt a fizzle of electricity run through me.

"Stephanie!" warned Trishna as I uncorked the vial of purified water.

"What in all the little fetid minions does she think she's doing?" snapped Jamal, dropping the now unconscious Timpsk and trying to get back over to me in time.

I dipped my finger into the salty water and then daubed those three important letters on my own forehead — A N I.

"I possess myself, soul, and will. I am mine, all mine. Soul, will, the whole damned lot." And as I said these words I put all the truth and meaning I felt into them. I belonged to me and me alone. No one had the right to possess me unless they *were* me. The fizzle of electricity increased for a moment and then disappeared with a bit of a head spin. The world seemed bleary for a moment as if I was watching and feeling myself do things as I did them. And then it all settled back down and I realised I had a league of demons and a young Chinese man looking at me with open mouthed awe. What? Hadn't they ever seen anyone possess themselves before?

# Chapter 15

"THAT should *not* be possible," one of the demons from the crowd announced as the others continued to stare at me in a rather disturbing manner. They seemed to be trying to focus on me, but not be fully able to do so.

"No, it shouldn't," mused Jamal stepping forward and poking me in the shoulder.

I slapped him away with a frown and then turned to Trishna for some reassurance I'd not just done something really stupid.

"Don't look at me!" Trishna said uncertainly, actually taking a step *away* from me. "I can't tell if you actually pulled off such an insane act." His reaction toward me worried me more than the bunch of bewildered demons now shuffling from one foot to the other nearby.

"Oh she did it all right," Timpsk said, once more conscious and being propped up by another demon. He held a mixture of awe and concern in his voice. "Damned if I ever thought it possible, but she really *has* bound herself to... herself. She is fully protected from possession and soul deals."

There was more whispering and shuffling sounds from the league of demons as I stared around at them all. Why were they all taking this to be such a dramatic thing? So I had protected myself from them all, big deal? I turned to seek Mr Vontant out to see what he thought and was even more unnerved to find him missing from the crowd. What now?

"We can still take him though," Jamal mused, eyeing Trishna over casually. "And even if we can't possess her, I'm sure there are plenty of things we can physically do to her that will be just as much fun without being in possession of her soul."

I looked back at Trishna, trying to tell him silently that now was the time to let me possess him, for his own good. Pretty sure my expression didn't quite say it that clearly though as I still wasn't too sure it was such a good idea myself.

"No Stephanie, you've done enough damage to your soul today already," Trishna warned, but he did move closer to me as the demons started to press in on us once more.

"It's better me than them," I tried to explain. I really wasn't too sure why possessing Trishna was so damned important to me, but it really was. I wanted to protect him, wanted to keep him free and not a slave to another bad guy of Darkness.

"You possess him and you can kiss your 'Walking in Light' accreditation goodbye," Jamal sneered coming in too close for my liking, again.

"Meh, what happens in Hell stays in Hell," I replied, really not feeling as bold as I was acting. I waved my vial of purified water at him and got some twisted delight in how he — and the demons near him — reacted in terror to it. Oh please, so it stung a little when splashed on a demon. Maybe they should try being nicer people and it wouldn't hurt so much.

"We out number you, even if you take control of both minds," Jamal warned. "Just because we can't possess you, doesn't mean we still can't have a bit of fun making you knit your own intestines into a hat."

Ick. Not exactly the sort of thought I wanted in my head right now, thanks so much.

"I don't suppose any of you would be up for a deal?" I then asked. "I mean, you're going to get summoned top side at some point in my life, I'm sure. Be nice to me now and who knows what help I can give you there." Even as I said this lie — I wasn't ever going to *help* a demon — it tasted nasty in my mouth. Pretty sure they could tell I was lying too as I was met with a stony wall of silence and some rather condescending looks.

"As if you're getting out of here alive to even offer such deals, let alone truly adhere to them," Jamal scoffed, seeming to voice the general consensus of the crowd.

"I say we take control of him and let him do the initial softening up before each taking a turn ourselves," said a new voice from the crowd and Benjamin, the rat fink bastard, stepped forward.

"How's the hand, newb?" I asked him in a mocking tone. What can I say, I felt I was doomed either way so why not go down bitching and scratching? He scowled at this but didn't reply.

"What's wrong Benjamin? Oh that's right, Mr Vontant currently *owns* you. How's that working out?"

"Stephanie. . ." warned Trishna, taking hold of my shoulder and calming some of the death wish hysteria that seemed to be taking control. I turned to him pleadingly, knowing this cat and mouse game the demons were playing with us could end at any moment.

"Please, let me protect you. Let me be the one to invade your mind so that they can't. Surely that has to be the better option than being owned by a demon?"

He gave me a pained look I really couldn't understand and shook his head.

"Humans possessing humans is *wrong*. It is done in Darkness, never in the Light. Please Stephanie."

Before I could answer, rough hands grabbed us and pulled us apart.

"We'll play with him first and let her watch I think," Jamal announced, still in charge.

"Back off!" I shouted and managed, somehow, to struggle free and move back toward Trishna.

"Let me protect you!" I shouted at him as we both struggled against the demons manhandling him.

"It is wrong" Trishna snapped through gritted teeth. I elbowed a demon out of the way and wiped at the still wet blood on his cheek and then wiped it on my own, over my own blood.

"As you didn't stop me, I take it that this blood is given of your own free will," I said to him while stomping heavily on the foot of a demon trying to separate us again.

"Stephanie, don't!" begged Trishna as he freed himself from the demon holding him by cracking the back of his head into the demon's nose.

"Don't let her take him!" growled Jamal coming too close and copping a foot in the genitals for his attempt.

"Back off bad breath," I hissed, then turned my attention back to Trishna.

I dodged another demon's attempt to grab me by flicking some of my precious, purified water in his face. The realisation I would use it as a weapon had the crowd around us lessen a little. Were they really that afraid of purified water? Or was it what I could do with it? Did they *really* think I had enough to possess a whole frickin league? Demons were starting to appear a lot dumber than I'd originally thought.

"Trishna, I'm doing this to protect you, to keep your soul safe from the demons and their Darkness. I'm possessing you in the name of those who walk in the Light, I'm doing so to keep you safe from dark forces," I babbled while daubing my name on his forehead, trying to ignore him struggling against it, *begging* me to stop.

"You are mine, owned by me to *protect* you. Mind, body and soul. May the Goddess forgive me as I do it with the best intentions."

I tried to ignore the tears pricking my eyes as I thought of owning Trishna, of being in charge of him to protect him, to keep him safe. I hated myself for what I was doing when I saw the torment in his eyes, but then it was done and his expression went blank, showing I had succeeded.

There was a hissed intake of breath around us and the demons once more backed off.

"We have lost both souls now," one of the demons spat angrily at Jamal. "First you let them in by being useless at your job, and now there is nothing to take as a reward."

"We can still play with them," Jamal tried, but was met with dismissive noises from the crowd.

"We have a kingdom of the tormented that we can *play* with any time we like," the angry demon replied. "But having *living* people here with souls to feed off. . . that's what we turned up for."

"Tathal has a point," Timpsk said. "You summoned us to watch you take control and possess those who dared defile our sanctum. Now what?"

While this discussion was going on I manoeuvred myself and Trishna back over against the wall and out of the way of the majority of demons now arguing with Jamal. Obviously I'd spoiled his chance of making amends, and hopefully if I kept quiet enough we might even be able to slip away.

"I'm pretty sure he just invited us here to bolster his own will with ours to stop her beating the pants off him. . . again," Benjamin said. As much as I didn't condone the punch in the nose Jamal gave him, it was better Benjamin got it than me.

As much as I was trying to keep up with what they were saying and trying to sneak away, I was finding it hard to focus on it all as the reality of possessing Trishna started to sink in. I could *feel* him, his mind fizzling away beneath mine. Feel his anguish at what I'd done, his anger, his frustration. There was a tight black ball of something else within it I was sure he was trying to hide from me and I had to fight hard against attempting to pry it open. If he wanted to keep it a secret, that was fine. I really was just possessing him to protect him, not sneak a peek into his inner most thoughts. Heck, I doubted they would be G-rated or something I'd be likely to forget. So best not to peek. . . no matter how enticing it was suddenly getting, growing in intensity with every passing moment.

As the demons now raged around me, I felt sick with the realisation that my mind wanted to take over Trishna's, pull it apart and look into all his thoughts, memories and ideas. I was not a nosy person and so this urge, this desire to pillage his mind was abhorrent. If I could recant the possession and still keep him safe, I would. But, for the moment, the only way to have the demons lose interest in us seemed to be by me owning both our souls. All the same, this feeling of greed and desire to know his every thought kept nagging at me and distracting me from trying to escape.

"Souls from a living human always taste the sweetest, and their life force ignites an addiction to delve into their every thought," crooned a voice so close to my side that I was reminded of my bladder and the state of my underwear.

I glanced over into what I had thought were empty shadows, and was just able to make out the shadowy shape of a man. . . of another demon. I tried to focus on him and see him more clearly, but the shadows seemed to be moving about him, changing his shape and appearance every few seconds.

"You should relish your first time taking a soul," this new demon said. "The rush and high you get from it is never replicated. No matter how many other lives you taste and destroy." It was a pleasant enough voice, eager in what it was saying, but I still wanted to be sick from what I heard.

"This is my first and last soul possession of a living person," I hissed angrily at the shadow man, "And I did it to *protect* him. Not rape his mind of every thought." How could he even think I would stoop so low? Oh wait, he was a demon.

"Pity. You're so good at it, and even a goody two shoes like you has to admit the. . . *sensation*. . . is quite intoxicating."

I gave up trying to sneak away and had to screw up my eyes to concentrate on not listening to him, and more importantly my brain bypassing that and agreeing. The sensation of *owning* a living soul was indeed starting to give me a rather pleasant tingle. The knowledge their very thoughts and being were there for me to mentally run my fingers through. To feel, to taste those hidden secrets of Trishna's inner being. It felt like a building pleasure and calm, like your first chocolate of the morning. It was also, however, making me as sick to my stomach as it had done when I'd possessed Jamal. And as much as part of me didn't want to, I found myself focusing on the queasiness rather than the thrilling pleasure. Possessing someone and taking control of all their thoughts, feelings and actions was *wrong*. This had been done only to protect — Trishna's thoughts were his own and I would not pry. I believed that to my very core and was shocked I now had to fight against this new sensation of pleasure that disagreed.

"Tut tut," the shadowy demon next to me said with a shake of his head. "You shouldn't fight it like that. You'll never get a high as strong as this again. Embrace it, enjoy it, breathe it in and suck his thoughts clear out of his head."

"Oh will you just *shut up* you sick little bastard!" I hadn't really meant to yell that, but venting my anger in such a way had felt nice all the same. That was, until I noticed the other demons had gone quiet. . . and I was pretty sure they were now all staring at us. Damn.

I was a little surprised they didn't rush me though, until I realised they weren't really looking at me, but more staring at the shadowy form next to me. I decided to risk another glance at the demon myself, now he had moved out of the shadows, and sort of wished I hadn't. Looking at him made me want to go cross-eyed. Even as I focused on the demon he seemed to shimmer and change his appearance. Sometimes tall, then short, fat, thin, dark skinned, light. . . it was as if he was flickering in between beliefs of those around him. I swear I even saw cloven hoofs, horns and a tail at one point before he seemed to take control of his appearance and settle on a rather good-looking middle-aged man. Tall, tan skinned and brown hair with flecks of grey at the temples. I was pretty sure my nausea increased as I realised he had taken on an appearance I found rather attractive. That was just *sick*. Most demons had a well-groomed and not-too hard on the eye appearance at the best of times. But to *know* one could manipulate its appearance to match my taste in men? Ew. Never ever in any dreams would that be my preferred scenario. I'd sooner hook up with Trishna.

"No offence," I found myself murmuring to Trishna, as I moved us closer together. Why I bothered I don't know? He could only hear me if

I let him. . . and I didn't really want to share my current insane train of thought with any other passenger.

"My Lord?" Jamal asked this new demon timidly.

That took me back a bit. Reverence and timid nature in one demon to another meant this shape shifting hunk — ew — was a more superior being. Uh-oh?

"What brings you here?" Jamal tried again, and I realised he was probably looking a little worried because he had taken responsibility for our being there.

"It's not every day a living human successfully binds herself to herself," the new demon replied, his tone calm but condescending. "That titbit of energy rippled through the whole Dark World and I simply *had* to come and meet her."

Double uh-oh.

"I apologise for the incursion into our realm, my Lord," Jamal said. "I had left the gate duty to one of my minions and was trying to clean up his mess just now. I can assure you he has been dealt with —"

"And smeared from one end of your home to another?" the new demon interrupted. "Yes, you minion *are* rather tiresome with your mistakes at times, aren't you?"

Jamal was a minion to this guy? Who in hell — literally — was he?

As if he'd been able to read my mildly hysterical expression, the new demon turned to me.

"But of course, you'll be wanting to know my name." He gave me a smile and I tried to ignore the weak tremble in my knees this caused. "You will understand that I don't give my actual name to just any casual visitor. Even one with the potential to become a new demon in a manner I've never seen before. So I will allow you to know me as the Supreme Imperial Demon. Ruler of this Dark World."

There were just so many things in his last statement that had me wanting to blink rapidly to concentrate on, that I ended up simply closing my eyes to work my way through it. I then realised I was standing with my eyes closed in Hell surrounded by demons and quickly opened them up again as it was better to see them than feel them in the darkness.

"Let me get this straight?" I told Mr tall, dark and handsome. "You won't give me your real name, and instead want me to refer to you as the Supreme Imperial Demon? Yeah no, nice try buddy. How about I just stick to Sid for short, just because I'm willing to meet you half way?"

I felt he had lost some of his thrall over me when trying to suggest I was a demon in the making. Of all the insults a demon could give me!

"I will not answer to Sid," he said coldly.

I shrugged as my death wish mood took over again. "I can assure you I've hung around with Other World folk long enough now that there are some pretty colourful phrases I could call you instead. And I have quite a repertoire of them too. It's either Sid, or you just deal with the alternative."

I tried to ignore the sharp intake of breaths that happened in the surrounding league of demons. Obviously even *they* thought I'd chosen the wrong demon to smart mouth.

"If I didn't find you such an interesting new plaything, I'd smite you for that," the demon now known by me as Sid purred at me. Ew, he was turned on by me being catty? How on earth were we meant to communicate now I knew this?

And then I remembered smite had two meanings, as I'd actually looked it up after having been threatened with it for so long. I mean, words were important to these folks. Smite meant not only to strike down with a heavy blow. . . but to form an attraction or affection to someone. Hence *smitten*. Okay, time to try and avoid both types of smiting and get myself the hell away from all these demons.

"Now, I feel we would be much better suited at my lodgings, rather than out here with the rabble," Sid said, and before I could object, he'd clicked his fingers and our surroundings changed.

I wasn't too sure if we had been teleported to a new location, or whether Sid was powerful enough to just change our current surroundings to these new ones. Either way we were now in some faux-wood-panelled, book-lined Edwardian style library. Wing chairs, roaring open fire and hissing gas lamps on the walls, the whole lot. Part of my brain cringed at how fake it all felt, but a bigger part tingled with excitement as it realised it was one of my favourite fantasy settings to be seduced in. Triple Ew! As unnerved by our new surroundings as I was, I was relieved to discover Trishna was still with me. How we'd ended up holding hands I don't know. But as long as he was safe and with me, things weren't so bad, right?

"Time to make ourselves more comfortable," Sid announced. His suit morphed into something more casual that included a quilted smoking-jacket. I tried to explain the shiver I then got as being around his stronger belief, rather than how *good* he looked in that jacket. Damn I was getting tired of his thrall and what it was doing to my better judgement!

"Refreshments?" he asked as a door at one end of his library opened and two women entered with trays. I was taken aback for a moment by the huge contrast between the two women. Though both were obviously demons, one was short, stocky, middle-aged and wearing a dull tweed skirt and jacket over a white blouse. Her dull mouse-brown hair was up in a severe bun and her face seemed to naturally wear a look of disdain. She placed a tray holding a tea pot and cups down on a small table before moving to stand to one side of a winged chair closest to the fire.

The other woman, in comparison, seemed to ooze into the room on well-oiled and sexually provocative hips. She was taller and, under a flowery cotton summer dress, she was rounded and curvy in all the places men seemed to like. She had a mane of slightly curly black hair that cascaded down past her dark and sultry eyes, and a rosy red-lipped mouth. Damn, her thrall was almost as bad as Sid's as she winked at me while placing a tray holding plates of sandwiches down on another small table and going to stand on the other side of the chair.

"Allow me to introduce the two main women in my life," Sid announced, moving to sit in the chair, while indicating I should take the other across from him. "My wife and my mistress. More commonly known as Duty and Pleasure." He kissed the wrist of each woman in turn, showing an equal amount of attention to them despite their names.

I tried not to cringe at such demeaning descriptions as I carefully sat myself down on the very edge of the chair. As there was a foot stool next to me I piloted Trishna onto that, clenching my jaw against the nausea of being his will.

"It gets easier, controlling your toys, if you just loosened up a bit and enjoyed it for what it was," Sid said in an amused tone. He snapped his fingers at Duty and pointed to the tea tray.

Duty moved obediently over to the tray. "Milk and sugar?" she asked.

I nodded dumbly, not wanting to actually accept anything from these demons, but not wanting to offend them either.

"Duty is the demon I had to marry to ensure the right stock of souls and balance of power," Sid calmly explained as his wife served him first before moving over to me. "Female demons control most of the souls in our Dark World, but they need a man's touch to turn those souls into power. I feel it has worked out for the best. Don't you agree my dear?"

Duty was silent until she had passed me my tea. "Men have their uses, why not go for the most powerful?" she said as she returned to his side. Her look of disdain changed briefly to a look of amusement and I found it a little unsettling that they appeared to actually love each other. Demon love, not something I wanted to think about. Unfortunately I suspected I'd be having nightmares about it for a few years to come.

Sid snapped his fingers at Pleasure and she gyrated forward to the tray of sandwiches, again serving him before offering them to me. I declined as politely as I could, not wanting to think of what demons actually put between two slices of bread in Hell.

"Pleasure here is a succubus who used to be in my minions. I took such a liking to the dirty little thoughts she was able to pop in my head I simply had to have her as my main plaything."

Pleasure gave a flirtatious giggle as she returned to her side of the chair, but said no more. I eyed her warily, pretty sure that succubi were both canny and cluey demons. So the airhead persona was obviously an act for Sid. I then realised he probably had to play his cards right around both women as I got the feeling female demons were a lot more powerful than the men. Possibly why you never saw them up in my world? They seemed too smart to let some mere human summon them like that. . . and if they already controlled the souls down here, why go up looking for more? How long did souls stay in Hell anyhow? I was pretty sure it wasn't an eternity, not for all of them.

I realised there had been an uncomfortable pause in conversation as I'd been thinking through all this and wondered if I'd missed a question. None of them wore a questioning look though, they simply stared at me as if I was an amusing and interesting new part of the furniture.

"I'm not a demon, I don't want to be a demon, I walk in the Light — no matter *what* some may say. And all I really want to do is get the soul I came here for and go home. Okay?" I felt that covered pretty much all the answers I had been willing to give. Now what?

"Pity about the 'not wanting to become a demon' part," Sid mused. "Given the way you're straying from the path you might not have a choice."

"You do know that carrying your own torch to see by isn't the same as 'walking in the Light'," Duty added with a sneer.

I waited for Pleasure to add her two cents but all she did was twiddle with the ends of her hair and stare blankly around the room.

Finally Pleasure gave herself a little shake. "What I want to know is what's to stop us just keeping you as our little pet and seeing just how demonic we can make you."

I really wished Abe Lincoln's quote about being thought a fool was correct for her. Damn she was sharp.

"I mean, the ankou doesn't want you sniffing around and taking his souls. He's actually quite worried about it now he knows you're here. The minor demons don't see you as much entertainment now there are no souls to pillage. That really does just leave us and our desires," Pleasure said, focusing on me as she said it, cocking her head to one side and allowing a small smile to play across her face. I wasn't too sure if the shiver I felt ripple through me was from fear or delight.

"Well, you could always just let me go and deal with the ankou, demons, and all the rest of it so I can then leave you alone and head on home. There is *that* option." I had hoped I kept the 'oh who am I kidding?' out of my tone, but from the laughter that ensued from the trio I guess I hadn't been that successful.

"Where is the fun in that?" Sid said, giving me a teasing smile. Damn! He snapped his fingers at Pleasure, making her go get him some more sandwiches. "I mean, what is in it for us if we just let you go?"

"You want me to make a deal?" I asked astounded. I had been expecting torture and the demand I plead for mercy and for my life. Not tea, sandwiches and a deal. Then again, these were demons I was associating with, so who's to say whether the torture and pleading wouldn't just happen after the tea?

"That's one way of looking at it Stephanie." Sid smiled as he said this and looked me directly in the eye. This was the first time he'd shown he knew my name and man it didn't feel good when he used it on me.

"Oh, like you're really giving me any other options," I snapped, I had been trying to keep civil but polite and amused demons really seemed to push my buttons.

"But there are my dear," Duty corrected me, noticing I'd not touched my tea and tut tutting at the fact. "There are several options you could choose. Such as trying to escape, setting your minion upon us, trying to kill us with your tiny vial of purified water and powerful words, killing yourself and your minion, giving yourself over to our wills and pleasures or sitting here until your tea goes cold and we bore of your intrusion and decide to teach you the lesson you so deserve for thinking you had the right to come into our world and attack our way of life."

"Trishna is *not* my minion! He is a soul I am merely protecting within my own will until I can get him home to safety," I growled angrily at her.

She sniffed her disdain at this. "If you say so my dear, those options are all still there and viable. I, personally, am hoping for the last one as there is just something about you that makes me want to see how you tick. And opening you up nice and slowly would be the best way to do this."

Ew.

"Oh I *do* like your style my love!" Sid exclaimed, looking up at Duty with adoration. "Further proof as to why you're my wife, when you think along those lines."

"I do so hope you will let me play with her first," Pleasure pouted, obviously put out by Sid's lavish attention on Duty. "Cut her open all you like, but let me play in her mind a little while first. I've never sucked the soul out of someone who has bound themselves to themselves. I'm curious to see how it can be done."

"Another excellent option," smiled Duty, "As I don't necessarily require her soul intact to do some slicing and dicing of her body."

As panicked as the majority of my brain was getting from this small talk, part of me caught the amused look from Sid as it went on and I suddenly felt like they were just goading me. *Was* there anything they could actually do to me while I was in possession of my own soul?

"Actually, I'm going to go with the option where you just let us leave so we can get on with the ankou situation," I said suddenly. I made a show of uncorking my vial of purified water and pouring it into my untouched tea. It fizzled and turned a nasty black colour. Was that just purified water reacting to something made in Hell? Or had there really been something quite nasty in the Darjeeling? I shrugged and tried to hand it back to Duty. She stared coldly at me, refusing to budge so I simply shrugged again and let the fine china cup and saucer fall from my out stretched hand.

"Oops," I simpered, to show Pleasure she wasn't the only girly one in the room, and blinked as a hole into blackness appeared in their rather nice looking Persian rug. It seemed to be a hole leading out of the room. Really — it was that simple? Or was this just another trick?

"You dare try to insult our hospitality by making a mess and then leaving before you clean it up?" Duty bristled.

I got to my feet and thought Trishna to his, taking his hand as I did so. "You're a demon, like I care if my actions insult you."

I took a closer look at the burned out hole in the middle of their floor. Yup, it definitely looked like an opening down into the stone tunnels I liked Hell to look like. Had my desire to go back to that Hell, aided by the purified water spilled in Sid's reality made it happen? Or were they still just playing with me? Despite the peril I now found myself in I was still a little tentative about just jumping through boots and all in case it was a trick. . . It was so hard to tell if it was, or whether I'd just got really, really lucky again. Could I ever take anything for what it seemed to be in Hell?

"We simply *live* for bad behaviour, don't we darling?" Pleasure said, smiling at Sid with her thrall on full blast. She stepped toward me and, despite my attempts to try and smack her away with my free hand, linked arms with mine and moved toward the hole.

"I always enjoy finding an opening in my day for exciting new friends and conquest," she told me with a grin. Then, before I could stop her, she gave me a hard tug and I found myself and Trishna falling with her through the hole, with Sid calling all manner of insults above us.

Why did I suddenly feel I'd just gone down the rabbit hole with a rather X-rated Alice?

# Chapter 16

THE Pleasure who helped me up off the ground was a little different to the one I'd just plummeted through the floor with. She'd somehow changed her clothes to those skin-tight, black leather outfits so many men seem to like their supernatural heroines in. I was amazed it could be so tight, fitting over all those curves and bumps, yet still be flexible enough for her to actually move in. The stiletto high heeled boots just looked ridiculous though. I mean, seriously, how was she meant to run in those? Maybe that was the point? Even with a sprained ankle and Trishna I thought I'd get a pretty good head start on her. That is, of course, if it wasn't for the way her arm was still looped through mine in a rather possessive manner.

"There now," she smiled at me as if we were two friends having a cosy gossip. "Much easier to have a chat now we're away from those two. We may even be able to come to some sort of arrangement."

Oh, fat chance lady!

"You do not own me, so just let me go," I said coldly, giving my arm a hard tug. She pouted but reluctantly let me go, though I was pretty sure she was only doing it for show. Even possessing my own soul wouldn't stop a demon from doing whatever they physically wanted to do, if it came down to it. So what did she want?

"If you want to make a deal with me sweetheart, you better be making it a doozy or just get lost," I warned her, and taking Trishna's hand again headed off down the rocky corridor. I had no idea where I was going, but I needed to keep moving. Standing still for too long in Hell just seemed like a very bad idea.

"You do know we're all playing nice with you until we figure out what it is we can actually do with you," Pleasure said conversationally, trotting after me on those ridiculous heels.

"And so I'm meant to be nice and civil to a bunch of demons until they decide in what order they want to rape, draw, and quarter me?" I asked her cynically. What can I say? I obviously wanted to go down swinging.

"My, aren't you the tough little nut," Pleasure said, having caught up with me and now matching me stride for stride. "Most people in your position would at least be trying to show some respect."

"I seriously don't think you get many people in my position, so I'm pretty sure I'm allowed to make it up as I go along," I replied, trying to be polite. And it was true, ever since falling in with the Other World crowd I seemed to make things up as I went. Not the important things I'd learned from the texts, about summoning, dispelling and all that. But when it came to how I handled the rest, winging it seemed to be working for me so far.

"Do you even know where you're going?" Pleasure snapped as her tottering shoes tripped on a rock. I'd not made it appear there with my belief, honest.

"I'd like to *believe* I'm heading toward Wroth's place. Surely that should make it happen down here."

Pleasure snorted her amusement and I tried to hide my expression of uncertainty. You mean this new idea about believing I could find Wroth wouldn't make it happen?

"Despite being a belief based realm, it does still have its own physical locations that you can't just magic up," Pleasure jeered, side stepping another sudden rock in her path. "You have to *know* where you're going to actually get there. Otherwise you'll just continue to wander these corridors until you die. Whether that be by natural causes, or at the hand of a rather bored succubus."

I stopped thinking about how dangerous Pleasure's shoes must be to walk around in on the rocky ground and tried thinking up something more useful to say.

"So this is where you offer to show me where Wroth is through some rather cack-handed deal that ends up with you get everything and I end up with zip?" At least my tone held mostly sarcasm and not the scorn I'd wanted to use.

"Something like that," Pleasure smirked. She grabbed me by a shoulder to stop me, and turned me to face her.

"Do you want to learn something very interesting about demons first?" She smiled winningly, and I felt her thrall bubbling just below the surface.

"What's it going to cost me?" I asked sceptically. Information from a demon was rarely free.

"Nothing — just a few moments of your time while you listen."

I quirked an eyebrow at her as she said this. As doe-eyed and innocent as she was coming across, Pleasure was still a demon and I just didn't trust her.

"What do you know about female demons?" she asked, assuming I'd agreed to hear her out.

"Not a heck of a lot, we don't seem to get you topside. And Sid said something about the women owning the souls down here?" I replied cautiously, keeping Trishna close to my other side and wishing he could be himself once more and join in. Despite him still physically being with me, I missed him actually *being* there. I wondered if I could possess him while letting him be himself. Doubtful or it would have happened by now, right?

"If you've finished playing with your toy, I *would* like your attention for what I'm trying to tell you" Pleasure complained, her true demon personality showing from behind her bimbo facade for a moment.

"Fine," I sighed and tried to focus on her, rather than Trishna. "So what is so damned important about female demons?"

The slap stung, but I feel most of my reaction was from the surprise that she'd dared hit me. That and the fact Trishna stepped forward and punched her in the stomach. Gee, did I do that?

I moved him to stand behind me as Pleasure and I eyed each other, both nursing new bruises.

"I expect more respect than that from you mortal, no matter who you are," Pleasure hissed as she rubbed her stomach. Straightening she shook out her hair and pouted. Through her vacuous bimbo expression, however, her gaze flashed with a steel edge and I knew I'd pushed enough of her buttons for now. She was seriously trying to tell me something important so I had better listen.

"Okay then, tell me what's so important about female demons."

"We control Hell," Pleasure said earnestly. "It is our ability to hold a soul here, rather than letting it pass into the new life, that gives us the power. The more souls we have, the more life energy we have to control and wield."

Okay, that didn't sound too good. I had guessed the powers of demons came from the souls they owned, but I had wondered exactly how the souls transferred into power. It was obvious now, the life force we carry with us from one life to the next. Capture that and it'd be like walking around with a battery in your pocket. Ghosts were only a smaller version of this.

"Then why do the male demons wander about as if they own the place?" It seemed a valid enough question, but Pleasure's face darkened.

"We females may have the ability to hold souls in this plane of existence but we have no control over accessing their life force without the help of a male. We also don't have the ability to collect the souls ourselves. Something else we need males for."

Gee, she didn't sound too happy about that.

"So why don't female demons rule the roost?" I asked, my natural curiosity kicking in once more and making mental notes for later.

"What use is a bunch of souls without the ability to draw upon their power? The men get to choose which women they add to their harem. Which ones have the better cluster of souls, the age and quality of the souls, the ones best suited to care for the fresh souls the male harvests, and so forth." She scowled unhappily.

"And I'm sure there is also that whole barter system of who gets what between prospective son and father-in-law when it's time to build a harem?" It seemed like a valid question but Pleasure's blank stare confused me.

"Fathers? Demons do not have fathers you silly trollop. We are *created* from pure evil. Souls corrupted beyond measure and mutated by the Darkness into a living being. Some of us are simply the manifestation of a heavy belief of the Darkness. Demons do not *breed* to begat demons!"

She actually seemed appalled at the idea of making babies. And she was a succubus saying that. Despite not liking the idea, I was pretty sure she knew all about the process.

"But let's not forget the fallen angels in that mix." I decided to give Mr Vontant a plug to show I knew *something* about the history of demons.

"Yes, the corrupted remnants of those who used to walk in the Light," she said and smiled meaningfully at me. "We don't see that happening as often as it used to now the Darkness and Light have balanced out. And it's even rarer when it is a *female* who has the ability to both contain a soul and the ability to possess it to utilise its power."

Oh shut the heck up! Pleasure may as well have punched me in the stomach by saying that. I was *not* a demon. I was not about to *become* a demon. I was a protector of souls and here to grab Simon's and get out of the place as fast as I could. I was pretty sure she could tell from my expression what I had been thinking as she gave a tinkling laugh and gently patted me on the cheek she had slapped moments before.

"So glad to see you've finally caught up with why I wanted you so badly," she purred. "Teaming up with the likes of you, I wouldn't need an annoying male in my life anymore. If you let me share my souls with you, just think of the power and pleasure we could have together."

I shivered from how much that thought made my skin crawl. I think I would have been less disgusted if she had just propositioned me for sex. So I possessed a demon last year and happened to have sort of possessed Trishna today — but only to protect him. It was no biggie. And it didn't mean I was a demon in the making and ready to start my own legion of flunkies with Pleasure. Then again, it really did feel so good to hold and control someone. To manipulate them from within their very being and bend them to my will. . .

"I walk in the Light," I said through gritted teeth. I was protecting Trishna, not using him for my enjoyment and dominance. Pleasure's expression hardened with disappointment.

"Such a waste of talent and ability," she snarled, her thrall dropping and her true demon side showing. "Well, if I can't have you, I'll leave you to the waifs and strays down here in the lower dungeons." And with that she was gone — and so was my calm, soothing, rocky tunnel.

I don't know how Pleasure had done it, I had assumed my stronger will had been controlling our surroundings, but gone was the darkness and rocks and we were suddenly left standing in a honeycomb of red and orange corridors. Rather than solid stone walls, the place was a series of columns that appeared to have been created by stalagmites and stalactites meeting. The heat was oppressive, the smell was appalling, and the distant wails and cries that filled the air jarred my ears. And then there were the shadowy forms that flitted between the columns, their insane jabbering and giggles really had me worried. So not in Texas any more Trishna!

"Typical of Pleasure to just discard her toys in the most unsavoury of places."

I literally jumped on hearing that voice behind me. I turned to meet the look of disdain on Duty's face with a wary look on my own.

"I'm no demon's toy," I said as calmly as I could, ever aware of the shadows around us and their unsettling hysteria.

"Oh but you *are*," Duty mocked, her tweed outfit and stern hairstyle making her stand out more in this weird world than Pleasure's leathers and spiky shoes. "We're all just going to play with you until we've decided what to do with you."

Yeah, no, still didn't like that idea.

"What? So you're not here to deal with me?" I tried a mocking tone myself, but in reality I was more wary of Duty than I had been of Pleasure. I guess it was the strict school mistress look. "Not here to sell to me the idea of how great it would be for us to join forces and rid ourselves of men?"

Despite being shorter than me, Duty gave me a great impression of someone looking down their nose at me.

"When you are at the top of the harem for the Supreme Lord of Hell, do you *really* think I would want to swap my allegiances to someone who can't even decide which side she's on?"

"I'm on the side of Light." I wondered why I felt I had to keep saying it? It was almost as though if I didn't it would stop being true.

"If you say so," Duty sniffed.

I really didn't like her attitude. If she wasn't here to deal or to convince me to join forces, what was she here to do? Before I could ask her, one of the shadowy forms I'd been trying to keep tabs on out of the corner of my eye leaped forward and took a swipe at me before giggling and crying its way back into the shadows. What in the hell was that? Part human, part smoke, and with eyes like that of a dead fish. I tried to supress a shudder and look as calm and indifferent at Duty.

"This is where all souls and corrupted beliefs come to fester," she told me casually. "Where they either crumble and fade within their own tortured self or pupate into the most beautiful creature known."

"That thing is a baby demon?" I asked, I felt it politer than pointing out how wrong she was with her description that demons were beautiful. How could evil contain true beauty? Wasn't beauty your inner Light shining through?

"We can't all be banished from heaven for getting up to no good," Duty answered, but I got the feeling she wasn't talking directly to me anymore. "Some demons are the manifestations of man's evil, some spring from the fear and belief of Darkness —"

"And some of you were just horrible people left to ferment in your own juices for a little too long," Mr Vontant cut in, as he stepped out of the shadows. It was a little unsettling at how relieved I was to see him.

"You're never too far away from Ms Anders are you?" she sneered at him, "Always watching. But it's what stupid old fools like you do best."

Now I know Mr Vontant was an evil being, I'd seen him go demon on me enough times to know he wasn't really a good guy in disguise. But he still scared me when he lashed out and backhanded Duty for her remark. Actually *seeing* him commit violence against a woman, even a female demon, just seemed so wrong.

"I don't care whose harem you're the top of," Mr Vontant spat viciously, "My kind has been established here for millennia longer than yours, you anthropomorphised by-product!"

I had expected Duty to fight back, I really had. But I'm guessing that barely audible sound of ruffled feathers and silence from the demon nursery was enough to shut everyone up. Heck, it had done me. But only just.

"If you're so unafraid of Sid, why did you let him take me before?" Yes, I came up with the dumbest questions at the oddest times, I know.

"You ask me that as if we have a deal going in this Dark World," Mr Vontant sniffed and straightened his suit. "Just because I don't give a damn what the mutants get up to doesn't mean I'm going to save your sorry arse for no reason."

"See how he disrespects you," Duty pointed out coldly.

"Oh and as if she who just called me a demon's toy is paying me the highest compliments right now," I snapped. What can I say, I *really* didn't like her.

I then gave both demons my best squinty-eye, after checking Trishna was still with me.

"Why are you both so damned interested to get me on your side?" It was an obvious question actually.

"If you have so much on offer Duty, why pick up where Pleasure left off in trying to befriend me? What's in it for you?" Duty had the decency to look uncomfortable for a moment while Mr Vontant looked smug.

"And don't think I've not noticed you mister!" I scowled at him too. "If we don't have a deal going and you're in no way inclined to help me, what are you doing here now?" A terrible thought then hit me. "Oh Goddess, you're not here to offer me a spot on your harem are you?"

I don't know what was worse, the snort of amusement from Duty or the appalled look on Mr Vontant's face.

"I can assure you that you're the wrong gender to be deemed suitable for such a title as *harem member*," Mr Vontant said coldly.

"Yes, you should see his two favourites. Supply and Demand aren't they? Big, butch fellows," Duty teased, getting another look of vicious warning from Mr Vontant.

He was gay? So you could get gay demons. . . not something I'd ever really considered. They were all about depravity, evilness and being nasty. Something as natural as gender preference simply seemed — weird. Although, now I knew Mr Vontant was gay. . . it suited him. And explained why he was about the only demon I knew who hadn't tried to hump me. I was actually more surprised you got gender-specific demons. Hell, I was surprised they had any preferences to male, female, alive, dead, animate or inanimate objects. . . as I felt they were all such perverse degenerates they'd do anything to, well, anything.

"It is called being of the Classic Greek persuasion," Mr Vontant told me, as if I really wanted to know. Which I hadn't, especially after *that* description of it. "Females are simply there to do the tasks best suited for them, while I can take my —"

"Yeah, let me stop you right there Mr Vontant," I burst in, as I really, *really* didn't want the mental images of him being sexual with. . . anything. "You like boys, er, men, um male things and we mere females are just there to 'do' for you. Got it! Perfectly acceptable choice in life, if not a little demeaning to we women folk, but you don't need to paint me a picture because I really don't want to think of you in such situations. With anyone. Ever."

Another snort of amusement from Duty had me scowling at her again.

"You're such a prude," she teased.

Nope, not really winning me over to want to listen to what she wanted from me.

"Yes, how stupid of me to forget demons will do anything to anyone, anytime as long as they come out on top." Damn, I wish I had thought that sentence through before saying it out loud.

The gibbering around us had returned and had possibly grown louder, indicating there were more demon pupae — ew — gathering around us. Time to change the subject, and my location.

"And I wish to point out that whichever one of you gets me out of this particularly unpleasant part of Hell will get more attention from me when it comes to deal time than the one who keeps me here any longer."

"But what is in it for us?" Mr Vontant asked politely enough, actually sharing a look of 'is she serious?' with Duty. Reminding me once more that I wasn't dealing with a good demon and a bad demon, just two demons.

"What do you *mean* what's in it for you?" I snapped, finding it hard not to in that location. "You want me to consider whatever deal it is you're about to hit me with so you want me in a good mood don't you? *That* is what's in it for you."

"But I'm not here to deal with you," Mr Vontant said, and turned to Duty.

I realised I wasn't the only one in the party unaware that he was really there to see her. But Duty's surprised was short lived, as she suddenly dropped Mr Vontant a regal curtsey.

"Well then, pray parlay sir," she said.

This unsettled me even more than my current location and situation did. Both demons took on such a formal stance toward each other I knew some serious stuff was about to go down.

"I want your ankou," Mr Vontant said. "The rebel one you've been helping to interact with the Impa Shilup."

"I've done no such thing," Duty replied evasively, "I have not once interfered with how my ankou serve their time."

"No, but you didn't stop or discourage one when it came to the New World centuries ago and learned a loophole that allows it to exist beyond the normal twelve month life expectancy."

"Wait a minute," I butted in, "Wroth works for *her*?"

"Please Stephanie. Unless you have something intelligent to say, I honestly feel it's better for all of us if you just stay quiet," Mr Vontant said with a weary sigh.

I still got the feeling he was telling me about Wroth without actually telling me though.

"Impa Shilup, they are a dark-spirit from the Choctaw tribes of North America and known to possess people and steal their souls and replace them with their own. How's that for intelligent?" I gave them both a smug look, having done a little researching on those little buggers before heading off on this journey to Hell.

"And from what I forced you to tell me about Wroth the other night, I'm guessing he came across some of these little spirit guys on his first visit to the New World a few centuries ago. The loophole you've just mentioned being that if he worked *with* the Impa Shilup he could extend his time as an ankou by collecting souls from bodies still deemed alive as they now housed the dark-spirit. And as long as the bodies stayed alive, the souls of the 'dead' weren't technically collected and so he has to wait around until body and soul are both dead. In the meantime he keeps extending that tentative lifespan of his by continuing this alive/dead trick with the Impa Shilup. And the actual souls collected can't pass on to their new lives until their bodies expire too. . . meaning they stay here and their energy can be used by the male in control!"

"Of all the leprous whores in hell, does she always have to state the blindingly obvious?" Duty snapped. She appeared a little unnerved I'd put two and two together and ended up with several thousand.

"And how do female demons get so many souls, but by controlling the reapers! And of course you'd be on a sure fire winner with a constant stream of prime souls if you controlled the rebel ankou in question!" I shot her a triumphant look as she paled slightly. I tried to ignore the unsettled feeling I often got when the answers just came to me like that, but it all made so much sense now. The female demons maintained the souls, owned them, and used their life force; but only through the help of male demons. They would, of course, want only the best and most powerful male demon to aide them, and how to attract the cream of the crop? By having your own sneaky ways of ensuring your source of souls didn't dry up come the end of the year where you'd then have to find a new reaper to employ. "I *knew* there was a bloody demon helping that little turd!"

Duty lunged at me, a look of murder on her face. "You little bitch!" she shrieked. "How do you know this?"

I ducked again and fought against the urge to use Trishna to protect me as I moved out of her reach.

"Now, now Duty. If you keep acting like this she might cotton on that what you're doing with Wroth isn't exactly. . . allowed. And if it were to get out. . ." Mr Vontant warned, as he stepped between the enraged female demon and me.

Mr Vontant's threat must have got through to Duty who stopped, smoothed out her suit and tidied her hair.

"You mean Sid, Pleasure and all the rest don't know?" I gasped, a little tone of glee in my voice. "Now isn't *that* something useful to *deal* with."

"Stephanie. . ." Mr Vontant said wearily as he grabbed at Duty to hold her back as she lunged for me again.

"What?" I asked innocently, though knowing I must have my death wish look in my eye again. "It's not as if I said I was going to summon them up and tell them all about it."

Duty screamed and tried to lunge at me, and was promptly slapped so hard by Mr Vontant she fell backward and landed on her backside in a cloud of dust.

"That is enough!" he spat at her. He shot me a warning look that would have cracked a mirror. "Wroth's ownership is still a secret, to most. If it wasn't he'd have been stopped by now. And if Duty doesn't wish for others to become aware that she is responsible for that abomination she would be wise to hand his ownership over to me."

"Male demons cannot control a reaper," Duty replied, as she heaved herself to her feet. "They simply cannot horde or maintain the souls they bring to Hell."

Mr Vontant gave her a withering look. "That isn't the point, please remember I *don't* need the life force of a soul to get my powers. Besides, I do happen to own a few of you silly female demons — created in my early years of experimenting with the Darkness — perfectly capable of nurturing your rebel and his collection of souls. If I let him live."

"You would just give his ownership to *her*," she spat, giving me a filthy look.

"Oh come on! I'm having a hard enough time possessing myself and Trishna right now. Why in the hell would I want to own an ankou as well?" I mean to say, I doubted I could even own or control a reaper.

"If Stephanie wants to truly keep her 'walking in the Light' status, she could not take ownership of Wroth," Mr Vontant told her coldly.

"And as I *do* walk in the Light, and plan on staying there, I don't want him. Just Simon's soul."

"What if I make Wroth give you back just that soul, and we keep the rest a secret?" Duty asked, seeming to clutch at straws now.

"I want Wroth," Mr Vontant said bluntly. "He is an abomination, even among present company, and I weary of the imbalance he is bringing to you lesser demons."

"How dare you call me a lesser demon," Duty screamed, she obviously had a short fuse. "I am the wife of the Supreme Imperial Demon!"

There was a rustling noise and I had Trishna and I step back from the demons as Mr Vontant grew taller, more skeletal and daunting. All in all he really looked the scary demon he was.

"And I," he said in a strange, rasping voice, "was with Satan the day our Lord closed the doors to Heaven upon us and cast us into this pit." Even Duty cowered away from this new Mr Vontant who towered over us.

"I went with Light in my heart and the belief we were *helping* mankind. Then spent millennia here, snuffing that miserable Light out and churning it into the true Darkness you grew from. I took my anger and revenge out on the souls of those who had me banished. Corrupted them and bred fear and evil in their hearts. If it was not for my kind, you mere misguided thoughts and beliefs turned animate would not exist."

There was an uneasy silence as Mr Vontant slowly shrank back to the form I was used to. When he had returned to the small, dapper demon he normally appeared as he seemed to give me a nervous look and straightened his suit.

"Your husband can call himself whatever he likes," he told Duty, "But he will *never* be a match to the first demons."

Despite the total fear and dread Mr Vontant had just put me through — again — I almost felt sorry for him. Here he was, an angel of the Light cast out for attempting to help mankind. But best intentions had caused his expulsion. And as a way to survive, he had become the corrupted, evil being I now saw before me.

"Don't go getting the wrong idea Ms Anders," he warned me coldly. "Just because I was exiled from heaven, doesn't mean I've not enjoyed the freedom, the death and the wickedness I've been part of since starting my new life. There is a spark of Darkness in all Light walkers. It's only those of us brave enough to embrace it that truly get to *live*. Why be good when your only reward is to walk in the Light? When you quench that spark, the Darkness you end up with is just *so much better*. . ." Well that squashed any sympathy I had had and brought back the fear and dread.

"I want that ankou," Mr Vontant told Duty, who appeared to have composed herself better than I had.

"What is so damned important about having him now? You've obviously known about it for some time," Duty huffed.

"He has something she wants," Mr Vontant said, pointing at me coldly, "And I want her out of Hell and back topside where she can continue to keep her side of the deal and keep me out of any old wastrel's summoning circle."

Well, that explained a lot. I *knew* Mr Vontant was helping me for a reason. As much as my deal with him protecting me was null and void with us both in Hell, so was his with me protecting him up in the normal world. And I have to admit, he was a rather favourite demon to summon and earth. Even in the short time I'd known him I'd had to rescue him almost as often as he'd had to help me.

"As much as I can see the benefit of getting her out of Hell, that is not a good enough reason to take my prime reaper. I've had him for centuries now. Her removal from our world is simply not worth the deal."

"Well, there's always the possibility of me happening to mention your relationship with that particular ankou the next time I see Jamal. . ." I admit I am useless at such threats, but it was worth a try, right? Both demons gave me a withering look.

"I personally don't see *why* we should even let her leave," Duty said, eyeing me with disdain. "She should be punished for daring to enter our domain without permission. I feel Pleasure had the right idea to put her down here among the babies, a place for her to fester and turn into something far more appealing."

She wanted to keep me down in Hell until I turned into a demon? Yeah right, as if I was going to let that happen.

"But now I know a few things you'd rather the other demons *didn't* know, do you really feel leaving me here to my own devices is the best choice?" I asked, honestly amazed she felt she could even consider keeping me here.

"You're right," she conceded. "I may as well just kill you and be done with it. You've caused nothing but trouble since you got here, and now you think you can threaten me to make me let you leave." A large, sharp-looking knife appeared in Duty's hand.

"My good woman," Mr Vontant said in such an icy voice I shivered. "As I have already mentioned, you really don't have the power to decide what happens to Ms Anders. I have already decided to return her to the World of Light Above. And as I know she won't leave until she gets what she's come for, I want Wroth."

Duty froze, then turned slowly to face him, and the warning look in his eye.

"I know you think you're better than my kind —" she began.

"That is because I *am*," Mr Vontant cut in before she could finish.

"Just because you think you're better than my kind," she began again, "do you really think you can stop me if I want her dead? I could cut you down where you stand in such a way it would take you a very long time to heal." She actually hissed the last part.

"Really?" Mr Vontant said quietly. I shivered as the hysterical gibbering around us abruptly died away. And then Mr Vontant added in almost a whisper: "To me."

Suddenly I found we were surrounded by a dozen rather burly, well-muscled and oiled demons baring sabres. It was pretty obvious they were oiled because they weren't in the normal demon business suit and wore nothing more than a leather loin cloth and a threatening look on their faces. They turned to Mr Vontant, who nodded briefly at Duty, and these new demons immediately surrounded her, sabres at the ready.

"I must say I like your taste in hired goons." I had only meant to think that, but it had popped out. For demons, they really weren't that bad on the eye. Mr Vontant gave me a curt nod before turning back to a rather worried looking Duty.

"If you're just thinking of wishing yourself away to safety my dear, let me warn you that I will take it as a deal declined and will go public with the knowledge I have about Wroth."

Duty's face went a dark red and I couldn't tell if it was from embarrassment at being about to do that, or anger at Mr Vontant.

"I don't parlay well when surrounded by greasy men with sharp swords," Duty spat angrily.

"Of course you do, you're a demon. We like grease and sharp things. Is our parlay at an end?"

"Are you telling me the deal is I either give you my precious reaper and the source of endless souls for the last three hundred years, or you will tell the others I own him? How is that a deal?"

"Well," Mr Vontant replied calmly, "You can either hand over Wroth's ownership to me, and leave a free demon with an unblemished record. Or you can keep the ankou and be thrown upon the mercy of the other demons and hope they don't bring the Arbiters in to balance the level of souls you have been stealing."

There was that name again, the Arbiters. I *really* needed to find out who they were and why even the demons were scared of them.

"You bastard!" spat Duty, going an even deeper red. "There is *nothing* I get out of that deal!"

"You get to live," Mr Vontant replied coldly. "I admit my little army here can't immolate you while you're here, in Hell, but I'm pretty sure Stephanie could, if told the right tricks of the trade."

I suddenly felt as cold and shocked as Duty looked as we stared at each other over the shoulders of the goons. But I didn't want to know how to kill a demon. Well, it would always be a good thing to know, I admit *that*. But it's not as if it's something I wanted to know, or do, right now!

"Keep me out of your threats Mr Vontant," I warned him shakily. "Not that I don't mind any free info on demon slaying. . . but maybe not right now, okay?"

He quirked an eyebrow at me in response before turning back to Duty. She, however, couldn't take her eyes off me.

"You would kill a demon?" she asked, as if already resigned to her fate.

I shrugged and tried to add a bit of light hearted tone to my voice. "I'd have to take a look at the 'how to' first. I mean, I don't want to cock it up and become a vampire or anything stupid. But why not? I walk in the Light and protect souls. You like to take souls and use their power for evil. I can see one of us having to take the other out at some point."

Duty physically shuddered and then turned back to Mr Vontant. "You're right, she needs to be sent back up to the World of Light Above. If this is what she's like when still classified as one of the 'good guys', I shudder to think what will happen to Hell if we did turn her."

Hey! I was *right there* you know? And besides, as if I was about to turn my back on the Light and come play on their team.

"We deal then?" Mr Vontant asked, moving closer to her through his guards.

"With much protest and disgust, we deal," Duty growled and held out her right hand to Mr Vontant as her knife dissolved from her left.

With a nod from Mr Vontant his small army also disappeared and he shook Duty's hand. Weirdly, a rolled up piece of parchment appeared between them as they did this. That had never happened when I'd made a deal with a demon. . . then again I'd never made a deal in Hell where your beliefs could literally change the world.

"He is yours," Duty said, literally spitting the words at Mr Vontant as she released the scroll. "Do *not* let that human have him or I'll be the one going to the Arbiters." She shot me a spiteful look and vanished. The cavern we were in started up with its gibbering again and I felt a little worried Mr Vontant was about to disappear on me as well, leaving me with near zombie Trishna to face the cavern's inhabitants alone.

But surely, if Mr Vontant wanted me out of Hell and back up where I could save his sorry arse from the misguided folk of the Other World, he'd help. Right? Catching the studying look said demon was now giving me I got rather worried, if he helped me now. . . what would that mean I owed him in the future?

# Chapter 17

"I'LL have you know, I don't plan on doing any parlay without my High Priestess being present," I blurted out, as I watched Mr Vontant cheerfully tuck the scroll into his jacket's inner pocket.

"I do not parlay with mortals, Ms Anders," Mr Vontant sniffed, showing me exactly what he thought of my open cowardice. "Especially you. The outcomes of our deals are bad enough."

"Well then, what now?" I decided to try the blunt approach as the demon nursery was really starting to get to me, and there was always the chance Mr Vontant might actually decide to help me get out.

"Now, Ms Anders," Mr Vontant replied indicating his current mood toward me in how he addressed me, "We go find Wroth and get this whole stupid mess sorted out. You would think that if you're going to go around calling yourself the Supreme Imperial Demon you'd be able to deal with a simple mortal infestation. But no, obviously not."

"You mean you're going to help me?" I asked cautiously, not wanting to commit myself accidentally to any new deals.

"As much as it pains me, in a way, yes."

"For free?" Yes, give it to me straight, demon.

"That is yet to be decided, Ms Anders." Mr Vontant gave me his best withering look, actually making me shiver, before turning on his heels and walking away through the cavern. "Come on then, and don't forget your possessed pet."

Not that I had forgotten about Trishna, but with that I grabbed his hand again and followed Mr Vontant. The cavern soon turned back into the rocky corridors I preferred Hell to look like and with it, thankfully, the gibbering and howling faded and our underworld sojourn was silent once more.

"Seriously though, why are you helping me?" Well, silent except for me.

Mr Vontant merely glanced over his shoulder to where I was walking a few steps behind him and then looked forward again. I don't know if he was simply showing he didn't want to talk to me, or if he was still thinking of exactly how to word what it was he had to say.

"Do you know the difference between the sorts of demons found in Hell Ms Anders? Although there are a myriad of causes and reasons for our existence, the three dominant ones are corrupted souls, the anthropomorphic personification of pure evil and other powerful emotions that thrive in the Darkness, and the fallen angels."

As much as this didn't answer my question, Mr Vontant giving me free information on demons was never something to be sneezed at so I kept my mouth shut and hoped to learn something new. Though part of me did still wonder why it was he hadn't answered my question.

"Despite our numbers when Heaven first closed itself to us, and our inner Light was extinguished, not many of us survive today. Quite simply, too many of those who first set out could not give up their desire to stay in a place in the Light. They were the first to die."

Was it wrong of me to want to know how one killed an angel? Or should I only focus on how to kill the bad guys? Well, those who lived in the Darkness. It was a strain, but I managed to keep quiet for fear he would stop talking.

"Others of my species enjoyed the freedom and ability to leave the restraints of the Light behind and embrace parts of life that had before then been unattainable. I can assure you it is an exhilarating feeling, almost as good as your first possession, first virgin sacrifice in your honour, well. . . first of most of the important things."

I really didn't like the pleasure and satisfaction in Mr Vontant's eyes as he recalled these memories. It did, however, remind me that he was definitely a demon and not an angel anymore.

"All beings corrupted by the Darkness become demons." I stopped in my tracks, so startled I'd said it out loud. And that I'd said it as a statement of fact, rather than a question.

Mr Vontant turned and raised a quizzical eyebrow at me. "Those powerful enough to survive the process, yes." He gave me a knowing smile.

"I don't want to become a demon," I said, tears in my eyes. What the hell was wrong with me? Why did it feel like a great big door had just been opened in front of me and I was able to see the Light in the distance through it?

"Funnily enough, I don't want you to become a demon either," Mr Vontant replied, ignoring my tears as I scrubbed at my eyes with the back of my free hand. "I really don't think our worlds are quite ready for that sort of upheaval just yet."

"But the longer I stay in Hell, in the heart of the Darkness, the more inevitable it is." Again, a statement and not a question. It was all becoming clear to me and I wasn't liking the answers. Both Duty and Pleasure had been hinting at this all along. As if they all knew this is what happened to mortals when they came to Hell. Why on earth had I come down here? What the heck was I thinking that I could just stroll into Hell and not get affected? Oh, that's right, I had been asked to save someone's soul and, that being my job, I had just run into the fire I was now burning in.

"Precisely, Ms Anders."

I met Mr Vontant's studying look with one of my own. "I need to get out of Hell before it's too late," I said, now realising what he had been hinting at.

"Within four days of entering, or there is no 'out' until your trans-formation is completed."

"But I've hardly been here more than a few hours." I tried to sound confident with this statement but was worried by Mr Vontant's raised eyebrow.

"Really? Can you be so certain of this? Time isn't something that easy to keep track of in the Darkness unless you know how."

Sweet Goddess, how long *had* I been down here? I was guessing longer than I'd thought by the way Mr Vontant was studying me. I gripped Trishna's hand tighter for comfort. Oh why had I possessed him and turned him into this mindless puppet? I really needed him here right now, telling me what an idiot I was. Not that I really needed him to remind me of the mess I'd managed to get us into.

Subconsciously needing a hug I didn't object when this caused Trishna to tuck me into a comforting embrace.

"I really wish I knew how to make you *you* again," I sighed into his neck. "I need you back." No response, but seriously, what did I expect? This wasn't some fairytale where wishing for something long and hard enough would make it happen. I'd possessed Trishna, removed his own will and replaced it with my own. He wasn't about to suddenly snap out of it and return to normal. That would only happen when I released him. . . something I wasn't about to do in Hell where an unpossessed living soul seemed to shine like a beacon to every demon close by.

"I'm so sorry Trishna, I was an idiot to take my job so far," I whispered before noticing Mr Vontant watching us with a rather bemused looking expression on his face.

"When you're quite finished playing with yourself. . ." he commented icily, "If you want to get out of Hell, why don't we just go get you to the closest portal?"

I blinked a few times trying to focus on the red flag suddenly waving itself at me.

"Not without Simon's soul first," I told him, wondering if Mr Vontant had deliberately just tried to get me out without taking me to Wroth first. From the look of frustration that briefly flickered across his face, yeah he had.

"The longer you are here, the harder it will be for you to leave," he warned me, but we both knew I was onto him now. My sudden hands on hip stance said it all.

"Listen Mister," I warned him, letting my fear warm into anger so I could control it better. "I just watched you blackmail a literal bitch queen from hell into giving over her prized possession under the pretence it was to get me Simon's soul and get me out of here. If you don't now make that happen I'm so going to give her a summons and make sure that the saying 'hell hath no fury like a woman scorned' has a ring of truth to it."

"As you wish, Ms Anders," Mr Vontant said in such glacial tones that the air seemed to chill around us. Boy I'd annoyed him big time! He turned on his heel and we walked on in silence. So I'd been given a little titbit of info about Hell's main occupants to try and scare me into leaving without what I came for. There had to be something in that.

Before I could think it over much more Hell changed around us once more and we were walking down a long stone corridor bathed in a sickly green light. No, not my idea so something stronger than my will was in control here, as it had been in the demon nursery. That, or there were just parts of Hell that weren't belief based and simply always looked the way they did. There were heavy metal doors set along the corridor, which gave the sense of being in a prison or dungeon. But there was no wailing or pleas of help from behind the doors, and no barred windows to peak through to see what was within. I was about to ask what it was all about when we rounded a corner and came across a booth like desk that somehow reminded me of the information kiosks you get at the big shopping malls. The seat behind the desk, however, was empty.

My non-possessed companion addressed the empty chair. "You may address me as Mr Vontant and I am here to see my newly acquired reaper and do an audit on his collected souls before adding them to my own."

All right, so there was something there I couldn't see. I mean, I'm not *that* stupid.

"And can you make yourself visible for those of us unable to see you. . . please?" I added, hoping there really was someone there and Mr Vontant hadn't actually been talking into some sort of demon intercom.

The demon in question flashed me a look of disdain at the same time as a stereotypical reaper — skeleton, tattered robes, scythe leaning against his desk, the lot — came into view.

"What on earth have you been doing with your time down here?" snapped Mr Vontant, "I would have assumed learning how to see into the spirit world would be one of the first things your sidekick would have taught you. Or, once you possessed your sidekick, at least used his eyes and abilities to do so. Seeing Hell without it must have been pretty boring."

"Uh, don't you have to die to be able to see into the spirit world unaided?" I asked. Our conversation might have continued if the reaper hadn't cleared his throat — how I don't know when it was just bones — and Mr Vontant returned his attention to him.

"Papers?" rasped the skeleton, holding out its bone hand. "You want into one of these rooms, I have to ensure you've got the right papers."

Mr Vontant promptly pulled out the scroll he had been given by Duty and handed it over. I swear the reaper looked surprised as he recognised the details. . . but how I don't know as his face was just a skull.

"Wroth? How did you manage to wrangle that prize out of her high-ness' tight fisted grip?" he asked, amusement and wonder in the reaper's voice. He was also, obviously, not a fan of Duty's.

"There are just some things one doesn't discuss with the desk clerk," Mr Vontant replied crisply, straightening his suit. "Please just advise me of his location so he and I can get acquainted and I can do a stocktake of his existing unclaimed souls."

"As you like," the reaper rasped, now sounding a little huffy. He turned in his chair to open a large, old-style, card reference drawer and thumbed his way through the W's.

"Up the corridor to the left, fourth door on the right," he announced, before closing the drawer and turning back to us.

Mr Vontant thanked him but as we were about to leave the reaper spoke again.

"Before you go, Miss, here is something for you," he held a wooden stamp out toward me.

I was hesitant to take it, being bare handed and all since losing my gloves. But Mr Vontant watched on expectantly, as if knowing I would take it. Obviously, not being a demon or dead I needed the stamp to get me through this area? I gave in, hoped I wouldn't regret it and held out my hand. The stamp felt cold and then searing hot before he lifted it again. I looked down at the stinging spot to see a silver ouroboros snake symbol left on the back of my hand. It shimmered for a moment before dissolving, sending an icy shiver down my spine. I darted a glance at the reaper and a smug looking Mr Vontant before I realised something else. . . the corridor wasn't as empty as it had originally seemed. There were creatures *everywhere* — and not just reapers. There were dark-spirits and even some ghosts. Not a pretty sight. The doors around us now also had writing shimmering over them, obviously designating what was within. I blinked a few times as the world seemed to swim in this new vision before it started to fade to a more subtle level of existence.

"So rare we get the living down here, please accept the gift of spirit-sight as a welcome," the reaper said politely.

How kind. . . right?

"That way, we get the better experience of scaring the life out of you when the demons give us permission to show you what we do to the living when they turn up in Hell, uninvited," he said. Despite his face just being a skull, I could feel his anger and visibly shivered. Okay, so not so kind then.

"Classic," Mr Vontant chuckled as he walked away. "I've always enjoyed the humour of the reaper classes."

Yeah, I really didn't feel much like laughing myself as we continued down the new corridor, especially with all these, until recently nicely invisible, creatures glaring at me as I walked past. What? So a living person got into Hell and was now here to grab a soul before leaving. So what? If they didn't like it happening, they shouldn't make it so damned easy to do!

"What's with all the attitude?" I muttered to Mr Vontant as we arrived at the fourth door on the right. He raised a questioning eyebrow at me.

"Really, Ms Anders. She whose job it is to keep the Darkness at bay in the land of the Light and therefore keep those of us who live in Hell in our place, wants to know why she's now not that welcome in their natural habitat."

I scowled at the demon, he had a point but I wasn't about to let him know I could see it as easily as I could now see into the spirit world. The wicked gleam of amusement in his eye showed he knew all the same, as he turned back and rapped on the door in front of us.

There was a moment's pause, and then the door swung inwards slightly, indicating we could enter. Not that I really wanted to, now that I could see a lot more of Hell than I'd previously known about. But, not wanting Mr Vontant to give me the slip and fail to nab me Simon's soul, I held Trishna's hand a little harder and followed the demon inside.

I really didn't know what to expect. . . I mean, I'd seen some pretty nasty things in Hell so far that day but was sure there were worse things to come. My imagination could only stretch so far before the demonic reality of cruelty, horror and pain filled in the rest. What I did see though was a stone like cell not much bigger than my old office cubicle, back in my accounting days. There was a small wooden bed, table and chair; all had a rough, homemade look. A few books sat neatly stacked on the table and that was it. Except for a second door at the back. . . and Wroth standing in the centre of the room, arms crossed and looking more murderous than angry. Hopefully not entirely at me, I mean, it's not as if I was his new master or anything.

"I am your new owner," Mr Vontant announced, ignoring the aggression emanating off the reaper. "If you wish to continue this unnaturally extended life of yours, you will do as I say at all times. You may address me as Master or Sir. Do you understand?"

I could hear Wroth grinding his teeth from where I stood, and it caused me to take a few steps back. Not even my sarcasm could make me brave enough to be in here facing him solo.

"Yes, Sir," Wroth answered after a moment. Although said politely enough, his stance and anger did not change.

"Good," Mr Vontant replied continuing to ignore Wroth's attitude. "I want to see the stock and to know the totals and ensure the quality is worthy of adding to my own."

"You'll not find better souls than those of the half dead," Wroth said, an edge of anger creeping into his voice. Catching the look on his new master's face he added "Sir."

"That may be," Mr Vontant replied, "But I would much rather see them with my own eyes than take a reaper's word for it. Pride can often blind the collector so."

I was pretty sure Wroth wanted to rip Mr Vontant to pieces at that point, but I could also feel a new sensation in the room over his anger. . . power. An iron rod strength of will so solid it was getting almost oppressive. And it was coming from the demon before me. As scary and powerful as Mr Vontant had always seemed, this was new to me and rather unsettling given the number of times I'd smart mouthed him. Perhaps I should start to show him a little more respect. Then, remembering he was a demon, I thought — screw that.

"Show me," Mr Vontant said again in tones so icy the room seemed to chill. With a last look of pure hatred, now mostly aimed at me, Wroth stepped over to the other door and swung it open. More of the sickly green light poured out into the room. And through this eerie light I could make out what looked like a long corridor pantry. It stretched away into the darkness, stone passage down the middle and floor to ceiling wooden shelves down both sides. It was then with a chill that made me break out in huge goosebumps that I realised the shelves were stacked full of heads. They were translucent and of varying shades, no doubt matching the aura colours of their owners. Glowing heads, staring blankly into the distance. Thousands upon thousands of them. I personally wanted to let out a scream and only managed to bite it back when Mr Vontant let out a low whistle of appreciation at the sight before us. Yes, okay, I *know* they were really souls I was looking at, but still, there was a heck of a lot of them. I tried to ignore the smug look from Wroth as Mr Vontant approached the room before us. It was then that the chittering and knocking sounds started. And, from the darkened other end of the corridor, came long black shadows. . . oh what fresh hell was this?

# Chapter 18

THERE were a dozen or so of the shadow-like creatures. There really was no better way to describe them as they looked like the long, thin shadows one casts in the setting sun. Except, unlike true shadows, they had visible eyes and mouths. Both stark white against the skeletal creatures' darker skin. I then realised I'd seen something like them before. The creature attached to Simon when I'd first met him in the park. It hadn't looked so shadowy up in the real world, but otherwise they were identical.

"Call your Impa Shilup to heel," Mr Vontant told Wroth disdainfully.

Of course, they were the creatures that possessed people and took over their bodies, allowing Wroth to remove their souls. *These* were the true Birdfolk. My sarcasm wanted me to ask why exactly these strange stick figure people needed to dress their victims all in feathers but I bit my tongue, not wanting to bring attention back to myself at this time.

With a nod from Wroth the dark-spirits stopped their approach and just chittered near the darkness they had come from.

"How many souls?" Mr Vontant asked as he stepped into the corridor pantry to assess the heads closest to the door.

"Forty-two thousand, give or take," Wroth replied proudly.

I was shocked. There were *that* many Impa Shilup wandering around in my world? The Priestess of Isis had told me there were hundreds of Birdfolk and I'd thought that was bad enough. But *thousands?* That was just wrong. Those poor people, even if they had been ones who walked in Darkness, did they really deserve this fate?

"Don't look so disgusted," Wroth grunted, seeing my reaction. "They are souls given freely. The bodies in question get to live far longer than they would have originally and get to enjoy a life of wealth, happiness and prosperity."

"Yeah, but without their own soul or free will being attached to enjoy it," I snapped back. How could he get away with twisting the words so much? I know they were important in both our worlds, but it just seemed *wrong* he could get away with it. Oh, hang on, person of Darkness — wrong was what they did. How could I have forgotten?

"They should have questioned us on that part. Nowhere in the deal has anyone ever specified that they wanted their soul attached to their bodies while it enjoyed this new life."

"Surely that assumption should be obvious?" I said, trying to not grind my own teeth, or Trishna's for that matter.

"They assumed wrong," Wroth said bluntly.

"That's right Stephanie," Mr Vontant smiled. "What is that old saying about how one should never assume?"

"The day humans realise how important it is to read the fine print and state in full exactly what they want out of a deal, rather than blindly go with the golden carrot waved in front of them due to their own greed is the day I go out of business," Wroth said.

Oh to be able to smack him a good one right now, and then live to tell the tale. "You disgust me," was all I said, though I can assure you I was thinking far worse from the Trishna school of potty-mouthed insults.

"I am merely the go between," Wroth replied with a shrug. "It is the Impa Shilup that make the deal, I merely get to take the soul once it becomes surplus to need after the possession is complete. It is humanity that is to blame for allowing it to happen. I would not have lived all these centuries longer than my designated time if it wasn't for the human greedy desire for power and possession. It leads them into temptation and deals with the Darkness."

"It is still wrong." So I was speaking in single syllable sentences, I was *that* angry.

"But that is what we who walk in the Darkness *do*, Stephanie," Mr Vontant pointed out from deeper in the room as he continued to count his newly acquired souls. "We feed off the greed and cruelty of mankind, occasionally bending it to our will to ensure we get the most out of it. How is it any different to those of you who think we should all be fair, polite and *kind* to each other?"

He said 'kind' as if he was spitting a bad taste out of his mouth. I refused to see the logic in what he said, I mean screw that! Darkness bad, Light good and good is far better than bad any day of the week. How could they expect me to agree with them?

"How often can I expect these souls to fully become mine?" Mr Vontant then went on to address Wroth, ignoring me as I stood there fuming.

"The Impa Shilup grant the bodies a further one hundred years of health, wealth and good living from the time of the deal," Wroth replied, "Though that doesn't include accidental deaths, murder or other similar fatalities. It's not as if they're immortal."

"But surely your dark-spirit friends would take better care of them?" Mr Vontant continued, eyeing the shadowy creatures again. Wroth shrugged before replying.

"The Impa Shilup may possess the body and replace the soul, but there is still a remnant of the original person left in the link and sometimes that remnant gets control and has too good a time... there is only so much the spirits can do to keep them safe. It's not as if they get harmed in the death. They simply return here to await a new body."

The callously casual way they were discussing living people, as if they were no more than a new set of clothes was sickening. I just wanted to get out of there. And to think, if I spent a few more hours in Hell, this sort of thing might start to appear okay to me.

"How about you both just stick to the job at hand? Get me Simon's soul and get me out of here."

"His soul is mine and belongs here," Wroth said angrily.

"Yes well, you're technically mine. . . so what's yours is mine," Mr Vontant cut in before I could reply. "And, besides, I was present when you told Ms Anders here she was welcome to come to Hell and take it back. . . so you've left yourself open to her claim as here, she is."

Wroth glared at me and ground his teeth some more. I glared back and went as far as my arms folded in front of me stance to show I wasn't about to be intimidated again.

"Well, that all seems in order," Mr Vontant said straightening his suit as he re-joined us. He snapped his fingers and a young, female demon appeared next to him. Her head was bowed so I couldn't make out her features, and she was dressed in almost a peasant style get up.

"Wroth, this is Obey. She will be the female demon in charge of you and your souls to enhance my will. Obey, ensure he behaves and don't go getting ideas above your station."

The young demon nodded quickly then glanced around the room at Wroth, Trishna and myself, shooting us all an evil glare. As cowed as she may be by the presence of her master, I definitely didn't ever want to come across her alone as I was sure I'd not walk away in one piece.

Wroth looked confused for a moment.

"You're not giving me over to *her?*" he pointed to me as he spoke.

"Oh please, I just want *one* soul. Simon's! Not a whole damned army of feather clad freaks!" I snapped back before Mr Vontant could reply. I know I was starting to sound like a broken record, but how hard was it for them to understand? I came to Hell to get Simon's soul and then I was going to go home, figure out how to pop it back inside him and send the stupid sod on his way. I wasn't here to steal anyone or anything else, to become a demon, or to embrace the damned Darkness and take over from Sid. Not a big deal people!

"As if I would be so stupid," Mr Vontant muttered coldly. "She is not mine to control, nor a demon."

But from the look he gave me I almost felt as if he wished I was both. Not a nice thought boys and girls.

"And are you certain she can be trusted with the soul of another?" Wroth asked, although I was pretty sure he was just playing for time now.

"Look at her!" Mr Vontant snapped. "She has possessed that man, possessed herself and still just wants to take that soul back to its original body and go on walking in the Light."

He sounded disgusted, as if I was wasting a good opportunity or something. What can I say? We who walk in the Light do the right thing, even when it's not the thing that we actually want to do. Otherwise I wouldn't be where I currently was having this stupid conversation.

Wroth watched me for a moment longer and then turned to Mr Vontant. The reaper was powerless against the demon and knew he had to do his bidding.

"As you will." He left the room to return a short time later with Simon's head-shaped soul. Not a pretty sight, but then again even when it was attached to the rest of him I'd never thought Simon that good-looking. Giving me a death stare Wroth handed the soul over to Obey. Obviously there was a protocol to be followed. As she took it, Mr Vontant produced a hessian sack out of nowhere and commanded she place the soul inside. The female demon did so and stepped back, head still bowed toward Mr Vontant.

"Here," Mr Vontant said, and handed the sack over to me. "Simon's soul."

It all felt rather anticlimactic. Not that I wanted to say anything in case he changed his mind. I'd come to Hell, *been* through Hell — figuratively as well as literally — and all for this soul. And this was it? No great thunderclap, no trumpets or sparkly lights. Just a soul in a sack handed over and we were done. Why did I almost feel let down by that? He could have at least done it with a flourish, rather than just shove the bag at me.

"And now to get you out of here and ensure you never come back."

"Actually, I think I can take it from here," Sid announced, suddenly appearing from out of nowhere. Then, before anyone could stop him, he placed his hand upon my shoulder and I found myself no longer in Wroth's cell, but somewhere totally different. Well, I had been feeling the whole situation had been lacking something. Next time I would just be thankful for the dull moments in my life.

***

What was it with caverns and the underworld? I mean, I hadn't really thought Hell actually *was* underground until all this started. But here I was, in yet another large, dark cavern. Just me and my hessian sack, a large candle burning in the centre of the lit area in which I stood and Sid lounging on a throne nearby. No Duty and Pleasure, no Wroth or Obey, no Mr Vontant and, worst of all, no Trishna.

"Could you make an appointment before simply snatching me like that?" I snapped at Sid, refusing to show how worried I was by the latest development. "I mean, I was *right* in the middle of something important."

"Talk to me like that again and I'll show you just exactly what it feels like to have the skin ripped from your back and force-fed to yourself," Sid said, eyeing me over with a look of entertained delight. "I've let you play among my children long enough, and now that you have what you came here for, I felt it was time we finally got around to chatting. It was obvious I wasn't going to get any sense out of you before then."

I did my best not to boggle at him. He *allowed* me to get kidnapped and brow beaten by Duty and Pleasure? He was aware of their power play with me as the new pawn? He was okay with Mr Vontant now owning Wroth and Wroth's forty-two thousand souls? Yeah, I didn't think so. Sid may indeed have been able to flay me alive, but he was still all show and no blow when it came to being in control of *everything* that had been going on down here. The look I gave him indicated as much and he snarled before leaping from his chair and stalking toward me.

"You dare to doubt me in my own domain?" he demanded, looming over me in the flickering candle light. Well, when he put it like that —

"You knew your wife had a rogue ankou who has been accumulating thousands of souls for centuries, keeping them charged to their full potential by keeping their bodies still alive but possessed by dark-spirits? And you let her *give* his ownership away?" I replied, attempting to stay calm, even if I couldn't quite prevent myself from sounding a little catty. "You can see how I'm finding that hard to believe. I mean, losing forty-two thousand souls just so I could have one before I talked to you. . . I'm finding that a little hard to swallow."

Sid blinked at me a few times and it was obvious he wasn't as on top of the whole situation as he thought he had been. Oh boy was Duty in for some trouble. This caused a small smirk on my face and another snarl from Sid as he then lunged at me, swiping at my face with a clenched fist. I ducked and stepped back, suddenly remembering all my combat training with Smith. As I straightened I longed for my sword and suddenly there it was in my hand. As Sid approached again I lifted it, pointing it at his neck with a mean look of warning in my eye.

"Just back off," I warned him. "I'm still new to the whole 'how to kill a demon and not become a vampire' deal so it might take me a few swings to get it right."

Rather than wishing up his own sword and facing me in some sort of clichéd Dark versus Light battle, Sid simply growled again and did indeed back away. He slunk to his throne and threw himself into it once more.

"I will not waste my time fighting you Ms Anders," he announced as I slowly lowered my sword, still watching him carefully. "I need you intact for what I have planned for you."

"And what exactly would that be?" And why had I asked that, given that I really didn't want to know.

"I plan on keeping you here, watching you go through the transformation and then taking the end result as mine. I am done with Duty and Pleasure, backstabbers the both of them. You will become my wife and your powers will ensure I never lose my place as Supreme Imperial Demon." He was actually gloating as he said this, as if it was the only true option and seriously about to happen.

"Yeah no, think again Sid," I replied as casually as I could. "I don't belong to anyone, demons included. And I can assure you I'd kill myself before letting any changes take place." I walked in the *Light* damn it, and I was *not* going to turn into a demon simply on someone's whim.

"How dare you!" Duty spat appearing from the darkness outside of the candle's light. Obviously she had been listening and wasn't too pleased with her husband's plans.

"Silence!" roared Sid, leaping from his throne and storming toward her. "You kneel before me you traitorous hussy."

Really? He's the Supreme Imperial Demon and that was the worst insult he could come up with? Even I could have done something better.

"Traitorous?" snapped Duty, refusing to kowtow for a single moment. "I have supported you for *centuries* with the finest souls I could accumulate. And this is how you repay me?"

"You also lost your best reaper simply to save face," Sid snarled back. "That was not the plan."

"But he would have told *everyone*. The Arbiters would have been called. . . the balance of Darkness and Light could have been shifted out of our favour."

Duty was now almost pleading for her husband to understand her reasoning. He had obviously been aware of Duty's sneaky dealings with Wroth and had turned a blind eye. Heck, he got all his power from the souls owned by his women. Why wouldn't a slimy little sod ignore the underhanded tactics used to get them?

"You were only worthy to be my wife due to the purity of his souls from their linked life force, without it you are a nothing," Sid said dismissively and turned his back on her. I was expecting a scream of rage and for Duty to launch herself upon his back to beat some sense into him. So was a tad disappointed when this didn't actually happen. She just stared after him with torment in her eyes as he stalked back toward me. I raised my sword again as a warning and he stopped a good distance out of my lunging zone.

"Don't look at me like that," I warned him. The look of lust he was giving me was more than a little disquieting. "I don't want you either. And as much as I don't plan on staying down here and turning into your kind, if it happens I can assure you I won't be choosing to be any male demon's tool."

"She can choose me instead, allowing the women to finally rule," Pleasure said, appearing out of nowhere and sidling up to stand by me. For the love of Isis would demons stop popping into existence around me!

"Fat chance sweetheart," I snapped at her. "If you're all going to keep me down here, which you're not, I'm going alone. I don't need any help."

"I'm afraid you're wrong there," Mr Vontant said, as he too — amidst a groan from me — came into existence in the cavern. Shortly thereafter followed by Timpsk and Benjamin, carrying Trishna between them.

"What is this? The grand central station of hell?" I snapped in exasperation. Despite the size of the cavern, I was starting to feel claustrophobic due to the numbers of demons now around me. Still, at least I'd got Trishna back. "And why do you have these two carrying Trishna? Did we really need them? Don't you have flunkies for that sort of heavy lifting?" Oh the things I focus on when in such weird situations.

"Our Supreme *Leader* over there made it a flunky free zone," Mr Vontant replied, pure disdain dripping from his voice. "You can't imagine the deal I had to make to get them to help, despite owning Benjamin's powers right now."

Yeah, he was right. I probably didn't want to know.

"And what did you mean I can't go it alone if you guys turn me into a demon?" I went on at Mr Vontant, ignoring all other demons around me, much to their fury.

"Firstly, we would not turn you into a demon Ms Anders, that would just happen by you being trapped here in Hell. Secondly, to be a demon of calibre enough to live how we do, you need flunkies. Yes you will no doubt be a rather powerful creature come the end of the transformation, but only demons backed by other demons have the ability to move between the worlds. It is the only way out of Hell."

I blinked at Mr Vontant a few times, was he telling me what I thought he was telling me?

"A demon can only leave Hell with the support of other demons?" I asked him cautiously, wondering just how thick everyone else was to not get what Mr Vontant was saying.

"Not just demons. Any powerful being in Hell can only leave with the willing help of at least thirteen demons."

"That is enough!" snarled Sid, the not-so-quick-on-the-uptake Demon Lord. I was starting to see why some of the other demon breeds didn't think so highly of him.

"Stay with me, let me protect you as you change and I will bring the men flocking to your feet to serve you when you arise," Pleasure butted in, trying to take me by the arm that didn't have a sword on the end of it. I shook her off at the same time as Sid lunged at her calling her all manner of names under the sun. Obviously he did know how to insult a woman, just didn't do so to Duty. That tweed clad demon stood on the outskirts of the group, watching me with hatred in her eyes. Turning her eyes from me she stalked over to where Pleasure and Sid were screaming abuse at each other and slapped the other female demon hard across the face, knocking her to the ground.

"Remember your place. He is still our husband and master," she snapped at Pleasure. Then giving Sid a withering look, she grabbed Pleasure by the hair and began to drag her out of the circle of light.

"I will deal with you two later," Sid growled in the way of thanks before dismissing the females. They blinked out and I was down to just four demons. . . and Trishna.

"My answer is still no," I stated to no one in particular. I pointed my sword in warning at Sid once more. "I have Simon's soul, I have Trishna. . . mostly, and I now want out of Hell. And you would really *not* like me as a demon. If you think I'm a pain in the arse to deal with now, just wait until I'm really grumpy. And I can assure you, allowing me to turn into a demon is *really* going to get me grumpy."

"As much as it pains me to agree with you Stephanie, I sadly do. Hell is no place for the likes of you and the sooner we get you out of here, the better," Mr Vontant said wearily. He glared at Sid, who obviously wanted to protest. It was starting to become clear that despite Sid being in charge of Hell, there were still some demons that he couldn't control. I also got the feeling that the fallen angels must have been outnumbered by those he *did* control, for the schmuck to have any power at all.

"Even if that's what you think, she still needs twelve other demons to back her before a portal will open and she can leave."

"I'm sure that can easily be arranged," Mr Vontant sniffed as if he'd just been asked to do something quite simple rather than convince a dozen demons to help me leave Hell. I shuddered to think of what it was going to cost me.

"Then there is the —" Sid started to say before Mr Vontant cut him off mid-sentence.

"Yes, I am perfectly aware of what opening a portal for a living soul entails."

The sly look that spread across Sid's face worried me a little. "And here I was thinking you were such an innocent these days," Sid quipped, rubbing his hands together. "Fine, your plan amuses me enough to let you try. But you need to bring twelve willing demons before me within the hour before I will allow any souls to leave my domain."

"Before you do what!?" I'd been silent long enough and obviously felt it was time to put my foot in it and remind them all I was there. "I don't need *your* permission before I do any damned thing, let alone leave Hell." The sigh and weary look from Mr Vontant made me worry a little.

"I shall leave you to discuss that *minor* point while I go arrange the others," he said, then he, Timpsk and Benjamin disappeared. Of all the downright rotten things he could do! Walk out on me when there was clearly a rather important thing I'd missed about leaving Hell. Why on earth had I thought this would be easy? Why had I thought getting into Hell was the hard bit and the rest would be a cake walk?

"Alone at last," winked Sid as he went back to lounging on his throne while ogling me. I scowled at him and made a point of sticking my sword in the dirt and walking over and taking Trishna by the hand and leading him from the shadows into the strongest area of candle light, and my sword.

"Cut the crap and just tell me why you're so happy to know something I don't," I snapped. "Obviously there's something about me leaving Hell that you need to give the green light to."

"That's right my dear Stephanie, the words themselves are written into the very walls of Hell. He who reigns supreme controls the souls." Sid gave me another smile.

This was new. "I thought all the demons had their own collections of souls they drew power from."

"Ah, but they do. Think of me more as the head of a prison. . . Although I may not be in charge, and therefore draw my power from, all the souls here, I do have the final say as to when they may leave my domain — whether to move to the Light, be reborn, or shift to that timeless void of a waiting room known as purgatory. It means I can take any demon's power away from them in an instant, simply by releasing their hold on their accumulated soul's power." He smiled again, "What can I say? It's good to be the boss!"

"And that's why even Mr Vontant has to, mostly, obey you?" I asked, pretty sure he was just giving me the basics as I didn't think it would really be that easy for him to remove another demon's powers by releasing their souls. Mr Vontant, I would have thought, would show him far more respect if this was the case.

"Oh, I may be glossing over it a bit to ensure your small, feminine brain can understand," Sid said with a shrug. "But that is the gist of it. He who rules Hell has the final say on which souls stay and which ones go. And I'm not totally convinced about releasing you yet, as I'm still interested in seeing what sort of demon you would turn into."

That didn't fill me with hope. No wonder it had been so easy to get Simon's soul from Wroth and Mr Vontant. Sid could still turn around and declare they were in the right and I in the wrong and keep it. That thought was so frustrating it almost brought me to tears, but I held it in as I didn't want Sid to know it was all finally starting to get to me. I'd come so far, seen a lot of stuff I'd rather I hadn't, and risked my own life and place in the Light to do my stinking job as Protector of Souls and free stupid Simon. Hang on. . . I was a Protector of Souls. . .

"Surely being blessed by Isis as a Protector of Souls means I'm here on a job and therefore don't come under your jurisdiction?" Hey, it was a shot in the dark but hopefully a good one. Or so I had thought until Sid starting laughing at me.

"Oh please! Those titles only work when you're in a place those of the Light can come and protect you. You're a soul, you're in Hell, you're *mine*," he replied, biting the last words out and leaning toward me menacingly.

Startled I dropped Trishna's hand, grabbed my sword and took two steps toward him, weapon outstretched to his neck. I'd moved fast enough to have caught him off guard and took my own turn to menace.

"Then let me put it this way, Sid," I hissed. "I don't want to be in Hell anymore and I want out. *Now*. With Trishna intact, as he is now, and Simon's soul too as the one package and deal. No messing me about, no mishearing me and finding a loophole. Just out! Because if you try to keep me here and I turn into a demon I'm so going to kick your arse off that throne, take over and then set *all* the souls free!" A sudden wash of anger rippled through me and caused my arm to shake a little but I gritted my teeth against it and glared at him. Instead of being afraid, Sid just smiled.

"It's happening already," he announced quietly. "That was the Darkness you just felt my dear Stephanie. Hold on to it, it feels good the stronger it gets."

The shaking returned to my arm, this time as much from fear as the new sensation burbling just below the surface and I found I had to take a step back and drop my sword arm. I felt sick. Even worse than when I controlled Trishna and became his will. Was this really happening to me? Or was Sid trying to stir me up a bit?

"It's been a slow nagging sensation in the back of your mind since you've been here," Sid went on, ignoring my sudden discomfort. "You've been doubting your right to be in the Light. Being surrounded by the Darkness as you are, it slowly seeps into you, down to your very soul where it will coil and nest to grow stronger."

"I. . . I walk in the Light," I stammered, trying to ignore the sensation now moving through me. I hadn't really felt it that strongly until he had mentioned it and now I *really* felt sick to my stomach. My cynical side kept me upright at that moment, scoffing at the very idea of the Darkness being able to touch me. It was probably just another type of thrall, right?

"I must say you are fighting it well," Sid continued. "I guess stubborn stupidity has shielded you enough, but you've now been in the afterlife and Hell for so long that even those are crumbling away."

"*IwalkintheLight!*" I said in a rush, turning it into a mental chant that seemed to make this new, horrible sensation ebb away. My hands stopped shaking and I felt more in control again.

"Oh you *are* good!" Sid said, with an appreciative clap and a look of glee on his face. "But I fear you're already tainted my dear. And even if I do let you out, that taint is going to stay with you and there won't be many in the Light who will want you to walk with them."

I ignored this jibe and kept chanting. It wasn't true, Roxanna would always stand by me, right? I was blessed by Isis. Could Goddesses unbless you?

"You don't believe me do you?" sneered Sid, leaning forward on his throne as I cowered slightly away.

I tried to focus on the Light and the good in the world. Darkness, demons, dark-spirits — all bad. I wasn't one of them, I walked in the Light.

"Here, let me show you," Sid said, getting up from his throne and moving over to a large shrouded shape that had appeared as he rose. He tugged the shroud away to reveal a large antique looking mirror. It sat in a dark frame of the most grotesque looking figures doing all sorts of nasty things to each other. As much as I didn't want to look into the mirror at myself, I found I couldn't focus on that horrific frame either.

"This is a mirror of truth," Sid said. "We often use it as a way to show our clients what their lives will be like if they accept a deal and sign over their souls to us. It's a classic prop but still works so well." As he spoke his words drew my eyes up from staring at my feet to look at him. Anything but look at that mirror.

"Look into it Stephanie," Sid urged, and this time I could feel his old thrall at work and my eyes nearly itched out of their sockets to stare at the silver backed glass before me.

"It will show you as you are, and as you will be," he whispered. Finally my will couldn't fight him any longer and my eyes snapped to my own reflection within the glass. I looked as bad as expected. My bruises still prominent, my clothes dirty and ruffled, and my blouse ripped and showing more cleavage than I'd anticipated. Damn Jamal! I wasn't pretty, I never thought I was, but right now I looked like I'd really had a bad day. Part of me almost snickered at the thought that I looked like I'd been through hell as I sure had. . . but was still there. I then noticed the blue marks on my forehead and found myself leaning in closer and realising I was looking at the backward reflection of 'ANI' that I'd daubed there when possessing myself. The blue was a lot darker than I remembered it to be when my aura had given the ghost Trishna his colour.

"That's right Stephanie, your soul has been in Hell too long and the Darkness has put a lovely tarnish to it. Just think of what it must be doing to your poor friend there?" Sid smiled, obviously enjoying breaking this to me. Oh Isis, poor Trishna! I had thought I was keeping him safe by possessing him to stop the demons from taking him. . . but of course *keeping* him here would mean he was changing too. What had I done? How many negative restitution points had I racked up?

"And this, my dear, is what you will become. . ." continued Sid. "That tarnished soul will change you forever." And as he spoke my reflection morphed and, although I was still looking at myself, I was also seeing someone I barely recognised. Dressed in black leather from boots to pants to gloves, the lot. My hair, which I always kept long and a mop of messy curls was gone. Yes there was hair there, but it was so closely cropped to my head that it couldn't even twist into those annoying Shirley Temple curls that made me keep it so long and messy. My face was gaunt and my expression grim. I admit I'm not someone who smiles a lot, but this face looked like it had forgotten how to. She, as I couldn't believe it was me, rested my sword upon her shoulder while her other gloved hand rested on her hip so that her overall stance was one of menacing attitude. Upon her forehead the reverse 'ANI' now glowed an almost midnight blue hue, darker again than how it appeared on my own skin.

"Whether I let you out or not, the damage is done," Sid smiled, "It's not exactly a flattering look, but I can assure you not many would want to bother you. Especially not those who truly walk in the Light."

"That is not me," I spat, trying to tear my eyes away from this stranger in my own skin.

"Oh, but it is, and it gets better!" Sid smiled. "As this is you again as time passes and that taint matures."

The reflected figure changed again. It was still a semblance of me, but colder, harder and darker. This version stood there passively in a pant suit, similar to the ones I saw the smarter demons wear, my hair was still short, but looked neater somehow. And although the expression was still grim, there was a deeper emotion showing. One of controlled power. Whoever she was, she'd obviously found her place in the worlds and planned on keeping it. Where I had expected to see 'ANI' in an almost blue/black shade, the forehead was bare. What did that mean? And did I care as I refused to believe this, and the last, image were truly me. They were just some hellish parlour trick Sid was playing with.

"My, don't you look so professional and demon like?" Sid smiled. "I simply can't wait to see you like this. . . I hope this future isn't too far off."

He winked at me and I found myself having to control the rush of anger with my mental mantra. *IwalkintheLight. IwalkintheLight. IwalkintheLight.*

"They are not me," I finally gritted out. "I'm better than that, stronger than that. I walk in the Light."

"If you say so," Sid scoffed, as he threw the cloth back over the mirror, breaking the spell.

As he moved back to his throne Mr Vontant reappeared. "Oh not the damned mirror!" he chided, as if it meant nothing to him, but the way he then straightened his suit showed me it was a bigger deal than he was making it out to be.

"Just a parlour trick," I muttered. I turned my back on the shrouded glass and shot Sid a filthy look. "I'm better than that and I'm going to prove it."

"Good to know," Mr Vontant sniffed, although I'd not addressed him directly. Turning to Sid he cleared his throat.

"I have the numbers. Shall I bring them in now or will you simply take my word for it?" he asked, removing a slip of paper from his suit coat's inner pocket. Even from where I was standing I could see things written in a red brown colour. Oh don't tell me they signed something in their own blood? Well, if it had to be blood, let it have been their own and not someone else's actually.

I think we both know the answer to that," Sid told Mr Vontant coldly.

Wise move, I thought, demons dealing with demons would be stupid to just take each other's word for it. I then realised, a little too late, that meant I was about to be surrounded by demons. I moved closer to Trishna as this happened and looked around me, trying to look more unafraid than I felt.

I recognised some of the demons from previous encounters. Timpsk and Benjamin were both back. Tathal was even there, and here I was thinking he didn't want anything more to do with me. What surprised me most was that Jamal made up the twelve demons now standing before Sid, Mr Vontant made thirteen.

"I'm sure you'll understand if I don't introduce them all," Mr Vontant said.

Words were important, names especially so. As a result I'd been pretty certain the only way I'd get their names out of them was by asking. . . or worse.

"Meh, if I need to address any of the ones I don't know I'm sure I'll find something appropriate to call them," I said, trying to seem tougher than I was. This didn't impress anyone and caused a scowl from a few of them. What? Like I was meant to be all nice and friendly to them just because they were here to help me get out of Hell. . . well, actually, that could possibly be about the only time I should be friendly to a bunch of demons.

"And before we do anything with these guys," I went on as a sudden thought struck me, "I would just like to point out that I'm actually yet to agree to any of this and would like to know up front what it's going to cost me."

Mr Vontant gave me a withering look while Sid snorted his amusement.

"Funny," Sid said, "As I seem to remember you holding a sword to my throat just now and stating in clear and precise terms you wanted out of Hell. If that's not agreeing to this in advance, I don't know what is."

Damn stupid 'words and important' nonsense. I bit back saying that, and then some, out loud and simply scowled. More at myself than the demons around me. The few that thought this all worth a grin soon copped the scowl too.

"Damned if you do and damned if you don't Stephanie," Mr Vontant pointed out in mock sympathy, but at least I could tell he wasn't too annoyed with me by how he addressed me.

"This is Hell, damning is what we do best!" Sid laughed from his throne. It seemed he expected the other demons to join in with his mirth and when he was just met by shuffling feet and stony silence he took his own turn to scowl around the room. "Just remember who has control over your souls," he hissed, causing a ripple of unease through the demons.

I could understand the unease as some of them were fairly young looking and, from the state of their suits, not that powerful yet. Yes, it was a sad but true thing that you could indeed judge a demon by the clothes he wore. I'd learned this early in my new career and it had helped me know exactly how much I needed to offer in a deal. A lesser demon meant fewer options before we shook hands.

"So I suppose it's deal time then?" I asked the group in general and they all turned to Mr Vontant with raised eyebrows.

"Not exactly Stephanie," the neat little demon replied, stepping closer to me. "For a living person to leave Hell under our current leadership, you must have the backing of thirteen demons before requesting permission from our. . . Supreme master." These last two words were said with a world weary distaste.

"And to convince thirteen demons to back me. . . what have I already agreed to do for them?" I asked cautiously, really wondering if my subscription to the Light was about to be cancelled. The smirk from Jamal wasn't helping right now either.

"A simple trade," Mr Vontant said. "We help you leave our world, you help us into and out of yours. All our powers intact. One year per demon, but we can all call upon you within those thirteen years for this favour."

Uh, that didn't sound too bad. . . did it?

"So similar to what you and I have going on?" I asked, still wary. Mr Vontant's face coloured for a moment before he said in a tightly clipped tone:

"It is not polite to discuss one's deals in front of other demons Ms Anders."

Uh-oh, touched a nerve there. . . must remember that one. I wasn't about to apologise though.

"Oh so now you tell me what a good thing I've done not blogging about all our deals then," I quipped sarcastically. Pointing out to Mr Vontant that if he didn't want me to act in such ways, a little forewarning would be good. I know he wasn't usually one to give information out for free, but sometimes it was in his best interest if he did. Feeling the weight of over a dozen demons now scowling at me I changed tack a little.

"So my choices are to stay in Hell and turn myself and Trishna into demons and have Simon lose his soul forever. . . or help thirteen demons come and go from my world for the next decade or so?" saying it out loud really didn't help make it sound any better.

"Only the strongest become demons. The rest just become torment-ed souls," Sid replied, pointing at Trishna. "And I can assure you I don't think he has what it takes to don one of our smart suits. But otherwise, that's pretty much it."

Sweet Isis, why had I thought coming to Hell would be easy? What would happen to me and my friendship with the priestesses if I were to let demons loose on the world? Again.

"How often must I help bring you into my world?" I asked Mr Vontant in a less bitchy, more subdued tone.

"We must each be allowed up once a lunar month, but can stay for no longer than the day in which we are summoned," he replied curtly, ignoring my look of defeat. "And you must be there to release us any time we are summoned to your region of the world against our permis-sion too," he added. I shrugged, this was pretty much the deal I had going with him already. I just hoped they weren't all popular in the summoning circles around my city otherwise I'd never get any other work done.

"I would like to add something, if I may," Sid smiled from his throne. "Something these gentlemen may *forget* to mention is that you may also summon them to help you as needed. And any summoning of that nature would count toward your monthly quota of bringing them into your world." This brought a lot of muttered swearing from the group of demons before me. I flashed a surprised look at Sid and then back to the group.

"You mean, if I call on them to go clean out my attic or something, *that* counts for me summoning them into my world for the month? And if it takes them all day to clean up, they then pop back down here before they get a chance to go off and get up to no good?" Mr Vontant's look of utter disgust as he glared at Sid over my shoulder said it all. What a loophole!

"What?" asked Sid innocently to the neat little demon. "I said I would consider letting her go if you gathered the right amount of demons. I didn't say I wouldn't point out how much control she could then have over you when it came to summoning you to her world."

"You utter bastard," Jamal snapped from the crowd.

Sid shot him a look and then shrugged. "The duty of being the baddest of the bad down here does sometimes mean I have to shoot my own kind in the foot. Such is life when you decide to turn from me and side with another for your own power and glory."

I let the insults fly between them all as I thought over what was said. So if I wanted to get out of Hell here and now with Trishna and Simon's soul, I had to gain this demon posse. If I didn't leave. . . no, that wasn't an option. I *was* leaving and that was that. I already didn't like what this hell taint on my soul felt like and didn't want to stick around and see what else would happen.

So, right, I have a demon posse and they're going to get me out of Hell. In return, for the next thirteen years, I had to let them into my world once a month as well as free them from my world anytime they needed it. . . within the city limits of course! But I could summon them to — urgh — do my bidding and it counted toward them being summoned for the month. So if I found them something to do that would keep them busy for a whole day, *that* would let them be in my world, but not off doing all the terrible things to it that they obviously had planned. I could live with that. And surely Roxanna and the others would understand and see that I was simply trying to do my best in a bad situation and get my job done.

It was about then that I'd noticed how quiet it had become and looked up from where I had been thinking while drawing flowers in the cavern's floor with the tip of my sword.

"You done?" I asked, as if it was I who had been waiting for them to pay attention, and not the other way around.

"It seems she's finally come to a decision," Sid said. "And?"

"And we do it. We leave Hell as previously described by me with the help of thirteen demons. And in return I promise to summon them to my world once a lunar month. . . but can't promise they'll have much free time when they get there. I also promise to free them from my region of the world whenever they are summoned and held there against their will." I ran through what I'd just said, it sounded like I've covered everything. Though I was up against fourteen demons having just heard it and I was sure a few of them were cluey enough to try and find some sort of loophole there to squeeze through. I then waited impatiently for their answers, gritting my teeth against another wave of nausea caused by the Darkness trying to get to me. Fat chance there — I walked in the Light damn it!

"I don't agree to that," Jamal snapped. "She can't just summon us and then keep us from having some fun. That isn't what I signed up for!"

"But, sadly, you have indeed already signed and so the deal is done," Sid smirked. He held out his hand and Mr Vontant handed over his list. Sid read over it and did a head count. As if ensuring all the demons on the list were indeed now here in the room with us.

"And now for you my dear Stephanie," Sid said. "I will need your blood on this contract too before I can agree to let you out. He showed me the piece of paper with unintelligible writing scrawled all over it. So much for me using it to learn all their names!

"I don't have a pen," I replied, deciding to play dumb.

"You won't need one," Sid said with a touch of menace in his voice. "Just a thumb and a pin. . . and oh looky here. I happen to have a pin." He reached into his coat pocket and withdrew something that looked more like a rather large meat skewer than any pin I'd ever seen. I didn't really want to do this. I didn't want to willingly give my blood to anyone, particularly not in Hell and surrounded by a lot of demons. But as another wave of Darkness twisted through me I jabbed my sword back into the ground and held out my thumb to Sid. My last thought, before the sharp pain of my digit being sliced silenced me, was that I hoped the damned 'pin' was sterilised. Who knew what you could catch from a dirty dagger in Hell?

The minor pain had caused me to take a sharp intake of breath. I then physically shuddered at the echoed intakes of breath from the demons around me as they scented my blood. What a time to remember how wild it made even the calm sorts like Mr Vontant.

Without spilling a drop I turned my thumb over and pressed it down onto the piece of paper still being offered to me. There, deal done. I was now the *proud* owner of thirteen demons for a good whack of time. Not something I could see me putting on my Other World CV any time soon.

While Sid, disgustingly, blew on my blood print to make it dry, I ripped a piece of my already ruined blouse off the bottom and wrapped it around my thumb to stop the bleeding and ensure no extra blood was left behind. Then, as an afterthought as Sid went to tuck his 'pin' away, I snatched it and wiped it clean on the rest of my blouse.

"My blood, and I say who gets it and for what," I snapped, handing the implement back. I caught a look of approval and amusement in Mr Vontant's eye, just briefly, as I turned back to other demons.

"So, do we have a name? Doesn't every group need a name or something? Maybe Stephanie and her ragtag gang of goons?" I asked, letting my sarcasm autopilot kick in while the rest of my brain was still catching up with what I'd done.

"Don't even *think* about such things," a rather disgruntled Jamal said. Obviously still smarting over the fact this new deal didn't give him all the freedom in my world he had hoped for. I shrugged and turned my attention to Mr Vontant.

"So now what?" I asked him, I mean they had my blood, they had me agree to it all and I had Trishna and Simon's soul. Surely I got to leave now!

"Now that I have the numbers and the signatures, do you grant permission for Ms Anders, the man she has possessed and the extra soul she carries to leave Hell?" Mr Vontant asked of Sid.

"That man being Trishna and that spare soul being Simon's," I added quickly to cover all bases. They both gave me a look as if to say they were fully aware they knew who we were talking about. But I wasn't about to glaze over such important details in case they were still up to something.

Sid then eyed me over in mock sadness.

"It seems like such a shame to let her go," he pouted. "But the way she is going, it won't be too long before I have her back. And having her here without her sidekick would be more preferable. So, yes. I grant permission for the living bodies and souls of Stephanie Muriel Anders and Trishna Duhkha, along with the disembodied soul of Simon Gordon Herberts to leave my domain and travel back to the Above World of Light."

Hallelujah! I almost did a victory dance knowing I had the ability to now leave. There was just something in the mannerisms of those around me that told me it wasn't all quite that simple and there was still a big step to take. I looked around and found myself moving into impatient hands on hips stance.

"Okay, it's obvious there is yet another big *but* about to happen so out with it." I gave as many of them the squinty-eye as I could without seeming too foolish.

"No more buts. We just need to take up our positions to open the portal," Mr Vontant replied a little too quickly and lightly for my comfort. There was a *big* but still to come. The second shoe to still drop, so to speak.

"Oh do let me tell her!" exclaimed Sid with one of his nasty little grins.

Mr Vontant pursed his lips in annoyance, but I could clearly tell he didn't really want to have to tell me himself. "Very well," he finally answered and Sid clapped his hands with glee.

"When a living soul is to leave Hell for the Above World of Light, they not only need thirteen demons to position themselves around them in a circle to focus enough energy to create the portal. They need the blood of a human spilled in the centre to actually open it."

Yeah, no, that didn't sound good. Though it could have been worse, they could have needed a virgin sacrifice or something, right?

"Exactly how much blood?" I asked, not entirely happy to be asking but needing to know. We'd come so far and I wasn't about to let a few drops of my own blood stop me now. "I'm sure if I squeeze my thumb a bit I can still get something out of it." The look of delight on Sid's face didn't fill me with hope.

"Merely a litre, in your local measurements," Sid replied. "Though it does need to be from an *unpossessed* soul."

I was starting to see why he was so happy about it all, and why Mr Vontant had been so quiet.

"But I don't think I know *how* to unpossess myself," I said warily.

"I know!" grinned Sid with delight. "Can you guess what that means? Or would you like some flashcards?"

I blinked at him a few times and then shot a look at Mr Vontant, who gave a tiny jerk of his head toward Trishna.

"You want me to release Trishna from my soul and will so you can spill a lot of his blood?"

"Technically it would need to be *you* who do the blood spilling for you to then be able to leave," Mr Vontant replied calmly, seeming unrepentant to have put me into this position. How could he? Why didn't he tell me about this before I went through all of that? I mean, I was pretty sure Trishna was going to be pissed with me as it was when I released him. To then point out I needed to stick him and take a lot of his blood? Dear Isis, I would be paying back his restitution for my next four life times at this rate.

"You have no other choice," Sid murmured in my ear. How he had moved from the throne to by my side so quickly I don't know. I shrugged him away and gave Mr Vontant a belligerent look. Then realised I had no right to be so annoyed or disappointed in what he had done. It's not as if he was my friend or anything, he was a demon. They all were and they would all murder their nearest and dearest to ensure they got what they wanted.

"I hate you." I said these three simple words with such emotion and power that Mr Vontant took a step back and straightened his suit. Good to know even those words had power against one so evil. I then realised something and looked to Sid with a mixture of concern and relief.

"But I don't have any purified water left. I can't release Trishna without it."

"Mr Vontant?" Sid enquired innocently over my shoulder to the neat little demon. "You've often been known to keep little souvenirs of your trips up top. Got anything to help us out?"

The fallen angel tried to look surprised and offended for a moment, then sighed and reached inside his jacket pocket once more. How big was it in there? He pulled out a vial containing a clear substance that appeared to be purified water and handed it over. I looked at the corked top and recognised the symbol of Isis branded into the soft wood.

"This is one of mine!" I snapped, offended more than I could say. I then started thinking about the other little things I'd misplaced from time to time and gave him my best squinty-look.

"I don't suppose my favourite hairclip from my mother is in that pocket of yours?" I asked coldly. Mr Vontant simply shrugged.

"Nowhere in our deal did it say I wasn't to take a few keepsakes when I visited," he replied in a rather aloof manner.

Damn I really hated him right now. Why did I have to keep reminding myself he wasn't a friend, he was a demon. I wanted to call him all manner of bad words right then but I realised it would be a waste of breath. He was what he was and did what demons do best — bad things that pissed us good guys off.

"Are we going to get this portal open today or what?" Jamal then asked rather rudely. "Some of us have other things we could be doing you know."

It took a lot of effort to *not* turn and flip him the bird. Instead I focused on the two main demons of concern right now.

"Okay, so I have the purified water and I can now release Trishna from my soul and will. How about you all back up a bit and give me some space to do it." When no one moved I added, "There will be left over water you know? Nowhere in our deal did it say I wasn't allowed to possess any of you."

"I like her more and more every moment," Sid grinned, although he did move back to his throne to let me get on with it. The other demons, on Mr Vontant's instruction, then took up places around me and Trishna in a circle and I was left in the middle feeling scared and worried about what was going to happen next. It was time to free Trishna from my soul and will, and then hope like hell I didn't have to chase him about the cavern to spill a litre of his blood. Boy, my day was just getting better and better.

# Chapter 19

I UNCORKED the vial with my teeth, as usual, and dipped my finger into it. Then, wiping said finger across Trishna's forehead I said the words:

"Trishna, I release you from my soul and will and return you to yourself. You were possessed to protect you from demons and not to do my bidding so I hope you forgive me."

He was reeling away from me and swearing in his best style before I'd even finished asking for forgiveness.

"You stupid, stupid cow!" Trishna barked at me as he turned back to glare at me. It was then he noticed all the demons and he swivelled in a small circle to take them all in.

"This doesn't look good," he added suddenly sober. "What have you gone and done now you frizz haired bimbo?" If he kept this up, cutting him wouldn't be such a bad thing. I then clenched my teeth against that thought as I was pretty sure it was more from the Darkness curling within me than my normal sarcastic self that it had sprung from.

"I'm trying to get us out of Hell before being here turns me into a demon." It wasn't exactly what I had planned to say, but it seemed to sum it up. "And the only way out is to now own a demon posse to create a portal back to our world."

"You don't *own* us," Jamal butted in from where he stood. "We're simply working on a deal only basis."

"Whatever," I snapped, keeping my eyes on Trishna the whole time. I was still trying to say the biggest part of news. The blood part.

"And you felt you not only needed to possess me against my will, but now you go and unpossess me to do what? Stand in the middle of a circle of demons and watch you become a demon yourself?" Okay, so there seemed to be a mild amount of hysteria in his voice. Would slapping him to calm him be a good thing or just add to my negative restitution points? I tucked the purified water away in my cleavage, shoved the sack containing Simon's soul under my arm and grabbed hold of Trishna's face in both my hands.

"Just. Listen." I said. "I'm really sorry we're in Hell. I'm truly sorry I possessed you, but it meant I kept you safe and not a demon chew toy. I have Simon's soul and I need to get out of here as I can *feel* the Darkness within me, turning me."

Trishna blinked at me for a few moments, seeming to take it all in. "You can't become a demon," he blurted. "I don't want you becoming a demon."

"The feeling is mutual," I replied with a cracked smile. "But I can assure you you're not going to like what I need to do next. Though I will add I'm so very sorry for it too." At this Trishna smacked my hands away and backed off. "How do I know you're not already a demon and just toying with me?"

"Oh please, if she was a demon do you think she would be apologising?" Sid asked in a bored tone from his throne. Trishna looked to him for the first time and his confused look deepened.

"Who's he?" he asked, and I had to bite back the frustration of having to fill him in at a time like this.

"He's the ruler of Hell," I replied quickly, "But that doesn't matter. What matters is you listen to me as you *really* need to hear what I have to say about how we get out."

"Actually, I *do* matter," Sid snapped. "She hasn't even left and yet she's forgotten me already."

He gestured theatrically, which copped a scowl from me. This was not the time. I needed out, and I needed out *now!* Something wasn't feeling so good inside me since unpossessing Trishna, and even my anger and cynical thoughts were taking on a nasty edge I didn't like.

"Trishna!" I snapped, bringing his attention back to me. "To open a portal back to our world I need to spill the blood of an unpossessed human. And, sadly, I can't unpossess myself."

"You shouldn't have even been able to possess yourself in the first place," Sid quipped, obviously the sort who always had to be the centre of attention.

I clenched my teeth and ignored Sid, watching Trishna the whole time as my words sunk in.

"You need to bleed me?" he exclaimed, and then let loose another tirade of paint peeling curses.

"If it helps, I'd rather have done it while you were still possessed and apologised about it afterwards," I answered, though then wondered how that was meant to have been as comforting as I'd hoped it would be.

"Gee, ta," Trishna snapped back. "Of all the stupid arse things you do Stephanie, you're in some really deep shit right now and I can't see you being able to dig your way out."

If he was trying to anger me so that I wouldn't be so upset at cutting him, he was doing a good job. As he stood there fuming at me, waiting for my next banal reply I plucked my sword from the ground and wiped it off on my pants.

"There is no way in hell you're using that on me," Trishna warned me, backing away as far as the circle of demons would allow. "Possessing a human was bad enough Stephanie, but spilling someone's blood against their will to complete a spell — that's dark magic. There's absolutely no way back from that."

My determination faltered. I needed to get out of Hell. I needed to stop becoming a demon. But more than that, I needed to be accepted to walk in the Light when I got home as I *really* needed that Light right now.

"I have to do this," I said, my voice breaking with anguish as I did so. "I walk in the Light Trishna, you need to believe me. But right now this is my only way home and I need to leave here and return to that Light before all is lost."

"You stick me and all *is* lost," Trishna warned. "Especially between you and me. Don't you realise what you've already done to me? You may as well have cursed me and left me to die."

This hurt me more than a punch in the stomach would have. And I found myself backing away from Trishna, dropping my sword and willing it away as I did so.

"She will become a demon if you don't let her go," Mr Vontant said, having been silent and watching until that moment. "And your soul will be her first victim and power source."

I looked toward the demon in question and found myself blinking back tears. "I won't take Trishna's soul," I stammered, trying to get a hold on my swirling emotions. I didn't need all this girly crying right now.

"You won't be able to help yourself. You have a taste for it now you've possessed him. And in your early stages of metamorphosis you won't be able to stop yourself as you will need his power to complete the change."

"I would rather kill myself," I answered, in a firmer tone now. "I will not harm Trishna more than I have to to get out. I *won't* become a demon."

"I think the lady doth protest too much," Sid grinned, butting in once more. "You keep saying that my dear Stephanie, but you're still here! You've got your demons, you've got my permission to leave and you have your unpossessed human blood sacrifice. And yet you linger on. Why, if you don't want to become a demon?"

I clenched my hands at this. It was not true, I was doing everything I could to get out right now and I really would give up my life to stop myself from killing Trishna. But then what? If we were both dead what would happen? Our souls would still be in Hell and for any demon to then claim.

"I don't want to do this anymore," I finally whimpered as I crumbled into a heap in the dirt. I had been so stupid thinking I could come to Hell, rescue Simon's soul and be home in time for breakfast. So very, very stupid to think all this Other World stuff was so easy. So what if I killed a vampire and saved my sister's soul last year? That didn't suddenly make me an expert in all this rubbish so why had I felt it had and I could just swan about in Hell and get what I want without such negative consequences? Maybe I really did want to become a demon and I'd just been denying it all? Maybe I'd wanted to come to Hell to check it all out and see how well I fit in? I mean, everyone kept telling me I wasn't suited for the Light, so maybe it really was the Darkness that I belonged in?

It was during these ever depressing and desperate thoughts that I suddenly felt the tingling pinprick sensation upon my shoulder that had comforted me so many times before. I looked up to see Trishna crouching down next to me, ignoring all the impatient looking demons around us.

"You really are just trying to save us, aren't you?" he asked in awe. "You are willing to sacrifice *so much* simply to get us home. I can feel it in my mind, in the scars of your possession, that you're just trying to do the right thing."

"I was the dumbarse who got us into this mess, so it's my job to ensure we get out again too," I replied, stifling a sob. "I'm sorry."

"I know you are." Trishna replied, sending another encouraging tingle through me. He didn't look happy, I could tell he really wished there was another way out but could tell now there wasn't. So it surprised me when he then held out his spare hand and a small, plain knife appeared in it.

"It's not much, but it's the best I can think up. This way I'm giving you permission, so hopefully you won't be in as much trouble when we get back," he said, frowning in concentration at the effort of producing the knife from nothing.

He helped me to my feet as I took the knife from him, stunned he was letting me do this. I didn't *want* do to this, but I didn't want to stay either. Then, as I watched, Trishna shrugged out of his jacket and tugged his shirt off, before putting the jacket back on.

"What are you doing?" I asked as he started ripping his shirt up.

"Bandages for when you're done," he answered logically. "As there is barely anything left of your top I felt I should sacrifice some of my own clothing."

Thoughtful to the last. I nodded dumbly as he finished ripping his shirt into strips. He then nodded too and held out his wrist.

"I only need a litre," I said to him, as if that suddenly made it all okay.

Trishna just nodded, his expression tight.

"I would rather you were taking none, as I still don't like doing this. But as it's the only way safely home. . ."

I could tell he was bracing himself for the pain and what was to follow. But was still willing to let me go ahead, knowing it was the only way to escape.

"You owe me big time woman!" he then muttered as my shaking hand descended upon his wrist and the knife dug in.

The cavern around us was silent, which was a scary concept in itself, seeing it still contained fourteen demons. Were they all holding their breaths as the knife entered Trishna? Thankfully, when the blood came, it was more a heavy trickle than a spurt, meaning I'd not hit an artery. It was a small comfort as I watched Trishna wince in pain while, around us, the demons started sniffing the air as if picking up the finest of scents.

As Trishna's blood started to drip upon the earthen floor, the circle of demons started chanting and the ground began to tremble.

"Oh! One more thing I forgot till now," Sid suddenly called.

From his grin I knew he'd waited until the last moment before mentioning it.

"No soul can leave Hell and be of any use up in your world unless it leaves protected by living form."

"I have it in a sack under my arm, it's protected," I replied angrily, knowing full well this wasn't going to be enough. But now that Trishna's blood was flowing, did I have much time for anything else?

"How droll my dear Stephanie. No, it needs to be *within* a body to leave and be returned to its own body."

Damn.

"Being a woman, that should be simple enough for you to do. Women have built in parts of their body for souls to live for up to nine months."

I stared long and hard at Sid at this point, realising how much I hated him too. Was he unaware of how hurtful he had just been? Or was he being deliberately callous to remind me how much of a jerk he really was?

"Not all women," I said, biting back my own inner Darkness to stop it mingling with the newer, stronger Darkness infesting my body. "Some of us don't even have a choice as to when we lose it."

Sid looked truly shocked and almost even saddened for a moment as what I said sunk in. I wasn't about to go into the nitty gritty of it all, but there was a reason I'd never truly become a mother again.

"Then you will need to wear him under your skin," he announced as if it was a simple task. "Come here, it will be my parting gift until we meet again."

I looked at him doubtfully and then at Trishna kneeling in a slowly increasing pool of his own blood. When the ground had started to vibrate along with the other demons' chanting I had guessed we didn't have long. What was I to do? I needed Simon's soul to be returned to Simon or all of this would have been a huge waste of my time.

"Do it," Trishna hissed, obviously thinking along the same lines. So I stepped toward Sid on his throne and, when he held out his hand, passed him the hessian sack containing Simon's soul. He removed the head-shaped soul and examined it closely.

"This is the type of guy you like?" he asked with surprise. "I'll look more like this for you when I get you back."

"He is *nothing* to me," I growled. "Just some dumb idiot I stupidly decided to try and save as a Protector of Souls." I raised my eyes to Sid's face. "And I am *never* coming back here."

"If you say so," Sid replied with a shrug. "Lean forward," he said, and made to put Simon's soul onto my head as if crowning me.

I hesitated for a moment but, as the ground trembled harder, I did as I was asked and felt a horribly familiar sensation of pinpricks as another's soul touched my own. Rather than wearing him as a hat I felt his soul go into my own head and felt rather dizzy and ill for a moment until the implantation was done. I then blinked a few times and realised I could *feel* Simon's soul now within me. It was an uncomfortable feeling, but not actually as bad as you would have thought it should be. I could feel his thoughts bumping about inside my head, but it was almost as if I was watching a sleepwalker fumble about in the dark. No consciousness was there. . . just thought. On top of that I could sometimes actually feel him moving about within me as my body was superimposed over his soul. The skin on my arms or face would feel suddenly stretched for a moment as if his form was trying to turn one way and I actually turned the other. It was weird to describe, but it really felt as if Simon was wearing me like a too tightly fitted suit. And still this didn't freak me out. I didn't feel possessed, simply occupied by a benign creature. There was no fear within all these weird sensations.

And no, it wasn't like pregnancy. I had held my baby within me long enough to feel her being, feel her moving about in the ever shrinking space. What I felt now was like that. . . simply all over my body. Yes, I was now going to need a few, large glasses of red wine when this was all over to wipe the sensation from my mind.

I returned to Trishna's side as the earth moved again and looked at the amount he had lost to make this happen.

"How will I know when you have enough of his blood?" I suddenly asked Sid, turning my attention to him one last time.

"You won't," smiled the reigning demon. "Toodles!" he waved as the ground shook further and we were suddenly falling into blackness beneath it.

*\*\*\**

I wanted to scream, wanted to release my fear in one loud, lung emptying banshee cry. . . but I couldn't. Instead I found myself fumbling for

Trishna who was falling with me and trying to tie off his wound to stop himself from losing more blood. Surely I should have been more afraid of the sudden impact that usually came with a fall, but I wasn't. With the uncomfortable feel of Simon beneath my skin, and the long and fast fall through complete blackness, all I could think of was finding Trishna and stopping the blood flow. How I could even *see* him in this total lack of light I don't know, but he was the only thing I could see and he looked pale and drawn, but still managed a smile when I finally managed to tie up the wound enough to stop the flow.

I wanted to speak, but holding a conversation in such a situation seemed wrong. I should have been screaming and flailing my arms around in fear and concern, instead I had ensured he was okay and now we just stared at each other in the whistling Darkness. I even found my body start to relax and almost embrace the falling sensation, like I had done many times when it had happened in my sleep. No doubt a weird response, as I'd heard most people freaked at the falling sensation in their dreams, but it had always comforted me. I don't know why.

As the seemingly unending fall continued I finally found my voice.

"Why are you so calm?" I asked Trishna as I thought he at least should have had a few choice curses to give.

"This feels like dying," he replied giving me an odd look. "I've done it enough times to know. Though I do usually fall through existence alone."

Yeah, no, not the most comforting thing he could have said. I found it made me lose my ability to speak again but not my feeling of relaxation. So I often dreamed I was dying and falling through existence and that made me feel good? Man I was even more screwed up than I'd originally thought.

It was then that I noticed the blackness around us was fading into grey. And the longer we fell the lighter our surroundings became.

"Not long now," Trishna said to me, reaching out and taking my hand. He seemed to have accepted that we were dying. I, however, did not. The demons had said they were returning us to our own world alive and well. Or had I just taken what they'd said to mean that? I tried to go over again all that had been said to ensure I'd not missed something important but I could no longer think straight. As the nothing world around us continued to lighten, my relaxed mood had ebbed and it felt as if it was being dragged from me the further I fell into the light. At first it had just been yet another uncomfortable sensation — I was having so many at the time — but it was now becoming more of a burning pain. Trishna noticed me wince and squeezed my hand to comfort me.

"That's the Darkness being ripped from you as we move into the Light," he explained. "And knowing the amount you undoubtedly absorbed while being both of our soul and will, it's probably going to sting a little."

That was the understatement of the year. The further we fell into the light the stronger the burning sensation on my skin become. It got to the point I needed to release Trishna's hand before I hurt him by squeezing it too hard. As our surroundings continued to lighten it felt as if my whole body was being burned by the Light. I found myself having to squeeze my eyes closed as it seared into me, burning the Darkness away and setting my entire being on fire. Oh dear Isis! And I had thought a drug free birth had been painful.

As the pain grew, the Light around us grew even brighter. So bright I could see it inside my head despite how tightly my eyes were shut. It hurt, it really, *really* hurt and I felt as if I was about to literally burst into flames I was burning up so much. That was when I remembered how to scream. The searing pain got so bad that I could feel the scream coming even before I opened my mouth. And that was the last thing I remembered before the Light seemed to burn me into pieces, the screaming letting the pain, anguish and Darkness leave me. I was nothing but a blinding white flame of agony and scream. There was no more.

# Chapter 20

"YOUR new password will need to be between eight and twelve characters in length, and be a mixture of uppercase and lowercase letters, numbers and symbols. No English words can be used."

Not exactly the first words I had expected to hear after burning to death in the searing white Light. But there you have it. As my brain woke further I was aware of the chatter of other voices too, with a background noise of the clatter of keys on a keyboard. I cracked an eyelid, when I realised I still had one and it hadn't been burned away, and looked around me. I was lying in a crumpled heap on the floor of . . . an office cubicle? Pink carpeted partition walls studded with thumb tacks, hard plastic floor mat, dodgy wheeled chair, desk and all. What fresh hell was this?

I found myself having to shift position as Simon's soul within me stretched me the wrong way. That was when I bumped into Trishna next to me and he groaned. The voice in the next cubicle, struggling to be polite while obviously helping some computer illiterate soul change their password, paused. The head that belonged to the voice appeared above the partition and quirked an eyebrow at me. Yeah, I would have too if I'd just noticed two dishevelled folk lying on the floor of the empty cubicle next to me. Her head disappeared again and, as I struggled into a sitting position that suited myself and Simon, I could hear her hurriedly finishing her phone conversation. This was going to be good.

"Hello" beamed the head as it reappeared over the top of the partition. I was pleased to see it was actually connected to a body when she stood up and leaned on the flimsy wall to get a better look. As soon as she did that I heard other voices go mute and, craning my neck, noticed more heads — also attached to bodies — appearing from the other partition walls. In my office days, this had been known as prairie dogging. Why I remembered that just then I have no idea.

"Uh, hi," I replied, keeping my attention on the first woman in the hopes it would stop me scowling at my other audience. I may have been out of it a little, but she seemed pretty human to me. She wasn't even wearing feathers, so not a Wroth follower.

"You must be the new managers. We go through them so often. Every time the 'regime' changes and they come up with new, and improved instructions on how to flog the dead horse. At the moment we seem to be getting a new one each week."

Phones were ringing and being ignored as more heads appeared. And that was one of my pet peeves, ringing phones being ignored.

"Isn't someone going to answer those phones?" I asked, starting to haul myself to my feet. Had they not *noticed* our tatty appearance and that we were on the floor? If not, possibly why they were going through so many managers?

"Definitely our new manager," sniffed one of the other heads as it disappeared. I could hear them answering the phone as if whoever it was had just rudely interrupted them.

"This is a help desk," I blurted out, finally getting it all to fit into place as I leaned heavily on the desk.

"Please, as if we're ever helpful," grinned the initial woman. "We're an ITC Service Desk, so that way, by only offering a service, we're allowed to forego actually being of any help."

Oh, sarcasm! I was beginning to like her. In my old job in the 'normal world' I had been seconded to audit a help desk. I had been stuck there for six months trying to sort it all out.

"ITC Service Desk. . . portal leading from Hell. Things are starting to make so much more sense," Trishna muttered from the floor as he sat up.

He had a point though. I mean, I wasn't saying all help desks and service desks were portals from hell. . . but I was no longer ruling out the possibility that all portals from hell could be found in them either.

"Oh my God, he's bleeding!" cried one of the other prairie dogging staff, ignoring her phone and taking gleeful delight in the situation. Though whether it was simply from having an excuse to avoid having to answer her phone, or whether she liked the sight of blood, I really couldn't tell. We had just left Hell and who knows what those who lurk around its portal were like? I gave her a filthy look she blatantly ignored, too busy taking in as much of the situation as she could.

"As you're obviously not about to actually do the job you're paid for, how about you go find us the first-aid kit," I said in as polite a tone as I could manage. I really had hated my time on the help desk. There had been three types of people there. Those who truly were helpful and did their best to actually get the job done right the first time — so that they didn't have to fix it again later. Those who thought they were an expert on everything and were useless instead — they kept the first type in work. The third type were the ones who were just there to be paid while trying to do as little work as possible. Again, the first type of person seemed to carry them as well, too polite to outwardly tell them off and too busy actually doing all the work to be noticed and therefore elevated to positions they deserved. Yeah, I know which group I'd been in. It had still taken me six months to escape back to the boring world of accounts payable. If it hadn't been for my strong willed sarcasm I probably would have left handcuffed and up for mass murder of incompetents. The more I thought of it the more I wondered *how* I'd not connected it with hell and portals before.

"Tough day, huh?" asked the first woman again as I helped Trishna to his feet and checked on my mid-fall bandaging.

"I wouldn't know where to start," I replied as politely as I could as Simon's soul twisted within me again. I really needed to get us out of here and back home. Though figuring out where *here* was would be a good start.

"I found it!" came chirpy Miss 'let me find ways not to work' as she appeared in the entrance to our cubicle and thrust a small first-aid kit into my hands. "While I'm on my feet I could, you know, make you some tea or coffee? Or maybe run down the road and grab you some morning tea?"

The woman we'd first met sighed at this and sank back down into her cubicle as soon as her own phone started ringing. How was I not surprised she was one of the first type of staff I'd mentioned?

"How about you just get back to your desk and actually answer the phone and do the job you're paid for." I know I'd said this already, but maybe if I kept saying it she actually *would*. I mean, this cubicle was a tight enough fit with just me and Trishna in it.

"Oh well, I suppose so," the time waster smiled and, I swear, walked as slowly as possible back to her own cubicle just in case I suddenly changed my mind. I, however, ignored her and opened the first-aid kit to grab some disinfectant, gauze and bandages. I mean, who knew what nasties there were in Hell? I wanted to ensure Trishna's wound was cleaned and dressed as soon as possible. And wound tending had been something I'd learned since becoming a Protector of Souls.

"So you lost the boss fight, huh?" the first woman appeared leaning on her side of the partition again. "We don't normally get two sent back at once so it must have been a doozy."

I had to stop in the middle of bandaging Trishna's wrist to blink at her a few times.

"Excuse me?" I asked as I really wasn't too sure she and I were on the same wave length. I mean, this looked and felt like a normal part of the world, no Other Worldly sensations at all. I glanced around to see who else was paying attention and if this was a joke.

"Ignore them, they just pretend to work here," the woman smiled. "But I cottoned on early that I wasn't actually insane and we actually *were* getting managers from Hell — literally — turning up to run and ruin us for a while before being transferred into more suitable roles in upper management."

"And why would they be coming from Hell?" I was trying to choose my words carefully, ignoring that knowing look in her intelligent eyes. This lady was sharp and obviously didn't miss a trick.

"What else would you do with a bunch of ego maniacs who thought they were good enough at being so nasty, greedy and evil they deserved to rule Hell? I mean, they don't enter here, but those who didn't quite make the cut get dumped here all the time. It's amazing how frequent it's getting."

I blinked a few more times. Maybe I really had died and this was just a different area of Hell I'd not yet visited.

"Uh. . ." It was all I could manage. I mean, she seemed so normal, this *all* seemed so normal. So why was she talking about the Other World as if it too was normal.

"Relax," she said smiling warmly at me. "You're not insane and, as I said, neither am I. My uncle is a layman for the Temple Thoth and although I'm not a card carrying Other Worlder, I know the basics."

Now that started to make some sense. Especially as Thoth was one of the Arbiters of good and evil and all that. Of course someone from there would know about portals to Hell.

"You mean people actually *willingly* go to Hell to try and become demons?" Not exactly the most important question in the world but it was the one that sprung to mind.

"Yeah, you can't feel so special now can you?" teased Trishna, "Thinking you were the first living person in centuries who wanted to go to Hell."

"But I did it to save a soul, not to take over the place," I snapped back. He was obviously feeling better if he could pick on me.

It was now our new friends turn to blink a few times.

"You're not beaten contestants then?" she asked curiously. "You mean folk still do that whole going to Hell to rescue their loved ones thing? I thought that was ancient Greek history."

"He wasn't, and never will be, a loved one." I frowned, feeling Simon's soul stirring again and really *really* wanting to get him removed. "It's just my job to rescue and protect souls as asked for by Isis."

"Ah, Isis. Now that would explain it," our new friend smiled, as her phone began to ring again. She started to move to answer it and I stopped her with a hand on her shoulder.

"I don't suppose you could tell me where we are so I know I can call a cab and get home do you?" I asked, really not wanting to wait around until she finished another phone call.

She smiled. "Of course," she said, giving me the address.

I closed my eyes with relief when I realised we weren't just in Australia, but that the portal had dumped us back in our own city, and that the Temple of Isis was only a couple of blocks away. When I opened my eyes she'd already disappeared back into her own cubicle.

"You'll need to dial nine to get an outside line," chipped in our original time wasting helper as I picked up the phone on the empty desk in the cubicle we were in. I thanked her through gritted teeth before dialling Roxanna's number. As normal and sane as this place seemed — despite it housing a portal that regularly dumped demon rejects on it — I really needed to get out. I actually think it was because it was *too* normal for me. There was just something about the Other World that seemed so much more safe and sane than the insanity known as normality.

As Roxanna answered the phone I suddenly realised how much trouble I was going to be in. I'd not told her I was going to Hell, I didn't know how much time had actually passed and, well, I didn't know how much she'd appreciate me using her white van as a taxi service to come and get us.

"Stephanie! Thank Isis you're okay. Since finding the note Trishna left us, along with his last will and testament, we've been worried sick about you. Can I assume that by being able to use a phone you never actually made it to Hell and are still here, safe?"

"Safe is optional," I answered in as calm a tone as I could, scowling at Trishna. Had he had so little faith in me he had to leave a note *and* a will? Sheesh! "And we did go, just got back a couple of minutes ago, but rather than getting a t-shirt I've got Simon's soul stuck under my skin and I'd really appreciate someone coming to get us and getting it out of me as quick as they can." I could feel Roxanna's disapproval and shock in the silence now on the phone. Thankfully it only lasted a moment or so.

"Where are you, I will send some priestesses to get you." Her tone was glacial and I felt myself cringing.

I covered the mouthpiece of the phone and asked our time wasting helper for the address again. Which she promptly gave, also offering to nip downstairs to call us a cab. I scowled at her while turning back to the phone.

"Wait out the front, my priestesses will be there as soon as they can," Roxanna said, her cold, crisp tones telling me just how pissed off she was. Boy was I in trouble.

"Roxanna. . ." I tried but she cut me off.

"We will discuss it when you have returned and I can assess exactly how much damage you've done to yourself and your soul from this latest act of stupidity," she snapped sharply.

The line then went dead before I got a chance to say more. Damn I was in for it. I wonder if Isis herself would fire me? Or if Roxanna had the power to do it alone?

"Help's on the way," I told Trishna. "Let's wait downstairs."

"Finally," Trishna sighed with relief, "someone is on their way to help me who isn't going to force their will upon me, bleed me or use me as a chew toy." The look he gave me as he said this made my stomach twist. Despite getting us out of Hell alive and in one piece, it was obvious he still hadn't forgiven me for what I felt had had to be done to protect him. He *would* forgive… right? Hopefully I could start racking up the positive restitution points again soon and we could get back to how we were. The way he jerked away from my touch as I tried to help him out of the cubicle though made me wonder if this was something that was going to happen soon.

"Hold on," it was my favourite staff member again, who'd finished her call. "I've got a break now so I'll come down with you."

"Are you the team leader or something?" I asked as we took the elevator to the ground floor.

She snorted, amused. "Don't be stupid, I'm too busy actually knowing how to do all the work to be given such a role."

There was just something about her that made me want to friend her on social media or something. But then again, things were already borderline insane in this situation and I got the feeling that reality wouldn't make it any better.

As we left the building she stopped me and handed over a small business card.

"You walk a fine line in your job Protector of Souls," she told me with a knowing smile. I hadn't even told her my name and — in true Other World style — she'd known not to ask. "My family are known to sometimes be helpful to those who find themselves caught in the Grey between the Darkness and Light. Give me a call if you ever need me." I took the card, searching her face for. . . something. I couldn't tell what, but she was suddenly giving off a very Other Worldy vibe now she was away from the office. The name on the card read Rebecca Szary. I felt it should somehow mean something to me, but I drew a blank.

"Uh, thanks," I answered, going to tuck it into my shirt's front pocket and then realising there wasn't really much of a pocket left to tuck it into. She nodded, smiled again and went back into the building.

I was still pondering the whole weird situation when the white van from the Temple of Isis arrived. The two priestesses in the front didn't look very pleased to see us but they wrapped us in blankets and ensured we were safely stowed in the back before taking off again.

So, that was Hell huh? Despite feeling I'd only just made it out of there as myself, I suspected this little adventure of mine was far from being over. Still, the Darkness I'd picked up in Hell seemed to have been burned from me on the trip home and, if I sat just right, I could barely feel Simon within me. I actually nodded off on Trishna's shoulder on the journey through mid-morning traffic as we made our stop-start journey back to the Temple. I hadn't meant to, but even the van held some of the peace and safety of Isis' home. Did I feel jubilant that I'd achieved what I'd set out to do, handbasket and all? Not really, as I was obviously in *big* trouble with the High Priestess and I still needed to ensure Simon's soul *could* be removed. I mean, Sid put it in there. . . but could anyone up here get it back out without causing either of us too much damage? Or more dealings with demons. At least Trishna was letting me rest upon his shoulder and not flinch away from me again. How was I going to make it up to him? He had to know I'd done it to protect him because he meant so much to me. Why was I suddenly so worried about how I felt over Trishna's anger at me?

These were the thoughts that kept me subdued until I dozed. Not the happiest return, but at least we had made it. I just hoped I got a chance to have a shower and grab a change of clothes before the next lot hit the fan.

# Chapter 21

———————— ⑨ ————————

"IS THAT you or Simon elbowing me in the ribs again?" complained Trishna, later that day. I rubbed my eyes coming awake, wondering how I'd managed to fall asleep again as Trishna and I were currently sharing the rather confined space of the stone altar under the Light of Isis. The place my undead sister had rested last year, just before I killed her.

"I'm blaming Simon," I said, and did my best to turn onto my side away from Trishna without falling off the edge. We'd been brought down to the Cavern of Isis as soon as we'd arrived. Although Roxana had overseen it all, she'd not hung around to chat. She was obviously upset with me, but probably felt our conversation should wait until we'd both had a good cleanse under the Light of Isis.

I mean, she had a point, I'd had to use the Light a few months beforehand after I got nicked in the ribs by a stray silver bullet — long story — and the Light had healed me up nicely. This Light was also controlled and soothing, unlike the bright, white Light I had burned up in as we had left Hell.

Still, I was unhappy with having to share the dais with Trishna. It was large, but not quite big enough to fit us both comfortably. I had told them to heal him first and I would wait. But Roxanna insisted we both be cleansed at once to ensure safety. The Temple's safety or our own, I wasn't sure.

They also wouldn't let me have a sheet to cover up from some of the drafts. Going by their clothing, you would have thought the Priestesses of Isis would have a spare sheet, but oh no. So my barely there top, ripped and dirty slacks and itchy skin from sharing it with Simon was adding to my discomfort.

"If I started chanting 'are we there yet?' do you think I'd get us in even more trouble than we already are?" Trishna asked, bored.

Oh Isis I hoped he didn't start chanting, I really felt quiet respect for the Temple's ways were in order right now.

"How about we play a game to see how long we can go without talking?" I muttered. Yes I was uncomfortable up on the stone slab, but most of my unease came from not knowing what was going to happen next.

"As if you'd ever win anything like that," Trishna snorted, then realising his mistake groaned at his own stupidity.

I rolled over on to my other side, facing Trishna, as he continued to lie on his back, and quirked an eyebrow. "I just did," I replied smugly. Yes, we were both bored and it was starting to show.

"If I can't chant, can I at least sing the bottles of beer song?" Okay, so he was now officially being annoying. Did I even *need* to worry about losing restitution if I deliberately elbowed him? I mean, I was obviously so far into the negatives did it truly matter anymore? Could I take it as a positive he was still talking to me?

"Surely you could at least make it about bottles of purified water," Roxanna said, as she appeared on Trishna's side of the dais and assessed his nearly completely healed wound. "Right, sit up."

"You're sounding friendlier," Trishna said.

"It's amazing what meditating with a moonstone and a large cup of spearmint tea can do for you," the High Priestess replied. It was obvious to me that she still wasn't one hundred per cent pleased with us, but she had thawed a little. We eyed each other briefly and I was about to say more when I realised the cavern was beginning to fill up with priestesses. Obviously something big was going to happen.

"Uh, do you need us to move so you can get on with Priestess Aggie's funeral or something?" I asked, trying to find *something* neutral to say.

"We held that yesterday and dispatched her body accordingly," Roxanna replied coldly, but there was a look on her face as though she was wondering how we knew of the elderly woman's passing.

"We saw her in the afterlife," I explained. "She and Isis said hi just before we headed off into Hell. She looked happy to be with her Goddess." For a moment Roxanna's face softened back to the happy expression I was used to. There was even a brief glisten of a tear in her eye.

"That is good to know she went in peace and found her way to her new home in the Light," she replied huskily. She seemed to shake herself, studied me for a moment longer as if wondering what on earth she was going to do with me, before turning to join the other priestesses as they started chanting and pacing about the cavern. Something big was obviously about to happen. I'd not seen them do this sort of thing since we last spoke to Isis. . . Oh. Geez sometimes I was a bit slow on the uptake.

My nervousness increased along with the usual build-up of mist around the Pool of Isis that always heralded her arrival. I'd only ever met her three times in this cavern and so the experience was still rather daunting and awe inspiring at the same time. Though looking at the mixed expressions on the priestesses around me, I got the feeling that it didn't matter how often you met your deity, the awe and slight fear of not being worthy never faded. Then, as the mists parted, there she was. Our Mother Protector in all her plain, simple, and ethereal beauty.

Roxanna moved to greet her and they hugged briefly before Isis turned her patient, watching eyes to me and Trishna. I felt him tense at my side and I didn't know whether to hold his hand as comfort, or let him deal with the situation himself. Yes he'd met Isis before, but he'd been a ghost at the time and I was pretty sure her effect on the living was far different to that of a spirit. In addition, while we'd just spent a few hours together on the stone slab, it had been pretty obvious he hadn't been happy to be around me. He'd kept his back to me most of the time, leaving me with the feeling that I was going to have to do some big time apologising to him later.

"Welcome home my children," Isis said, as she smiled at us. Once again I was amazed at the motherly-warmth and kindness I felt in her presence. She made you feel welcome, made you feel safe. As much as I usually hated being in the presence of the truly powerful Other Worlders, when it was Isis, it just seemed *right*.

We returned her greeting as she reached out and gently touched Trishna. Ignoring his flinch she ran her long, slender fingers down his arm to his former wound. Then, holding his head in her hands, she looked steadily into his eyes.

"Your soul is only mildly tarnished. The possession protected you as intended and absorbed most of the Darkness. You are safe and may go in peace."

Isis gave another smile, and helped Trishna down off the dais. So *that* was it! Roxanna had called in the big guns to ensure we'd not brought something bad back from Hell with us. Well, this should be a doddle, right? I'd had all the Darkness burned out of me on re-entry. I smiled as

I moved to her side of the dais for my own examination. Isis turned her attention to me and gave me a look that held both amusement and mild reproach in equal measure.

"Good to see you made it back from the afterlife," she said, "You took a great risk in saving Simon's soul. And although he may never thank you enough, know I am truly grateful."

I blinked at this a bit as there seemed to be a 'but' about to happen. There wasn't meant to be a but — I went, I got him, I came home. That was my job and what everyone had said I should do. Bless me, get him out of me and let me go home to bed please.

Isis' smile widened as she reached out and stroked my cheek and I could tell she knew what I was thinking.

"My child, you absorbed a great deal of Darkness while in Hell. Although you possessed another living soul against their will, you did it with the best of intentions. While I cannot condone it, I appreciate your effort as it kept Trishna safe." Isis studied me a nerve wracking moment longer before adding: "The possession of yourself has me intrigued. However, although you strayed further into the Darkness than one of my followers should, this self-possession has protected you too. You are still safe and blessed by me in all you do in the Light." She said the last gently to Roxanna as she summoned her over with an outstretched hand. It was obvious she was assuring both of us of this fact.

"Stephanie," Isis said, as she turned to give me a final warning, "you seem determined to sometimes walk a little too close into the edge of the Darkness. You must realise I cannot vouch for you if you choose to stay there."

I fixed a smile on my face, worried if I let it slip they would see my fear at losing my place at the temple. It wasn't just a job. It was a life with loving and caring friends.

"But I walk in the Light," I replied, trying to keep my voice steady. "It was that belief that got me there and got me home. I will not dwell in the Darkness."

Isis lay a reassuring hand on Roxanna's shoulder as the High Priestess looked about to speak.

"Peace Roxanna, Stephanie speaks the truth. She is a child of the Light. . . but it appears she may also be a little more." Isis turned back to me and took my head in her hands. She studied me closely.

"Despite your love of the Light Stephanie, your soul does now bear the marks of Darkness upon it. And not even I can remove them. You have aligned with demons, possessed a living soul, and made a blood sacrifice of an innocent to open a portal from Hell. These are actions that *cannot* be ignored." And then Isis smiled at me as she released me from her gentle examination. "But you are still a daughter of Isis and still welcome within my home."

"But. . ." Roxanna interjected, apparently concerned I was getting off so easily.

"Peace, High Priestess," Isis told Roxanna gently, using her title rather than her name to show who had the greater power. "Stephanie is not one of your priestesses, who must always stay pure and white in the Light. She must be allowed to tread her own path, as her journey to where she really belongs has only just started."

Yeah, no, that didn't sound that good to me either. I'd just come back from Hell and was pretty sure my travelling days were over. Isis flicked a reassuring smile in my direction before taking Roxanna's hands in hers.

"I assure you Stephanie walks in the Light. She is still who you think she is and she still deserves your trust and friendship. Let it not wane until I tell you otherwise."

Wow! Now if that wasn't an affirmation I was still the good guy I thought I was! Oh the relief I felt as Roxanna nodded and smiled at Isis. She released herself from her Goddess and turned to embrace me long and hard. So that had been the problem? It wasn't that I had got into huge amounts of trouble, Roxanna had been angry with the thought of no longer being able to trust me. . . of losing me to the Darkness. I'd never really been one for the whole touchy-feely thing, but for once I clung to her tightly. It hadn't been until that moment that I realised the biggest reason I hadn't felt so alone since losing my flesh and blood sister was because Roxanna had filled the void. She was family now, and about all that I had in this weird Other World. Yes I had friends and associates, but Roxanna was what kept me strong in my faith that I belonged here and truly did walk in the Light. Having her angry at me, reject me, and think I had descended into Darkness had really hurt. And I'd not even realised this had been why I had been feeling so crummy around her until that hug and the release of fear and tension it gave.

"There now," Isis smiled as Roxanna and I finally parted. "Sisters in love make sisters in life. Be happy my children and know you are worth it."

I looked to Isis and then to Roxanna and nodded, wiping away a tear. Gee I must be getting old if I was letting this girly stuff get to me.

"And before I go, I will resolve settling the soul you so bravely went to rescue," Isis announced. She leaned forward to where I sat and gave me a motherly kiss upon the head.

"Like the prince awakening his bride, so too will be the way you return Simon to how he should be," Isis announced cryptically. "May he wear a crown of blackberry, rowan, ivy and agrimony to remove the spirit that enslaves him."

Gee I hoped someone in the crowd of priestesses was taking notes and knew what she was saying as it was a little jumbled to me. Still I smiled and nodded, we all knew I'd do what had to be done. . . even if it meant someone else would have to point me in the right direction first.

"It will come to you as it is needed," Isis said, seeming to know what I was thinking. But then again she was a Goddess. She gave me another smile. "Peace be with you, you are safe to leave my Light and go once more into the fray." She had said the last bit rather cheekily and winked at me after saying it. Isis and I embraced before the Goddess moved off and began to travel about the cavern, stopping to talk to each priestess in turn. When she was done the chanting began once more and, as the mists began to rise Isis turned one last time to me.

"Be yourself Stephanie Muriel Anders, warts and all — you are loved and as long as you are doing it your way, you are right." And she was then gone.

I wasn't too sure how to take that last comment. I mean, yes I was worth it, but what was this about warts?

When the ceremony was over Roxanna came back to my side with a smile of greeting. She seemed to be trying to say something but I cut her off.

"No apologies and no regrets," I told her firmly. "We are what we are. You have a Temple to protect while I have some acts of stupidity to uphold, all in the name of saving souls."

She smiled, taking this the way I had intended it to be and helped me down off the dais.

Oh if life was only this simple always. But sadly there was more to come before I would be able to catch that shower and next nap.

# Chapter 22

IT TURNED out we'd been away for three days. It scared me to think I had been so close to being in Hell too long to leave. Mr Vontant had said beyond four days, I wouldn't have had a choice about becoming a demon. Still, I'd made it out in time. . . just. It really hadn't felt like we had been in Hell for that long either, but I was feeling pretty funky by the end of it and was shady on one or two things. Trishna was of no help either because, as he'd pointed out in an overly rude manner if you ask me, he'd been possessed for most of his time down there.

Still, three days is what is was and now I was back home and slipping into an old t-shirt before tackling the next part of my job. I had wanted a shower, and was even told I would have time. . . but had baulked at the thought of being naked in the shower with Simon's soul moving beneath my skin. I mean, yes he was just a benign force for now, no consciousness to perve on me. It just seemed ew, okay?

Stepping out of my room and heading down into the kitchen I was surprised to find my home a bustle of white-robed priestesses. Trishna and I had arrived with Roxanna to be greeted by priestess Yolanda, who'd been on duty watching Simon's still sleeping body, but other than that the place had been empty when I'd gone to change. It now had three priestesses in the kitchen making up tea, sandwiches and all sorts from food they'd obviously brought with them — my fridge rarely had things like fresh bread, milk and salad in it. On my smaller dining table sat the Apothecary twisting and weaving plants into a wreath and I could see at least two of her assistants out in my jungle of a garden, no doubt collecting more plants essential to what was going on. With the large dining table still out of commission until it could be cleansed by the next full moon, I propped myself up against the island bench that separated the kitchen from the dining area and tried to look pitifully at the kitchen workers in the hopes I'd be given a sandwich and some tea. It worked, bless them.

"I can't believe you're calmly feeding your face with what you've got ahead of you," Trishna teased coming out of his room fully dressed in new clothes, still towelling his hair dry. Yeah, I might not have felt like a shower, but it hadn't stopped him. What concerned me though was that in his other hand he was carrying his bag.

"What have I got ahead of me?" I asked, gulping down the last of my ham and cheese, "And what's with the bag?"

"Well, if I had to kiss someone I truly hated as the only way to get their soul out of me, I wouldn't be chowing down. Who knows the barf capability of puckering up to a douche canoe?" He dropped his bag by the island. "And the bag is me moving out," he added awkwardly. " No offence, but I just don't feel comfortable living under the same roof as someone who possessed me, used me as a blood sacrifice, and would have eaten me if allowed to turn into a demon."

I choked on the tea I had been drinking as he replied. To the point where one of the priestesses had to come and pat me hard on the back for a few moments until I waved her off.

"I have to do what? You're doing *what?!*" I just didn't know which bit of that dreadful information I wanted to know more about first.

"Were you even paying attention when Isis was telling you how to finish this stupid soul saving mission of yours?" Trishna asked, obviously choosing politer words in the presence of the priestesses. Also obviously avoiding half the conversation.

"Isis told you the way you would return Simon's soul would be by kissing him. I did wonder at the time if you actually got what she was saying as I was expecting a bigger reaction than you just smiling and nodding like some limp-minded twit."

I scowled at Trishna for that comment, and tried not to react too badly as the bigger lead weight in my stomach right now was him leaving. . . because of what I'd done.

" 'Like the prince awakening his bride, so too will be the way you return Simon to how he should be.' Ick! I suppose it's too late to decide this whole soul saving thing is a bad idea," I said, smacking my forehead. I *knew* those words should have been setting off alarm bells when Isis had said them. What did the prince always do to wake the sleeping princess? Kiss her. Ugh! The priestesses who didn't know me too well gasped with shock at this concept while Trishna gave me a withering look and the Apothecary just shook her head as if trying to ignore the wittering of a silly child.

"Okay, so I admit I didn't realise I was going to have to *kiss* the cretin!" I snapped at the room in general. "But if that's the last damned thing I ever have to do to him I will. I mean, I hadn't wanted to go to Hell and save his soul, now I've done that and it's crawling under my skin, kissing him to get rid of it is probably worth it." Yes, I was trying to pep talk myself into believing it. If I didn't I'd be stuck with Simon's soul within me until I don't know when. And I was pretty sure it wasn't healthy to be walking around with more than one soul inside you for too long. Who knew what it might attract from the Other World.

"You're still such a newb," Trishna snorted in an almost disappointed tone. He turned away from me and moved into the kitchen. I caught his arm and stopped him before he got much further.

"Why are you leaving? I. . . I didn't mean to do all that stuff to you to hurt you. I did it to protect you. What about all this restitution I'm meant to be helping out with?" I was floundering now, still more upset at the thought of losing Trishna than I was at planting a wet one on Simon.

Trishna looked at me long and hard for a moment and then gently removed my hand from his arm.

"It's complicated," he said. He shot a glance at the priestesses scattered around the room, all studiously trying to pretend they weren't listening. I nodded to show I understood that this wasn't the time or place to talk. He would tell me when we were alone. . . well, I hoped he would tell me and not just walk out. He and I couldn't end this way, I'd done what I'd done to keep him safe, to keep him with me and *protected* from the Darkness. And I'd not made him come with me, that had been his own choice, right? But still. . . if Trishna was now afraid of me after what I'd done to him, what else could I do? We weren't a couple, we weren't *together* and the thought of us ever being mistaken as being in a romantic relationship still worried me more than having to kiss Simon. Not because it was as gross as kissing Simon, but because romance and I didn't gel that well together. Trishna was just Trishna. . . and I needed him in my life to make me a better person. Be that speaking conscious to keep me going in the right direction. But that need for him to always be there was starting to make me nervous.

"You better talk to me before you go. That's all I ask," I finally managed. The disappointment in his eyes made me cringe. Had he wanted me to say more? Demand he not go? Without saying another word, and really not wanting to be in the room with any of them anymore, I went and hid in my study until I was needed. Gutless, but the best I could manage at the time.

***

I looked up from my doodling on some note paper when Roxanna tentatively knocked on the study door.

"Trishna said I would find you sulking in here," she said.

"I call it preparing myself for the final Simon ordeal, rather than sulking," I replied, trying to mask the huffy tone in my voice that would prove I really was sulking.

I threw my pen on the table. "He's leaving me!" I exploded at Roxanna, venting my frustration at the whole stupid situation.

"I would have thought you'd have wanted Simon to leave as soon as you'd fixed him up," Roxanna answered calmly. She leaned against the bookshelf next to my desk as I had the only chair in the small, narrow room.

As I turned to give her a glare for not understanding, I caught that cat and mouse look in her eyes and stopped myself from biting back and sighed instead. I *hated* sighing as I seemed to do it a lot, but sometimes it was the only thing I could do to keep from swearing and going all Trishna on people. Trishna. . . damn it. I *needed* him to stay.

"Why is it everything I do to make things right always has me end up alone and sorry for myself?" I said turning away to say this at my scribble pad, not wanting Roxanna to see the tears I was fighting back. I am not a weak person and the tears springing up from nowhere just pissed me off further.

"Would you be happy to be around someone who can possess you against your will whenever they feel like it? Who soaked up so much Darkness she almost became a demon? Who used you as a blood sacrifice to get you out of a place you didn't want to go to in the first place?" her voice was calm and kind, no form of judgement in it. Still they made me wince.

"He didn't have to come with me, it's not as if I held a gun to his head or anything. I *told* him he didn't have to come. He chose to," I muttered. "Plus he let me take his blood, even gave me a damned knife."

"And the possession?" Roxanna prompted in her motherly tone.

"I was trying to keep us safe," I said quietly, trying not to think about it. "I possessed myself too you know. I did it to make us safe, and it worked. No demon got him and, by possessing him, I sucked up most of the Darkness that would have otherwise ended up in his soul. Isis herself said he wasn't damaged because of me."

"Without even going into the fact you shouldn't have been able to successfully possess yourself — an ability that probably came from the Darkness you'd absorbed — taking control of one's own soul and will isn't exactly the same as taking control of someone else's. Is it?"

I sat in silence for a moment, angrily scribbling at the paper before me to release some of the tension I was using to keep that terrible fact from myself. I had taken away Trishna's ability to be himself. To think, act, move and even defend himself. I had imprisoned him inside his own head and used his body and will without his permission. I'd taken away his ability to *be* while giving myself the ability to use and abuse him — mind, body and soul — in any way I so desired. Even if I hadn't used him for anything, simply possessing him as I had was heinous enough. If the normal world's court of law could get their head around it being possible, I was pretty sure I'd be up for some nasty charges right now. Imprisonment, brutality. . . rape? I had taken control of Trishna to keep him safe, but what I'd done equated to locking someone up with no food as a way to help them lose weight. No wonder he couldn't be around me anymore. Thinking on it, I really didn't want to be around me either. . . and yet I had no choice.

"I need him." Saying these words out loud to someone else, especially Roxanna, surprised me.

"Why do you need him? What's so important about keeping this man with you, even against his will?" Roxanna's motherly tone had taken on a stern edge. I looked up at her, groping for an answer.

"I. . . I don't know." And that struck me as painfully as what I'd already done. I didn't *want* Trishna in a sexual way; but if I didn't want him as a lover, if I didn't want him there against his will. . . then what was it I wanted? What was it in our relationship that made me *need* him?

"I do know I would *never* keep him against his will," I finally added, realising the truth as I spoke it and knowing what I had to do.

"Well, may I suggest you let him go for now — not far, just to the Temple — and when you figure out why it is you need him, you come and let him know?"

Roxanna gave me a long and hard look that made me realise she was right. I couldn't just expect Trishna to stick around and be my sidekick for no reason. What was in it for him if I just did what I liked, when I liked and didn't think of how he would feel about it? But was I ever going to figure out why I needed him to be there?

I slowly nodded agreement to her statement when there was a knock on the study door and the Apothecary poked her head around it.

"We're ready," she told Roxanna, then gave me a nod before disappearing. Roxanna opened the door and I rose to follow her out, stretching and feeling Simon's soul press against my skin as I did so, making me feel like I was wearing clothes two sizes too small.

"Okay Simon, pucker up, it's show time," I muttered as I followed Roxanna out of the small room and down the corridor to where we had been keeping him.

I really did hope this was the final thing I would have to do with Simon before I got him out of my life for good. I mean, if I *had* to I would possibly offer him a cup of tea when we were done, but after that I didn't want him anywhere near me. I wanted him gone, for good.

And then my stomach twisted at the thought that when it *was* done, it wouldn't just be Simon who would leave. It would be Trishna too. That was just the crappiest two for one deal I'd ever heard of.

# Chapter 23

THE bedrooms in my cottage weren't the biggest at the best of times. But when you put a double bed — with associated chains to hold it and its occupant in place in the centre of it — an Apothecary, her assistant, the High Priestess, two of her aides, Trishna and myself in there as well. . . it was a rather snug fit. And I wasn't even allowed to crack a window, despite the room really needing it after Simon having been in there for so many days. Add to that someone had drawn all over the walls and I was starting to feel rather irritated. Well, having Simon's soul under my skin, and knowing I was going to have to kiss him to get it out wasn't helping my mood. And neither was avoiding Trishna's gaze in the hope he wouldn't see how his departure was hurting me.

"Who the hell drew all over the walls? I hope they realise I'm not about to be held responsible for that!"

"I'm pretty sure your landlady will understand," Roxanna told me sarcastically.

So did she mean that she'd been responsible, or that she, being my landlady didn't mind, or that I was finding the dumbest things to complain about to ease my tension? I was pretty sure it was a bit of all three, so I held my tongue as the priestesses geared up to get the ceremony going.

As they started chanting a simple prayer of protection I looked at the walls. From what I could tell the artist or artists, whoever they'd been, had also concentrated on protection glyphs. Some were for good health and harmony, others to defend yourself against dark forces. The priestesses seem to have been trying to cover all bases with what they'd put there.

As the prayer came to an end I noticed Trishna wince.

"What?" I asked him as he put his hands to his ears.

"It's the Impa Shilup. It's screaming for help. I think it's cottoned on to what we're trying to do."

"Well, tell it to shut up," I replied, feeling flustered. If the dark-spirit felt calling for help was needed. . . would help actually arrive? And what would it be?

"You tell it to shut up!" snapped Trishna, pulling another face at the noise only he could hear. "You're the one who now has spirit-sight installed with a switch to turn it on and off."

I winced as I remembered the mark on the back of my hand. I had told him about it while we had been stuck under the Light of Isis down in the cavern. Not wanting to make a big show of how I could do it, I hid my hands behind my back and rubbed the near invisible small circle on the back of my hand. Immediately the room filled with a piercing scream and the black, shadowy spirit form appeared crouched over Simon on the bed.

I found myself having to cover my own ears at the noise and, without meaning to sound too childish, screamed back at it to be silent. . . or words to that effect.

It stopped briefly and gave me a baleful look.

"You have been given the spirit-sight," it hissed at me with disgust.

"I've been given a bit more than that buddy. So how about you just go away now and let us get this room all cleared out."

"This body belongs to me. My Master now holds the soul. We traded it fair and square."

"Wrong again," I grunted and held out my hand. The priestesses around me gasped as the skin along my bare arm rippled and writhed. "I have Simon's soul and it's time it went back where it belonged."

"I will kill this body before letting you take it back!" the dark-spirit hissed, and thrust its hand *into* Simon's throat. Simon's unconscious body started to splutter and cough as the Impa Shilup cut off the air supply.

"The wreath, quick, put it on his head!" I have no idea why I suddenly felt this was the right answer, but Isis had said it would protect Simon and he really needed it right now.

The Apothecary said a quick second prayer and then placed the wreath — unknowingly stepping *through* the Impa Shilup to do it — upon Simon's head. The dark-spirit screamed again and fled to Simon's feet, trying to get as far away from the wreath as it could, while still staying connected to Simon.

"If you return his soul, you release me into your home untethered. You yourself have said only those of Darkness given your permission can leave. I promise you I *won't*. I will stay and I will bring as much Darkness as I can into your home."

"Is he threatening me?" I asked the room in general. The priestesses all gave me a blank look, being unable to see and hear what I could. "Did that creature of Darkness just threaten me with harm and bad luck?" I asked Trishna.

"You know, I believe it did," Trishna replied, catching onto what I was saying.

"Hmmm, being threatened by dark forces like that. . . sort of brings to mind a certain deal I have going with the certain owner of a reaper. . ." I went on.

Roxanna groaned as she finally realised what I was up to. Her aides gave a startled jump as the door behind them opened and a rather angry looking Mr Vontant stood in the doorway.

"Yes, yes, spell it out for the idiots in the room why don't you," he said as he assessed the situation. "I suppose you want me to do something about. . . *that?*" he asked me in near glacial tones while pointing at Simon's feet.

"I'm sure you have a flunky or a reaper you could call up to clear it away for me," I said smugly.

"As long as you realise this doesn't count toward my monthly summoning," the demon sniffed.

"Actually I think it does," Trishna mused. "She needed you, you came. You now have to do what she asks and can only leave when she says you can."

Mr Vontant swore as he realised Trishna was right.

"See! *This* is why I need you!" I blurted out. "I'd never have realised that on my own." I don't think I'd ever seen Roxanna face palm, but she did it right then.

"Now is seriously not the time for that," she said, never too happy to be in the room with a demon, or have me openly discuss my deals with them in front of the other priestesses. Trishna and I exchanged a final look before I moved my attention back to the Impa Shilup cringing on top of the feet of Simon.

"Time to go," I said to it, pointing a finger at it to emphasis I meant it, jerking it back just in time to avoid getting it bitten.

"Look, threatened by dark forces again. Do something about it" I snapped at Mr Vontant, before giving him an apologetic look for losing my temper. Damn it, being apologetic to a demon? Of all the stupid things I was doing that afternoon.

"Wroth, I summon thee in plain sight of all," Mr Vontant muttered and the room became even more crowded as the ankou appeared by the side of the bed. He looked rather annoyed to be there, though whether that was because of what he was being asked to do, or that he had such an audience to do it with, I don't know. But as the priestesses all gasped and moved as far away from him, and Mr Vontant, as the small room would allow, I found myself caught up in a rather unladylike shuffle as people repositioned themselves around the room. I felt like telling the Priestesses of Isis to take a chill pill, it's not as if these guy's Darkness would just rub off on their pretty white sheets. . . would it?

"You know, for a soul cleansing and returning ceremony, this reeks of an amateur production," Trishna muttered as he found himself pushed out of the corner he had been in and squashed up against the door with me. "If I'd known the tea and sandwiches made this into a dinner with a show I'd have dressed more appropriately."

I shot him a dark look, and tried to keep my professional game face on.

"Wroth, take this Impa Shilup away from Simon, he's no longer needed and I don't want him cluttering up the place." I tried to sound stern — but not too bossy — as I said this. Wroth, however, just scowled at me.

"Make me." He folded his arms as if to prove he didn't plan to do a thing.

"Mr Vontant. . . your *lackey* isn't helping me remove a threat from dark forces toward me."

The small, neat man sighed and rolled his eyes. "I would like it known, for the record, just exactly how demeaning this is. Seriously, I can't see how any of this is covered in the deals we have."

"He has a deal with him," I replied, carefully pointing at the dark-spirit and then at Wroth. "And he belongs to you." I then pointed from Wroth to Mr Vontant. "And you have a deal to protect me from threats from dark forces. Please don't make me spell it out any further or it's just going to embarrass all of us."

The demon glared at me a moment longer, but I refused to back down. I'm pretty sure there was some more professional way to deal with this type of situation. . . but this was how I was doing it. The sooner the bad guys realised that, the better.

"I really do wish you would play by the book," Mr Vontant said as he straightened his suit.

"The day someone bothers to actually show me the book and give me a chance to read it, I will," I answered back blandly. "But until that day, I'm writing a new one as I go. Deal with it."

"Very well," the demon sighed, a pained expression on his face. "Wroth, remove your cohort from the body. Stephanie here has done what she said she would and has returned the soul to its owner. That is the deal you set and so must it be."

Wroth scowled at us for a moment longer and then turned to the Impa Shilip.

"Come away. There are better bodies for you out there," he growled and, surprising all of us who could see him, the dark-spirit jumped down from the bed and scrambled up Wroth's back to sit on his shoulder.

I bit back my desire to thank them, I mean come on! They were dark forces retreating after being beaten. No thanks were needed, right?

"You may go," Mr Vontant told Wroth, before remembering the wards that prevented this. He sighed at this and pointed out the door. "Wait by the back door, we will be leaving soon."

I could tell how undignified this all seemed and I had to fight to keep the smirk off my face. All the strict rules and ceremonies held in place with those who lived in the Other World all thwarted by me having to open a door to let them out.

"And if I'm finished here?" Mr Vontant asked as around me the priestesses sprang into action and started what looked like CPR on Simon while shooting me urgent glances. I was distracted by this for a moment before turning back to Mr Vontant with a worried expression. He gave me a look that was at first withering and then amused.

"When you take away a body's soul, as well as the spirit possessing it in the soul's absence, what else is it meant to do but die?" the demon asked with a smirk and I cursed myself for not realising this. I should have put Simon's soul back in *before* I had removed the damned Impa Shilup. Of course a body needed a spirit or soul to make it work, otherwise it was just a lump of meat.

"Oh shit!" I exclaimed, leaping forward toward the head of the bed and hoping it wasn't too late. If Simon's body went and died on me now, where did that leave his soul? Everything I had just put myself —

and Trishna — through would have been for nothing. Just a corpse and someone else's soul making my skin itch from here to eternity.

There was no time for one of those soft focused Disney moments where pretty music played as the prince calmly leaned in and brushed his lips against the sleeping princess. Nope, I needed this soul out of me and back in Simon to ensure his heart, lungs and all that other stuff kept working and the schmuck lived so I could get him out of my house and my life as soon as possible. So I flung myself on top of Simon, straddling him, took his head in both my hands and leaned in and crushed my lips onto his, willing his soul to leave me and return to his own body. It was all I would allow myself to focus on: Simon's soul, leave me, return to Simon's body. I tried to keep it as plain and simple as I could so as not to cause some sort of karmic cock up later on — see Trishna. I refused to let any other thought in to make it backfire and I squatted there, kissing him and feeling my skin rippling until Simon's chest beneath me expanded in a huge intake of breath.

I only stopped when I felt Simon's manacled hands rise and run themselves down my back to rest rather rudely on my backside, giving it a squeeze. That and I realised he was kissing me back. I jerked my head away to see a glassy eyed Simon staring up at me.

"You know you didn't have to chain me to a bed to get your way with me Steph love. I knew you weren't picky, but damned girl you took your time to make a move." Then the jerk tried to pull me in for another kiss.

I don't know exactly what sort of karmic backlash I may have then have created as I slapped him hard before I scrambled off him and the bed, scrubbing my mouth madly as I did so.

I bit back the extremely bad words I wanted to say as next to me Mr Vontant sneered and Trishna did his best to hide a smirk. The priestesses across from me held a mixture of shock and concern. What? Like they'd put up with being felt up like that by a guy they were trying to rescue.

"Well done Stephanie," Roxanna finally said, finding her voice at last. "Perhaps you can finish some of your other. . . business. . . elsewhere while we clean up in here?" She shot Mr Vontant a look and I knew she was telling me to remove him, Wroth and the Impa Shilup from her Goddess' cottage.

"I want him out of here," was all I said coldly.

Roxanna may have thought I had been referring to the demon, but my look of disgust at a bewildered Simon spoke volumes as to who I was really talking about. I knew I wasn't going to get a thanks from Simon. In fact I seriously doubted he even remembered why he was even here. And so I just walked out and left him to the priestesses to deal with. Let him get all handsy with them and get away with it. I think not!

***

I found the reaper, dark-spirit, and demon waiting impatiently for me by the back door, like a bunch of annoyed cats crossing their legs and jiggling to get out. I gave them all a good scowl before crossing to the door.

"Don't let me catch you around here again," I warned the cowering dark-spirit and Wroth as I opened the back door for them and bade they leave. Wroth looked to Mr Vontant for permission before going. When the demon gave him a dismissing nod the ankou turned back to me.

"We must all die at some point. I hope I'm there to witness it, if I can't be the cause myself." He leaned in a little too close for comfort. "There's no way he can defend you from dark forces if you're dead by the time he gets to you. And I can assure you, I can snatch a soul in seconds."

Uh, was it wise for a reaper to be threatening me in front of its master? I would have asked this if I wasn't so unnerved about the whole situation and possibility of Wroth waiting for the right moment to pounce. Wroth turned to leave but was stopped by Mr Vontant clearing his throat.

"I had really hoped you wouldn't go and say something like that," Mr Vontant said, in a disappointed tone. Then, before Wroth could stop him, Mr Vontant grabbed him by the wrist and snapped a strange looking bracelet upon it. I have no idea what it was, but the Impa Shilup took off into the night howling in pain and Wroth reeled back swearing and tugging at the bracelet.

"I had it made up especially for you," Mr Vontant told him, "just in case you decided to become a threat to my plans. It's made up of silver, blackberry, rowan, and ivy; and studded with rock salt, tigers eye and agate, inflected of course."

"'Of course'," Wroth said, and looked ready to snap Mr Vontant in two. "You do know you've removed my ability to interact with another's soul, and broken my connection to my spirits! Without those I am *nothing*."

"Then let that be a reminder as to exactly where you sit in the order of things," Mr Vontant told him. "To me you are just another reaper, an abomination. Ms Anders on the other hand. . . I have a *use* for her."

"I am nothing now until it is removed. You cannot do this to me." Wroth was now begging, and I *almost* felt sorry for him.

Mr Vontant smiled tightly. "Prove to me over the next few centuries that you'll behave and maybe I'll remove it."

"You cannot do this to me. If my soul contracts come to fruition in that time, I will cease to be!" Wroth had fallen to his knees in front of the demon and I was feeling uncomfortable witnessing it all.

"Deal with it!" Mr Vontant snapped, and kicked the ankou hard in the face, laying him out flat across the back door's threshold. "You may go."

I shuddered over what had just happened and took a few unsteady steps away from Mr Vontant, who was wiping something off his shoe and trying to straighten his suit as if nothing had happened. I then realised something amazing. As long as Mr Vontant owned Wroth, the ankou wouldn't be able to harm me. But, surely, this wasn't the reason the demon had taken ownership of the reaper. . . right?

"Mere coincidence, I assure you Ms Anders," Mr Vontant said, seeing the look on my face. "May I go now?"

"Well, I'm not being threatened by dark forces anymore, so I guess so," I answered warily. Part of me wanted to thank him for all his help. Whether he had meant to or not, Mr Vontant had helped me survive Hell and get home with the soul I'd gone there to get. He'd then helped me return the soul to where it belonged, removed the threat of Wroth and all up had. . . *helped* me throughout. Surely this was all coincidence? And as much as I wanted to give him some small measure of thanks I simply couldn't bring myself to say the words. I felt if I did I would not only be showing a vulnerable innocence to a demon, but embarrassing him by reading more into our relationship than what was already there.

"And I want you to go straight back to Hell. No mucking about topside and claiming it was part of the deal." Was what I actually came out with and I swear I caught the flicker of a smirk on the demon's face before he stepped through the door.

"Oh the things I do to annoy those in charge of Hell," Mr Vontant announced with a theatrical sigh. He bowed his head to me, almost as if saying 'you're welcome' to the silent thanks I'd tried not to give. Before I could muse over this some more he followed the ankou and disappeared into the evening's twilight and, hopefully, back down to Hell where he belonged. I took a moment to lean my forehead against the cool glass on the veranda's door, before sliding it closed and locking it.

"You did good Stephanie. . . well, mostly."

I jumped, startled to realise Trishna had followed me out into the dining room to witness me dispatch those who dwelled in Darkness out my back door.

"Mostly," I replied in agreement, turning to look at him, eyeing the bag that was back in his hand. He followed my gaze and supressed a sigh as if he was about to try and explain why he had to leave.

"I know," I cut in before he had a chance to say a word. I needed to get out what I had to say first, in case I never did put it in words. "You need to find some space, to find your feet. You've had one hell of a week — what with re-awakening as Trishna, finding me again, following me to Hell and having me. . . do all that stuff to you. I know." We looked at each other for a long moment and I tried to keep the sadness from my expression. I couldn't tell Trishna how I really felt, as I really didn't know. But I was pretty sure the link my possession had caused would share it all the same. I wasn't too sure if that was a bad thing or not. I mean, *yes* I needed him, but for what? We both knew it wasn't so he could point out all the Other World stuff I failed to spot. There was something else there and until I discovered what it really was. . . I couldn't talk to him about it. I was worried about what would happen when we did talk.

"Roxanna has invited me to go stay at the Temple with her. So I won't be too far away. . ." Trishna said, trailing off as he was clearly unable to commit himself to much else to do with me right now either. I mean, how were you *meant* to act toward someone who just held you prisoner in your own mind for three days? A cup of my best Buddha's Tears tea and the last Tim Tam simply wasn't going to cut it.

"Don't be a stranger." I winced at my attempted humour. Really? I abused this man, held him against his will and *wanted* him to call me? How stupid I must sound right now. "Actually, be a stranger. Be Mark, be Trishna, be yourself. . . find which one suits you best. Let the priestesses pamper you — but don't take advantage of them — and find where you're meant to be in this world. Be free and only talk to me if you want to." Yes, if I hadn't seemed stupid before, that definitely confirmed it with that gibberish.

Trishna snorted his amusement and gave me a hesitant smile.

"Be true to yourself too Stephanie," he finally said. "You're a whole lot of something I don't think anyone has seen before and the sooner someone figures out what it is, the safer the world will be."

I mused over these words for a moment as I wasn't too sure if they'd been meant as a compliment or an insult. . . and really didn't want him to clarify which, in case I didn't like the answer.

There was a sound from the passage and we both turned as the priestesses all entered the room, with a slightly more presentable Simon than the one I'd seen moments ago.

"He needs sustenance before we pitch him out on the street," the Apothecary warned me, obviously expecting me to lose my nut over seeing Simon still there. I just shrugged and went to leave them to it and see Trishna to the door.

"Uh, Stephanie?" I turned and glared at Simon as he said my name. Yes I'd just literally gone through hell and back for this man. . . but I still didn't like him. Actually I liked him even less now than I had when he'd originally begged me for help. But beg he had and some stupid part of me linked to this whole Protector of Souls things had responded before the sensible part of me had had a say in the matter.

"Yes?" I replied coldly, refusing for one moment to be nice to him. I could still remember his grope, after all I'd done to be the good guy and save his soul.

"I don't remember everything," Simon began slowly, "But I do re-member I was in a bad way and somehow knew you would help me. Despite it all."

I bit back what I wanted to say. Despite all what Simon? The fact you used and abused my ex-husband's friendship for years and then dropped him when he was no longer fun? That you couldn't understand the emptiness I felt over losing my unborn child and instead poisoned my ex-husband's mind until he too couldn't understand and so just left me to deal with it all alone? That you have always been the biggest, manipulating jerk I'd ever known and yet I *still* did my best to save you — as that's what we who walk in the Light do? Rather than voice all that I just stood there, hands on hips and glaring. Maybe these words were emanating off me, perhaps he could hear them from his soul having shared my body, I don't know. . . but for a moment he did seem to cringe a little. Sadly, he then bounced back and returned my look with a cocky stare of his own.

"Yeah, okay. You helped me and that was. . . nice. I just wanted to know who I make the cheque out to so I can be on my way. You know, payment of services and all that."

My hand itched to slap him again at that moment and even the priestesses around us looked taken aback by his words. Maybe now people would believe me when I said he really was the biggest douche canoe in town.

"Talk to the priestesses," I finally muttered, after gaining control over my voice once more. "They were the ones who supplied the *services*, I was just the dumb schmuck who did the fetching and carrying." And with that I gave Simon one last look of complete disgust and then stalked out of the room. I didn't know where I was going. I just knew I couldn't be here while he was. Everything I'd done had been to save his soul, and for what? I'd known he was the way he was before and I'd still done it? What was wrong with me? Everyone had told me I'd done my best as Protector of Souls, but once his soul was in Hell I couldn't do a thing. Why had I been so gung-ho about going to Hell? Had retrieving his soul just been an excuse? Had I needed to prove to the Other World I could do *anything*, especially when told I couldn't? I didn't need these sorts of questions swirling around within me right now and so I had to leave and hope they stayed behind with all those who caused them.

It was over. I'd been to Hell, had come back with more problems than I'd set out with and Simon's soul was returned to him. I had done what I'd set out to do. That should have been the end of it all.

# Chapter 24

"HIDING from your acts, both good and bad will never help anyone. Especially not yourself," Roxanna said the next day as she joined me on the park bench I'd been occupying in the predawn gloom in the park just down the road from the Temple.

"I'm not hiding, just thinking," I replied wearily. And honestly I hadn't been hiding. Unless walking around the city all night and drinking endless cups of poor quality tea at twenty-four hour fast food places is what they called hiding these days. I had just wanted to get out. Be outside, be *topside* again after all that time in Hell. I had been me, alone, no prickly soul beneath my skin, no nagging feeling of ownership as I dragged possessed people along in my wake. Just me, my thoughts, and I.

She eyed me warily from the opposite end of the bench. It hurt more than I could say, knowing she still didn't fully trust me.

I leaned back to look into the sky to watch the shapes of the buildings around us emerge as night became day, and wondered once again why I had gone to Hell? Had going there to save Simon's soul just been an excuse? Had I wanted to see how the other half lived? Gone to check out the Darkness to see if I fitted in there better than I did in the Light?

"I suppose you're about to warn me that those who walk the streets all night tend to be those who walk in the Darkness rather than the Light, aren't you?" I said.

"Sometimes the best way to seek clarity in the Light is to first dwell within the Darkness," Roxanna replied calmly.

I shot her a look. With all the thoughts swirling around inside me right now, she seemed to have just given me my answer.

"You know I walk in the Light, don't you?" I said, staring back into the sky. "I mean, I might not be your orthodox Light walker, but I do what I see is the best thing to do in any given situation. I'm one of the good guys and my aim is to ensure the good guys always win."

"I know you do everything with the best of intentions in mind, Stephanie. But I also fear for you. The path you walk isn't always well lit and I'm afraid one day you might trip and fall. . . and not remember how to get back to the Light."

I winced at this and found myself holding back tears. I was a good person, we both knew it, but we both also knew I had the potential to be a bad person too. And what I currently did for a living really was a fine line between the two. The High Priestess gave me a moment to compose myself again as the city started to come back to life around us.

"What was it like? Hell I mean," she finally asked in a very quiet voice.

I turned back to see her watching me carefully in the gloom. Again I fought those stupid tears back as I remembered it all.

"Hell is what people make it. If you wanted it to be all fire and death and pain, that is what you saw." I shuddered at the memories of what I'd seen there when allowing someone else's will to be in control.

"And what did you want to see?" she asked, still cautious but genuinely curious.

"I just saw Darkness and a lot of demons," I said softly. Yes I'd seen more. I'd seen creatures so much like the humans I lived among it had been scary. The people of the Light I'd got to know seemed so different, so alien to me. But in Hell. . . well, take away the heat and stone walls and I could have been anywhere in the real world with its greed, envy, selfishness and hate. I hoped it was because Hell was what you made it. . . rather than the sadder possibility of real life being closer to the Darkness than it was the Light.

"Hell made me a better person," I said sombrely.

Roxanna looked both startled and scared. "How so?"

She looked even more taken aback when I smiled at her, everything starting to make more sense as the world around us lightened and the day began.

"Like you said Roxanna, I needed to go see the Darkness to make it clearer to myself why I walk in the Light. It showed me who I am, what I could be and how best to live my life to ensure I didn't become *that* person." I guess Sid had helped me figure a few things out after all.

"Will it mean you stop dealing with those of the Darkness so often?" Roxanna asked tentatively. I tried to return the smile but ended up sadly shaking my head.

"I can't," I replied. "I made a deal. And besides, how better to control them than ensure they have me to answer to?"

Roxanna shook her head in disbelief over this but also let out an amused cough of laughter at the same time.

"One day I hope to truly understand you and why you have been brought into my life," she said, standing and offering me a hand up.

"When you do get that memo, please pass it on to me so I know as well" I said as I took her hand and rose. I was still mentally a mess inside, there was still much I needed to sort out over what I'd just been through. But at least I now had time, and friends, to help me through it. I stopped, mid-step, at the thought of having friends to help me.

"You are doing the right thing and he is in the best place to recover," Roxanna assured me, giving my hand a squeeze as if reading my mind. So Trishna was gone from my life again right now. But this time he, at least, wasn't gone forever. Well, I at least hoped he wasn't.

As we turned and headed back toward the temple the sun rose over the old roof and spread its glory and warming light over us both. Sometimes karma had a bit of poetic licence to make it all seem better.

# Epilogue

IF ONLY real life could just be ended as easily as all that. Unfortunately I couldn't just draw a line in the sand and walk away into the sunrise and be a better person.

I'd been to Hell, and learned more about the Darkness while there than I had ever expected — or wanted — to. I was now bound into a deal with thirteen demons every month for years to come. And someone I had come to think of as my best friend — despite only knowing him such a short period of time — had come into my life and then left it again. All because I kept doing some pretty bad stuff to him. . . in the name of keeping him safe.

Add to that the fact that the Birdfolk of Wroth were *really* pissed off at me now they had no Wroth, Other World folk who walked in the Light tended to cross the street rather than talk to me, and my soul had darkened from duck egg blue to a rich peacock. And, yeah, life wasn't going to be that easy for a while.

Other Worlders from both the Darkness and Light were now paying far more attention to me than I felt I required and it was making the Priestesses of Isis a little edgy. For one thing, I'd had to stop attending the weekly services to Isis as I seemed to be attracting a lot of rubber neckers, while scaring off the true congregation.

Layman Smith, on a positive note, had recovered well from his run in with me. I'd written him a rather good letter of apology — with Roxanna's help — and had been told he had appreciated it. The restraining order he'd then whacked on me meant I was unable to hear from him in person. I was pretty sure he'd never agree to teach me how to fight again.

And Trishna? We sometimes came upon each other in one of the many corridors of the Temple. I always did my best to hide the longing I felt to stop and chat and just *be* with him. He always just seemed wary and wanting to leave as soon as he could so maybe he could still feel it?

Yes I was frustrated that the longer we stayed apart, the worse his feelings toward me seemed to get. But what could I do? I had abused his trust and friendship and now I had to let those wounds heal. And when they had, maybe I could get back to earning restitution. At least I hoped so.

Had going to Hell to save Simon's soul been worth it all? Well, he was still himself, unfortunately, but at least he'd left my life as quickly as he had arrived. And the school the temple helped fund had received a lovely new music room and kitchen garden from the hush money he'd thrown at us. I hadn't even got some simple words of thanks.

But what else can be done when you're the Protector of Souls: leather gloves, running shoes, and handbag clinking with bottles of purified water? Yes I still felt alone in a room full of people who might care for me but were still scared of me at the same time. But I'd been to Hell and back. I walked in the Light; I kept the good guys safe and the bad guys in their place. Nobody was about to take that away from me. And for anyone who tried, get in line.

The End.

Thank you for reading
THERE'S NO PLACE LIKE HELL
we hope you enjoyed it.

If you would like to be kept informed of further releases in the
Other World series, or other new books from Hague Publishing, why
not subscribe to our newsletter at:

**www.HaguePublishing.com/subscribe.php**

And if you loved the book and have a moment to spare we would
really appreciate a short review.

Your help in spreading the word is gratefully received.

# About The Author

JANIS grew up in and around Darwin and its rural surrounds. As a child, she spent a lot of time in her own imagination as there wasn't much else to do when living in a swamp and dealing with fires or floods.

Janis now lives in the Adelaide Hills with her husband and 3 children, lovingly referred to as the 'Demonic Hordes'. She is a work from home Haus Frau and carer of neuro diverse children. When not writing, she enjoys turning rags into yarn and other recycling eccentricities. One day she would like to live in a home made of mud and straw. But for now dabbles in the art of translating century old cookery books into modern recipes to experiment on her family with.

For more information visit https://janishill.wordpress.com/

Hague

Publishing

www.HaguePublishing.com

PO Box 451 Bassendean
Western Australia 6934

www.ingramcontent.com/pod-product-compliance
Lightning Source LLC
Chambersburg PA
CBHW071514110726

47908CB00003B/839